THE OUTING

FABIAN FOLEY

With Gratitude… for Tom and Madelaine and Paul, who always believed in me. And me, for finally believing them.

***

"Power without love is reckless and abusive, and love without power is sentimental and anaemic. Power at its best is love implementing the demands of justice, and justice at its best is power correcting everything that stands against love."
Dr Martin Luther King, Jr.

CONTENTS

PROLOGUE

Brisbane 1986

On the verandah overlooking the front yard, Robert absentmindedly fingered the outline of the watch nestled in his pocket, wondering why he'd thought time off work was a good idea. He flung his half-finished tea over the railing and watched as it turned into a liquid starburst, holding itself in the air, before plummeting onto the floral starbursts below. *What were they called? Agga-something. Agapanthus.*

After rinsing the cup, he headed to the backyard, retrieved the washing, and then paced with the folded bundles from the pile to their various cupboards and shelves, trying to ignore the phone. Marnie had promised she'd call once they had the new coroner's report. Harry had promised to call as soon as the update came through from his private investigator, on the search for Alan John Peters.

All he had to do was be patient.

If he vacuumed, the kids would wake up from their afternoon naps, and he'd have something else to think about. He shoved the plug into the wall socket. Nothing. He looked at it vacantly, before noticing the switch. *Fuck.* He reached down and flicked it on. The vacuum whirred noisily to life before settling into a loud drone.

He'd finished the back of the house and thought he heard the kids. He

1

started to lean over to switch off the vacuum and check, but then, over the drone, vocal tones registered. It sounded like 'I can hear the vacuum cleaner. Go and get mummy', and 'No', and 'Mummy's at school'. That was Emma.

Then quite distinctively, "It's not school. It's una— univer-city."

He smiled. Thomas.

As he turned the corner into the central hallway, pulling the machine by the flexible hose, he saw his children in the open front doorway of the house. The sunlight pouring onto the verandah was brightly obscuring two other figures, making them all look haloed at the end of a tunnel.

"Hello," he said.

Emma and Thomas heard his voice and ran back towards him.

He took a step forward.

In the changing play of light and shade the image cleared.

Something was trying to claw out of his chest.

"Robert Carson?"

He nodded.

Hands holding shiny metal badges waved across his vision, "I'm detective…"

The words were lost. Drowned in the thumping echo of his heart, reverberating inside his head, and the whining drone of the machine. He bent down and switched it off.

PART ONE

1985

CHAPTER 1

Arriving at his boss's office Robert expected to return Duncan's oh-good-you're-here smile, with his own of-course-no-problem one. Instead, he found himself in slack-jawed confusion, transfixed by the back of someone's head.

His heart thumped. His memory lagged.

He continued to stare at the shoulder-length chestnut hair. He knew the voice. Where from? The head tilted, and auburn highlights became visible amongst the softly curling waves.

Suddenly he was sitting on the darkened stage in the Schonell Theatre, his last day at university. The twinkling bands of riser lights heading to the foyer, made the stairs look like a gently cascading waterfall. A figure shimmered, and seemed to be floating up them towards the door. As it opened a spill of light blazoned the image into a secret corner of his memory.

"Ahh, Robert." Duncan's voice brought him back. "Come in."

The person with their back to Robert stood and turned, and time and his breathing stopped.

"This is John Saunders," said Duncan, then put his hand up correcting himself. "I mean, Johnny Saunders. He said you know each other."

As they gripped each other's hand, Robert suppressed a shivery tingle and his foot nudged the chair next to Johnny before he sank gratefully into it, "Yes. Yes, we do."

"Nice to see you again, Robert," said Johnny. "I often wondered if you'd stay, with law, I mean, as a job."

Robert managed a subdued nod and ignoring the clamour of unasked questions, turned to Duncan, "How can I help?" He hoped it sounded like his usual relaxed and confident. Professional.

"Well," said Duncan, "it's rather— and I don't want to cause you any," he pressed his lips together and nodded. "I'll be straightforward. Johnny here is— He's homosexual. Gay. And," his hand made a traffic stop signal, "as far as I'm concerned, that's entirely his own business."

Robert offered a slight nod, waiting, not breathing.

"Mmm-yes. And because of your," he searched, "association," up came the hand, "he filled me in. You were in the same classes? At university?"

Robert inclined his head further.

"I only bring it up because," Duncan stopped talking and coughed to mask the pause. "He assured me you wouldn't be offended, that in fact you'd been friends. So I decided to bring you in on his case."

"Go on," Robert tried not to sound relieved.

"It concerns Judge Matthews and Johnny here."

Robert's eyebrow was the only thing that moved.

"The police have been covertly investigating the judge," said Duncan.

"Why? Don't they need a reason to follow people?" Robert's brow creased. "Not these days I suppose."

"Mmm-yes. He said something to upset them. It was in the news, Judge Matthews commenting about a case. About crucial and already entered evidence being *misplaced* by the police. The clearly guilty party was let off. That journalist from the *Courier Mail*, what's his name?" Duncan turned to Johnny then answered his own question, "Yes, Simon Draper, had a few words to say. Something about what was the point of the Lucas Inquiry, if this sort of thing kept happening."

"I remember," said Robert.

"I believe," said Duncan, "that this is their way of keeping him quiet. Judge Matthews. Not the journalist. Obviously."

Duncan paused for breath or clarity or both, and leaned forward, "And so, here we are."

"Sorry, I'm not following," Robert shook his head, wondering if the shock of seeing Johnny had made him miss something, or it was just Duncan being uncharacteristically inelegant.

"To keep him quiet, or maybe punish him," Johnny shrugged, "the police are using me."

"But why you?" Robert frowned.

Johnny ran his hand through his hair, scrunching it behind his ear.

Robert remembered he did that when he was upset or nervous or afraid.

"They can't arrest Harry," said Johnny. "It'd be too obvious. He makes some comment in the press and wham he's arrested for being gay."

Robert still looked blank.

"The judge, Harry. He's my boyfriend."

"Oh," said Robert. "But how?"

"You probably don't remember. I thought I might get some paid roles if I did a stint at New Theatre in Sydney. I didn't. But I met Harry and—"

"No, I meant how did this happen? Why did they arrest you?"

"Oh," said Johnny.

"I've checked the QP9," Duncan intervened, reading the police report. "DS Nichols and DC Andrews, off duty, were in the same bar as Judge Matthews." He shook his head, "Of course they were." Then continued reading, "A young man, John Saunders, entered and engaged the judge in unwelcome conversation."

"Not exactly a crime," Robert commented.

"But," said Johnny, "soliciting is. They made up a story that's what I was doing."

"How would they even know?"

"They don't," said Johnny. "That's the whole point. They made it up. And that I posed a threat to other patrons. Nothing's happened, but they wanted something over Harry."

"That's extortion," Robert's voice rose. "A trap. He's implicated. They could use this any time they choose."

"Exactly," Duncan's lips soured. "And this allegation—"

"Not an allegation Mr Eldridge, sorry to butt in. They charged me, fingerprints and all." Johnny turned to Robert, "Remember? You said, it won't disappear. Ever."

Robert hazarded a searching look into Johnny's eyes. He glanced away looking for composure, then turned back, "So you want us to represent you?"

"I want someone to." Johnny's smile broke like a winter sunrise.

Robert basked in its hesitant warmth for a moment too long.

This time Johnny looked away.

Duncan, apparently oblivious, ruminated, "It's about leverage of course. But while Johnny can't prove his innocence, not that he should have to, they can't prove his guilt. The QP9 is on record, so their story can't change." A pause. "Well, it could. They seem to lose and find statements and witnesses and evidence to suit these days. But in my estimation, it hinges on whether this gets treated as a summary matter or something more serious."

"You mean criminal, not *more serious*," Johnny's face sagged.

"So where is he? Judge Matthews," Robert asked.

Johnny's hand pushed his hair back again.

Robert's heart flooded with the same tenderness he felt when Emma or Thomas's bottom lip quivered. His averted eyes found the formal portrait photo of them both with he and Lauren, on Duncan's desk. He wondered if Johnny had noticed it.

"I'm staying at my own place for a while," said Johnny, while Duncan looked at something riveting on the back of his hand. "Harry said to see his old friend Duncan Eldridge. Something about a favour."

"I'm happy to help, of course." Robert glanced towards Duncan, "It's not my field but—"

"I know," said Duncan. "It isn't anyone's field, is it? But I thought, given the circumstances, people's attitudes…"

"I'm assuming," Robert filled the space, "you'll direct me with the relevant statutes?"

Duncan was already nodding.

"OK then," said Robert standing. He went to put a hand on Johnny's shoulder then quickly lifted it away. "Is there a plan, besides no proof either way?"

"It should merely be a matter of making an appearance. But we need to be prepared for whether it's treated as summary or," he stopped. "And we can't antagonize them. I hate to say it, but if we start making waves, they'll start making evidence. No. We go along with it. You'll see, it'll be thrown out. We don't want to open up a can of worms," said Duncan.

"Would that be so bad?" Johnny said. "I mean I'd rather it wasn't me, but all this paying off and secrets. Nothing will change."

Robert frowned, "What? A bribe?"

"Of course! What do you think?" Johnny scoffed, "Two grand."

"That's half a car. So, if they've been paid off, how come you're still—"

"In the shit?" Johnny finished. "They're making a point? I don't know. Evidence *not* disappearing?"

"Regardless," Duncan said, "we'll focus on miscommunication. Mistakes can be made. Perfectly understandable. They were doing their job. You expected it to be sorted out at the station. It wasn't. You're an actor, Johnny. You're going to play it straight."

"Meaning?" Johnny's question synced with Robert's eyebrow.

"OK. Spelling it out. You'd met the judge before. You chat, something's misheard, misconstrued. Simple. You two," he looked at Robert, "need to set up an appointment and do a preliminary statement. We'll go from there when I've briefed you."

"I hope it's going to be as simple as you say," said Robert, but his face remained tense. "I don't want them thinking we tried to bamboozle them. I don't fancy being on their wrong side. I'm sure Johnny doesn't either."

For Robert, the walk to his office seemed like it wasn't going to end, and then that it would end too soon.

After a distracted, "No disturbances please, Anna," to his secretary as he closed the door, he faced Johnny, wooden and wondering what he was supposed to do, or not supposed to do.

Johnny hesitated then took both Robert's hands in both of his, "Thank you," he scanned Robert's face. "Just, well… thank you."

Robert's eyes lingered on their hands and then he turned abruptly, breaking the hold and reaching for the phone, "Sorry Anna," he said staring at his reflection in the window. "Would you mind coming in. Mr Saunders needs an appointment. I made a mistake," he paused. "He can't stay today after all."

Johnny's eyes moved from his empty hands to Robert's averted face and then the photographs on Robert's desk.

"Your kids?" said Johnny.

"Yeah. Pigeon pair."

"Lauren hasn't changed. Still stunning."

Robert's smile wavered, "Ahh," he said when Anna tapped and opened the door, "good, what have we got free in the next few days?"

CHAPTER 2

"You OK?" said Lauren as Robert walked into the kitchen, placed an absent-minded kiss on her cheek and reached for the fridge door-handle.

"Big day. I'm a bit uptight. Fancy a drink?" He didn't wait for an answer.

"Well?" she said as he handed her a glass.

"Remember when we first met?" It wasn't really a question.

"You were tipsy as I recall."

Robert raised his eyebrows, "I was celebrating."

"Haha. Of course I remember," she said. "You know, I was always a bit surprised you two weren't an item back then."

Robert looked up sharply.

"Marnie, I mean." She reached past him and turned off the stove. "Before that night I thought the baby was yours. We met her brother as well."

"Johnny," said Robert.

"That's right. You two were in the same tutorial or something. He was very good-looking." She peered sideways at Robert. "You do realise if he'd been available, you wouldn't have stood a chance," she grinned.

Robert smiled too, remembering Marnie, noticeably pregnant, despondently drowning her sorrows in lemonade. Her dad had insisted Johnny come with her. To keep me out of trouble she'd said, then added, bit late for that. They'd all half chuckled in sympathy and he'd slid across the banquette, bunched up next to Johnny, forcing his attention to stay on the gorgeous, self-assured blond opposite him, now his wife, who was saying something to him. Shifting his attention back to her now, he caught the end of what she was saying.

"…used to see a fair bit of him, didn't you?"

"Johnny? I suppose. Apart from our theatre stuff, we used to go jogging together." And then he drifted back. He and Johnny, after one of their runs, looking out over Brisbane from the top of Mt Coot-tha. Johnny had been going to ask him something and changed his mind.

"Well," she said again, "your day? That's how this trip down memory lane started."

"He came in today. To the office. He was arrested."

"What? I don't suppose you can go into details. Are you representing him?"

"Yeah. Yeah," he repeated.

"But," she started.

"No," he said. "It's nothing to do with commercial or business. Your dad asked me to do it. Seems Johnny's boyfriend, partner whatever, was an old friend. Judge Matthews."

She shook her head, "Never met him. Must've been a long time ago. Not that Dad's the social type, as you know. It was mostly just me and him growing up. What happened?"

"Nothing. That's the thing. The police concocted a fake charge to get back at the judge. You know that story? It was all over the news. The SP bookie who was arrested and then the evidence disappeared. They had to abandon the case. That was Judge Matthews."

"Yeah, I remember, and he made those comments about the ludicrous idea of corrupt police in charge of an inquiry into corrupt police. What a joke."

"Except this isn't a joke."

"No," she said. "I didn't mean…"

"I know. I know. Sorry. It all just got to me."

They were interrupted by a shriek from the living room.

"You go," Lauren said. "I'll finish organising dinner. They're already in their pyjamas. Oh, and can you hang up the wet towels in the bathroom. I didn't get to that yet."

The television was on. James Dibble's judgment-free face reassuring everyone that despite the disappointments and disasters he was reading about, everything would be OK. It's only the news. There will be something else to tut about tomorrow. "Come on kiddoes, Daddy's reading your story tonight." He pushed the dial to off.

Their excited squeals made his heart clench, "OK, OK. Isn't this supposed to be quiet time?"

They each pressed a forefinger against their lips, "Shhhh."

"That's better. Now, let's be quiet as little mice and tippy-toe to bed."

They tippy-toed down the hall. The two equal-sized smaller ones in front, the big one following, rocking slightly from side to side on long spindly legs with oversized feet.

With the closed book on his lap, Robert sat on the reading chair between their beds, watching the covers rising and falling with a soft even rhythm. He could smell the lingering fragrance of soap and closed his eyes. Fleeting images of the day moved around and he lifted his chin towards the ceiling to dispel them and conjure his favourite hit of happy.

He smiled as he watched himself coming into the kitchen in their old house, with a bottle of Great Western Champagne even though Lauren couldn't have any.

"The flutes are up there." She'd pointed to the overhead cupboard, seeming to have caught the mood without him saying anything. "But how did you know?"

"What? They rang me." The cork popped, and they'd laughed, catching the foam. "Did they call here too?"

"Who? No," said Lauren rubbing her bump. "Who are you talking about Robert? Who was supposed to ring here?"

"The bank. We got it. We got the loan. They rang ten minutes before close of business. Their business. I've been sitting on the news since three. I wanted to see your face when I told you."

She put the glass down and hugged him. As they drew apart, he'd noticed her tears.

"What's wrong?" he said. "What's the matter?"

She sniffed, "No, no, go on… what happened? How?"

"Your dad. Remember he'd said my billings were way higher than almost everyone else's and he was going to put up my pay at the end of the financial year?" He'd waited for the nod. "Well, I asked him if he'd bring it forward because with the recession and interest rates moving into double figures it was looking like the bank would say no."

"And he did?"

This time he'd nodded. "The pay lady did up a letter and well, now it's a matter of signatures. We'll be in our own house before the baby arrives."

They'd clinked glasses.

"Well, that's a relief," her voice was surprisingly flat. "But you've got it slightly wrong."

"What?"

She'd taken a tiny sip of her champagne and grinned, "We'll be in our own house," the grin broadening, "before the babies are born." And she'd watched his face.

"Joking," he'd said. "You're joking! Babies?"

"Two, Robert." She put her glass down, and he'd picked her up and swirled her. "We're having twins."

He waited. But the expected glow of contentment was missing, a creeping hint of something else in its place. He started counting. Annoyed, he stopped himself.

He'd have a chat to Duncan tomorrow.

CHAPTER 3

"I didn't expect this from you, Robert," Duncan's lip's pressed together. "He's an old friend for goodness sake."

Robert lifted his head, "And that's why I should remove myself."

"And this is serious," Duncan seemed not to have heard. "Lives and careers are at stake. When Johnny said you'd been friends at university, despite well, I knew you'd be the only one here I'd trust on his case." He shook his head. "When's his appointment?"

"Tomorrow. Eleven."

"Give this some thought, Robert. If you're still of the same opinion, I'll make myself available. Let me know by four if I'm going to have to rearrange my day, will you?"

Returning to his own office, Robert leaned back into his executive swivel chair, interlaced his fingers behind his neck and did what Duncan said.

He thought.

He was a professional. His personal life, past or present, should not interfere with his work. And he'd acted rashly going to Duncan with his demands. He wouldn't have done it if Marnie had been the client. And except for the last time he'd seen Johnny, they'd been easy in each other's company. Good friends. He huffed aloud, hearing Lauren's voice saying, and it's not like you have that many. *No*, he agreed, *not since*—

He shook off the memory and his resistance. He was used to his own company but it had been nice to have a friend.

Surely you could just be his friend.

He reached for the phone. He might as well tell Duncan now.

***

A few days later Robert was reaching for a new case folder when Duncan's arrival broke his momentum. Robert waved him in.

"No," said Duncan. "I only have a minute or two. What have you got?"

"Not that much. He and Harry have been living together at Harry's in New Farm for about three years, since he came back from Sydney, but Johnny has his own place too. It's rented out to cover the repayments. His dad helped him with the deposit, but I wouldn't expect that to come up. Main thing is, it gives them separate addresses."

"Excellent. And he's living there now?"

Robert nodded, "Johnny's tenant left recently. It was still empty, so he moved straight in."

Duncan waited.

"That's it really. I made sure there'd be nothing the police could pick on. Not that they have any jurisdiction over anything occurring outside Queensland. And as far as work goes, he went back to uni, volunteers at a shelter, and works part-time at the Park Royal Hotel."

"In the bar?"

"Mostly front office."

"Good. Good. The magistrate will like all of that."

"There's something bothering me," Robert paused. "Johnny said that their relationship had changed. That it was more like he and Harry were best friends, who live together."

Duncan half-chuckled, "A bit like an old married couple."

"Really?" The irritation in his own voice surprised Robert.

Duncan straightened, "Harry and I, we're about the same age. That's pretty normal."

"Except it's three years, not twenty. And with respect, your situations are completely different."

"Granted, and it's none of our business unless it has some bearing on the case."

"Maybe it does."

"Go on."

"Purely conjecture," Robert hesitated, "but I was wondering why Harry isn't supporting Johnny more. Why is he banished? Yeah, I know. Different addresses for appearance's sake. But, he's fending for himself completely. And the just friends thing, before this happened. Something's wrong. Maybe the judge was involved in this. In deliberately setting things up to get rid of Johnny. Or using it anyway."

Duncan frowned.

"It's well, the police were paid off, so you'd assume all this would be put to bed. But as yet, there's been no 'oops, sorry, we made a mistake,' from them," Robert shrugged. "Did you get Harry's statement? Were you right? Is the whole thing a sham to put the wind up Harry and get some quick dollars at the same time?"

"Here," Duncan handed Robert the statement.

Robert glanced over it, "Damn."

"You could be right," said Duncan. "I mean about their relationship, but that doesn't have any bearing on the case as it stands. And the statement? Read it again. I read it through a couple of times. To me it's intentionally worded to look like it's supporting the arrest. It's hinting, pointing, which is obviously to appease the police—"

"But without checking in with Harry, we don't know for sure. Are you still planning to contact him?"

"I thought not. That," Duncan pointed at the document in Robert's hand, "is supposed to support the prosecution, so for us he's a hostile witness. We can cross examine him, but he's not about to admit to anything. His career would be over. That, I believe is part of their twisted plan, so what purpose would it serve?"

"Yes. But aren't you supposed to be old friends? Why tell Johnny to see you?"

"We were. Years ago. He was never fond of Lauren's mother, and well, even after she passed away, different circles..."

"Perhaps a chance meeting, friends of friends?" Robert suggested. "Somewhere public where people would expect you both to unexpectedly meet up."

"Don't hold your breath. With the press he's had, I doubt Harry's social calendar is brimming at the moment. And I wouldn't blame people for keeping their distance. No-one wants to get their faces in front of the police these days."

"Do you honestly believe it's that bad? The corruption."

"On top of turning blind eyes where it suits them to, heavy handed thuggery when it's not warranted, and interfering with the justice system, all of which have been splashed about on the pages of the Courier Mail recently by our friend Simon Draper, they're blackmailing a judge. And you can bet your bottom dollar there's more. A lot more. So yes. I do."

Robert sighed, "I caught something on the news last night about a crackdown on prostitution, massage parlours."

"I wonder what our illustrious Premier Joh is up to?" said Duncan. "That kind of news is usually bandied about when there's something shady happening and he wants to divert the public's attention. They'll arrest a few of the girls and call it a triumph of law and order, very loudly so we all hear it, and everything will go back to normal with the real crooks sitting pretty. As usual."

"I've always tried to stay away from all the hype around Joh Bjelke-Petersen. Force of habit. Dad never liked to talk about it at home," said Robert. "Anyway, we have our own problems."

"Yes, indeed," said Duncan. "But," he pointed again at the document in Robert's hand, "to me this says Harry's tendering a statement in lieu of making an appearance. That way he can't incriminate himself, or Johnny. And depending on how the questions on either side are put, everything can be made to fall within the bounds of truth-telling. I'm sure you get my point. When's the committal?"

"Two weeks," said Robert.

"Make an appointment with Johnny," said Duncan. "We need written character references to offer the Magistrate. The person in charge where he volunteers, that kind of thing. But stipulate the detail you want. This defence is completely do-able Robert." Duncan's eyes glazed as if he was reviewing an imaginary courtroom scene. "But Johnny needs coaching. I said before, he's got to come across as a straight man. No dramatic camp gestures. There must be absolutely no doubt the police have made a mistake. And Johnny must also be sympathetically supportive of them. Understanding. The police were only doing their job. That kind of thing."

"I'll call him."

"Good." Duncan turned to go then turned back, "Robert, this has to be low key. It's not about political point scoring or news stories. I know I'm just stating the obvious, but do you think it's worth having a chat to your dad, or Simon Draper, make sure he doesn't make a hullaballoo out of this. It's his story that got Johnny arrested. We don't want Johnny to become a target when it's over."

Robert half nodded, "Don't worry about dad. Lowly back-benchers get as much look in with Joh and his parliamentary cronies as they do in the media. Not that I'd discuss any of this with him. And Simon? Warning him off would be like waving a flag. My thoughts are, it hasn't reached the news, so why broadcast it?"

Duncan started to leave again.

"Oh," said Robert, "I'm also putting together a submission to expunge the arrest record."

"Excellent. Does Johnny know? That this will follow him forever?"

Robert nodded.

"Well, here's hoping your submission does the job and he doesn't need to worry about that."

***

Robert allowed a self-satisfied smile to hover as he jotted billing details onto a cover-sheet and placed the file he'd been working on into a neatly stacked tray. It hadn't been that way when he arrived as an article clerk, but he'd soon put it right. And it had stayed that way.

He reached for the phone, and pushed the flashing orange button, "Hey Johnny, what kept you?"

"Sorry. Uni."

"Of course. Duncan's given us some work to do. Can you come in?"

"Now? Only, I've got an extra shift today. I'm a bit skint without Harry and I don't want to blow it off," Johnny stopped. "No, it's OK, I'll get ready for work and come to your office."

"Have you got a video player?" Robert asked.

When Johnny said yes, Robert checked his watch, "Good. You're sort-of on my way home. I'll come over to yours instead. Start thinking about character witnesses. Your boss, lecturers, people who'll vouch that you're kind, honest and hardworking. That sort of thing."

"Meeting?" Anna asked.

"Yes. Then home. In fact, you should leave early too."

As her surprise softened, he realised that after seeing her almost every day for two years, he had no idea if there was a Mr Anna, or children.

"I couldn't."

"What? All the overtime you do for me? Come on. Pack up. What's the matter?" he said when she looked away.

"Nothing. It's, that's really kind. I think I'll do something extra special for my mum. She's usually pretty tired when I get home."

"Oh. I don't want to pry."

She looked back tearily, "The doctor says it's MS."

"Oh, Anna, that's dreadful." *Nice boss you are.* "Look, we can make this a regular thing. Once a week, hey? I'd better be off, but we'll talk about it tomorrow."

His hand reached the elevator button without his foot kicking the door, and he smiled at his unexpected grace.

CHAPTER 4

Robert's eyes wandered around Johnny's apartment. He was pleased at its ordered cleanliness. There'd been a moment on the drive over, when it occurred to him that Johnny might be slovenly, and he'd felt queasy until the door opened on Johnny's smile.

"We'll start with some ad-libbing," said Robert after explaining what he and Duncan had discussed.

"OK," Johnny's head tilted slightly, giving his profile more prominence.

"That's it," Robert mimicked him. "See? A straight guy wouldn't do that. Change of plan. Videos first. We'll pause and replay the mannerisms in slow motion."

Johnny held up two videos.

"Doesn't matter. Either. And we can use this," Robert pointed at the mirror hanging to capture and reflect the view of the parkland, river and the cityscape beyond.

"I've got a cheval mirror. Marnie gave it to me."

"I haven't seen her in ages," Robert's eyes softened. "But, that's not why we're here. Let's get started."

Robert felt a triumphant flush when Johnny gripped him by the shoulder and said, "Later. OK mate? Let's take ten minutes, have a drink, and then get on with the paperwork."

"Excellent," said Robert. "You'll be great. Keep practicing though, with the mirror. And it's probably a good idea if we do a few more sessions."

They'd been working at Johnny's dining table for about half an hour when Robert checked his watch, and started packing and arranging the notes for Johnny's character witnesses, "I've been thinking," he said, "maybe we could—"

Johnny interrupted him, "I've got plenty of time."

"This," said Robert, "is exactly what I mean. I know it's unconscious."

"What?" Johnny's jaw lifted higher.

Robert replayed the manoeuvre, with pointed exaggeration.

"This is not going to be that easy," Johnny said.

"Just get into character. And stay there. Don't come out."

"Well, you'd know about that," Johnny's mutter was barely audible. He masked it by changing his posture. "Hold on. OK. How's this?" He grabbed the back of the chair with both hands, leaned forward, and in excellent macho said, "I understand perfectly well what you said, mate. But that's not what I meant."

"I meant us," said Johnny, "spending all this time together now. What about us?"

"What about us? We're friends, Johnny. We've always been friends. That's not going to change because I'm your lawyer," Robert's tone was even. "I was going to say, let's meet up and go running again. I really miss that. When this is all finished and done with."

Johnny looked at Robert, his eyes probing, and then they blanked, "Look, I have to get to work."

"I thought you said," Robert stopped talking as Johnny picked up their coffee mugs and turned towards the kitchen. He pasted a smile on his face and stood up, "OK. Of course. Will you be able to get those references by Monday? Bring them into the office. First thing. I keep it free."

CHAPTER 5

Stop-start traffic shunting into the commute stream on the Story Bridge wasn't the distraction Robert was hoping for. And it was hot. Spotting the beer garden at the appropriately named Story Bridge Hotel, he decided to stop.

Sitting under a shady canopy of red flowers, he remembered running with Johnny and slipping on the mushy mess they made when they dropped. Johnny had helped him limp to the car.

He hadn't been keen when Johnny suggested they run together. He'd said the only sound he liked to hear out running was his own feet hitting the ground. But racing against Johnny, certainly hadn't hurt his times, even though, at least in that instance it had hurt his pride.

He looked up into the branches as a welcome breeze sent a handful of red petals fluttering groundward. Enjoying the sweat cooling on the back of his neck, he drifted into the past again. He'd raced ahead and had finished warming down when Johnny caught up, and was bent over holding his knees. He'd said, 'Don't you feel great after?'

Johnny had given him a look, and between gasps had said, 'After a beer I will.'

They'd sat on an aging wooden bench, and Johnny had suggested a drive to the coast next time, and a swim afterwards. He'd asked Johnny if he was going to change his mind and add a teaching diploma to his course.

"Shit, I dunno," Johnny said, taking a greedy swig of his beer, and looking out to a not so distant future, "I didn't sign up for acting and theatre to teach it. I mean, I've got nothing against kids. I like them."

"But?"

"I'd feel sort-of cheated, you know if I didn't at least try to make a go of it in Sydney."

They'd sat. Quiet.

Then, "We still gonna see The Chant of Jimmy Blacksmith?"

Robert nodded, "I've heard good things."

"So now you're a film buff?"

"Hah. I've always liked movies. You know that. What made you say that?" he'd bumped his shoulder playfully against Johnny's, as if they were kids.

"Robert?" Johnny had turned his face away as Robert turned towards him. "Doesn't matter, I'm, doesn't matter."

Nursing his beer, Robert contemplated. Johnny had been his friend, but he wondered how much of a friend he'd been to Johnny. *You were so wrapped up in your own thoughts and concerns and— Narcissistic. You never really thought about what was happening for him. Sydney, putting yourself out there, that was a big thing and you never even asked him.*

A man nodded hello as he sat, intruding on Robert's thoughts, and his personal space. He mustered a polite nod back.

"You come here often?" The man wore the sleeveless body builder t-shirt favoured by those with muscles to show off.

Robert instantly nicknamed him Muscles. *Hah, hardly original.*

"No. No," Robert repeated. "First time. Usually still in the office now." He looked away.

"Live close by?"

Robert pretended the words weren't for him.

"Hey, I said do you live close by?" There was an edge to the iteration.

"Me? I-ahh, no. No. Cooling off. Better here than stuck in traffic, eh?"

"Why here then?"

What is this?

"What? Why not here? Good a place as any," Robert resurrected his pasted-on smile. "Anyway, I suppose," he swallowed some beer and was about to add he'd be off, but he'd hardly touched the drink. He looked around again and caught eyes with two men who were watching them.

They nodded. *Friendly lot.* He nodded back.

They came over, one of them giving the muscle-guy a reverse head-

22

nod, the other one spoke to Robert saying, "So, you made it," as if they'd been expecting him, or he'd been expecting them.

What?

"Maybe later then," Muscles stood. "I'll be at the bar."

"Name's Pete, mind if we sit?"

"No. Go ahead."

"Jimbo." The other one put his empty glass down and added, "Haven't seen you here before."

"You-ahh," Pete's head turned quickly left and he looked around slowly, "looking for something?"

"What? No. Beer. That's all. Robert." Robert raised his glass, turned his embarrassment into a smile and said, "You come here often?"

"It's our local," said Jimbo.

"Another?" Pete nodded at Robert's almost empty glass.

Robert looked at it, surprise at his unconscious hurrying him along, except there was no need to rush now, and there was a relaxed buzz to the place. Or maybe it was the beer. "Thanks," emerged unexpectedly instead of no.

Beer foam drizzled towards the coaster and Robert picked up the glass, "Thanks mate."

"No worries, mate," Pete and Jimbo unisoned, smiling like he'd made a joke, and pretended to high-five.

They seemed much more relaxed.

A slight, athletic man wearing a black singlet, its cut-off end nuzzling the waistband of faded flared jeans, headed their way. Feeling beerily expansive, Robert smiled, shifting to make room, "Here, pull up a pew."

"Coming to the show Friday night?" the newcomer addressed Pete and Jimbo.

"Tank here, does a drag show at the Wickham."

Robert coughed.

They laughed.

"Really?" Robert asked recovering a fragment of composure.

"I'm quite famous in some circles," Tank lightly touched his chest, looked Robert up and down, smiled, and slugged his beer. He turned to Jimbo and Pete, launching into a conversation about people Robert didn't know from Adam.

As Robert's eyes scanned the beer garden, it slowly dawned on him that he'd found himself in a gay bar, and then he realised his long gazes were attracting attention. He turned back to the conversation he hadn't been following and finished his beer, in a hurry again now to leave.

"Let me buy you one before I leave," he said into a lull in the conversation.

"All good, mate. Next time," said Pete.

Tank sent him an air-kiss, "Come and see my show, Lovey."

"Will do," Robert nodded with apparent enthusiasm.

Tank smiled graciously.

"Thanks again. For the beer," Robert converted his formal hand extension to a more appropriate half-wave.

"See you around mate," Jimbo and Pete pretended to high-five again.

Tank laughed at them and called out to Robert's disappearing back, "Don't forget Lovey. Fridays. The Wickham."

Robert turned to acknowledge him and bumped into someone.

"Watch where you're going. Fucking poofter. You spilled my beer." It was Muscles, waving his almost full beer at Robert who suddenly felt sick.

"Oh, it's you." The flash of contempt disappeared from Muscle's face, something like encouragement in its place, "Looking for some action?"

"Sorry mate," Robert wasn't sure what for. Looking around self-consciously, he noticed two men at the end of the bar watching them, and looking distinctly out of place. One tallish with eyes that looked like they'd forgotten what a smile was. The other one, was unsuccessfully trying to keep a cream and hairy mountain of belly from escaping past the straining buttons of his public service style, short-sleeved white shirt.

He hurried past them, relieved to be exiting onto the verandah. As he turned, he spotted someone else. A tall redhead polishing glasses from inside an alcove doorway. He'd no doubt seen the beer-spilling side-show too.

Crossing the carpark in the afternoon sun, Robert shivered. And after a few gulps of hot stale air inside the car, he shivered again.

A thump on the car roof startled him. The sick feeling returned.

The creeps from the bar.

What the hell do they want?

Something wasn't right. He debated telling them to shove off. They

24

could be cops nabbing people for drink-driving. But they'd be in uniform, wouldn't they? And there'd been no sign of a badge.

Maybe they were after something else.

This time he shuddered, and started the car, inching forward.

Nothing happened.

He marginally increased the pressure on the accelerator. Another thud on the roof.

He flinched.

At the curb, he remembered to indicate. Glancing to the rear-view mirror, he was surprised not to see a flashing blue light.

***

"You should've gone straight to the nearest station," Lauren's cheeks wore pink highlights. She finished drying her hands on the tea-towel and plonked it onto the kitchen benchtop. "They're probably looking up your licence plate now. You know what they're like. What were you thinking?"

"Shit, I don't know. It was all so weird."

"Go to the station now. I don't want any unexpected knocks on the door."

"What should I tell them?"

"Seriously, Robert? You're the lawyer. Just tell them you wanted to do the right thing. Hurry up. I'll get the kids ready for bed."

"*You* should be a lawyer. Honestly, you think like one." He turned to go, "Hey, thanks."

"False alarm," he was home in under an hour. "No cops there."

"Maybe you dropped some change or something," Lauren shrugged. "You know, I've been thinking… what you said earlier, about I should be a lawyer. I'm inclined to give it a go. I mean, I like my job at the Assistance Centre, but let's face it, it's not going anywhere."

"Really? You've got a lot on. Honestly, I don't know how you manage as it is."

"Yeah, you're right. I have, haven't I?" Enthusiasm ebbed from her voice.

Robert noticed, "No. No. Look into it. Maybe part-time?"

"God, that would be what? Eight years. The kids would be in high-school."

He shook his head, "You've got a degree already. It could be lots less. Promise you'll look into it. I can help more at home and I don't go anywhere. Well, not usually. And Mum could," he faltered. "You could do it."

"What made you such a kind and thoughtful person?"

He found something on the cupboard to wipe.

"I feel so lucky," she said. "And at the same time I feel, I don't know, like there's something missing. That I'm missing something or missing out on something. Then I wonder what's wrong with me. I should be happy with what I've got. And I am, mostly. It's just—"

"Normal," he said. "It's normal. And I don't know about kind and thoughtful. Though nice of you to say."

"Are you happy, Robert?"

"What?" *Did she mean with her, with life in general, with his career, or the whole package? Was she picking up on his recent lapses in concentration and moments of melancholy?* "Of course."

Her scrutiny demanded an explanation.

"I have the most gorgeous children, a fantastic job, prospects, one day we'll even own this house. My parents have learned to hide the burden of their disappointment and I sometimes think they love me, a bit, despite me choosing law instead of following dad into politics. Against all expectation she'd say bugger off, I married the most beautiful woman in Brisbane and— What?" he asked when her head tilted. "Everyone says you are. And, even if she's a bit over-ambitious and tells me what to do, that doesn't change the undying gratitude I have *bursting* out of my heart every moment of the day," he finished with a hand on his heart.

"Nice speech," Lauren smiled. "Glass of wine?"

He nodded, "Seriously, I'm happy too. Mostly."

"That's it though, isn't it?" she said, filling the glass from the box in the fridge. She'd been standing in its open door when the speech started, "Something in me knows there's more. I just don't know what it is. And that makes it even harder, doesn't it? How are you supposed to get what you don't even know you're looking for?"

"I don't know," he said. And taking the glass he forged a smile,

"Cheers."

CHAPTER 6

"Here," Johnny passed an envelope over the desk to Robert. "The references. And sorry about the other day." He turned surprised as Anna came back through the open door with a tray and put it on the sofa table.

"I'm still a bit clumsy," said Robert. "I try to avoid liquids near my desk. Can't trust myself."

"I meant isn't this a bit fancy?"

As soon as they were sitting together on the sofa, Robert wondered why he'd asked Anna for tea. His thoughts and nerves were zinging erratically. He distracted himself with Johnny's references. He started to get up and knocked the edge of the tray. Johnny reached to stop his cup rattling on its saucer.

"I'll put these," Robert pointed the references towards his desk in lieu of finishing the sentence. *I should never have let Duncan talk me into this.*

"Are you going to sit back down?" Johnny said looking at Robert standing mid-room. "Or should I?" he started to get up.

"No. Yeah." Robert moved, sat and picked up his cup. "We'll go over procedure, a kind of run through. Familiarize you with what they might ask, and prepare your answers." Robert's voice was even, but his heartbeat wasn't. "I want you to be as comfortable as possible, at the hearing."

Robert put his cup down. Then picked it up again. He glanced over to his desk, at Lauren looking back at him from inside the silver frame, and remembering his conversation with her; her question, 'are you happy?' repeating itself. And then Johnny's voice was asking him something. "Sorry," said Robert. "What did you say?"

"I said, the other day, I'm not really sorry," said Johnny. "And I asked you, are you happy?"

Robert's eyes stayed on the photograph while he replayed the question again, and then again. Are you happy Robert? Are you happy? And the answer wasn't coming. He changed the words. *Am I happy?* And in the small space between the threat of tears and the first fleeting need to blink, a kaleidoscope of emotions converged into an undeniable no. *Not really. No.*

The knowing why was evasive, but the feeling was, like Lauren had said, of something missing. That even though from the outside it looked like he had everything, it was a lie. Or at least not the truth. There were things about his life, in his life, that made him happy. Yes. There were moments of gratitude. He fostered them. They were his go-to place for when knowing threatened to foment. But there was a hole in his life. And he'd been covering it with planks and patches and stepping carefully over it.

He and Johnny sat on the couch in the corner of the office, suspended in a timeless silence, and in full view of the inlaid leather-topped desk and the shelves of books and ribboned files. Robert's testamur gazed at them indifferently from above a hefty filing cabinet with brass shell-like handles. And side by side, their thighs and shoulders reacquainted, becoming a touchpoint for when he and Johnny had sat wordlessly together on the edge of the stage after their last performance together before graduation.

"You're remembering, aren't you?" Johnny's voice was quiet.

Robert nodded, "I came after you. To apologise." He paused. "And you weren't there."

There was silence.

"We should get to work." Robert stood and bent to pick up the tray.

Johnny went to get up.

"No," said Robert. "Stay there. I'll get rid of this and come back."

Johnny continued to stand and reached for the tray. He set it back down, then put his hand on Robert's shoulder.

Its familiar weight dragged Robert's eyelids down. He thought he felt the backs of Johnny's fingers brush against his cheek. He was unconsciously leaning into the touch when he opened his eyes and they looked at each other, neither one wanting to move. The perfection of this moment could disintegrate if a breath was taken. And then it was.

"What about the judge? Harry."

"What about us?" It wasn't petulant, but Johnny's hand fell.

"I'm married you know."

"Fuck's sake Robert," Johnny's eye travelled to the photograph of three year old Emma and Thomas on Robert's desk with their mother. "Your pigeon pair, they're twins? They're more like Lauren than you."

"Duncan's her dad."

"Oh? I thought— something Harry said. Doesn't matter. The judge, Harry, we're, he's, it's been a bit weird lately. I told you. Not only since this happened. Something else. He hasn't said. But he's my best friend. More than that. And I love him. It's hard to explain. Anyway," Johnny frowned, "are we working now, or is this just stuff you want to know."

"I don't know, I didn't—" Robert's shoulders lifted, but didn't settle into their professional stance. "I..." Johnny's hand was back on his shoulder. Robert looked down as it moved and softly framed his jaw. It didn't feel in the slightest awkward. He noticed the heat coming off it and spreading up across his cheeks, and he closed his eyes again. It felt like a gentle sun warming his face, and from somewhere, came the smell of cut grass competing with flowers. *Where was he?* He didn't know. He was watching a butterfly. It landed on his outstretched arm, its delicate feet stepping on the soft hairs, making his skin shivery.

There it was again. Now. On his cheek. He stayed perfectly still. It lifted and landed again, searching for a place to settle. He ached for it to land on his lips.

Ever so tenderly, it did.

Then a tentative tapping on the door.

Robert's eyes flew open, and Johnny stepped back.

"Hello," Anna's voice came through the closed door, before the tap-tap-tap repeated.

"Sorry," she said after Robert opened the door. "I couldn't get you on the intercom. There's someone waiting. They said it's important and," she stopped. "Are you OK Mr Carson?"

"Who? Never mind. Tell them I'll be a while longer. Or, could they come back in half an hour."

"It's OK," said Johnny. "I have to go."

CHAPTER 7

Robert didn't recall Johnny's departure at all. There was a vague idea that somehow he had to get through the day.

"Shall I take the tray?" Anna's question seemed to be asking more than it was.

Unexpectedly, the day passed in intense highly productive concentration. Whatever was in charge of this feat, also managed to stuff his emotions and confusion somewhere out of reach. It was like a switch had been flicked and any gaps through which a feeling or a thought might escape, was instantly and automatically puttied over.

His exuberance began waning though, on the drive home. Mental inactivity opened a fissure, and the automatic puttying of gaps switched off. He was left forcing everything back himself.

The respite of bedtime story was brief and by the time Emma and Thomas closed their eyes and he'd tilted his face ceilingward searching for the familiar welling of gratitude, he couldn't hold back the remorse. It flooded in.

Getting up to leave, a searing nasty jab under his ribs made him slump back onto the reading chair, surprised he was still breathing. He turned the book in his hand over without seeing it, and the pain jabbed again, holding him cramp-like. He imagined this is what happened when you drowned. Then remembered, float, don't struggle. Let the water hold you.

He floated, with his eyes on his sleeping children, but the flat water that he thought was holding him, sucked him into a riptide. *It was only a kiss. Not even. Was it? You had your eyes closed, fuckwit. Who even cares what it was. They will disappear. Lauren too. All of it will disappear. Everything. But Johnny?*

Was that real? Did I imagine it? You can't go there. Leave it. What the fuck were you thinking? Hah. You weren't. Breathe. I can't.

The air stuck.

His eyes found the corner of the room. He started counting, *one, two, three, four, five…* and rocking gently, pressing the book against his lap, his fingers curled around its spine. He tried to get to fifteen but panic clawed at the numbers and images from the past stole their places, jerking him into doorframes and corridor walls; trying not to notice the jeering faces as he fished his books from amongst the decaying lunch scraps in smelly rubbish bins; his school jumper muddied in the middle of the rugby field; the wedgies; and the smile you pasted on because everyone was just having a bit of fun. Then his mum's pursed lips and hard eyes, 'have you got no respect? I'm not made of money,' when he'd confessed to yet another accident with his belongings. And Terry's face, pink with shame, 'you won't tell my dad will you?' then slowly turning grey.

Doggedly he kept counting and the images faded. He noticed he was still clutching the book. Something more than, deeper than sadness, welled. He didn't want to contaminate the air with it and rushed out of the room heading unconsciously for the shower.

And now I'm supposed to chat with Lauren about her day. Fuck. Just, fuck.

He let the warm water mingle with his tears, flushing away the surface angst and welcomed the lethargic calm of emotional letdown.

For now, right now, this moment, he could simply do nothing. And then more nothing as the next moment arrived. He could contain this. He was daddy. Nothing had changed for Emma and Thomas. He was Lauren's husband. Nothing had changed for her. He was Mr Carson, respected lawyer. He could do this. And he could do with a scotch.

Lauren handed him a wineglass, "I didn't wait."

It would do.

"Did you switch off the exhaust in the bathroom?" she said. "It's started to drone and clunk again."

"Yeah. I didn't notice."

"Not straight away," she smiled. "But if you leave it on, it really makes a racket. There must be something wearing or loose."

"Mmmm," he said, "I'll have a look on the weekend."

"Good. Oh, and the new neighbours moved in," she said, putting the lid back onto a saucepan.

"What?" He stooped to look out the kitchen window.

"Oh, Robert," she frowned. "At work. I told you. That gay group. CAMP. You've heard of them?"

"Why? Should I?" Robert arranged his face, "Yeah. Yeah. I remember now. You said a couple of doors up. Probably good."

"Meaning?" she said.

"Meaning nothing. Just you get a pretty mixed bag at your office. Some of your lot might be a bit anti."

"My lot? Really?" Sarcasm and humour vied, "Yes, my lot would all be somewhat homophobic wouldn't they?"

"You know what I mean," he said. "Anyway, are we talking advisory or activism?" He didn't wait for an answer. "I don't suppose it will take the Premier long to send the boys-in-blue around to give them a shake up."

"No idea. But it's about time things changed, don't you think?"

"Of course I do." He forced a smile. *How was this even a conversation for tonight.* "What's that smell. Dinner, I hope."

"Are you hungry?" she said. We can eat now."

"Yep," he lied, "starving."

CHAPTER 8

"The hearing is next week," Robert was concentrating on keeping his voice low and even. "We need to talk before then. I've asked Anna to pencil you in last up this afternoon, if you can make it."

There was nothing.

Robert changed the receiver to his other hand, "Are you there?"

"Yeah, I'm here," said Johnny.

There was another lengthy silence, then Robert spoke, "I could come to your place again if you'd prefer."

"No," said Johnny. "It's OK."

"Are you sure?"

"Why would I say that if I," Johnny paused. "Unless you want to come here. Is that it?"

Robert held his words and his breath. He wasn't even sure.

"It would be easier for me," said Johnny.

Robert felt the air he'd been holding in, leave his body.

***

"I don't think you need any more coaching," Robert said. They'd gone over Robert's list of questions and answers and Johnny had delivered them with poise and humility.

"Are you worried?" asked Robert. "About the proceedings. What might happen, you know, if…"

"You said Duncan's opinion is that they have an agenda, we're just going through the motions, and this will quietly disappear."

"I wanted you to know though, I've looked up precedents."

"I'm not sure what you mean," said Johnny.

"I mean there's really nothing specifically like your case to go by, so we'd know what outcome to expect."

"Well, I'm trying not to worry. No point. I talked to Dad, he knows a few lawyers, they've said the same as Duncan. From a purely practical point, the police won't want this going any further." Johnny's shoulders did a slow rise and lower. "Harry's too high profile. People would be asking questions. And they, the police, don't want that. And, I didn't do anything."

Robert said nothing, but his face was sombre.

"I can almost see what you're thinking," said Johnny. "But if they can manufacture evidence to say I'm a notorious gay, then I can manufacture some to say I'm not. Marnie's got half the women who come to her salon lined up to vouch for me. They'll all swear I'm the best they ever had."

Robert couldn't help smiling.

"And Dad said I should have called him sooner. He's going to pay you if Harry doesn't."

"I don't want any money, Johnny. That's not what this is about. Duncan is happy to help free of charge, and I don't need the billable hours. So no."

"There is something I do want to talk about though," said Johnny.

Robert turned away from the window, "The elephant?"

"We need to. Don't you think?" said Johnny.

"It's really not necessary. There's Harry. There's Lauren. The kids. We sort of talked about this before. A while ago granted, but if anything, things are more complicated. That's it, as far as I'm concerned. We have to be practical."

"Obviously. Why do you always jump the gun?" Johnny said.

"What's that supposed to mean?"

"It seems like I'm always saying something like that's not exactly what I mean."

"Sorry," Robert looked down.

"It's OK. Let's talk about the practicalities then. Will I be seeing you after this hearing. Do I disappear? Are we going to be *just* friends again? You said we could go running together. Is that it? Do I get invited over for dinner? Is that something you want? Is that something I want?"

"I don't know," said Robert. "I don't know. No, yes, I do. Way back, you said you weren't interested in that. And well, I'm not interested in," Robert's words fell away, and so did his dramatic arm wave. "There's never going to be an us. Not in the sense of… Realistically you know that. We both do."

"And what about the other day, in your office. You felt nothing? *Realistically*, it didn't feel that way to me," the yellow flecks in Johnny's eyes glittered.

"I was confused."

"Ohhh, that's how you do confused is it? Hah! Good thing you don't get confused very often."

"Poor choice of words. I wasn't thinking," said Robert.

"What? Then? Now?"

"I let my emotions, the past, take over. It was unprofessional. I'm sorry."

"That's it? You're sorry. Sorry it happened or sorry for me? Or sorry you are lying to yourself. *Still* lying to yourself. When are you going to get real, Robert?"

"First things first. This," Robert slapped his briefcase, "is what's real. You and Harry is real. Me and Lauren is real. Emma and Thomas. My job, my family, my responsibilities." The self-righteous arm-wave rose again and this time it crested his words. "That's what's real. It doesn't go away just because in a haze, I don't know, a momentary lapse of judgment, I let you kiss me."

"You let me kiss you. You let me kiss you. You had plenty of opportunities to stop me. All you had to do was step back. Put up your hand. Oh! And there's a word. What is it? Yeah, I remember. Two letters, starts with N. N-O. You didn't even hesitate! You wanted me to."

Johnny leaned against the wall with his forearm and rested his forehead on it.

Robert searched for a reprieve. He slumped into a waiting armchair, found the corner of the room and closed his eyes. He rocked back and forward, "You're right." Robert opened his eyes, "I did want you to."

"Well?" Johnny wasn't willing to let this opening seal over. "This, what's between us, what's always been between us, this is real too. As real as everything, as everyone else. I'm real too."

Johnny closed his eyes and his fists bunched at his sides. When he opened them, his eyes found Robert's, "Don't I matter?"

Johnny's anguish hung in the air.

After a while, a soft sigh from Johnny, "Have you ever put yourself first?"

"I thought I was," Robert sounded slightly incredulous. "By saying no, to you. I thought I was. What the hell? What am I supposed to do?"

"For a start, at least admit it to yourself," said Johnny. "Make me real to you. Even if that's all I get. To know it's real and it matters. That I matter." He paused, looking at Robert's face, searching, checking, "I deserve that much, don't I?" The waiting tears welled.

Robert closed the gap between them, "You do. You do matter," he whispered as his arms encircled Johnny. "You always have. It's just..." his hand moved to the back of Johnny's head and cradled it, gently reassuring, guiding it onto his shoulder, *not possible, too hard, too complicated, too...*

He didn't finish the unspoken excuses, but as Johnny shook with a silent sob, the waiting tears rolled, unnoticed down Robert's cheek too.

"What happens now?" Johnny eased out of the embrace.

Robert's finger brushed the damp from his own cheek.

After a few moments, he said, "Let's not try to figure everything out in five minutes. First we have to get past the hearing as client and legal representative."

Johnny nodded.

"And I was thinking, on the way over, I should probably call you John. For the hearing. It's more masculine. I want everything we can, working in your favour."

"Do we need to talk about that now?" said Johnny.

"We sort of do."

"I probably won't answer you," said Johnny. "That's my dad's name when it's not Jack. I've always been Johnny. But hey, I'll try. Do I need to call you Mister Carson?"

"I don't know," said Robert. "That would seem weird too."

"You're overthinking Robert," Johnny said. "I think I should stick with Johnny. I can't be anything else."

Robert's half smile faded.

The lingering anguish seemed to close in around them.

They were silent.

"I can't promise anything," Robert said finally, "I don't mean about the case. Although— I mean after this is over. I can't go there in my head right now. I need to be clear and do my job. But when this is over, I," Robert hesitated, "I may not be able to tell you what I think, what I know, you want to hear."

Johnny sighed, "For now, it's enough you want to."

CHAPTER 9

Robert spotted Johnny walking away from the entrance of the Magistrates Court in Roma Street, and then retracing his steps, stopping to stare at his watch then turn again. When Johnny spotted Robert, hurrying towards him from the big end of town, where all the important buildings bunched together around Queen, Adelaide and George Streets, his relief was audible.

"Am I pleased to see you," said Johnny. "I know I said I wasn't worried, but all of a sudden—" He looked around at the faces waiting with him, they both did, and Johnny added, "I keep thinking what the fuck am I doing here."

In front of the unmoving eyes of the guards, Robert put his hand on Johnny's shoulder. He could almost feel Johnny's rising panic. He wanted to hold him. "Come on," he said.

Their early-afternoon shadows followed them into the building, hanging off them as they waited at the duty desk. The grey-ended fluorescent light above them, draped everything in an extra layer of gloom.

On the way to Number Six Courtroom, Johnny flinched as leftover sounds seeped through the air gaps of the heavy doors. Then sitting outside on the bench, he hunched over holding his forearms against his middle, "This place gives me the creeps," he whispered. "I feel like I'm going to be sick."

"Breathe. Try to relax," said Robert.

They said nothing for a while, then Johnny said, "What if those arseholes—?"

"Stop it Johnny. Don't even look at them."

"But—"

"That's if they're even here," said Robert. "If Duncan's right, which he usually is, it will be the statements, quick review, nothing important going on here, and with a bit of luck we're done and dusted."

"I'm fucked then. It's not like I've had much luck lately," Johnny said. "What about Harry? If he's not here to be questioned about making a mistake? I know Duncan said it's better if he's not here, but…"

"It depends."

"Yeah. My point."

"I wish," Robert looked for the right words on the ceiling. "You'd think, it's the law, cut and dried. But for us, right now? It's good that it isn't. Gives us wriggle room. Of course, you shouldn't even be here."

"And yet, here we are," a grim haze blanketed Johnny's eyes. "I really don't want to stand up there, answering their questions. Can't you answer for me?"

"If I can. But honestly—"

"Fuck's sake Robert," Johnny's eyes rolled.

"Sorry. Be respectful, and forthright and don't embellish. And Harry's statement is clever. It's sort of hinting nothing even happened. He says things like I thought. You've read it."

The tight skin around Johnny's eyes loosened, "I should be OK then?"

"Should be. But, we've gone over this," Robert frowned. "This charge, it's not like jaywalking. It comes under the criminal code. It's just supposed to be rubber stamped here and go straight up. But like I said, we have wriggle-room."

"And times are changing blah blah, I know," Johnny leaned back, "yay Bob Dylan and all that. But jeez, it's the twentieth century and for all intents and purposes, I talk to a guy in a bar and my life could be over."

Robert couldn't think of anything to say except, "Try not to worry."

The doors clunked and groaned.

"Remember to nod," Robert whispered, as the Clerk called them in. "And it's your Honour," he said.

"I've got it," Johnny hissed.

"My client would like to present his case your Honour," Robert handed his documents to the Clerk and bowed his head.

"So advised."

While the judge read, Robert scanned, pleased to see no arresting officers. It was a sign they weren't interested. He spotted the *Courier Mail* reporter, Simon Draper, and scowled. If he'd kept his opinions to himself, this wouldn't be happening. He mustered an acknowledgement, lowering himself back onto the seat next to Johnny with the grace of an uncomfortable spider.

"Excellent references young man," the Magistrate said, and Robert and Johnny breathed. "Commendable. How long have you been volunteering there?"

'Is it OK?' flashed across Johnny's face. "Your Honour. About a year, your Honour."

"Tell me, how did this come about?"

"Your Honour," said Johnny, "I used to walk Fuzz, our— my dog, in the mornings. There was always a queue outside this building, the 139 Club. I thought, I figured they were homeless. Fuzz broke the ice. They loved him. Anyway, when he died last year," he momentarily veered into the past, "Fuzz, I mean, I still walked in the mornings for a while. We'd nod and smile. Chat y'know. And one day I walked in with them, and offered to help. Your Honour," he nodded.

"And this situation. I'd like to hear what you have to say about it."

Robert's shoulders relaxed.

"Do I?" said Johnny.

The Magistrate indicated the adjacent witness box.

Johnny's hand rested on the Bible, and he promised to tell the truth.

Robert stood, "Mr Saunders, can you tell us in your own words what happened the night you were arrested?"

The words came with the easiness and earnestness of unpolished truth, eliciting approving nods from the Magistrate.

The prosecutor presented a few yes-no responses to some concisely unambiguous questions, and followed with a friendly, "You said, Mr Saunders, and correct me if I'm wrong, that you didn't know the complainant."

"No sir."

The prosecutor didn't hide his smarmy smile and began speaking again.

Johnny interrupted, "Excuse me, sir. Mr Prosecutor, but you said correct me if I'm wrong. I meant no, that's wrong. Sir. Is it OK to say that?" Johnny turned towards the magistrate.

The Magistrate nodded, "Continue."

"I'd met him before. That's why I was talking to him. If I'd known he didn't want compan—" Johnny saw Robert's hand close to the table-top, hovering. "I was extending a social courtesy to someone I had met before."

"And yet when you were told you were under arrest, you agreed to go with the arresting officers," the prosecutor sounded soothingly reasonable, "so I contend that you were, as charged, soliciting."

Expecting this implication of guilt, Johnny presented mildly aggrieved shock, "No sir, Mr Prosecutor. I agreed to go, yes, but I didn't want to, and I certainly didn't agree with the charges." Johnny half turned so he was also facing the Magistrate, "I know that resisting arrest or obstructing police officers in the course of their duty is wrong. I didn't have any choice except to go with them. I fully expected it would all be cleared up at the station. I understand, though," quickly flicking his eyes to Robert, "the police were just doing their job. But I definitely wasn't doing what you said. And I fully expected they would see a mistake had been made."

When the prosecution had finished, the Magistrate shifted his attention to Robert.

After Robert's 'nothing further', the Magistrate's hand floated regally from the witness box towards the defence desk, "You are excused."

Everyone watched as the Magistrate leaned back, supported his elbows on the ample armrests of his chair, and tapped his fingertips together underneath his deliberating chin. He stared at a spot halfway up an imaginary wall.

Eventually the silent tapping stopped, the fingers pressed together and angled forward pointing at Johnny.

"Your testimony is compelling, Mr Saunders, and I don't find any evidence that you have actually committed any offence." The hands came down contentedly to his midriff, as if they were signalling the end of a satisfying meal, then moved abruptly to his armrests, "And under any other circumstances, I would dismiss this case. However, this is a criminal offence, the complainant is a judge, and I feel bound to send it up for committal. Where it rightly belongs. Perhaps with clarification from the judge." A slight shrug filled the pause. "Mmm, well." He looked at Johnny, "You will receive notification of the court date in due course but not more than six months hence."

He pushed against the armrests levering himself out of the chair, "This court is adjourned."

As the robes swished through the door at the side of the courtroom, Johnny's hand raked through his hair.

He bent his nod lower into his hands, fingers pressing against his forehead and whispered, "Fuck, fuck, fuck."

CHAPTER 10

"This was *not* supposed to happen," Johnny glanced at Duncan and Robert, and tugged at the hair behind his ear, "Harry paid them. It wasn't supposed to go up to anywhere."

"You're right," said Duncan, "But it was always a possibility. A criminal—"

"It's a setback," Robert cut him off. "That's all. You heard the Magistrate. He said there's no evidence to say you are guilty of an offence."

"He wants someone else to rubber stamp it," Duncan said.

"But what if that's not what he wants. What if next time there is evidence?" said Johnny. "They could easily find someone else to blackmail into saying or doing whatever the hell they want, and we wouldn't know." He looked over at Robert, "I know I joked about Marnie's clients. But I don't think they'd willingly perjure themselves."

Duncan pulled out a chair for Johnny at the boardroom table and then sat down himself, "Let's take a moment here. It all depends—"

"I'm sick to death of hearing that. Depends. Depends and fucking possibilities," Johnny gripped the back of the chair with both hands. "It's like I'm a chess piece. And the game, it still looks like chess from the outside, and unless you are one of the pieces, you'd think it was. But it isn't."

No-one disagreed.

Johnny's face was grim, "I need a drink."

"I could do with one myself," Robert said, still standing in the doorway.

"We can have one here. There's," Duncan stopped when he saw the look on Johnny's face.

"No, don't get me wrong," Johnny said. "I didn't mean— Really, I owe

44

you one, for all this. It's just I meant out."

"You don't owe me," Duncan said. "And out isn't my thing. But you and Robert, you should go and-ah, unwind," he stood up to cover his embarrassment. "It's been quite a shock. And this whole thing," his head wagged from side to side, "isn't over yet."

Johnny's hand moved upwards and Robert raised an eyebrow.

"Apologies, I shouldn't have said that, I'm," Duncan stopped.

"Tell you what," Robert filled the gap. "You and Johnny have a boardroom drink while I call Lauren and tell her I'm going to be late."

"Good idea," Duncan looked pleased.

Robert wasn't sure if it was the prospect of a shared drink or the attentiveness to Lauren, till Duncan added, "Gotta keep my little girl happy."

Robert was suddenly defensive, "I haven't had any complaints."

In his office he stared at the phone, contemplating his life keeping Lauren happy. He hadn't thought about it like that. Ever. He loved her. He loved his kids. It had never felt like a burden. But there's that something. Shifting. Shapeless. Out of reach. She'd said it herself. *Except yours has a shape. A Johnny shape.*

Eventually he picked up the handset and pushed the button for an outside line. It was Anna's early day. At least he'd made someone happy today.

***

"That was a bit awkward," said Johnny as they emerged from the office building.

"What? He can't have any idea about, you know," Robert kept his eyes on the footpath.

"What?" said Johnny. "It's not always about your secret Robert. Other people have secrets too. Maybe that's why he was OK about helping me."

"What do you mean?"

"I mean," said Johnny, "Duncan's gay."

"How do you know?"

"Gaydar. I suspected earlier. I'm not a hundred percent, but…"

Robert slowed, "I would never have guessed."

"Obviously."

"So does he know he's gay?"

"How would I know? Johnny shrugged. "How long's he been married?"

"Lauren's mum died twenty-odd years ago. I thought you knew. Lauren was only young. Cancer."

"No. Maybe Marnie knew. If she told me, I forgot. Anyway, we have something else in common, me and Lauren. And he never married again?"

"Lauren said he never even dated anyone. 'Only have eyes for one girl now,' he used to tell her. I know," Robert acknowledged the eyebrow raise. "But it made her feel special. Still does. I suppose between working long hours and taking care of Lauren it never seemed strange to anyone. Maybe him too."

"It explains why he has an affinity with you."

"You don't think he's subconsciously attracted to me?" Robert shuddered, "That would be weird."

"Hah. Get over yourself. I meant, straight guys, they tend to keep us at arm's length," Johnny said. "Hadn't it ever crossed your mind?"

"No. I thought he was nice to me because of Lauren. And I am good at my job."

"But how would he know that, before you started working for him? Seriously Robert, how many jobs *didn't* you get, before you got this one?"

Robert frowned, "Do you think Lauren knows? About her dad. Not me."

"How the fuck should I know? You're the one who's married to her," Johnny rolled his eyes. "Hey, I didn't mean it to come out like that. I doubt it. To her it would seem normal. Like that's just dad."

"What about other people?"

"I don't think he's passing." And to Robert's vague look, "Pretending he's straight, like some—" He turned away, "At work, he's himself. The boss. To clients? They wouldn't give a rat's arse as long as he's sorting their problems for them. And they wouldn't be looking, would they? They'd be completely preoccupied, with what's going on in their life. Even if he was sending signals, they wouldn't notice them."

"But you did."

"Yeah," said Johnny, "but not right away. Other people might too. Probably why he's not into pubs and socialising. Anyway, why are we talking about him?"

"I don't know. Better than talking about— Where are we going?"

"Somewhere I don't have to pretend being something I'm not."

At the next intersection Johnny turned towards a line of taxis and raised a finger, "The Valley mate. Drop us off in Ann Street near the Station."

When they got out Robert looked around, "Are we catching the train?"

Johnny shook his head, "Up a few hundred metres, The Wickham."

"Why didn't we get dropped off there?" the crease deepened on Robert's forehead.

"Not everyone's gay friendly in case you haven't noticed."

"The famous Wickham," Robert said.

Johnny made a sweeping welcome-to-my-world gesture on his way to get drinks. Robert sat at one of the tables on the footpath, outside the French-door side-entrances to the pub. Removable lattice fencing was decoratively separated by greenery-filled pots, and guarded patrons from the curb-edge.

"Thanks," Robert stared into the foam before looking up. "I'm really sorry about today. I don't know what else to say."

"Nothing you could do," Johnny's head swayed side to side, "unless you could've dragged Harry in to have a chat to that Magistrate."

"Are you worried?"

"Of course. They've got six months. Who knows what they'll get up to."

"But they can't introduce anything else, and even if they made something up, it wouldn't be allowed, admissible."

"Robert. Chess?"

"But things have been documented. In Court."

"You're still being a lawyer piece, in the *old* game. You think you know what's going to happen. Your experience, the past, the rules. It doesn't mean shit," Johnny paused. "I'm just glad those creeps who arrested me weren't there today. It's humiliating enough, I wouldn't want to give them the satisfaction. Urrgh. The thought of them makes my skin crawl."

"Reminds me," said Robert. "When you said skin crawl."

Johnny finished listening to Robert's encounter at the Story Bridge Hotel, "I'll leave the whatever you were doing there for later."

"Nothing. An innocent beer on a hot day."

"What can you remember about them?"

Robert squinted, "They were at the end of the bar trying to look like they belonged," his head shaking. "Ties and short-sleeve shirts."

"Really? Hah. I'm getting a fashion report."

"D'you know that cop show *Division 4*?"

Johnny nodded.

"Their clothes. Not them. And without those detective hats. Anyway, the older one, the buttons on his shirt, big gaps with belly hair poking through. Gross."

"And their faces?"

"Honestly, I was trying *not* to look at them," Robert closed his eyes, "Fat one, jowly; big nose, red and lumpy; dark piggy eyes, sneaky looking; greying hair at the sides, stupid comb-over. The other one, younger, skinnier, taller, darker. Angry-looking, like the world owed him an apology for slapping his bum on arrival." He opened his eyes, "They were both smirking, like they were in on some big secret, some big joke."

"You never asked me what the cops who arrested me looked like. Nichols and Andrews."

"I thought we'd see them in court."

"But we didn't. And that's them to a T," said Johnny.

"But those guys, mine, weren't police. I checked."

"You checked?"

After listening to the next episode, Johnny shook his head, "Robert. Think. They would have been checking for traffic cops or keep-the-public-safe ones. No-one in Coorparoo Station would have any idea what Special Branch or Licencing Branch were doing."

"You're right."

"Tell me what actually happened at the pub. Start to finish. All the details."

When Tank's name was mentioned, Johnny chuckled lightly, "So your gaydar does work."

"You wouldn't be talking about *moi* would you?" The voice came from behind a large red-headed man, and Robert's eyes narrowed in recognition.

Then a signature black cut-off tank-top appeared, "My shell-likes are burning." And spotting Robert, "Oh, Lovey. You made it!" His hand rested against the vee of his throat. He sent air-kisses to Johnny, then added, "This is Blue," he introduced the red-head to Robert.

"I saw you at the Story Bridge pub, didn't I?" said Robert.

"Can't stay," said Blue. "I'll send you out a jug. Nice meeting you," he nodded to Robert and waved himself off.

"Well," Tank topped up his beer from the jug as Johnny finished speaking, "I wondered why I hadn't seen you around. Those bloody stinkers. But there's fuck-all we can do."

They filled him in on Robert's encounter next.

"So, before I came along, you'd been propositioned by Muscles." He turned to Johnny, "He's fairly new on the scene. Nicknamed Muscles because, well," Tank flexed a slender arm. Turning back to Robert, he continued, "And then you were rescued by Pete and Jimbo. Then those creeps of Johnny's," he paused, "I wouldn't mind betting they were trying something like that on you. Like Harry and Johnny."

"But I'm not anyone important," said Robert.

"Yeah, but," said Tank, "they saw you with Muscles, and Pete and Jimbo, and you weren't exactly blending in." He turned to Johnny and mouthed, 'Sore thumb.' Then back to Robert, "Neither were they. Maybe they were just trying their luck, see what you'd do if they threatened to tell your wife or your boss where you'd been."

"Do you think?" The possibility spread across Robert's face.

"Why else would they be there?" Johnny's brow furrowed.

Tank bent forward, "Don't say anything. Blue hasn't exactly spelled it out, but I've seen him hand over the odd bulging envelope or brown paper bag. I call them unofficial licencing fees. Probably other things too, which I don't know about."

Johnny's fingers drummed the table, "I was going to ask you if you'd noticed them there before. Or since. Or anywhere else. Here even."

"I've seen them a few times, not here though," Tank said.

"Why do you need to know?" Robert said. "It won't make any difference to you. To the case."

"You don't know that," Johnny challenged. "Chess?"

Tank looked into his beer.

Johnny put his hand over Robert's, "I know you're trying to get this over with, no fuss but when Tank said there's nothing we can do," he shook his head. "Someone's gotta do something. Start to. And well, I am."

"What do you mean?" Robert glanced at his hand and left it there, using the other one to lift his beer.

"I called the journo, Simon. The one who wrote the news story that got me into this mess. He was there today. That's *why* he was there today."

Robert's unswallowed beer sprayed the table.

"Manners please, Lovey," Tank joked.

"*You* did?" Robert ignored Tank.

Johnny looked at Robert, "Journos protect their source. And anyway, if the police can do dossiers on me and Harry, and half of fucking Queensland, then I can help Simon do dossiers on them. Bastards."

"You're mad." Tank softened it with a pat on Johnny's hand, still resting on Robert's. "But in a good way."

"I've been thinking about it for a while. And," Johnny paused. "It's not just what happened to me. There's others. I heard this story, from one of my 139 mates. Maybe he picked up, knew it'd be OK to tell me."

"Because his radar works," Robert said flatly.

"Maybe," said Johnny. "But, these guys open up a bit when they know you aren't judging them. I don't know the whole story. It sounded like entrapment. Not that you could do anything about it. Anyway, my man is on a night out. Some guy won't leave him alone. My man's not really interested and leaves. But the guy follows him to the taxi rank. No cabs. Come on, says the guy, I'll give you a lift. In the car the guy comes on to him and well, my man didn't say no. Thought why the hell not. It hadn't got all that far when they were interrupted. What did he call it? Gross indecency. That was the charge I think."

Robert squirmed.

"Jail?" Tank asked.

"Yeah. But the harder part comes later," said Johnny. "He was a teacher. Can't teach anymore because he has a criminal record. No-one else wants to give him any other job for the same reason. So, money, house friends, all gone." Johnny scoffed, "Even his family. He's a dead-set outcast. Everyone deserted him."

"And," Tank added, "it'd be even worse for teachers, especially now. They've been flogging 'all gays are paedophiles' till it's mainstream. Everyone believes it."

"When did all this happen?" Robert's face had paled, he looked around nervously. "I should get going."

"Does it matter?" Johnny ignored the escape bid.

"I suppose not. But—"

Johnny interrupted, "Things haven't changed Robert. It doesn't matter if it was ten years ago or twenty or yesterday. They get away with it."

"I know. That's my point. I'd be in exactly the same place," Roberts eyes flicked around again in a hurried scan.

"Fuck. Sorry. I'm an idiot. I didn't think," Johnny's hand went to his hair.

"Don't worry, OK?" Tank held Robert's shoulder, "Those paper bags? That's what they're for. While you're in here nothing happens."

"It sort-of did though. Almost," said Robert. "You even said you thought—"

"But it didn't, did it?" Tank interrupted. "They must have thought better of it and remembered their part of the bargain. Or it could have been something else completely."

Robert breathed in and out slowly.

"You might as well hear the rest," said Johnny. "I also called CAMP. They're starting up here. In Brisbane."

No one spoke.

"Thanks for the support," Johnny huffed.

"You being straight and wrongly accused, that's our defence," Robert's voice was too loud. "Can't this wait?"

"It's people helping other people. I don't have to wear a badge or anything. They don't tattoo your forehead."

"Don't be angry," said Robert. "I'm on your side. Remember?"

"What's the go?" Tank intervened. "Is it a job? Volunteering? And what exactly is CAMP? Well, you know."

"It stands for campaign against moral persecution, it's like an advocacy service I suppose, and I don't know what I'll be doing," Johnny shrugged. "Maybe nothing. They said they'd be in touch."

"So," Robert herded the cats in his head, and started to relax, "all you've done is call them. You've only talked to Simon Draper, and the dossier business is just you planning on gathering info."

Johnny relaxed too, "I'll probably end up being mail-boy or tea-lady, hah. Maybe they'll want to know my story. Harry's and mine. It's," he looked up before continuing, "I just don't wanna be another helpless victim. We gotta start being proactive. You know?"

Tank was nodding into the silence of Johnny's faded momentum and said, "I've got two good ears and eyes. I can help."

"Would you?" Johnny's face brightened.

"Don't get carried away, eh?" Robert tried to sound light-hearted. "Both of you. Should we make a move?" He looked at his watch.

"I hardly think Lauren would be expecting you home before dark," Johnny scowled.

"I thought you'd be sticking around for the show," Tank pouted just as a foam-topped jug arrived.

Having the venue's star performer as a table guest had perks.

"I suppose I'm staying then," Robert grinned as Tank poured. "And anyway, it's a night out and I'm a grown man. I can do what I want. Can't I?"

*

Encroaching night had driven Robert, Johnny and the rest of the beer garden crowd inside. By the time Tank's first show was due to start, Robert was happily and loosely wilting.

"What are you smiling about?" said Johnny.

"Tomorrow's hangover," said Robert. "I've only had one. I discovered mum's secret stash. I even topped it up with her *ahem,* cold tea."

"I think we all have one of those memories," Johnny laughed.

"I 'onessly think she didn't notice. I—"

The lights flashed, and conversation stalled. In the darkened hush, a spotlight swung across the crowd, illuminating a figure on the stage. Tank. Looking like nothing Robert had ever imagined. Sparkling in a blue sequined gown. The iridescence was repeated on his eyelids, or what you could see of them through astonishingly wealthy eyelashes. The Marilyn

Monroe do, pinkly contoured cheekbones, and cliché but luscious, fire-engine-red lips completed the picture. And then the music started.

Everyone let Tank lip-sync Gloria Gaynor before joining in full throttle to proclaim they will survive, while boisterous hey, heys, bounced loudly off the walls.

Bodies moved and swayed, disco pointing congas formed and fell away, and choruses became heartier as the crowd's ABBA favourites came on, one after the other. Tank was a star entertainer. He selected people seemingly at random, to join him on the compact stage. The disinhibiting effects of alcohol mixed with unfettered letting-loose, smoothed out any embarrassing kinks and everyone who stepped off the stage met with exuberant cheers.

Taking his turn, Robert was delighted with his uncharacteristic finesse.

Far from wilting now, he felt like a disco queen and moved like one, almost matching Tank's turns and twists and sidesteps to *Mamma Mia* as if he were one of the originals.

When it was over and the applause and whistles had abated, Johnny met him, halfway up the stage steps.

"You were brilliant!"

Robert gave him a face splitting grin.

They stood there together as the lighting muted and Tank centre-stage, presented his back to the audience, his head down and sequins twinkling in the silence. The music started again, subdued with melancholy, and he turned slowly, lifting his face into the light.

Thank You for the Music was traditionally a solo with everyone floating in the emotion of Tank's final dramatic moment in the spotlight. A restrained silence followed the fade-out, no-one in a hurry to break the mood.

Standing midway on the stage stairs, Johnny squeezed Robert's hand and brought it to his lips. The spotlight included them at the edge of its glow, and picked out the tears in Robert's eyes. As the crystals fell onto his cheek, a finger on Johnny's spare hand reached over and touched them.

Lost in their own world, they turned in to each other and kissed.

And the crowd erupted.

CHAPTER 11

Robert rolled carefully onto his back, and felt for the sheet, pulling it up across his chest and smoothing it unconsciously. From inside the woolly haze of what felt like dreaming, he'd heard a door close, and opened his eyes. Awareness of waking in a strange room, brought up a churning mix of anxiety and remorse. What on earth was he going to say to Lauren? Oops? I got a bit drunk? I ended up, what? He started shaking his head and stopped. He felt sick.

He rushed for the bathroom.

"Feeling better?" Johnny fresh and apparently completely un-hungover, handed him a shopping bag, "Coke, crackers and toothbrush."

Robert peeked inside.

"There are towels in the cupboard," said Johnny. "And help yourself to aspirin and toothpaste. Take your time."

Johnny moved over on the bed as a towel-draped Robert perched on the edge, crackers in one hand and coke in the other.

"It's closer to lunchtime than breakfast," Johnny said taking the coke and handing Robert the phone. "Lauren will be worried. Should I leave?"

Robert's stomach was still fragile. He kept his head still, "It's me— I know. Yeah, I just woke up— It was. I honestly don't know what time— Way too many— Yeah, at Johnny's."

Johnny went to leave and Robert signalled him to wait.

"No, it's still in town, we'll get it later, I'd be way over the limit— Oh shit yeah, I forgot— OK, hang on, I'll put him on. And hey, thanks— Love you too. Johnny, can you give Lauren directions?" He handed Johnny the receiver.

"Is this going to be awkward?" Johnny said, replacing the handset.

"I don't think so. Guys at work talk about crashing at a mate's after a big Friday night. It'll be OK."

There was a pause, filled with awkwardness anyway, "Johnny, did, did we?"

"What do you think?"

Robert's head moved automatically upwards.

"Relax. We were both a bit past it," Johnny sighed.

Robert looked down in embarrassment and regret, "I had an amazing time. Only sorry it was on the back of such a disappointing day."

"Yeah, but good to have forgotten about it for a while, eh?"

"Johnny," Robert forced his eyes not to move, "I think, I really want, you know."

"I know. So do I. Now is not the time."

"Yeah. Right. It's," Robert looked away. "Did you tell Harry what happened? At court."

"Well that just killed the mood," Johnny sighed. "Sorry, I'm joking. Half-joking. Duncan called him from the boardroom, said the case was sent up. He said thanks for updating him. Not to phone. He'd be in touch. He's a bit paranoid. Don't blame him."

"I should get dressed."

"Don't. Not yet." Johnny patted the space next to him, "Lie down."

Robert hesitated, and glanced at the clock.

"I just want to hold you," Johnny shifted to create more space and Robert lowered himself and placed his head on the pillow. With his back to Johnny he closed his eyes, welcoming the arm curling over him, enjoying the spreading warmth.

"Turn around."

"I don't want to breathe on you," Robert protested.

"I didn't ask you what you wanted."

Robert turned and their foreheads touched. Then their noses, and then their lips. Softly. Johnny's hand trailed across Robert's shoulder, inching down towards the side of the towel, and finally feathering against the skin of his penis. As it thickened in response, Robert's chest tightened. An uncontrollable whimper escaped as he started breathing again. And then he turned swinging his legs over the side of the bed, sitting up, and pressed the towel against his erection.

"Get dressed," Johnny rolled over exiting on the other side, keeping his smile hidden, "How do you like your tea?"

"Strong," Robert said contemplating the nerve-wracking and incredulous thought that very soon, he, his wife, his kids and this man he also loved, would be sharing a table and a pot of tea, "and a dash of milk."

They could hear the kids clamouring along the hallway and Johnny opened the door to greet them. When Lauren's 'Shhhh' caught up with them, they reverted to their quiet-as-little-mice bedtime walk.

"You haven't changed a bit," she said looking pleased when he reciprocated.

Robert put his best husband smile on and much to Emma and Thomas's amusement, stumbled on the mat, before placing a kiss on Lauren's cheek, "Johnny made tea," he said.

"Here," Lauren handed a kiddy-tote to Robert. "Change of clothes. We'll go straight to the BBQ at your parents' place." She laughed at the pained look on his face, "Serves you right."

Robert hesitated at Johnny's bedroom door and walked past it into the spare room.

In the kitchen, Johnny held up a cup, a question mark on his face.

"Dash of milk, strong." Lauren turned towards the TV, "Would you mind? Saturday morning cartoons will keep these two occupied."

CHAPTER 12

Lauren was looking for a gap in the stream of traffic, "Johnny told me what happened."

Robert felt his stomach lurch. His face went clammy. He said nothing.

Merging into the lane, she continued, "Yes," she said, as if he'd asked a question, "he told me about Harry, the arrest, court, how he was completely," she mouthed, 'fucking', "shattered." Her eyes flicked to the review mirror, checking the kids, "And how you and Dad decided he needed cheering up."

"Oh. Yeah. I should've just had a couple of drinks in the boardroom."

She shrugged, "What are friends for? Even not-seen-in-ages ones?"

"Mmm."

"It's not a good place to be mentally you know," she continued, "Johnny, I mean. He must be feeling pretty vulnerable."

Robert started unpicking the knot of nerves in his midriff, "It's not like we're close friends. Used to be. But I hadn't seen him for years. Not since— till this happened."

"Obviously."

The wind buffeting their ears from the open windows filled the silence.

"It doesn't bother me," Lauren said after a while, "if you want to go out sometimes. I was surprised. Only because you never do. But I think it's healthy."

"Maybe not the hangovers."

"Hah. No. But that part's not compulsory." She changed lanes and continued. "I was wondering why you never saw him. He said he'd been back in Brisbane for a couple of years. I thought perhaps it was because he's," Lauren's eyes flicked to the mirror again, "gay? I thought maybe your dad? The National Party line?"

"What? No, of course not. We lost touch. Marnie too, I feel bad."

"Thanks for that. Now I feel like s-h-i-t." She drove for a while, silent. "It's, well, you start out with good intentions and then you find yourself in different worlds."

"Brisbane's hardly different worlds," Robert's eyes turned away from her withering look. "But I get it. Marnie's little girl, Nicole, must be about— God, I don't even know? Six? Seven? Crap friends, aren't we?"

"I'm going to call and ask her over. She might tell me to piss off, but…"

Robert stared at the windscreen thinking about Marnie. How she'd rescued him in his first weeks at the new school. He'd wondered why the boys harassing him were in such a hurry to leave when he heard the voice, 'I saw all that,' it had said, and he'd turned, embarrassed, a hand anchored under each armpit to press off the throbbing threat of bruises trying to break through the tight skin. He'd looked into her eyes, yellow flecks on blue, *the same as Johnny's*, her face framed on either side by two loosely held ponytails, the same auburn as her eyebrows, *the same colour as Johnny's*. She started picking up his textbooks from where they'd been kicked around the empty classroom, 'Arseholes,' she'd said, adding 'You're the cross-country boy aren't you? I can see if there's any ice in the tuckshop.'

But he hadn't wanted her to leave, and made a lame joke about at least he'd learned to run fast, and followed it with 'anyway, it's just good-natured teasing.' 'Bullshit,' she'd said, 'They were stomping on your hands. That's assault.' And added that half of them were probably gay too. He'd muttered, 'I'm not gay'. And she'd shrugged like it was nothing, and said are you sure, and that she wasn't bothered either way.

They'd exchanged names and he'd instantly gone back to the thought of Terry, scared and alone, sobbing in the boys' toilets, saying are we going to be best friends now? And he thought he recognized something in her or in himself. The same feeling.

She'd said, 'You should try not to be alone.' And he'd smiled, and said, 'Seriously,' then laughed. They'd both laughed.

She was the only other person besides Johnny who knew what he really was. Although he'd never actually come out and said it. Anxiously, he contemplated Lauren's plans, and that they might all soon be sharing a bottle of wine or dinner together, and didn't answer.

"What? You don't think I should?" Lauren's voice brought him back.

"No. No, I mean of course. You should."

"I'll make more of an effort with Dad too. He can't spend every weekend re-potting orchids. *And*," she said, "if you really mean you don't mind about Johnny, you should make an effort too. He could use a friend right now. Not just a lawyer."

"What? A boys' night out or something?"

"Exactly. It's not like you're overwhelmed with after work activities. And it'll make me feel better."

"OK. But I don't understand. Why? Why would you feel better?"

"Well, I'm going to need more help at home," she glanced at him and he remembered to smile. "I got the notification from UQ about Law. I've been accepted. I'd planned on telling you last night. But then I started to worry about what you said. Part time work and part time uni and the kids. I know the money comes in handy but—"

"You're right," Robert interjected. "Sorry, I don't mean about the money. We'll make do. No, I was thinking you should go full-time. Speed things along."

"Are you OK with that?"

"Yeah. Honestly. Have you told Duncan yet?"

"I wanted to talk to you first."

"Then it's settled."

"Of course," she pretended, "if you'd had any reservations, I would've ditched the whole random idea and gone back to the kitchen sink, in my bare feet. Of course, I'd need to be pregnant. Goes without saying."

"Have I told you how adorable you were bare-foot and pregnant?"

"Not in ages."

They both breathed more easily behind their smiles.

Lauren indicated.

"Looking forward to this," Robert joked, as they parked in the driveway of an elegant Colonial-Queenslander, accessorised by a jacaranda whose petals fell like melting mauve snow and had killed off the once green front lawn. "How long are we staying?"

"I imagine," Lauren's lip twisted, "at least until Big Russ decides everyone can go home. How does your dad stand it?"

"Practice? Honestly, I have no idea."

"Is he standing for the next election? Your dad."

"Yeah. Said this would be his last. But he said that last time too. It's so they have the numbers."

"I'm surprised. Don't the country votes carry more weight than the city ones? And I thought they divvied up safe electorates, made a few more National Party seats out of thin air." Lauren bounced out of the car and flashed him a spectacular smile, "How's my happy face?"

*

Barry Carson grasped Robert's shoulder and hand for a hearty father-son shake, "Easy Dad. Bit of a hangover."

"Hah! That's my boy." He steered Robert towards the men semi-circled around the BBQ and the esky full of ice and beer. The heat sheen above the hotplate had spread, seemingly condensating on their sun-pinked faces.

"Pass him a hair of the dog will you Russ?" Barry turned back to Lauren, a child at the end of each arm, "Jeannie's in the kitchen Love. With the girls."

Only Robert noticed the mischief in her eyes.

As she walked towards him, the conversation thinned and watching eyes widened.

"Gentlemen," she nodded. "You won't be needing this," she said taking the kiddy-tote from Robert's hand and turning back towards the house.

Robert watched till Russ Hinze's massive paw nudged a beer into his own, "Thanks. Bit early for me."

"No such thing." No-one argued with Big Russ.

Robert raised the bottle in the BBQ salute. "Cheers," he swallowed, and shielded his eyes so the grimace would be attributed to the sun, and surreptitiously appraised the Minister for Everything.

He imagined Russ's reaction if he said something, about gays, or AIDS or even street marches. He saw the blank face, and the open wordless mouth, and the slow lizard-blink, and speech resuming on a totally different topic. It made him think about Johnny's dossiers. Maybe it *was* time to be proactive. He might not be driving the conversation, but he could be a better passenger and take in the lie of the land. He just wished it hadn't been today, with a hangover, and that he'd brought a hat, and that they'd all want to leave early.

"Your old man says you're a lawyer."

Robert recognised Mike Ahern's face. Unsure if they'd actually met, he faked having a mouthful of beer and nodded.

"We could do with some of your type in the House. Place is full of old farmers," Mike flicked an upraised eyebrow in Russ Hinze's direction, "hell bent on modifying the laws to suit themselves. Or should I say, amending the legislation?" His chuckle tried to lighten the accusation.

"Anything in particular you don't agree with?"

"Got a list as long as your arm, mate," Mike stepped back from the circle and Robert accepted the invitation. "I've been in this game for a while. I keep expecting things to be about the good of the community, y'know, not for the good of the fat cats." He looked off at something on his mind's horizon. "But if you're not part of the gang, nothing happens. Even then…"

"Gang?" Robert frowned.

"Gang of Eighteen. The Premier's special club. And to be part of it, well, two things. You gotta have something Joh wants, and you gotta do as you're told. Ask your dad. He knows more than most how this system works."

"Can I ask *you* a question?"

"Fire away."

"The Lucas Inquiry?"

Mike winced, "I had hopes we'd get a police *service,* not an even more heavy-handed police *force.* I also kind-of hoped that the brown paper bags would disappear." Mike looked towards that imaginary horizon again, and back to Robert, "Anyone who wasn't just sitting on their arses and watching that Inquiry die, were actively killing it off."

"So it's well and truly dead?" Robert asked.

"No-one here's given it mouth-to-mouth."

"But they must know what's going on," Robert surveyed the yard's occupants. "It's not right in your face front-page headlines, but it's not invisible. Those journalists, like Simon Draper, who've dared put their hand up, their stories, they can't all be wrong. Why would they make it up?"

Mike squinted and smiled, "You've heard Joh talk about feeding the chooks haven't you?"

"Hasn't everyone?" Robert frowned, "But do you mean Queenslanders in general or the media?" He paused, "Or both?"

"Let me put something to you," Mike ignored the question. "You'd agree, that if you give a fox the key to the henhouse, you can't blame it for doing what comes naturally?"

Robert's shoulders and eyebrows lifted in unison.

"Bit of a shame. Couple-a dead chooks," Mike said. "Farmer's not happy. Wants the key back. But the fox says no, and his mates, they want keys too now. Of course, the henhouse would be empty in no time, and that doesn't suit anyone. You with me?"

Robert nodded.

"So one of two things has to happen. No more eggs and no more chickens, *or*, the fox and the farmer have to work together. Up the game so to speak."

"And," Robert said, "the more foxes, keys, chickens, and farms, the bigger it gets. So how? How does it stop?"

"It's tricky," said Mike. "I reckon we need to find a rare breed of vegetarian fox. One who doesn't have a key, *and* doesn't want one. Because," he added, "apart from those few die-hard journalists who every so often mention some squawking, or a few missing chooks, or a messy pile of feathers that soon blows away, *no-one's* interested."

"Except maybe the chickens," said Robert.

"Yeah. But," Mike said, "most of the chickens pretend it isn't happening. Or they hope it never gets to be their turn. Farmer throws down some pellets and they're contentedly pecking away. They have notoriously short memory spans."

"So why isn't anyone pointing this out. For real I mean," said Robert. "Why this coded analogy or metaphor or whatever? Why can't you just say what's going on? Do something?"

"I was just rambling on about the nature of foxes, farmers and chickens," Mike said.

"No. No. You said there's too many old farmers. That parliament could use a few lawyers."

"True. Fair comment," said Mike. "Another beer?"

*

The party followed the enticing smell of sizzled meat into the cool concrete-floored space under the house. The buffet table, dressed in red-checked plastic, was burdened with platters deposited by a succession of wives, whose arrival from the kitchen upstairs didn't augment the conversation so much as mute it.

Suddenly ravenous, Robert wrapped a slice of buttered bread around a sausage and scanned for Lauren. His Mother was nowhere to be seen either, and her signature pavlova was missing. Distracted, he bit down, cursing silently in time with air sucks, to cool the burning lump on his tongue. He searched the esky, in the vain hope it was hiding a coke, before heading upstairs to raid the girls' fridge.

Lauren's smile was only half there, "It's your mum."

"I was wondering," he said. "The pav hasn't made it downstairs."

Lauren passed a cup under his nose.

"Eww."

"Eww. Yes. She's having a lie down. I don't want them seeing her like this Robert," Lauren nodded towards Emma and Thomas perched on swivel stools at the kitchen bench.

"You there Jeannie," Robert's dad, called from downstairs.

"Pavlova is on its way, Barry," Lauren lifted the tray. Then to Robert, "I'll be right back and then you should check on your mum."

Robert gratefully sipped fizzing cold lemonade, while Emma and Thomas fed him pieces of sausage. Thomas walked his sausage across the plate towards the sauce. "Glomp, glomp, glomp and whoosh." Sauce splodged, pooling on the floor and Thomas's fork thrashed around as he giggled. The piece of sausage, precariously speared in the first place, bellyflopped into the sauce pool.

"Oops," his face wide-eyed in wonder, lifted from the sausage, to Emma, to Robert, checking they hadn't missed the action.

Their laughter stopped abruptly. Emma and Thomas had squeezed their eyes closed.

"What are you two doing? Come on, finish your lunch."

They shook their heads, eyes firmly closed.

"Is this a game? Come on," he said again.

"We aren't supposed to see Grandma Jee," Emma's eyelids fluttered. "Mummy said."

Robert swivelled on his stool, "Oh. I thought you were having a lie down, Mum. It's OK kiddoes. You can open your eyes."

"I'll have my tea, if you don't mind," she patted her pillow-squashed hair, and reached for her cup.

Robert took her hand, guiding her to his vacated stool, "I'll get it."

He picked up the saucer turning quickly. The unanchored cup launched itself, its contents floating above it briefly, on the way to joining the sausage and sauce with a loud crack.

"Now look what you've done!"

Robert spiralled into his childhood while his own children stared.

"It's OK. Mum. I'll make you a fresh one."

Jeannie's eyes narrowed.

He watched the debate behind them.

"Make me a fresh cup will you Love?" she said finally.

"I just said I'd make," Robert stopped talking and looked curiously at his hand before unclamping the fingers.

"Two scoops of tea, Robert," she said with a curling edge of scorn. "I'd like a double."

Returning, Lauren conceded a fleeting eyebrow twitch at the sight of Jeannie seated opposite the children.

"I was telling mum. About uni. You going back to do law," Robert said. "You don't mind do you? It's not a secret is it?"

"Not at all," her smile was uncharacteristically nervous. "I'm kind-of excited. Hope it's not too mentally strenuous. I'm a bit out of practice."

"Rubbish," Robert smiled at her. Then turned towards his mother, "She's already got a degree. She'll sail through. She's smart. And I'll help. I'm not useless around the house or anything." The words bubbled out trying to burst through a dense layer of undefined hostility.

"What on earth for?" Jeannie ignored him, her eyes intent on Lauren, "You have a job," her chin angling slightly towards Emma and Thomas.

"I'm resigning. Oh, you mean," Lauren wilted momentarily. "They'll be fine. Nothing much will change for them."

"I thought you'd be pleas—" Robert started.

"You girls now are never satisfied," Jeannie ignored him again. "Something always falls over, mark my words. I don't want my grandchildren, roaming the streets, getting into trouble. And it won't be cheap."

"It's basically free, Mum. Anyway, we'll manage. We don't exactly live the high life." Robert's eyes moved from his mother to Lauren, "And I'm sure Duncan will help if we ask. It's all hers in the long run. He won't mind giving her some ahead of time. You don't have to worry about—"

"Well don't expect me to be baby-sitting this lot. I'm not one of *those* grandmothers."

"No. It's OK Mum. We know," Robert's voice sagged.

"Mummy," said Emma looking at her grandmother, "I'm finished."

"Me too," said Thomas. "Can we go now?"

Jeannie lifted them from their stools, suddenly and inexplicably bright, "You haven't had your pav-o-lova yet."

Emma and Thomas put a plastic spoon on each serving, and Jeannie tapped the tray with her metal one, "Pavlova everyone. But first, an announcement. My daughter-in-law is embarking on a new career in law. Isn't that amazing? What us girls can do now?"

Her lips pressed together, desperate to look like she was holding back her pride. Her eyes found Barry and beamed into him, "Aren't we lucky? Our son's quite the modern man. It's so nice," she waved the spoon at Robert and Lauren's lowered heads, "to have a husband who wants you to be fulfilled and happy. I'm sure we all wish you good luck Lauren, dear. Now come-on everyone. Eat."

Emma and Thomas stopped clapping when they saw Grandma Jee's face.

CHAPTER 13

"Have you talked to Judge Matthews?" Robert said as Duncan was gathering his meeting notes. They'd been discussing an entirely different case.

"Are you psychic?"

"Not that I'm aware," Robert joked.

"Just got off the phone. Before this. It was a personal matter."

"Oh," Robert was turning back to the open folder thinking why mention it.

"He wants to set up a trust and a will."

"Doesn't he have his own lawyer?" said Robert.

"Precisely. Which is why I suspect it involves Johnny. He didn't go to the mention. If he had, this might have been resolved."

"He wants to make some kind of amends?"

"I suppose I'll find out next week. Perhaps I'll be able to broach his intentions now this thing with Johnny has escalated."

"Did Lauren call?" Robert asked.

"She did. I'm delighted. She should come in, start working here."

"Let's see how she manages first. Full time and kids. But I meant about you coming over."

"You can visit any time. You know that," said Duncan.

"I think the point was to get you out somewhere different."

"I like it at home."

"We know," Robert smiled in mock exasperation. "But it's so much easier with two kids if you bring the party to them."

"Granted, but—"

"And Lauren's asking a few people. She can't exactly tell them to go to your place, can she? It would make her happy."

Duncan opened his arms outwards from the elbow, palms facing up, in the universal gesture of 'can't-argue-with-that', "Then it's done. And if you're talking to Johnny, don't mention Harry's visit. I don't know yet if it's confidential."

Robert shook his head. *Again, why even mention it.*

Back in his own office Robert faced the stack of folders waiting for the undivided attention he'd only been able to sporadically muster since the disaster in Court. Since before then. Since the back of Johnny's head had blindsided him. Since that kiss. Right here. He closed his eyes and a soft moan escaped. His insides tightened exquisitely while reminders of being cradled in Johnny's arms arced through him. He shifted in his chair.

He should call Johnny. He reached for an outside line button and pulled his hand back. He wanted to call Johnny, and he didn't want to. He buzzed Anna and asked her to do it, then picked up his car keys and was absently tossing them as Anna came in.

She looked surprised, "Are you going out?"

"I—"

"It's just Mr Saunders asked if you could meet him, I said you didn't have any other appointments, and I was sure it would be OK. Do you want me to call back?"

"No. Good. Thanks." He groaned inwardly, then distracted himself with, "How's your mum, by the way. I've been, a bit," he searched, "preoccupied."

"I know. I could see that. Not the best."

"Oh, I'm sorry. I should have asked."

"It's OK. Mr Carson?" Anna hesitated, "You said it would be OK." A shorter pause. "Would you mind if I left early? I wouldn't be here when you got back."

Robert baulked, wary of the apparent and seductive good luck.

Anna mistook his silence, "Don't worry."

"No. You should go. Has something happened?"

"It's," she looked at Robert's face, "we've had a bit of a setback. The doctor suggested we look at homes, put her name down, so things are in place for when— it's so awful Mr Carson, I feel so helpless," her eyes filled, and she looked away and sniffed.

"I'm so sorry Anna." *Stupid selfish arsehole.* "Pack up now. If you need time with your mum, it's yours. I'll talk to Duncan. Work something out."

She sniffed again, "Thanks. I don't want to put you out. I feel really bad about all this."

"Don't. I know it's work, but we're sort-of a work family aren't we? Come on. I'll walk with you."

By the time they reached her car, he learned what he should have already known. That she was an only child, unmarried, that her father disappeared when she was sixteen and her mum's tiredness and clumsiness was given a name. That she'd traded school, plans and dreams for typing, shorthand and bookkeeping. That she'd then started and stayed at Eldridges. And that yes, it did feel like sort-of family.

CHAPTER 14

Outside Johnny's door, Robert listened to his pulse thudding. He bit his lip and swallowed. He told himself again this is just a meeting and to stop working yourself up. But he knew it wasn't. Not really. Was it? He knocked. The door opened as his bunched fist was lowering, and Johnny's hands closed over it coaxing him forward.

"Can you stay long?" Johnny walked half sideways, still holding Robert's hand.

"I don't know. I haven't got any appointments, I..." Robert wondered if he should stay. He wanted to stay. He wanted to go. They hadn't talked since he'd spent the night not doing anything.

Johnny stopped at the sofa, "Here, sit down."

Robert's eyes followed the join between the wall and the ceiling, stopping when it was straight in front of him. He could feel Johnny's eyes watching him. He changed directions looking down at the floor, his lap, and then his hand moving, picking at something imaginary on his slacks.

Johnny's hand rested on the fidgeting.

A long pause later, Robert lifted his head searching Johnny's face for a hint of what to expect. or what to do.

"I'm glad you're here. I want you, to be here. But we don't have to do anything. It's not compulsory or anything. We can talk—"

"It's just," Robert cut him off and then looked at his hand, encased in Johnny's, "I don't. I've never, I don't know what to do."

"About what?"

"What?"

"I'm trying to lighten the mood. Look at me," Johnny said.

Robert looked up again and sighed with relief. In Johnny's eyes he saw something steady, unwavering, and comforting whatever was frightened searching and hesitant in his own, with an intense reassuring stillness. The intermittent urge to flee he'd been fighting off abated. His shoulders relaxed, "It's, I'm kind of…"

"Scared?"

"Yeah, I suppose. Nervous."

"It's not rocket science you know. It's completely natural."

Robert's gaze had been lowering and he looked up again quickly.

"Been happening for thousands of years. Millions," Johnny smiled.

"But the actual mechanics. I don't…"

"You've got two kids, Robert."

"I know but—"

"But you're all thingy about doing it with a man."

Robert didn't let his eyes move from Johnny's face.

"Even though you want to."

Robert nodded.

"What do you want to know?" said Johnny.

"Does it hurt?"

"I know what you're worried about. It doesn't have to. We can work our way up to that. If we want. Look. Answer yourself this, have I ever done anything to hurt you?"

Robert shook his head.

"Then why the fuck would I start now?"

The tight skin around Robert's forced smile began softening.

"We have all afternoon. We have tomorrow or next week. We have all the time in the world," Johnny's voice was reassuring and gentle. He shifted preparing to stand, "Come on. Let's make tea. Or do you want something stronger?"

"I don't want…"

"What? Tea?"

"No," said Robert, "I don't want to wait. If I wait you might disappear again."

"I didn't disappear. You did. Well, the real you did."

"I," Robert stopped.

"It's OK. I'm not going anywhere. I can wait."

Johnny's hand which had been resting over Robert's squeezed slowly twice, and Robert knew that Johnny didn't want to wait either. He let his hand be lifted and turned and then he sighed into the kiss as it landed tenderly on his wrist.

"Trust me," Johnny whispered, as the next kiss was making its way to Robert's lips.

Kisses which had floated over his face, delicate as mist, had turned into solid weighty droplets, and like rain hitting a sun-scorched tin roof, released a steamy vapour. Robert floated inside a hot white cloud. His breathing, shallow and quick. His face felt full, pulsing with suffused heat. The same pulsing heat in his groin. His ears noticed Johnny's voice but not the words. His eyes saw nothing but a dim soft light which reminded him of the sun trying to penetrate closed curtains. Every now and again, shards of brightness flashing through as the breeze lifted them.

He was kissing Johnny back.

Johnny was guiding Robert's hand.

When it reached Johnny's crotch, Johnny pushed down hard and groaned. He used Robert's hand to squeeze and release and squeeze again.

Lost in the sensation, Robert didn't realise Johnny's hand was gone until he felt it on his own crotch, rubbing and pushing at the fabric, and then pushing right under him. He could feel Johnny's forearm moving back and forward, and then a bunched fist twisting and lifting. With eyes closed, his hands grabbed at the cushions of the sofa, fingers curling against the cloth before flattening his palms and pushing against it. His back arched and his neck extended, chin pointing blindly to the ceiling. He could think of nothing. Suddenly Johnny's other hand was inside his pants.

His mind wanted to focus on one sensation at a time, but it was beyond him. Briefly aware that there was a warm soft pressure at the end of his penis, he arched again, pushed down hard on Johnny's fist and rocked, sending his senses somewhere they'd never been. Then in one perfect moment instinct held him still. All that moved was his breath, and then it stopped too. He spasmed and shuddered and lost himself in the repeating interplay of light and dark behind his eyes until it slowly turned opaque.

When he opened his eyes, Johnny was looking into them, his face flushed with the heightened colour of lust. Then Johnny started to withdraw his hand and Robert moaned, and everything that had started relaxing, clenched again.

"Shall we move to the bedroom? Or have you decided you don't like it with men after all?"

"Not sure," Robert's breath was short. "Might need some more convincing."

***

Jittery muscles made him unstable, and Robert put a hand against the wall-tiles of Johnny's bathroom for support. As the shower rained on him, his mind started wandering. He found himself hurrying along an obscure trail, and some kind of dread rising up in him. He'd lost something. No. He was lost. Ahead was another path. An easy well-marked one. He took it, feeling relieved. But it circled back. Was this the right path or not? He looked around. There was something wrong.

Wrong. He was filling up with guilt and that amorphous dread. Now, standing at the juncture of the two paths, he counted and tried to breathe away the fear but it had become something solid in him, holding him in thrall and irresolute, trying to choose between what he wanted, and what he wanted.

The loosely belted robe didn't hide the ripple of muscle under skin, as Johnny reached towards the overhead kitchen cupboards. Watching him, Robert was able to momentarily shut everything else out and enjoy the reminders of their afternoon, randomly surfacing in different parts of his body.

"Are we having tea?" he asked.

"Actually," Johnny turned towards the fridge, "I got bubbles, you know, in case I had something to celebrate sometime. What do you think?"

Nursing his champagne glass in one hand, and leaning back into the supporting cushions of the sofa, Robert stroked the material and tingles spread through his abdomen. He stretched out, then retracted.

"Spit it out," said Johnny.

"I was thinking, hah, I haven't stopped thinking except..."

Johnny waited for a moment before saying, "Let's leave Lauren and the kids thing. Talking can't change it. So no point. Next?"

"Us?"

"You need to be a bit more specific."

"Is there an us? Is this going anywhere? Is this all? Today? Do I just go back to being Robert the dad? The husband?"

"We weren't going to talk about that."

Robert stared ahead.

Johnny ran his hand through his hair, "Look—"

"What? This isn't 'look, this was great *but*,' is it? Did I get it wrong?" Robert's glass wobbled on its fine stem as it came down against the tabletop, "I've taken a hell-of-a-chance even coming here and—"

"Bloody hell, Robert. Where the fuck did that come from?" Johnny handed Robert's glass back, "Here. I *was* going to say look, I don't *know* where it can go. Somewhere, I hope. I haven't got a crystal ball. All I am going to say is, I haven't loved anyone—"

"Harry?" Robert cut him off then looked away and muttered, "Fuck. What is wrong with me?"

"I don't know," Johnny sighed. And as Robert's shoulders stiffened, "I'm not talking about you. I'm talking about Harry. With Harry it's different."

"What if he asked you to come back?"

"What if he did?" Johnny made sure he had Robert's eyes. "I suppose," he said, "Harry is my Lauren."

"And so. What do we do?"

"Do we have to *do* anything? Can't we just be? Planning everything out doesn't mean anything. Things happen."

"Lauren was worried about you. Said I should spend more time with you."

"Not sure where that came from, but that's nice of her."

"She doesn't mean like this."

Johnny opened his mouth to speak and a breathy chuckle escaped, "Obviously." He squeezed Robert's forearm, "She's... you got lucky there."

"She's pretty special. Thoughtful, kind."

"Harry too. He's so... right, y'know? Without the righteous. Maybe that's how he got to be a judge. He's not judgy. You'd like him."

Robert nodded vaguely, "Lauren wants you to come over for a barbeque. Marnie too. How is she by the way? I keep meaning to ask. After you left, after we, after I," he stopped.

"After you dived into life with Lauren and fuck the rest of us."

"Not quite." And to Johnny's you're-kidding-me look, "You're right. I didn't want reminding. She was my best friend. She knew me. Too well. What happened?"

"Dad's practical. He's a silver linings guy. He just gets on with it. Had to, after mum died," Johnny looked away. "With Marnie he could have chosen blame and tears and whatever, but he didn't. Of course, he wasn't thrilled, I'm sure Marnie told you, but then when Nikki, Nicole arrived, he was besotted. We all were."

"And what does she do?"

"She has her own business now," said Johnny. "After Nikki arrived, mum's friend next door, Mrs Harris, sort of barged in and took over. Organised baby-minding and fast-tracked a hairdressing apprenticeship. It was her salon. Anyway, Marnie's arty. It suited her. She wasn't keen on going back to uni. That's what I mean about plans. They change."

Robert nodded then frowned, "Marnie wouldn't accidentally say anything would she?"

"Soul of discretion. They have to take an oath, hairdressers."

"Joking. Really?"

Johnny laughed, "Oh God you're cute. I'm more concerned about me. Keeping my hands off you. But it would look bad if I didn't come. Bit rude."

"Won't be easy. But I suppose we have to get used to it. If we're going to—"

The phone rang and Johnny winked, "Glad that didn't happen earlier."

Robert listened to Johnny's part, "Hello— Oh, Mr Eldridge— Of course. Yes— Thursday. Four. OK." He turned to Robert, "It can't be about the case. That's your department."

"I have an inkling."

Johnny's eyebrows lifted.

"You know that hairdresser oath? It's kinda the same thing," said Robert.

"It's Harry. Isn't it?" It wasn't a question. "I'd better get ready for work."

CHAPTER 15

Robert's head shifted from his notes to his watch, pleased he could concentrate again, but it was getting late, so Duncan appearing in the office doorway surprised him.

"Can I help?"

"Where have you been?"

Robert's throat pulse started tugging him into the past.

His mum standing at the front door. Her eyes dark, her voice harsh, 'Where have you been?' She'd bent over him and he'd tilted his head to avoid the rancid sweetness on her breath, "Sorry."

"Never mind. Come on." She turned towards the front room, which was for important visitors, and not for kids, and he hesitated.

"Hurry up," she said. "There's a policeman waiting. He wants to talk to you."

"Where's Anna?" Duncan's voice brought him back.

"What? Oh. She's—" Robert reminded himself not to add anything. Then changed his mind. "Actually, it's her afternoon off. And I've been meaning to talk to you about something." He waved Duncan towards his visitor chair.

"We aren't a charity," Duncan's face wore the slightest hint of flush, "I mean obviously we should do something."

"I know," Robert's eyes found Lauren's photo and Duncan's followed. "It was something Lauren said. That we get so caught up in our lives, we forget to think about other people."

Duncan nodded, and Robert waited.

"How long has she been with us?"

"The payroll lady said twelve years. She started here when she was a kid. Seventeen."

"I have an idea," Duncan leaned forward.

Robert tried not to smile.

"I've been thinking about getting computerised, we're too piecemeal when it comes to billing," Duncan said. Then adding, "Not you. Anyway, she's on the ball. She could manage it. Office Manager, perhaps?" He looked ahead at something invisible. "She can do some courses. What do you think?"

"Extra money?"

"Extra money *and* less hours?"

"She's more than worth it. And we pay for the courses," Robert encouraged. "They're tax deductible."

Duncan's forearms extended palms upwards.

Robert grinned, "When do you want to tell her?"

"Me? No. Your idea."

"Much as I'd like to take the credit," Robert said, "it's you who makes this sort of thing happen. I'll tell her to come and see you. You'll be free before Thursday's meeting?" Robert contained the wince.

"Hmmm. OK," Duncan didn't notice. "Apparently I'm expected Sunday afternoon, since we're scheduling all and sundry."

"This Sunday?"

"A family roast, I'm told," said Duncan.

"Oh. Good. Yes." Robert's heartrate slowed.

"And her old friend from uni is coming. You know her, Marnie. In fact, she's Johnny's sister."

Shit. He wasn't ready for these extended social gatherings Lauren had in mind. His heart hammered again, "Yes, yes, I'm looking forward to it."

***

Anna's head popped around the doorway as Robert was finishing a note.

"I don't know how to thank you," she said. "I know it was you who arranged things with Mr Eldridge. You didn't have to. It was kind."

"You and your mum deserve a break, Anna," Robert felt a surge of warmth. "We'll start sorting it out next week."

She nodded, smiling, "Mr Eldridge said to give him half an hour."

"Oh. OK. Good," the warmth became a chill. Thoughts about why bumped against each other. One kept pushing to the front, *Were Johnny and Harry having a private meeting? Why?* He remembered to breathe.

Anna was still in the doorway, her face a mixture of concern and confusion, "Is everything OK? Can I get you anything?"

"Yes. No. Thanks."

"Well. Thanks again, Mr Carson."

Robert stared at the closed door. *What the hell? Does Johnny feel like this every time Lauren is mentioned? Whoa. This is crazy. Come on. We talked about this. Harry is Johnny's Lauren. We both have our commitments. We both love each other. Now. Get yourself together. It's not like you don't know how to act.*

*

His foot hit the door before his knock. He breathed out heavily. *For once. Just for once, it would be nice.*

Duncan's come in sounded relaxed.

"Harry Matthews," the judge stood extending his hand.

"Nice to meet you, sir."

"Harry, please."

Robert joined them at the conference table and nodded to Johnny who looked upset and something else. Confused?

"I've been dealing with a matter for Harry," said Duncan, "but he wanted a quick review on Johnny's case, from your end."

Robert looked from Harry to Johnny to Duncan his mind whirling. *What would Johnny's lawyer do now?* "No disrespect sir, Harry, but you *are* a prosecution witness. It wouldn't be appropriate—"

"Things aren't always as they appear," Duncan said.

"Yes," said Robert, "I think we all know that, but—"

"I understand," Harry cut him off. "I'll make it clearer."

When he'd finished, Robert stifled his sarcasm, "We'd figured out Johnny takes the rap, you keep your reputation, by ourselves. And yes, things didn't go according to plan. But honestly, that's down to you. The Magistrate pretty much said if he'd been able to question you, clarify your statement, this would all be over."

"It was a judgment call. The written statement would make my presence redundant, whereas my actual presence might have caused problems. Part of me wanted to be there," said Harry, "but circumstances—"

"Harry's got cancer," Johnny interrupted. "He didn't come because he'd had an operation. And... and, he never said."

"I'm sorry. Johnny and I, we're old friends. I was, I shouldn't have gone on like that," Robert forced himself to keep eye contact with Harry, but now he understood the look on Johnny's face.

"You weren't to know," Harry said. "Heaven knows I feel, well, not the best, about any of this, but the saving grace is I've had time to think things through and make some decisions. One of which Duncan has helped me with. And you, can help me with the other. So if you'll be kind enough," he gestured to Robert.

"I was going to petition the prosecutor," said Robert. "We haven't received notification of the date, but I didn't want to push any buttons. I was hoping he intended to drop it."

"Obviously hope's not the whole strategy though?" Harry prompted.

"Well, you can't recant but your statement is vague enough to be interpreted in a number of ways, especially with the right questions when I cross examine. Their statements are worded as heresay. So, lack of evidence. A jury, if there is one, would have no reason to find Johnny guilty, and there's the character references. The magistrate loved them."

"I'm worried about the prosecution bringing in stories, made up stuff, or changing their statements," Johnny added.

"They can't," Harry started.

"Tell him about chess," Johnny's lip curled in distaste.

"Of course, you know about that first-hand," Robert added, after explaining.

"Mmm. The rules are, that the rules change," Harry mused. "But look," he scanned the faces around the table, "from a purely legal standpoint, it's impossible for me to perjure myself. Not only have I not given any testimony, we," he looked at Johnny, "are already a couple, which I'd make very clear. That makes the charge irrelevant. If that doesn't put an end to the matter, as you pointed out Robert, their testimony would confirm hearsay. And as it's a criminal matter they'll have to turn up and say so. They'd have to wear a bit of egg on their face for a while but they're good at scrubbing it off."

"But the whole point was to *not* implicate you, to protect your reputation, and your position," Robert said.

"Which," Harry shrugged, "doesn't seem quite as important now, as it did at the time."

"But what if afterwards, they arrest you, or me?" said Johnny. "Just for being gay?"

"They can't," said Robert. "What proof have they got."

Johnny rolled his eyes, "Chess. Fa-rk me. All they need is a junkie who doesn't want to go to jail to sign some statement. They could change theirs."

"As I said," Harry patted Johnny's arm, "I've had thinking time, so you stop worrying. They'll want this to disappear. My guess is it hasn't disappeared yet because they thought they'd be able to milk me for a bit more. But the risk for them is, I talk. And if they make a big song and dance people won't be able to turn a blind eye. If it's out in the open, all of it, if I'm out in the open, and I no longer preside over anything, which I won't because I'm retiring, blackmail will no longer work."

CHAPTER 16

"I don't understand why you're seeing that journo."

"His name's Simon?" Johnny said. "Why are you in a tizz? He's straight. His only interest in me, or Tank, is the information we can give him. Which isn't much. Sadly."

"I'm not. But we only see each other once a week and... doesn't matter. Sometimes I wish you didn't tell me everything," Robert mumbled.

"I'm not as good as you at keeping secrets," Johnny said. "It's fucking hard. I don't know how you do it."

"Practice," Robert lay back down on his side, cradling his head with one arm, so he could see Johnny. "Something came for you today. The court date."

"I know."

"You know? But—"

Johnny laughed, "We make a good pair, don't we?"

"Aren't you upset?"

"I would have been. But since I've been back living at Harry's and we've talked about it more... I'd been focussing on what-ifs and letting them scare the pants off me. Like jail. And even if there's some media circus, as I've said before, it'll be about Harry, not me. And if I do make it into a headline, anyone who knows me, well, knows me. Those creeps can't change that.

"So you're OK?"

"Well, at first I kind-of wished it had never happened. But then that's not true," Johnny said. "Dad's influence maybe, but as far as I'm concerned there's not so much a bright side, as a blazing sparkling sunburst side. If it hadn't been for Simon, and that story, we wouldn't be here now. You and me."

81

"So you really don't mind?"

"And neither should you," Johnny smiled. "And since we are all about not keeping things to ourselves... Harry, the Trust and the will thing. He said it's not *just* because he's feeling guilty, he's doing it so that his niece and nephew can't make trouble challenging his will after he, after he goes. And he's putting his apartment into my name, and a bunch of shares. They'll get something too, but not all of it. So when you ask if I really don't mind," he shrugged.

"Holy shit!" Robert's grin faded quickly, "Not that— but it's going to happen, no avoiding it. Wow," he drifted for a minute. "Have you met them? The niece and her husband?"

Johnny's eyes frosted, "I don't need to be accepted by people who look at me as if God had accidentally swallowed pond scum and vomited something out."

Robert felt a hot wave of shame wash through him. As it receded, he forced himself to smile, "And since Thursday is Harry's dinner with family night, we have our bright side." He gently stroked Johnny's arm.

"Yes," Johnny's smile returned too, "and you better be careful, or you'll turn into a regular Pollyanna. Hah, I can't wait to see them pick up their smug faces from the floor after they find out."

"Except will readings are reserved for family. You'll have to imagine it." Robert frowned, "You should have a word to Harry, get Duncan to have you included in some sort of care plan. Otherwise, you might not be able to see him, in hospital or hospice."

"So you're not jealous anymore?"

"I've tried." Robert's eyes softened. "But someone's rubbing off on me. And glass houses, and things like that." He turned to the bedside table and glanced at his watch, "Do you mind if I get us something quick to eat?"

"Will you stop with this do you mind, and may I shit." Johnny flashed an apologetic smile, "I thought that would stop when you got your own keys. I really want this to feel like we're at home together. You go shower, I'll tidy up here and you can take over in the kitchen when you're done. How does frittata sound?"

"Posh," said Robert.

"I simplified," Johnny said when he saw Robert. "Omelette with cheese, and some bread rolls. It's all in the oven keeping warm. If you're really starving there's some beans, you can put them in the microwave. And set the table will you. Don't forget to put mats down for the hot stuff. I'm off for my shower."

"I have been housetrained," Robert laughed, feeling buoyed and relaxed in their illicit domesticity.

***

"Lauren asked me if I'd rather change my night out to Friday," Robert said, a few weeks later, handing Johnny a bag of groceries and exchanging hello kisses. "Careful, there's a bottle in there too."

"Are we celebrating?" Johnny put the bottle in the freezer and handed Robert a vegetable knife, pointing at some already peeled potatoes and carrots, "You can do these if you don't mind. Chunks, for roasting." Then adding, "What did you say?"

"I said no. Then I thought maybe she had a reason and started to feel guilty."

"Did she?" Johnny nodded at the vegetables still waiting,

"No. She said she was thinking about giving up her Friday nights out. I asked her why?"

"And?"

"She said she's spending so much time on herself, assignments and lectures and whatever. That it wasn't fair on me. Just being her usual thoughtful self. And making me feel even more guilty."

"You can't do this Robert," said Johnny.

Robert shrugged, "I know."

"I mean it," Johnny put the vegetables into the baking tray, shook it so they coated in oil, and shut the oven door, "You're not hurting anyone. We're not hurting anyone. Not really."

"Invoking the age-old principle that what you don't know can't hurt you?"

"Something like that."

"But realistically," Robert caught Johnny's eyebrow raise. "Sometimes I wonder how long we're going to get away with this. And what will happen..."

"Fuck's sake Robert," Johnny shook his head, "If we weren't stuck in a time warp, where people have the right to lock you up just for being who you are, then this wouldn't be an issue."

Robert looked up into the corner of the room.

"Imagine," said Johnny, "what it would have been like if we'd been able to just be together from the start. How is it fair that can't happen? How is it fair that people like us have to live secret lives. Pretend. We're made to feel ashamed. I don't want to feel like that."

Robert could feel his eyes prickle.

"Come here," said Johnny, folding Robert into a hug. He pressed his forehead against Robert's.

As Robert's eyes closed, he could feel Johnny's soft kisses trailing down the side of his face. When they found Robert's neck, the kisses became nuzzles and nibbles.

Robert moaned and pulled Johnny's t-shirt free from his jeans, running his hands up along Johnny's bare back, then grasping his shoulders and pushing him against the wall. Then he pressed himself hard against Johnny.

Their breathing quickened.

Their bodies locked together. Moving slowly. Straining against each other.

Robert's hand found Johnny's jean's button and zip.

Johnny gasped, "Fa-rk me."

"I have every intention," said Robert.

When Johnny came back fresh from a shower to check on their meal, Robert was putting the finishing touches to the table in the living room. "I've been thinking that I should leave my car in town, at work or at the pub," he called through to the kitchen loud enough for Johnny to hear. "And get Lauren to drop me off the next morning. She has classes. Seems a bit weird to be driving home when I'm supposed to be out, drinking and having a good time."

Johnny emerged with a platter between two mittened hands, "Haha. Yes. As opposed to *in*, and *not* drinking. Well not drinking much and having a *really* good time." He couldn't keep the smile from his face, and then noticing the table setting, "Oh," he said, "we should toast."

They glowed in the candlelight and raised their glasses.

"Me first," said Johnny. "To Lauren and Harry, who helped make this happen."

Robert's eyebrow lifted and Johnny apologised with a cheeky smile and said, "I'm finding it a bit hard to be serious." When Robert smiled back, he added, "And to always being this fucking happy."

"To Lauren and Harry and you," said Robert, "and to always feeling this fucking happy."

When they finished eating, Robert was silent.

"What," said Johnny.

"I wanted to tell you something."

Johnny looked at him, turning his chin and narrowing one eye.

"Here," Robert topped up Johnny's wine and peered into his own glass, "That night at the Schonell, when you left, after we argued. After I insisted I wasn't gay," he looked at Johnny's face. "I went after you." He watched Johnny nod. "It wasn't to say sorry," Robert said. "I know that's what I told you. But it wasn't." He could feel his eyes moisten, and blinked, "I felt this, I don't know… this overwhelming 'yes'. Not just in my head. It was all of me. Urging. No. Insisting, I go to you."

The glass in Johnny's hand quivered as he placed it on the table, and after a breath, "Why didn't you come and find me?"

Robert shrugged, "You know. All the stuff I'd said. It all rushed back in. You weren't there."

Johnny nodded and reached across the table for Robert's hand, "Doesn't matter. Things have a way of working out."

This time Robert nodded.

"Come-on," Johnny picked up his glass again. "Cheers. To always being this fucking happy."

***

"Do you want to chill in front of the telly or chat?" Johnny asked putting the last dishes away and refilling their glasses. It was a couple of weeks later.

"I was going to ask you about Simon. What's happening?"

"So you're over that?" Johnny teased. "I haven't had anything to tell him and he doesn't say much. He did say that it's serious, and big, and gonna take some time."

"Is it for the *Courier Mail*? I wouldn't have thought so, given where they sit."

"You mean on the fence or in Joh's pocket," Johnny chuckled. "No. That's another reason it's hush hush. He's working with his mate, Tim Harper from 4 Corners. It's Tim's story. Simon's doing some prelim articles to stir up more interest and then the follow up print stuff. The paper will be wanting it then."

"Does Harry approve?"

"He doesn't know how they're gonna get away with it, but he said something's gotta give. It's not petty stuff. It's big league. Massive."

"I told you I'd talked with Mike Ahern at my dad's?"

Johnny nodded.

"Do you think Simon might be interested in talking to him?"

"Probably. What about your dad? He's not mixed up with these crooks is he?"

"I don't think so." Robert looked vacantly ahead, "If he was in the thick of it, he'd be part of the Gang. And he's not. I think he knows some of what's going on, the shady deals and whatever. Not that he could do anything about it. And there's this thing, they call it 'The Joke', but unless you're in on it, you don't know what they're talking about."

"I can see how they'd think it was a joke. On all of us."

"Did I tell you my mum fancied being Mrs Premier when Dad started out. He was a minister of something for all of five minutes way back when Joh first got in." Robert drifted into a memory, "I didn't know much about it, but I could tell she was proud."

They sat without saying anything.

Then Robert took Johnny's hand, "You know, I'm rather proud of you," he said.

"Meaning?"

"I meant," said Robert, "I admire you. What you're doing. Tank too. I know what I said, ages ago, but, well, I am proud."

"I love you," said Johnny.

Still holding Johnny's hand, Robert brought it to his lips.

They looked at each other.

"It's getting late though. We'd better get going," said Johnny.

***

"I've been meaning to ask," said Robert, several weeks later as they were leaving Johnny's, "if you're OK with this, with us going back into the city together on the ferry, and then cabs home?"

"For a boy's night out it makes sense," Johnny shrugged, and looking up at the blank end of the lamppost across from the apartment, he added, "I wish they'd fix that though. It's been like that for ages."

While his eyes adjusted to the dark, Robert tripped. The root of a Moreton Bay fig, sprawling across the parkland between the road and the river, was trying to break through the bitumen. Johnny reached out to steady him, too late.

He picked up his jacket and brushed the dirt from the knee of his trousers, a prickling sensation on his palm, made Robert stop and look. As the tree branch lifted in a breathy gust and the sliced moonlight broke through the leaf canopy, he could see little red droplets bubbling around a graze.

"You OK? Don't want you going home all banged up," Johnny joked, "or Lauren mightn't let you come out to play anymore."

Robert examined his hand again as they walked on, "I'll live. Nice neighbourhood."

"Will be one day. Courtesy of Expo 88." Johnny chatted as they walked. "Real estate agent said this will all be gentrified. The dockyard and workshops will be gone, and my place overlooking the city and the river will be worth a lot more than I paid for it. And I'll be rich. Not that it matters now, thanks to Harry. We should get a move on. The ferry only comes every hour after ten."

Robert looked down at his watch. Except it wasn't there.

"My watch. Bugger."

"Really, Robert?" Johnny's eyebrows arched.

"I can't go home without it."

"Why not?"

"Why do you think? Jeez Johnny. Lauren will notice."

"So? You left it at work."

"Why would I take it off? At work?" There was an edge of anxiety in Robert's voice, "I can't—"

"Go back to the apartment and get it. I'm not gonna argue with you."

"How much time do we have?"

Johnny looked down at his, "Twenty minutes or so. I can ask the driver to wait. Sometimes they will."

"I'll make it in time if I run. Here," he thrust his jacket at Johnny.

"I'll wait," Johnny called after him. "If you're not back when the ferry comes. I'll wait. Do you hear me?"

Robert raised a thumbs up and kept going, hoping Johnny had seen it.

CHAPTER 17

Robert fumbled unlocking the foyer door, and again at the apartment. His breathing wasn't slowing down, and he realised it wasn't only the running. He hadn't thought things through. Johnny should have come back with him. If they missed this ferry, or even if they didn't, he decided they were going to get a taxi. He pushed away the thought of shattered lamplight glass, and the slurping of thirsty mangroves. There'd be someone else waiting. Johnny would be OK. And he wouldn't be long.

Inside he went straight to the bedside table.

No watch.

Maybe you hadn't forgotten it. Maybe you put it in your jacket pocket. Maybe it fell out when you tripped. No. No. Think.

He tried tracing things backwards, but thoughts of Johnny waiting alone, of missing the ferry, of getting home late had him turning in unproductive circles. *Stop moving. Calm down. It should be right there on my bedside table.* In spite of himself he smiled. *My bedside table.* But still no watch.

Time wasn't standing still but he needed his mind to. He sat on the bed, then bent forward looking under and behind the bedside table. *Think. I was in the shower. Johnny was making the bed.*

He bent forward again, this time running his hand along where the valance brushed against the table. A triumphant sense of relief washed over him and he stuffed the watch into his pants pocket.

∗

Jogging steadily, Robert touched his pocket, *Stupid bloody watch. We're definitely not hanging around for any ferry. We're going back to the apartment. We'll get taxi's from there instead.* This arrangement had been niggling at him. It had started out as a nice stroll to the ferry after dinner, but with the missing streetlights it was way too dark and it felt more isolated. He breathed in and out deeply, to release some of the tension. *Come on. Relax. Won't be long now. It didn't seem to worry Johnny.*

Slowing down to a fast walk he let his mind wander. It settled on Johnny waiting patiently in the shelter for him, absently stroking his jacket, and glancing towards the big figtree in the way of the footpath. He smiled now thinking of Johnny's face alight with welcome, as he was spotted.

At the Jazz club, he stopped to peer at a car, its interior light on and someone inside. The headlights made it difficult to see. There was another car behind it with something on its roof. A taxi light? He put his hand up to block the headlights and started moving again. No, a police car. The man in the back seat had his face turned towards the park on the other side of the sparse hedging. He must have sensed someone looking at him and his head swiveled towards Robert.

The rear window was wound halfway down and Robert took a long glance at the man's face. As their eyes caught each other, Robert registered the dazed shock. Then the man turned back to whatever he was watching, and as Robert rounded the bend the pathway made to accommodate the huge figtree, it became clear what it was.

Four figures standing around something. Kicking it.

Robert's head jerked, shaking off confusion.

The thing on the ground jerked too. Oddly. Not stiffening against the blows.

A tall muscled figure stepped back with a small laugh, which didn't match his size. Something was sitting out of sight in a darkened corner of Robert's memory.

A fat-bellied skinny-legged figure patted the muscled shoulder, and Robert noticed the shirt gaping, straining at its buttons and its ends flapping above the lowered waist of the trousers. There was a hat, and something else, next to whatever was on the ground.

The awful thud of flesh absorbing kicks sank into Robert's consciousness.

He tried to make sense of what he was seeing. *Was that a person? What were they doing? Why?* Questions and images were pressing in on him.

90

Jumbled.

He pushed them aside. *Where's Johnny?*

One of the figures stopped kicking and moved, momentarily unblocking the shelter light. Was that his jacket, sprawled on the ground?

The horror dawning.

They were kicking a person. A man.

"Hey," he yelled. "What the fuck do you think you're doing? There's a fucking police car here. Next door. I'm calling the police."

The kicking stopped.

Four heads turned.

Laughter, bemused and bordered by hysteria, cut into the silence.

Transfixed, Robert watched the fat one bend down unhurriedly and pick up a hat, pushing it securely into place on the head of the slight figure next to him. Then light again. The band on the hat, blue and white check, blue and white police check. And the face jutting in his direction, he knew it. Nichols.

Robert stared unseeing, unthinking.

Then a thought. Familiar.

Terry will be OK.

A memory.

Run. Get help. Call an ambulance. Where? Where to?

He felt the heavy hand of Mr Sullivan clamping his shoulder.

Had he imagined it?

He looked over at Johnny. *Was that Johnny? What's wrong with him? Why wasn't he getting up?*

"Johnny!" he shouted. "Johnny! Get up!"

Johnny didn't move.

A voice from somewhere, 'Run. Robert. Go.' It was Johnny's voice.

He looked around.

He was sure it was Johnny's voice.

And then his own anguished, "Come on. Johnny. Get up."

Something was coming towards him. Navy pants, light blue shirt, police hat and another, tall, un-uniformed. He recognised Muscles from the pub. He put his face down, and stepped further back into the shadowy fold of the figtree before he heard it again, Johnny's voice, 'Run! Now Robert. Now!'

Robert didn't notice the tears as he sped down McDonald Street. His awareness filled with a familiar theme singing in his head, in time with his breathing and footfall. *Johnny will be OK. Please God. Johnny will be OK.* Footfall footfall, breathe. Footfall footfall, breathe.

PART TWO

1985 - 1986

CHAPTER 18

Footfall. They'd be listening for footfall.

He headed for the grassy verge, wary of tree roots.

Johnny will be OK, breathe footfall footfall.

He needed a phone. Passing the apartment, he stole a despairing glance. He wouldn't make it inside.

Keep running. *Johnny will be OK, breathe footfall footfall.*

How the hell was he supposed to get help, with them after him? *Breathe footfall footfall.* His mind settled into the blank altered state that came with running.

In a moment of clarity, he reasoned there were only two possible routes back to Johnny's and the phone, and the bad guys were on one of them. He changed tactics and bent over in the light of the street-corner lamp-post pretending to get his breath. When he was sure they'd seen him, he doglegged and ran past the Story Bridge Hotel. The lights were still on, the front door closed. He'd misdirect them. Make them follow him towards

East Brisbane. Lose them, and double back.

And the clarity stopped and the questions came. Where was Nichols? Even if he lost these two, he'd have no idea where Nichols was, and most likely Andrews. Would they wait at the park for these two to come back? Anyone getting onto or off the ferry would see them. Don't they have walkie-talkies? Would Johnny get away? Was that Johnny? Where was he then? *Johnny will be OK. Breathe footfall footfall.*

Checking they were following and could see him, he turned into a side-street leading out of Kangaroo Point. Partway along, he crouched between two cars, hidden by their shadows and the A-frame sign on the footpath. And then the sound of footsteps stopped.

Shit. What now?

He strained to hear the voices.

"That's it… tell'm… got away."

"…lie?"

"Well I'm not… all fucking night."

"B- But you can't…"

"Watch me."

Robert leaned against the car looking skyward. *Fuck.*

He waited. They had to be well clear. He closed his eyes, but the image of Johnny rushed in, filling the blackness. He opened them. *Fuck. Fuck this. Fuck them.* He had to get an ambulance.

The pub. There'd be a phone, and people, and… *they could be there.*

He got up. They wouldn't do anything stupid there, he reasoned. Even so, he took a roundabout route back, keeping to the shadows.

A car was parked in the bus stop opposite the rear of the pub, where it shouldn't be. His heart sank. So did he, crouching and inching blindly backwards, his painstaking progress making his heart go even faster.

Finally, around the corner he crept through the gap in the ti-tree fencing where the pub's bins were, and headed towards the verandah like any other patron who'd been taking a convenient leak where they shouldn't.

The lights were low, and wobbly with fear and crouching thigh-strain, he tripped on the step.

"You all right mate? Pub's closed."

Robert looked at the speaker, "Jimbo?" he said, scanning for Pete. "I need a phone."

"What's wrong? Oh, it's Robert, isn't it?"

"It's urgent, an emergency. Do you think they'll let me in? I need an ambulance."

"OK. OK... stay here." Jimbo looked around, "I'll get Pete, he'll call one."

"No. No. It's not for me. Can't I go inside. Make the call. It won't take long."

Jimbo's hesitation was brief, "Come on."

They stopped together at the closed door and Jimbo knocked, "Blue," he said, then louder, "Bluey?"

The door opened enough for Blue's head to appear.

"We need the phone. Emergency."

"What? Oh, I know you," Blue took in Robert's condition, and checking down the hall towards the back bar, steered Robert in the opposite direction. "Here, come into the office."

The phone sat between a wire basket of invoices and a spike of speared till receipts. Robert's hand stopped vibrating when it closed over the receiver.

He'd never called in an emergency and looked at the space above the door as if the instructions might materialise on its aging off-white paint.

"Ambulance," he said, "No. No, just ambulance— The ferry at Kangaroo Point— No. The other one at the end, I can't— Yes, yes Holman Street."

The door opened.

Bluey with a tumbler half-filled with brown-gold liquid. Robert swallowed his nausea and half the liquid and nodded a thanks as Blue left, "—no the park. A man. Injured. Between the shelter and the playground— No. I'm OK." He looked up again as Pete's face appeared in the doorway, "Yeah honestly, I'm OK," Robert spoke into the receiver. "My name?" he hesitated, Pete raised a finger to his lips and pointed to the phone, miming. Robert followed his directions and replaced the handset.

"Drink up mate. Robert. I'll get you a cab, eh?"

Robert stood, grateful for the warmth drifting down his throat.

"No. Wait here," said Pete. "I won't be a sec, I'll use the cab phone in the bar."

Robert slumped into the chair. The tears instant. He put the glass on the table. The icy fingertips, still shaking, were almost soothing against his closed eyelids. He sniffed, opened his eyes and drained the glass.

When Pete came back in, he put a coaster in Robert's pocket, "My number. In case. I told them to come around the front. We've got-ah, visitors out back."

Words had abandoned Robert after the phone call. He hoped he'd given Pete a grateful look, and then the white mist in his head turned into fog.

Pete guided him into the cab, "You got some money?"

Robert nodded, still mute.

The driver turned unsurprised but not pleased to have a non-vocal passenger, "Where to?"

Pete turned to Robert, "Where's home?"

"Camp Hill," the words struggled out.

"He'll give you directions on the way mate. Off you go."

The cab driver grunted.

As they approached the turning for the main road leading onto the freeway, an ambulance sped in the opposite direction, its siren pulling Robert's attention with it.

"Can you turn around please. The ambulance. I need to—"

"Are you fucking kidding me buddy?" The driver shook his head, "I can't turn around here."

Hope lingered on Robert's out breath. He closed his eyes and tried to pray. But after Dear God, words disappeared, except for Johnny will be OK. *Johnny will be OK.*

CHAPTER 19

Snippets of disjointed kiddy chatter, kitchen and mummy noise, broke through the whiteness of Robert's non-dream.

He opened his eyes blinking at the sight of a window where it shouldn't be and sat up. He was in the study. *Why was the phone on the floor?* His heart flickered sending a spurt of adrenaline to his throat and setting off a drumming pulse in his ears.

He'd put it there, the phone, then closed his eyes, waiting, before calling the hospitals again.

His eyes found the corner of the room. *Breathe, one, two, three...* the numbers drowning the drumbeat. *Breathe deeper.* His chest expanded and he held the breath while thought caught up.

You saw the ambulance. Breathe out now. Everything's OK. But his out-breath stuck in a strangled sob. He pressed his fingertips against his lips and the movement sent the sour smell of last night's fear out to maraud the room.

He got up and opened the window, and the door.

*

"Look, Daddy's awake," Lauren's smile was brightly out of place.

Emma and Thomas clambered past her in the doorway, and hugged a leg each, and he bent to ruffle their hair.

"You didn't have to sleep in the study."

"I didn't want to disturb you."

"Pee-eww. You look like s-h-i-t." She fanned the air under her nose, "Go and shower. We'll drop you at work. Is it still OK for tonight?"

"Tonight?"

"Robert. Girl's night. You don't get to have all the fun."

He shook his head, "Yeah. Yeah. Of course. Yeah."

"Want any breakfast?"

He shook his head again, more slowly, and patted his stomach, "No. Couldn't. Thanks."

Her smile was indulgent and sympathetic, and he turned quickly away from it.

Say something. "I'd better get ready."

The water drummed. His thoughts drummed.

You should have gone back. What the hell were you thinking? That's it. You weren't. Fuckwit. You could've... what? What? Held his hand? Stroked his forehead? Yes. Just been there. And what? Who would have called the ambulance? Them? But you should've gone back. And you'd have been next. You did the right thing. You got help. I don't know... Did I?

He turned up the cold tap. The water hit him like an open-hand slap. An afront, not an assault. He felt cheated. He turned the tap full on and the icy droplets pelted him.

*

The drive was silent in between Emma and Thomas's chatter, till Lauren switched on the radio and music wafted over them, softly filling in the gaps. Near the end of the expressway she said, "Work? Or do you need to pick up your car?"

"I, uh..."

"Robert?"

"Sorry, not with it."

"Work then. You shouldn't be behind a wheel if you aren't *with* it," she huffed. "Maybe you shouldn't be at work either?"

"I'll be OK." *Johnny will be OK, please God.*

"Hey, thanks," he kissed Lauren goodbye through the open car window, and forced his cheeks to drag his lips into smile position, before turning to the back seat. "Be good for Mummy."

"You be good for Mummy too," Emma giggled.

"You be good for Mummy too," Thomas took his turn.

"You don't smell at all boozy," she sounded surprised.

"Listerine."

"Hahaha. You don't smell Listerine-y either."

"Maybe it hasn't quite caught up with me yet."

Her shrug said not that important, "See you by five."

He stood on the footpath in front of his office building and watched till the car joined all the other dots falling into the horizon.

*

Anna was at her old desk outside his office looking cheerily expectant, "Good morning, Mr Carson."

He looked at her confused, half nodded and went into his office.

She watched his back as he closed the door on her disappointment.

Robert placed the handset in its cradle, then rubbed his forehead. Still no record of John Saunders at the PA or the Royal Brisbane hospitals. Emergency ambulances don't go to private hospitals, do they? Someone must have him. He'd tried asking about emergency admissions and describing Johnny and been cut off quickly, with we aren't a missing person's service, and we are very busy. We suggest you contact the police.

No chance of that. But wouldn't the ambulance service know? He dialed 000, quickly hanging up. There'd be an administration or an office number. He scanned his bookshelves for the white or yellow pages and sank back into his chair temporarily defeated.

When Anna's head appeared in the doorway with a coffee in hand, he turned to avoid the smell. The inside of his cheeks moistened. He swiped his forehead, and stared at the sheen on his fingertips, "I need some air."

He stood, without moving, as if he was waiting for permission.

"Is there anything I can do?" she asked, backing out.

"What are you doing here?"

She smiled. He did notice, "Your new girl quit, I—"

"I have to go," he looked past her, pale, sweating and preoccupied.

"I'm coming too. You don't look well."

"I'm fine. I'll be fine," he insisted. "I don't want to see anyone today. Can you make some calls?" Then adding, "Do you know how to call the ambulance if it isn't an emergency?"

Anna was about to answer, and he interrupted, "Doesn't matter. I'll go myself."

"No you won't." She picked up her handbag and appointment book, "Come on. You can fill me in," she glanced at his profile, "or not, on the way to wherever, but you're not going by yourself."

She pushed the call button and handed the appointment book to the receptionist, "Can you cancel Mr Carson's appointments for today. Tell them we'll call to reschedule."

In the basement, Robert started walking to his car and stopped, remembering it wasn't there, "Shit!"

Anna reached into her bag for her car keys and tapped his elbow, "This way."

Outside on the ramp Anna looked for a pause in the traffic, "Where to?"

"The Park Royal."

"What?"

"My car. I left it there last night. Can you drop me off? I need to—"

"Mr Carson," her head making an emphatic no, "I don't think you should be driving."

Robert pushed a deep breath incrementally past the obstruction between his ribs, "Honestly," he said, "I'll be fine. I need you to look after things at the office."

He looked at the set of her face and back to the road, "You should change lanes here. I'm feeling much better." And he was. For now.

She pulled into the loading zone outside the carpark entrance. As he reached for the lock, she put her hand on his forearm, "You can trust me, Robert."

He pressed his lips together and nodded, not trusting himself to speak.

She moved her hand back to the steering wheel.

"It's Johnny. Saunders. You know?" he watched her nod. Then turning to look ahead through the windscreen, "We, last night, he was hurt."

"I'll call Judge Matthews. Surely he'll know how he is."

"I don't know if he knows." Robert continued to stare straight ahead, except when he looked down at his hands, inert and useless on his lap.

Anna said nothing, she glanced in the review mirror at the truck with its indicator on. She was in its way.

"I called an ambulance. I don't know where they took him."

"Why didn't you go with him?"

"I," Robert paused. "It doesn't matter. I couldn't. I need to see if he's OK." *Johnny will be OK, please God.*

The truck behind them beeped, Robert jumped, and hurried out.

CHAPTER 20

"I'm sorry, I know you're busy, but I couldn't go with him. I was too far away making the call. I couldn't get back. Not in time. But I saw the ambulance. I promised his sister I'd check up on him," he looked at the duty nurse, pleading. It wasn't that much of a lie.

"I'll check again. John Saunders. Right?"

She upended the wire tray onto the tabletop. He waited .

"What if..." Robert paused, "if someone came in, an emergency, with no ID, what would happen? You know, if they were robbed or beaten up or something?"

"Is that what happened?" She glared at him, "Were you involved in this?"

"No! No. But it just occurred to me that maybe he'd been robbed, so he wouldn't have any ID and well, you know, if he was unconscious, or—"

The pain in Robert's eyes must have helped and her lips uncrinkled, "We'd notify the police. They'd check missing persons. From there it depends on the circumstances. They'd contact family."

"OK, I thought so. But were there any?"

"John Doe admissions?" she sighed and picked up the phone.

Robert listened to her half of the conversations.

She shook her head, "You've already checked with Royal Brisbane?" She watched him nod. "But not for any John Doe. And you haven't checked with St Andrews or the Mater?"

"No. No, they're private. I didn't think," he started to turn. "Thanks. Heaps. You've been great."

"Hang on," she said, "I'll call them."

When nothing came from her calls, he was starting to think that somehow, his entreaties to God had worked this time, "What about the ambulance. Would they be able to tell me? Us. His sister I mean."

"Family maybe. Or the police. I don't know. No-one's ever asked me."

"Well, you've been so helpful."

"I might as well make another call and ask them."

Robert pressed his prayered hands to his lips. He watched as she ran the button on the phone index up to 'A' and clicked it open. The top flipped up on its spring, and her finger followed a list then dialed.

He listened to her half of the conversation again "OK," she said and looked at Robert. "Thank you. I think."

"What?"

"I don't know if this is good news, but, she checked the call-out sheets. There was a dispatch to Kangaroo Point 22.29.38 but there was no-one there. The caller, you obviously," she arched an eyebrow, "didn't leave a name or a contact number. They marked it as a hoax."

CHAPTER 21

Heading back to his office, Robert felt like he was finally getting a good lungful of air after being repeatedly dumped in a shore break. Exhausted and grateful. He'd cope with the fallout; Johnny's anger, disappointment or whatever it was. *Thank God,* he checked the review mirror, *but please, if you're still in the mood for favours, let him not be too sore, or too pissed off with me.*

He imagined Johnny's face, disappointed but forgiving, telling him he'd heard him call out, and that he knew the police were after him, and that's how he got away himself. It was Friday. He'd be at uni. Would he have gone today? There was bound to be a message at the office.

Suddenly, he was feeling hungry.

*

"Everything OK then?" Anna said.

"The ambulance didn't pick him up. He must have been OK and gone home. Such a relief." He opened the packet and took a bite of his sandwich, "Where's what's-her-name?"

"Gone. I've advertised. Do you want some tea with that?" she was already getting up.

"Love some."

Anna came in with his messages skewered in reverse order on their spike, and the tea. He sipped and floated in the carb lethargy, sorting messages and then began flicking more hastily. No calls from Johnny, three, no, four now from Harry, and from Marnie. The plug holding his contentedness in, had been yanked out, and the warmth drained as quickly as the blood from his face.

He called Harry first. No answer.

"Marnie," he said when she answered, "what's wrong?"

"Harry called me. Johnny's not home."

"Not home?" Robert echoed. "When did he call?"

"Early. Before work."

"I just called there. No answer. But it's Friday. Uni. Johnny wouldn't be back before two. Let me think," he looked at his watch and scowled.

"You keep trying Harry. Remind him about uni. Tell him to stay there and to ring you as soon as Johnny gets home. Then ring me. Tell Anna if I'm not here. I'm going to the apartment. We went— he might have gone there instead of going home. Did you ring there?"

"Of course. I left a message."

"Don't panic." He could feel his own panic rising. There was no point in saying anything until he'd checked, "I'll leave now. I'll ring you from there."

"How? I mean, if he isn't there."

"I— spare key, I know where it is," Robert lied, scraping the unspiked messages into a jumble.

*

On the drive to Johnny's, questions came one after another with no gaps for answers. *Why didn't you tell Marnie about the hospital? Why didn't you tell her you'd been checking for him half the night and all morning? That you'd been together till you spat the dummy about your stupid fucking watch? Why didn't you tell her you called an ambulance, that you ran, you were being chased, that you didn't go back. Why didn't you tell her what you saw?*

At the apartment, he dropped the keys. The gap in the unlocking ritual caused a gap in the questions and into it fell an answer. Neither he nor Johnny wanted the world to know what was going on between them. They'd have to stop seeing each other. With that realization came Lauren's face. Harry's face. Terry's face, pink, 'don't tell Dad', and turning grey, 'nothing happened here'; the policeman, 'what were you doing in the water son?'; his mum's face turning away, and the phone thrust in his own face 'go to your room'. Words and images clamouring to escape. He pushed them back into the hole and rolled a boulder over the planks and coverings which were no longer strong enough. One, two, three, four, five, six... fifteen. He counted till they all settled into place.

Stepping inside the apartment, Robert knew no-one had been there since he left last night. He walked through anyway. The air was flat and still, like the walls hadn't been breathing.

Then he walked to the ferry-stop, and stood at the tree forcing himself to scan what was in front of him.

The grass was flattened in places. His jacket was nowhere to be seen. Nothing to be seen. He went to the jetty shelter. What if...? The glare outside made it almost impossible to see inside. He wrinkled his nose at the stale ammonia smell. When his eyes adjusted, he spotted the blanket stretched over something lumpy under the bench-seat. His throat seized, his head buzzed, and thought disintegrated. Then a wordless wish to heaven that it be Johnny, and then another that it not be.

He crouched, touched the corner of the blanket closing his eyes, opening them as he lifted it.

Seeing a pillow, greasy and adorned with dark-brown drool flowers; socks, stiff with dirt and skin dust; an empty bottle, and a plastic zipper bag, he crumpled into a pile of relief. Then thought returned. The man in the police car. He'd been watching. Maybe this was his stuff. Maybe he'd know where Johnny went.

Robert started to run. *Johnny will be OK*. His eyes caught the swings and he slowed to a walk. They seemed to be nodding, yes, Johnny will be OK.

Back at Johnny's apartment he called Harry. Still no answer.

Marnie answered hers, breathless with worrying or rushing, and Robert let the opportunity to say something slip away again. He had no business dumping his dread on her, and nothing made sense. He pictured Johnny having a beer with friends after uni, buying groceries for dinner. But the question lurked. Was that possible? He'd called and Johnny didn't get up. Was he playing possum with those thugs? Pretending, so they'd stop? That had to be it. He's got to be somewhere.

"I'll leave a note here and—"

"Robert," her tone caught him by surprise, "I know. I know about you two. OK?"

The stone in his chest shifted.

"Did you hear me?"

"Yeah," he blinked away the tears.

"Does anyone else know?"

"No. Just us. Johnny and me. And you."

*

"I was hoping you or Marnie might have heard from him," Harry said when Robert finally got him sometime after three.

Robert let Harry talk off some of his anxiety.

"I've called the hospitals. But I'm not family, they wouldn't tell me anything."

"I should have said. Sorry, look—" Robert started.

But Harry was talking again, and Robert half-listened wondering how long he could or should keep quiet or how he could say... *what? Don't be stupid. Harry has enough to contend with at the moment, without me spilling my guts just to make myself feel better. Johnny could turn up any minute and I would have ruined everything. Breathe. Now say something useful.*

"Harry, you need to be home, when Johnny comes back. Phone Marnie as soon as he does. OK?"

"Yes. You're right. Home. Yes."

"When did you see him last?"

"Last see him? Sorry, I'm repeating myself. Yesterday. He called me about five, left a message. He goes out most Thursdays. He was meeting a friend for drinks. I have a standing arrangement with my niece." Harry reflected, "Yes of course. Twenty-four hours. We can file a Missing Persons."

"I told you before, that we were friends, before all this. Johnny and I, and Marnie?" Robert waited for Harry's confirmation. "I'll go over to her place. She's worried sick. If he's not home by five, I'll look after Nikki while she goes to the police station. Her dad can go with her."

"I'm trying not to think about it. I know he's a grown man, but..." Harry's voice faded into the unsayable.

107

CHAPTER 22

Robert checked the map on the passenger seat and the number on the driveway gate-post.

Marnie gave him a quick hug in the doorway of her house, a mini version of its impressive neighbour, "Come in, Dad's here."

Robert followed Marnie into the TV room, "Nikki," she said, "Uncle Robert's here."

"Good," Jack said. "We'll be at Hendra Police Station. Pointless waiting around here."

Robert followed Nikki's eyes. She was watching Marnie rubbing the back of one hand with the fingers of the other one. *Say something. Say I saw him last night. He was on his way to get the ferry. With me. He was being beaten. I'm sure it was him. I called an ambulance. Go on tell her. I called out to stop them, but they came after me. For God's sake, say it. Don't be fucking stupid. You can't say that in front of the child.'*

"We won't be long I imagine," she stopped fidgeting, and picked up a framed photo of Johnny.

Robert sat on the couch watching Nikki watching the cartoons. He thought of Thomas and Emma. And Lauren. He had to call Lauren.

"I'll cancel," she said. "I couldn't go out now anyway. Call me, even if you don't know anything. OK?"

He called Harry, and went back to the cartoons, where violence was a bandaged bump surrounded by circling stars and perilous cliff falls only ever ended with a word. Splat.

He and Nikki both looked up when they heard the knock. *Did Marnie*

108

forget her key?

Two uniformed police were waiting.

"We were looking for the owner of the house," they glanced towards the big house, "John Saunders."

Robert frowned, "You mean Jack, Jack Saunders?"

"Do you know him, Mr Saunders? You called him Jack."

"Jack? Not really. I'm a friend of Marnie and Johnny. Jack's daughter, and son. I was assuming that if you were looking for John at the house, that you meant Jack. They're at Hendra Station. Marnie and her dad. Johnny is missing. They're reporting him missing."

"Ahh. I see."

Robert wanted to know what that meant. He rubbed his solar plexus. *It can't be a coincidence that they were looking for John Saunders. Why would they be here? Was there something they'd found. Had someone found Johnny?*

They stepped back.

One of them spoke on his radio, then turned to Robert, "Maybe we could sit down and wait? Perhaps some tea?"

He switched on the kettle, "Is that why you're here? But you didn't know Johnny was missing. You came about something else?"

"We'll go over everything when your friends return."

The kettle bubbled and whistled and switched itself off and Robert didn't move.

He was back in the front room, the day after his eleventh birthday, and standing in front of the policeman, his mother sitting in the other big lounge chair, "Well tell him," she'd said.

"What?"

"About your friend."

"Who?"

"Oh for God's sake, Robert. Your friend from school, Terry."

"Is he OK?" he turned and faced the policemen, his nose prickling and his forehead tensing and releasing, hands bunched at his sides, "Can I see him? Is he in hospital?"

"No son," the policeman said. "No."

"He had asthma, and—" nothing came out except a breathy huuhh.

"He died," the policeman paused. "I came to ask you what happened.

See if you could help with our-ah enquiries."

Robert looked up, blinking repeatedly, *this isn't real, this isn't happening, Terry will be OK.* His fingernails were trying to cut through his palms. *One, two, three, four... fifteen. One, two—*

"Look son, Terry's dad, Mr Sullivan, said you were both wet. It's winter. What were you doing in the creek?"

"They were playing," his mum said. "He probably slipped, you know—"

"He didn't," Robert interrupted. "We—"

His mother talked over him, "Chasing the ball or—"

"Mrs Carson, please. Go on Robert."

"I was trying to help him out of the water," Robert said.

"Was there anyone else with you?"

"Not at first," Robert looked directly at the policeman.

"What happened son?"

"Some big boys came. They teased us. They— "

"Robert's father is a Cabinet Minister you know," his mother interrupted again. "It wouldn't be appropriate for—"

"Did they hurt you?" The policeman cut in. "Did they hurt Terry?"

He looked at his mother's lowered eyelids. The warning peered through the slits left open.

"They were mean. They teased us and ran away." He turned back to the policeman, "And then I helped Terry out of the creek. I got his puffer and I went back to school to get his dad."

Robert's anguished face went back to his mother, "I tried to tell you yesterd—"

"Shhhh-shhhh." Her eyes fixed on the policeman, but she spoke to Robert, "It's OK. We know you didn't do anything wrong."

"Do you know the boys who-ah, teased you?" the policeman ignored her.

"He would have told me," his mother's nostrils quivered.

"It's OK," the policeman ignored her, "You can tell me, son."

He heard Terry's voice saying *it'll be worse next time,* and another voice, *nothing happened here,* taking turns. He found the ceiling *one, two, three, four...* The thud in his throat merged with the one between his ribs, getting louder in his ears and faster. He looked at his mum, his head making a slow no,

"I— Mum, I— please, I don't want to go back there. That school, I hate it. What if they think I know who—"

"Shhhh-shhhh," she stood pulling him to her, burying the rest of his words against her ribs. He felt her bones press against his teeth, "Shhhh." She looked down at the policeman, "Is there anything else? You can see he's upset. He didn't do anything wrong."

"Thank you for your-ah, cooperation, Mrs Carson, Robert. If there's anything you remember later. Here," he put a card on the occasional table.

They all looked at it as he stood up too.

"Let me help," the policeman in Marnie's kitchen reached past him for the mugs. "You want one?"

Robert shook his head. His face was hot. Then icy.

"You known John, Johnny, long?"

Robert nodded. The question was a diversion and the officer seemed decent, but the sickening images of last night swirled into his memories, "Do you mind?" He lurched towards the hall. Nikki was watching him, "Stay here."

He made it to the bathroom and retched.

He looked into the mirror splashing cold water onto his face. Stray droplets clung like tears to the image staring back at him, confused and grey and tight.

Emerging from the bathroom, he heard Marnie and Jack's voices.

"Do you mind Robert?" Marnie said. "We're going over to Dad's."

Yes, I do mind. I need to hear what they have to say. Why are they here? You hadn't even reported him missing. And they were looking for Jack. Not Johnny. He drew his dry lips back over his teeth in what he hoped was a smile, "No. Go."

***

"I don't get it Marnie. The police don't make house calls to return a lost wallet."

"Two things. The ID. It had his name and this address. Dad's."

"Yeah," said Robert. "My point."

"Let me finish. I'm barely keeping it together. It's procedure or

111

something, they ran a check on the name. The arrest stuff came up, with a different address. They started calling and didn't get an answer. They went to the apartment, no answer, then here."

Robert lined his ducks up, "They thought he'd given false information, that something was dodgy."

She nodded.

"But how did they get the wallet? Did someone find it? Who? Where?"

Marnie shook her head, "They said they're continuing to make enquiries. But," she took a sharp breath and her eyes welled. "Oh Robert, they're evasive and sombre and, and—"

He pulled her towards him for a hug. He needed it as much as she did.

"I have to go back," she said, wiping a tear. "I told them I wanted to check on Nikki. Call Harry, will you? Make some toast or something for Nikki?"

She started to turn, and Robert took her hand, "Marnie," he held her eyes, "I— he must be OK. Somewhere. I saw him."

"Are you sure it was him?"

"I— I thought it was." He peered into the space between them. "It was dark. I saw someone on the ground. There was a jacket nearby. I assumed— Johnny had my jacket." Pieces of picture rearranged themselves, "I don't know. I wasn't— it wasn't there when I went back looking for him. I don't know."

Her eyes clouded, "I have to go."

He made toast for Nikki and tried to ignore that the yellow flecks in her eyes were the same as her mother's and Johnny's. *Where's Johnny? Please God. Find him.*

He called Harry and then Lauren, from the extension in the hall.

"You're not my real uncle, are you," Nikki said when he came back into the kitchen, "like Uncle Johnny is?"

"No," he said. "It's a polite way for grownups to talk about their friends with their children."

"I know," she said. "But you *are* Robert."

"Mmmm."

"Are you sad about Uncle Johnny?"

"What?" Robert's face re-composed itself, "Worried, sweetie. We're all worried about him."

"Is that why the policemen are here?"

He nodded.

She rocked gently, "He was watching."

"Watching what sweetheart? Who?"

"Uncle Johnny. He said he was on the swings watching. And he said to tell Robert he was sorry."

"When did he say that, Nikki?" Robert's heart was moving but his breath wasn't.

"Last night. When everyone was asleep."

"Did he say anything else? Did Mummy see him too?"

She shook her head.

"What happened then? After he said he was sorry?" Robert's heart raced.

"Grandma came and they went to her place."

"Do you know where Grandma lives? Does Mummy know?"

"Silly," she looked at him as if he had forgotten something important. "Grandma lives with the angels in forever ever after. In Heaven."

"Oh, yeah. I forgot." He let this sink in. "I am silly, aren't I? Did you tell Mummy?"

"No," she frowned. "He didn't tell me to. He said tell Robert."

Robert calmed himself, "Can I ask you another question?"

"Mmm."

"Does Grandma come, to see you, to visit often?"

"No. Just sometimes. But she said she's always here. Even when I can't see her."

"How does that make you feel?"

Her eyebrows knitted, "Sometimes sad. Because she isn't *here*, here. But it's OK."

"And does Mummy know that she visits you?"

"I suppose," her shoulders lifted into a shrug. "Will you read to me?"

*

113

Marnie interrupted their story.

"The police want us to go to the station in Fortitude Valley," she said. "That's where they have his things. Someone found them on the Story Bridge. They're saying it's suicide Robert. I can't believe that Johnny would do that. But..." Her face went blank and her eyes dulled, "There's a body. They've found a body in the river. It can't be him, Robert, it can't..."

The words stopped flying, as the air carrying them out into the world stalled into a body jerking sob. Tears glided down her cheeks, and he folded his arms around her, trying to stop her from breaking.

He didn't realise he was crying too, until Nikki came in and hugged them both around the legs.

"Do you want me to come?" he asked when he felt her breathing change. "Lauren can come over. Someone should be here in case the phone rings."

Marnie stared at it, as if it would burst into life.

Robert did too, imagining Johnny apologising. He'd been out. Time got away.

He caught the end of Marnie's explanation to Nikki, "...you remember Emma and Thomas, don't you?"

Nikki nodded.

"And when they get here, Uncle Robert will come and get us. I don't know how long we'll be."

Nikki nodded again.

"Are you OK sweetheart?"

Nikki shook her head, her shoulders sagging under the weight of everyone's fear, "I don't want Uncle Johnny to go to forever-ever-after."

CHAPTER 23

Robert sat in the corner of the empty police station waiting area, on the last of the joined-together red plastic chairs. *Johnny will be OK.* Silence. *Johnny will be OK, please God.* Crushing silence. Then a thought. That the police from last night might belong to this Station.

He reached for an abandoned newspaper as two uniformed police came through the internal door separating the public area from the squad room. If they noticed him, they didn't seem to mind he was there.

Without even trying, his ears tuned in to their conversation.

"I'm telling you, it's not the same bloke."

"Who made you the bloody expert?"

"I didn't say I was. But, my Uncle's with the Water Police."

"So?"

"Tides."

"Well smart-arse. We've got a sighting; belongings lifted from between a girder and railing on the bridge, and a body, in the river. Sounds pretty simple to me."

"Just because it's logical doesn't mean it's true. My Uncle, he's an auditor, he reckons you can be out by a cent, and write it off, but it could be you're out a hundred dollars on one hand, and ninetynine-ninetynine on the other. So you've missed two pretty big numbers. What if there were two jumpers? What if—"

"How many uncles have you got?"

"My point is—"

"Yeah, but why make life difficult? We've got a missing person, a body, and a big flag waving us in the face."

"But, we're supposed to—"

"Put a sock in it, Kowalski. *My* uncle," pause for emphasis, "says don't let the truth interrupt a good story."

"Well you can laugh, but I'm telling you—"

"They went right back to the spot they'd reported sighting him and found the wallet and the jacket, all neatly stashed like he was at the pool for a swim, or some diving practice more like," he laughed. "And they've got a witness. A drunk. Wouldn't say he'd be too reliable though," another chuckle.

"Well why didn't they stop? They could have talked him down," Kowalski argued.

"How the hell would I know? Probably because they had a passenger. Anyway, we aren't a counselling service."

"But we're supposed to help people, it's our duty—" said Kowalski.

"Well I wouldn't be holding no-one's hand on the wrong side of that railing. Wouldn't wanna go swimming with them. Haha."

"Someone died arsehole."

"We all gotta go sometime."

Kowalski's jaw tightened, "My point was, he'd be miles down-river on the *out*going tide. Or stuck somewhere in between and *not*, back the other way, in the mangroves."

"What? Tides only go one way? Full of shit, Kowalski."

Robert registered the fight falling out of Kowalski's next words, "Nope. Doesn't add up. Something stinks."

"Hah. Your head's so far up your arse you think everything stinks."

Kowalski flicked through some papers on the counter, "Hey. You 'right sir?"

"Me?" Robert lowered the newspaper.

Kowalski sighed, "I don't see anyone else here."

Robert looked around, "Sorry. My friend and her dad are here. I'm waiting for them. They've come about a missing person."

Kowalski reached for the sign in book, "Got some ID sir?"

Handing the driving licence back to Robert, he said, "Need a new one soon."

Robert checked the date, "Hey, thanks," and obtrusively reading Kowalski's name tag hoping it signaled he hadn't been listening in, "Officer

Kowalski."

"All good sir. Just trying to be helpful."

"Well, you didn't have to," he found a smile. "Should I wait here?"

"Let me check for you."

He was back quickly.

"Mr Carson, they've gone to the morgue. To identify the body." He apologized when he saw Robert's face sag, "I'm sorry. Look. It may be. Or it maybe not."

"I'm… are they coming back here? Should I…I'm not sure what…"

"I'll let them know you're here. And basically, regardless of whether, well you know… The pathologist does an examination and gives it to the coroner. His job is who died, where, when, and what happened."

Robert nodded, he didn't want to embarrass Kowalski, "Mmm, thanks. I thought so." And then, "But is it only a coroner? Shouldn't there be an inquest?"

"Not necessarily. Unless there's evidence or suspicion of foul play. I'll radio now and see where they are with all this, eh?"

"Can I ask you something?"

Kowalski nodded.

"How would they know if there's suspicion without an inquiry."

"Hit the nail on the head there. But mine is not to reason why." Kowalski looked pointedly at his colleague on his way out.

He was a while.

"You look like you could use something stronger, but," he lifted up the hinged part of the countertop, and led Robert through the visitor door off the main lobby into the back, stopping inside by the CafeBar and handing over a plastic cup of hot water.

Robert sat watching the tea-bag blob on the surface and slowly sink, then took a grateful sip.

"Mr Carson," a concerned frown lined Kowalski's forehead, "I wanted to give you some privacy. They've made the identification."

Robert's head barely moved in acknowledgement and his mind stilled completely.

They sat in silence.

After what could have been moments or years, Robert's eyes moved down from the ceiling, and he stared at the cup he was holding. He put it on the table, and rubbed his hands on his thighs, before they moved, still of their own accord and grabbed hold of his knees. He couldn't think of anything to think or anything to say.

"So you been friends long? With the Saunders I mean?"

"Marnie and Johnny," somehow the words came out.

He fell back into silence.

No. No. No. No. NO.

His chest moved. Shuddering. He was rocking, little forward and backward movements. And then, noticing his hands gripping his knees, he loosened his fingers. He could feel moisture in the outside corners of his eyes, then sniffed. He looked at Kowalski, as if he couldn't understand what he was doing there, and then for some reason he took out his wallet and even though thought hadn't caught up, he said, "I'm more than friends, I'm Johnny's lawyer." He handed Kowalski his card, "He has, had, some history with you lot."

"Yeah, I know."

"You do?"

"Not that you're his lawyer. But the history thing."

"And what exactly do you know?" He didn't mean it to sound terse.

"Hey, I'm the cop here." Kowalski's smile was meant to be disarming. "Would it be worrying enough to jump?"

Robert pressed his lips together and shook his head slowly, till he could speak. It took every ounce of self-control not to shout, NO. "I can see why some people might come to that conclusion, but," the head shaking continued, "definitely not."

"How come you're so definite?"

Robert's forehead clenched and unclenched. He forced his mouth to open, "A conversation we had. Several. He was in a good place. Despite what was going on."

"Specifics? Off the record. Not that anyone listens to me."

For some reason it seemed that he should tell Kowalski. He went with the feeling. "To start with, the arrest, court, he was upset, worried. As you'd expect. After some time to think, it was more like an annoying hiccup. He had family, friends, lots of love, and career prospects, not that he'd really need it, because he'd just heard he was going to inherit truckloads of money. So," Robert paused, "happy, and *not*, by any stretch of the imagination, suicidal."

Kowalski nodded and held up the business card, "Got another one?" When Robert handed it to him, he wrote on the back, "I don't normally do this. In fact, I never do this. My personal number. I mean it. If you need anything."

Robert tucked it into the space in his wallet behind his licence. As he did, he noticed a torn off beer coaster and a chill crept up the back of his neck.

CHAPTER 24

No-one spoke as Robert drove Jack and Marnie home. It was like a fog had filled the car muting even the sound of their breathing. Small bursts of light from the houses either across the river, or along it, flashed into Robert's awareness and disappeared again into the dark.

When they arrived Marnie said, "You and Lauren stay. Don't disturb the kids. I'll go to Dad's."

He watched their shadows move across the lawn dividing their houses.

Lauren answered the door at Marnie's, "You need to go to Harry's. It's been on the news."

"It can't have. The coroner hasn't had time."

"I'm not arguing Robert. I'm telling you. Go."

He turned and stopped, "I'll let Marnie know. Ring your dad. Tell him to meet me there. They haven't seen much of each other in the last twenty years, but they were close friends. At least he won't have to explain himself to Duncan."

***

Robert's eyes roamed around Harry's apartment. He'd always felt smugly complacent, growing up in suburban middle-class ease, despite the discomfort of its defining and ill-fitting gender requirements, but today the sense of other-worlds was dramatically real and on top of everything else, completely disorienting. The living room was opulently subdued, like its owner.

The only thing out of place but completely appropriate, was the anger and hurt, thrashing around in Harry's eyes. He swallowed something golden brown from the crystal glass he held, "What's unforgivable, even more than being the last person to find out, is hearing it on the news," his words harsh and flat. "I feel so…" he didn't finish. "I've been sitting here listening to the newsreader over and over in my head. I wanted to punch a hole in the wall, but when I tried to stand up, I couldn't. Just devastating, devastating sorrow. Waves of it. And I kept asking myself why? What did I miss? What was so troubling he couldn't tell me? That he would do something so, so…" His eyes profoundly sad and bewildered, "My poor boy. My poor beautiful boy."

Harry had put his glass down on the art deco side table with such gentleness, that the sob which broke out of him took Robert by surprise. It made him think of metal tearing apart, jagged and resisting, trying to hold its original shape while something huge and forceful made it buckle and split open.

The sharp edges of Harry's grief cut through Robert as well. Fat wet drops oozed from their eyes. They sat in silence, opposite each other, two islands, their shores sharing the same ocean of grief.

"I don't understand," Harry said finally, "how they could come to a conclusion so quickly. There must have been absolutely no doubt at all that this was a deliberate and intentional act of self-harm. I just can't believe it."

He looked at Robert as if somehow the answers would appear.

Robert stood, "Excuse me, Harry, the bathroom?"

Harry pointed up the hall, and Robert rushed off, hating himself for the inanity of a bathroom excuse, but the grief was so raw and urgent and present, and he wasn't that good an actor. *Is this what you're going to do? Keep slinking away from the truth like this?* It was taking staggering willpower to keep the stone in his chest in place. It was exhausting. *Don't you dare say anything. You can't pile on more hurt. Talk about kick someone when they're down. But all this? It would be such a relief to say something.*

Robert sneered at the image in the bathroom mirror, *Yeah. For who? This isn't about you. How would you feel? If you lost Lauren and her lover turned up. Oh, by the way, I just wanted to say I'm sorry. We've been having a bit of a thing. I thought you should know.*

He gripped the basin, then hit the edge with his fist. Grateful for the physical pain, he looked down at his hand and wrist and took off his watch.

"Stupid fucking..." he stuffed the watch into his pocket, his finger tracing the crack he'd put in the face. *You didn't want to lie about it. Your entire fucking life is a lie. Oh Johnny, I'm so sorry. I'm so sorry. I'm...*

He looked back into the mirror. *Stop it. Just stop it.*

*

"Forgive me," said Harry, when Robert returned, "I've got cheese and crackers and some odd bits in the fridge, I'll fix you a plate."

"I'm not hungry. But thank you." It seemed unfair, shameful, to be eating or even hungry.

"All the same," said Harry. "But first, I want to say something."

"Actually, I," Robert faltered. "Harry, I don't quite know how—"

Harry raised his hand in a stop, and the intercom buzzing stopped them both.

Harry switched to leveraging himself from the chair, then de-tensioned, "I'm not expecting anyone."

"No, that'll be Duncan. Lauren, my wife, she, we didn't want to interfere, but we thought maybe some company. Someone you were comfortable with. Who knew Johnny and well..."

The buzzer went again. This time Harry got up.

Somewhere in Duncan and Harry's greeting, Robert's attention disappeared and something lurking at the edge of his mind began to emerge, "Can I ask you a question, sir?"

Harry nodded.

"We knew about the bequest, the will and the Trust set up, but does anyone else know? Did you tell him what it was? How much?" Robert silently berated himself for pretending not to know.

"I can see why you're asking," Harry tapped his lips to help keep the tears in place. "Makes no sense. You're set for a substantial inheritance, soon, not years away, and you kill yourself? And no. No-one else knows."

Harry thought for a minute, "I don't like to admit it, but frankly I was frightened by what happened. The ambush, the blackmail. I thought it would be better, safer, for Johnny and for me if he— if we were both to appear as if we had separate lives. And then well, I didn't want him to be my nursemaid. But as he rightly pointed out, that was his decision not mine." Harry swallowed and put his glass down, "Anyway, at first I didn't want the money to seem like a big financial carrot. A sorry please come back to me inducement."

"But he knew the details? You told him? What changed your mind?"

"We all make mistakes," Harry looked at Robert and they both looked away, "I'm not immune," he continued. "He changed it. Or I suppose love did. Johnny isn't the sort of—" Harry's eyes filmed and he tapped his lips before continuing, "*wasn't*, Johnny wasn't the sort of person who would hang around for money. I don't know why I got all thingy about that." He shrugged, "My own baggage I suppose, maybe because my niece and her husband think of me as some kind of cash-cow. Then I thought, if we were any ordinary couple, a legal Mr and Mrs, Mr and Mr, he *would* know the details at least in a general sense if not the specifics, and I wouldn't be making special provisions. I wouldn't have to. He'd get if not all, then most of my estate, and we'd talk about it. So I told him. And he knew I thought of him as my partner. Not that lately..." he shook his head out of its reverie. "And," he snorted, "I was supposed to die first. Instead, I'm sitting here only half dead, finding out on the news, that my Johnny, my special love, my..." he stopped, took a breath and shook his head, "... has jumped off a bridge."

"To be fair," Robert said quietly, and sniffing back his tears, "we all expected him to simply walk through the door. Marnie, Jack too. They wouldn't deliberately exclude you. They're not that sort of family."

"I know, I know, I'm just railing against it." Harry's anger and hurt needed somewhere to go. "I won't even get a copy of the report, the coroner's report. Family will. Johnny's," he paused, "Johnny's body won't be released to me. It will be released to *the family*. We aren't *allowed* to be family. Good thing he wasn't alive somewhere in hospital... I'd have been arrested breaking down the bloody doors to see him. Garrhh. What the hell. Here," he held his glass up, "do the honours would you Duncan?" His head moved slowly side to side, "We sicken them. Hah. They sicken me." His breath caught, and he rubbed his forehead, the anger dissipating into sadness, "They sicken me."

Robert had been absently twirling his glass while his heart was breaking for Harry. He watched as Duncan refilled Harry's glass and put a hand on Harry's shoulder, giving it a squeeze, as if the gesture could somehow ease the anguish. Robert watched as Harry's hand patted it thank you and something else started clicking into place. He needed some time without them talking.

"Harry," said Robert, "why don't you two have some time together, and I'll raid your fridge. It would probably be a good idea if you ate something too."

Harry pointed unnecessarily towards the kitchen.

"You told Johnny I owed you a favour," said Duncan.

"I thought you did," Harry's nod was directed at the decanter on the sideboard, "Help yourself, I'm slowing down... my treatment, and the edge is off, for now."

"Thanks. You were saying," Duncan prompted.

"I wasn't."

"Come on Harry, you're a professional arbiter of truth. Withholding it is as bad as telling an outright lie. I was hoping you know... between old friends."

"This isn't easy. No-one likes rejection."

"Who are you talking about Harry?"

"I loved Johnny, dearly," Harry stopped, his eyes damp and desolate. "He reminded me of being young, of us being young, but I'm not good at letting things go. Johnny is— *was*— expansive. He got over things quickly. Early on, I thought he was burying things, that they'd fester, that there'd be some lashing out to follow. But he wasn't like that. Don't get me wrong, he was no saint. But he didn't bear a grudge. He'd be... if something's wrong, let's fix it, not blame someone."

Harry fell silent.

"When he came back," he said, after a while, "he was, I don't know... aloof isn't the right word. Maybe there *was* some hurt or resentment. Me sending him away like that might have felt like a rejection and... I think I'm rambling. What if he hadn't gotten over things this time. And maybe that's why he..."

Supported by the doorframe in the kitchen Robert closed his eyes.
Duncan stayed silent.

"I've felt close to doing it too you know. Twice," said Harry. "The first time was when you married Lauren's mother. I was broken," he paused, "and then, when she died, I thought…"

"Julieanne," Duncan said, "her name was Julieanne. I had a child Harry. I had to work. We both had to work."

"I think that's why I sent Johnny to you. For a connection. Maybe at some level, he knew my motives weren't all pure."

"Are you trying to blame yourself for this?" said Duncan. "Because it was something you contemplated? I think most people have, if they're honest."

"I'm trying to find a reason, an explanation. But… the way things were set up. He seemed genuinely content. Except… I don't know."

Robert pulled himself away from their conversation and started making noisy progress in the kitchen.

It didn't take long, and he made his presence known with an off-hand, "Harry, I'm looking for a corkscrew," and emerging soon after with a couple of plates, and catching the last bit of their exchange.

Harry was shaking his head in a slow no, "Strange to say considering how much this is hurting, but I know he wouldn't do anything to hurt me," he sighed heavily and a glittery film smudged and softened the red veins of grief spidering the whites of his eyes, "…but I'm glad you're here Duncan. Thank you."

Duncan nodded.

A teary and uncertain smile hovered over Harry's face, "If there's one thing Johnny taught me it's that nothing is too bad. I loved him for that." His sniff couldn't stem the tears, "His hope." His shoulders sank, and he looked at Duncan and Robert in turn, in blurry-eyed bewilderment, "And now I don't believe him." His lip shook, and he trembled, "He lied. He lied."

*

"I'll leave you to it," said Robert. "But before I go I wanted to flag something you mentioned earlier, about the coroner's report. The family, Jack and Marnie, I know you said you hadn't told anyone but, do you have any idea if Johnny had spoken to them. Told them anything about the will and…" Robert looked for Harry's eyes. "They know you're back together, but…"

"Of course. That's why it was on the news," said Harry flatly. "The coroner will have the information from the police records. He'll be going by what they think they know. To them it's open and shut. Their story will be that he was depressed about the court case, the prospect of jail. The stigma and loneliness, and the fear, were all too much."

"You're right," said Robert. "The policeman at the station said they knew about Johnny's arrest and the circumstances. They'd probably already done fingerprint matches. The identification would've just been an added tick. So without any reason otherwise, the verdict was suicide, as long as the injuries," he stopped. "I don't want to upset you Harry, but, as long as they were consistent with, well… they would've shut the file." He looked at Duncan and then settled on Harry, "There won't be an inquest."

CHAPTER 25

"Wasn't expecting you, Lovey," Tank's reflection looked at Robert from between two rows of bright bulbs on either side of his dressing room mirror at the Wickham. He turned to peer around behind Robert, "Where's Johnny?"

"What time's the show?"

Tank looked at the wall-clock, "Fifteen minutes. Are you joining in again?" he wiggled his shoulders, turning back to the mirror, and adjusting his headband. His reflection changed dramatically when it caught Robert's expression in the mirror. "What's wrong?" He was up and guiding Robert into a chair. "Here, sit down. What is it?"

Robert's exhale vibrated on the air around it, "It can wait till after the show."

"Somehow I think not." Tank leaned forward. "It's Johnny isn't it?"

The wretchedness was now clearly visible, but the words were still hiding. The dull tick-tick-pause, tick-tick-pause of the second hand held them in its thrall, then one word, soft on the out-breath, and trying not to be heard, "Dead." And then, following an anguished hiccupping sob, "He died. Johnny died."

Tank tilted forward, rocking, a hand gripping each knee, and stared at the door, as if Johnny would come in, laughing, wondering why they were being so morose when the show was about to start. When the door stayed closed, he turned back to Robert, "What happened?"

"The show."

"Fuck the show. My friend is dead. I want to know what happened," his face twisted.

Robert unburdened himself from being custodian of the only full version of the events of the last twenty-five hours.

Telling it didn't lift the stone, but he got a deep breath down to his stomach without it having to claw past in several shuddering pushes.

"No-one else knows," he finished looking down at his hands.

"Come with me."

At the side of the bar, Tank whispered something to Bluey, who nodded and disappeared, while Tank made his way to the stage. The lights flickered and then, in the spotlight stood Tank, demure in his belted dressing gown, his headband a ribbon of colour above his unmade eyes. His bare lips shushed into the microphone.

"There won't be a show tonight." He took a deep breath. "We have news. Heartbreaking news." He looked around the room. "Another one of us, otherwise happy, full of love and life, has nonetheless managed to unexpectedly and inexplicably kill themselves." He blinked, bit his lip then continued, "The lights went out here on earth, for our dear friend Johnny Saunders."

As the shocked whispers fell away, "All of us who knew him will miss his beauty, his charm, his generosity, his wit, his kindness, his earnest sense of fair play, not that life was all that fair to him on occasion, but he managed in the face of everything that came along, good and bad, to maintain a sense of humour and of hope. Except, it seems, till now. To all of you who never had the chance to meet him, you have missed one of life's gifts." He bowed his head, "That was hard." Then looking up again, "Remember ladies, don't believe everything you see in the papers or on TV. If you hear anything, you'll find us, me and Bluey," he nodded towards the bar and Blue raised his arm, "here or the Story Bridge back bar."

Tank squeezed his nose, and then raised his hand. The speakers behind him sputtered, then the muted sounds of ABBA. *Thank You for the Music* floated and fell over the crowd soft and gentle like mist. Tanks voice overrode the last few bars, "To Johnny Saunders. Thank you for the music my friend. May your star shine brightly forever."

The silence swirled around them, the stage-light went out, and the pub lights came on. "I'll see you all next week."

In Tank's dressing room, a bottle of champagne and four glasses waited between the makeup and the wig. Blue stood next to them. He held Robert's shoulder and rubbed it softly.

When Tank came in after Robert, Blue wrapped him in his arms and held him. Then brushed the tears from Tank's cheek with the back of his fingers.

The bottle released its cork with a soft fwerp. Four glasses were poured. Bluey handed one each to Robert and Tank. The three of them stood facing the unclaimed glass, watching the strings of bubbles floating upwards. They raised theirs, "To Johnny."

Robert wrinkled his nose to scratch the fizz and the moist residue of unspent tears, "I wasn't sure you were the same Bluey, until Tank said that at the end."

"Surprised you remember."

"I don't think I'll ever forget anything about last night."

"I work here Fridays," Blue explained, "when Tank does. That way neither of us is out alone late. And every little bit helps too, jobs aren't easy to find for us."

"So you live in Kangaroo Point?" Robert said. "Is that how you know Johnny?"

"Met him in Sydney. He and Tank did some shows together."

"He never said." Robert imagined Johnny, sequined and stunning. He ran his fingers over the sharp edges of the watch in his pocket, "When you said *another* one of us has managed to mysteriously kill themselves, what did you mean?"

Tank looked at him with you're kidding lifting the corner of his lip.

"I only recently knew I was gay." Robert shrugged. "Maybe, I always sort of knew."

"But you aren't out, and you don't know the rules," said Blue. Then turning to Tank, "Give him a break love."

Tank's chest deflated, "There's this epidemic. Gay people jumping off bridges and cliffs. Not just Queensland. But the reporting, it sounds like they can't bear to be alive they're such a disappointment to themselves."

"Not just that," Blue said. "Not just the haters. We think there's something more organised, something deliberate."

"We talked about that, remember?" said Tank.

"We've been warning people when we can," Blue said. "But you don't hear about this, bashing and aggro, because if you report it, you'll be reporting it to the same people who did it, or at least condone it."

"The police," Tank clarified. "It's one of the reasons we volunteered at CAMP. Johnny and me. They're working on a safety campaign and being more visible."

"Johnny mentioned it."

Tank nodded, "You warned us to keep a low profile. But I'm not the shrinking violet type," Tank's hand came up to his neck and touched the vee. "Anyway, that strategy wasn't exactly successful."

"Meaning?" said Robert.

"Keeping a low profile was supposed to lead to some sort of public acceptance," Blue scoffed. "But it's getting worse if you ask me."

"But places like this—"

"Are tolerated at a price," said Blue. "What do you think those wankers at the Story Bridge Hotel were hanging around for?"

"You pay them, Tank told me."

"It's the same all over Queensland. More obvious here in The Valley. I mean, have you walked through here at night?" Blue's arm swept towards an imaginary street.

Robert shook his head.

"The main drag is lined with massage parlours, and what do you think happens in them?"

"Not massage," Tank quipped.

"Prostitutes?"

"And the gambling, casinos, drugs. All as legal as us!" Tank's proclamation was a combination of triumph and disgust.

"Everyone pays?"

Tank and Blue nodded.

"So Andrews and Nichols, who do they work for?" wonder and revulsion competed on Robert's face.

"They're the police, Lovey."

"I know. I know, Sorry. I meant who in the police? How far up does it go? Is everyone involved?"

"It's gotta be someone high up," said Blue. "They're too arrogant and cocky."

"Yeah. Brazen. And they're literally getting away with murder. But to answer your question," Tank shrugged, "Blue hands over the cash and smiles, like they're doing him a favour."

"But," said Robert, "why would they be in the park, attacking someone? What's that got to do with whatever protection money they're taking."

Bluey and Tank tilted their heads.

"Of course," said Robert. "Because they can."

"More than that," Blue agreed. "Our best guess, is that it's some kind of side thing, a hustle that probably doesn't go into the main coffers. And also, they have to get their own to do something wrong—"

"So then they have no way out without incriminating themselves. A kind of blackmail," Tank finished. "And who doesn't love a spot of poofter bashing?"

"Has this happened to you? To anyone you know?"

"Nah. But it's why we don't tend to go anywhere alone at night," said Blue.

"Were they there last night? Nichols and Andrews?"

Blue nodded, "Muscle too. They came back shortly before you arrived, but only Nichols and Andrews. I gave them their money, and they had some business or other with Pete. God only knows what. That's why I put you in the office. Then I gave them drinks while Pete got you a cab. I thought they'd roughed you up. I didn't want them to see you."

"You thought I'd been attacked in the park?"

Blue nodded.

"I'm not clear on all of it, but I know this much," Robert frowned, "a uniform, Muscle, Nichols and likely Andrews were all there last night. And all four of them were beating someone up, right where Johnny was supposed to be waiting for me."

"And then, no Johnny," Blue finished.

"He didn't jump," Robert was adamant.

"You don't have to convince me, Lovey," Tank said. "But if they've shut the book on it, and they are the ones who investigate it, then—"

"Then we need someone to investigate them," Blue said, "without them knowing."

"Exactly," said Robert. "Which is another reason I'm even here when I should be— I knew you'd be here tonight. Tank, remember Johnny said he was going to talk to Simon Draper. I know they've talked about a few things. Not the details. But I don't want those bastards getting away with what they did to Johnny. Do you think he'd help?"

CHAPTER 26

"You went to the pub," Lauren fumed. "What's gotten into you lately?"

Robert tried to look contrite, but confusion, guilt and urgency were competing with it, "Sorry. I know it looks... honestly, I don't know how it looks, but it wasn't for fun." *How could it be for fun? Why would I do that? What's in your head? Fuck.* "I have to make some calls. Sorry."

"The kids are all asleep, now. I thought... forget it. It's OK."

After leaving a message with Simon's answering service and wondering if he'd call back, he called Harry.

"Did you want Duncan?" Harry sounded tired.

"No. No. Sorry to bug you, but have you talked to Marnie or Jack about the coroner's report, arrangements or…"

"Not yet."

"It's just, I went to tell some of Johnny's friends what happened and this niggle about how fast it all was— We all agreed. There's no way this was given serious attention. I mean honestly, from the time Johnny's body was found till the 6 o'clock news?"

"You're right," said Harry. "It's probably not documented formally yet. But they couldn't release the information unless it was definitely going to be the official version."

"There's more. There's been a spate of gay suicides. Johnny's friends, others too, have their doubts, but the families, they're in shock. They're dealing with grief and shame and massive guilt. You don't get over this. And no-one wants to prolong the horror, but people don't even know they can question it. I doubt Marnie or Jack do."

"And besides the emotional toll, there's the financial fallout too. No life insurance, funeral costs, homes, loans," said Harry. "I don't mean to sound mercenary, but yes, navigating this while you're…"

"Harry, I know I could look this up, you know corporate and financial's my niche, but off the top of your head, can anyone ask for an inquest or only the family. Could I do it? As Johnny's lawyer? Because *if* he jumped, it's ninety k's an hour meets concrete wall. Did they just vaguely mention his injuries were consistent with that? And what does that even mean? Spelled out. Sorry…"

Harry was silent, then sniffed, "There should've been one anyway." After a pause, "Family can make a formal request. The coroner could dismiss it. It would go to Appeal if the family want to pursue it. I'll call them in the morning."

"We're at Marnie's, with the kids. She's staying with Jack. The lights are still on."

He stood next to the phone, wondering whether Harry would call Marnie and Jack tonight. Could it wait? Could he? Murder wouldn't make it feel any better, would it? It might stop everyone blaming themselves. That's something.

Lauren was watching TV.

"Sorry," he said, "I haven't got Jack's number. I'll walk over. There's something I need to talk to them about."

"Stop apologizing. It's cringy."

He winced, "I'll fill you in when I know more."

'It's not your fault.'

What?

He glanced back at Lauren, to ask what she meant but she was watching the screen. Did he just imagine it? It didn't sound like her voice. It sounded like Johnny's. He frowned.

*

Robert pounded on the door. When Marnie apologized, explaining the doorbell was outside the gate, he smiled sadly, "You had other things on your mind, it's kind-of why I'm here."

In Jack's study a teapot sat on a tray next to a bottle of red, "Help yourself."

"I've been thinking," Robert started, stopped, and started again. "After I saw Harry, I went to see some of Johnny's friends. Tell them." He blinked and took a long swallow of the red. "I don't know how to say this, I'm trying to spare your feel—"

"Spit it out," Jack interrupted. "We've taken a battering today. Another hit isn't going to knock us out."

"They, we, no-one I've spoken to believes Johnny killed himself. I don't."

He explained yes, Johnny had been worried and upset, but he'd moved on. He was active in gay rights and that he and Harry hadn't only made up, but that Harry had made up a new, hugely generous will, and that Harry was going to call, if he hadn't already, and tell them. "Everyone thinks it's ludicrous. Johnny told me that you'd taught him about silver linings, Jack. That there was always something to be grateful for. He didn't do it. I'm convinced." He watched as Jack's face softened. "Have you seen the coroner's report?"

"No," said Jack. "Probably sometime Monday. It has to be typed up. Did he really say that?"

"Yes. He was happy. He wasn't depressed. Not by a long shot. Did they tell you anything?"

"They said that everything was consistent with what they expected to find under the circumstances."

"And, that's the point. Under what circumstances? They don't know. They're assuming. Based on the inverted commas, known facts. The ones they have on file because of the arrest. Did they even ask you what his state of mind was?" He hardly paused. "Harry said an inquest should be standard. He can't figure out why it's not happening. That we already have the coroner's findings. Or he can. If you see what I mean."

"Why would they do that?" Jack sounded surprised. "They're the police for God's sake."

Robert froze, realizing that the average Queenslander over forty years of age had been brainwashed by Joh Bjelke-Petersen's rhetoric and propaganda about upholding law and order. He'd have to choose his words carefully.

"I know," he said. "But when I was waiting for you and Marnie, I overheard the two duty officers. One of them was saying an inquest wasn't just procedure, it was an obligation. Their duty. That facts have to be established. According to the other one? If it looks vaguely like a duck, then it's a duck. Even if it doesn't quack like one. Even if it's got fur instead of feathers. So it would be a waste of time."

"But what about the arrangements. The funeral?"

"They'd be delayed," Robert conceded.

Marnie's face was a kaleidoscope of blank, angry, confused, distraught, "Are you saying that something might have happened to him? That whatever you thought you saw—"

"Yes," Robert's eyes brimmed with apology as he cut her off. "It could have been an accident. Unintentional. Or it could've been," he had to stop. "Murder. And I for one think it should be looked into. If someone did something, I don't want them to get away with it."

Marnie and Jack exchanged glances, "I don't know about you Dad, but I have doubts. Yes, Johnny *had* been worried," she faded into her own thoughts for a moment. "And he *never* stewed. *And,* they didn't ask us if we knew what his state of mind was. They'd have to, wouldn't they?"

Jack nodded.

Marnie looked into the past, "And if he hadn't been OK, *I'd* know. He always told me stuff." This looking at Robert who held her gaze. "Even when we were little, and Mum… He thought he'd made her angry and that's why she didn't come home. Poor little boy." She pinched the top of her nose. "And when he first came out and didn't know how to talk to you. We never had any secrets."

Jack rubbed his fingers against his forehead, pressing all this into shape inside his skull, "What do we need to do?"

"You have to make a formal request." Robert watched as the pain Jack said wouldn't knock him down, did. "Harry said he'd help."

Jack's inhale didn't quite reinflate him, "I'll call him in the morning. I should've called him anyway. He should have been here with us." He looked from Marnie to Robert, "I'm not used to all this, you know."

"Call him now," said Robert. "He'll be relieved."

CHAPTER 27

Lauren called down from the upstairs railing when the mower choked off. She was wearing her it's-serious face, "You can't hide outside all day Robert. We need to talk."

They'd been home for a few hours and between interludes of playing with Emma and Thomas he'd been trimming, sweeping, weeding, mowing and ruminating. "Won't be long," he called up to her. "The kids are still—"

"No," her arms folded. "Now. Lunch is ready, then nap-time, and I want to know what's going on."

The hedge trimmer joined the cuttings in the wheelbarrow, "Come on kiddoes. You two hungry?"

Her voice, indifferently curious dropped onto him as he lifted the kids off the trampoline, "Who's Simon? There was—"

"What?" He plonked Emma next to Thomas. "Why didn't you tell me? When? Jeez. Can't you—" the skin was white and tight across his clenched jaw, the rest of his face flushed.

Lauren's face palled, "There was a message. OK? I checked the answering machine when we came home. He said he'd call back."

He nudged the children to the stairs, "Sorry."

"You should be. That was uncalled for. We've all lost a friend. Not just you."

*

He sidestepped questions by placing his thoughts, concerns and observations into other people's mouths, explaining the consensus was, that something had happened to Johnny that was at worst being covered up, or at least being ignored or overlooked.

"But you were out together. How did he seem to you?"

"He," Robert took a thought gathering breath, "he *said* he'd stopped worrying about the case, and was happy. I don't suppose it matters if I say anything now." He told her about Harry's health and his will. "So no money problems, now, or in the future," and finished with Tank and Johnny volunteering, and about helping Simon, "Whose story caused the problem in the first place."

"Yes," she smiled, "I can see why Tank. But why's Simon calling you?"

"At this point I don't know," Robert lied.

"I know you think you need to do something. Johnny was your friend, and your client, but hear me on this Robert, his family are in charge now. You have to let it go."

"Marnie's in no state and Jack—"

"Are his family."

"It's— I feel responsible. I was," Robert looked at her face, soft with love and understanding, and all he could feel was self-loathing. "I didn't— I couldn't see…"

"It's OK," she cradled him from behind where he was sitting hunched at the kitchen island. "None of us could."

"No," he protested from inside the cocoon of her arms, wishing he could hibernate there, till he could come out to a different world, or a different Robert. "No. I meant… doesn't matter. Thanks."

She leaned forward and kissed the back of his head.

The phone ringing interrupted them.

CHAPTER 28

While Simon and Robert waited for Anna to return with tea, Robert cleared a no spill zone and wondered if asking an investigative journalist to meet with you, when you had something you didn't want investigated, was akin to shooting yourself in the foot before a marathon.

As the door closed behind her, Simon leaned back, "So, why am I here?"

Robert stalled, bringing the cup to his lips, and absently swallowing, scalding his tongue and the inside of his mouth. "Shit," he said after letting the hot liquid dribble from his open mouth back into the cup.

"You OK?"

"If I can live down the embarrassment," Robert pushed his cup out of reach, in case any unconscious need to put something in his mouth instead of words arose. "You know, knew, Johnny Saunders?"

Simon nodded.

"You know what happened?"

"I heard."

"He said he'd asked you to come to the hearing, way back. And he mentioned you a few times since, so I knew you'd spoken. Not all the detail, but I knew he was seeing you because you don't make it easy for people who think they're above the law."

Simon's head tilted.

"So as a source I'd be anonymous wouldn't I? You can protect my identity, can't you?"

Simon's cheeks puckered, "Yes and no."

"But I thought…"

140

"Yeah. Everyone does. Don't get me wrong. If you don't want to be a named source and there's a good reason, we can. We do. But fair warning, I can be compelled, under a court's direction. It doesn't happen very often. But if it's a confession you have in mind, you'd be better going to a priest."

Robert rubbed his hands over his knees, clasped them, then noticing, brought them back to the table.

"You're uncomfortable. I can see, but I thought you'd have known."

"I did. I do. I was hoping it was more like us. Client confidentiality."

"There'd be leeway, something like, other sources confirm." Simon sat forward, "I don't want to force the issue, but you called me. I'm assuming you have something similar to Johnny? Extortion, false statements, lost evidence, bribes, drugs."

"Murder."

"Whoa. Whose murder?"

Robert pressed his fingertips to his lips.

Unexpressed, all this could remain a distressing and threatening maybe, instead of an unavoidable and highly likely real. *And he'll know. About me.* There was a thudding, blocking the sound of his thoughts and something was pushing at the back of his throat trying to choke him. He had to get it out, "Johnny."

His fingers were vicelike on his knees and he stared at them unseeing, completely ignorant his eyes were even leaking, until he felt a cold dribble at the edge of his nostril. He sniffed and an automated hand moved to stifle the drip. "I— It wasn't suicide. I saw them. Four of them."

Robert told the story, leaving out the intimate interlude, hoping Simon would observe the invisible boundary.

He didn't.

"I'm going to ask you up front mate. Context and all that."

Robert nodded.

"Were you and Johnny in a relationship?"

Robert nodded again.

"I feel for you. Tough hey? But I'm thinking this isn't merely a case of I don't want to be outed."

"I'm married, Lauren, two kids and my job, you know…" he paused, "and Harry, Judge Matthews. He and Johnny got back together a while ago," his face slumped. "It would be an epically pointless train-wreck. Hurt too many people and for what? It can't bring him back."

"I get it."

The silence was short.

"The other thing I have to ask," said Simon, "is, are you sure?"

It was expected. When Marnie had asked the same question, he'd doubted himself. But then he'd been desperate, clinging to the hope she was somehow right, and that Johnny was alive. Robert pressed his lips together nodding grimly, "I'd stake my life on it."

Simon jotted a note.

"Did Johnny mention Tank or Blue?" Robert asked when Simon's pen rested.

"I know Tank. Is this related?"

"Sort of. It's not only Johnny. There are others."

"What? Killed? Or just beaten?" Simon snorted, "Just..."

"Both, I'd say. Blue and Tank said there's been an awful lot of suicides. They called it an epidemic," said Robert.

"It's all slightly more than I'd thought. When Johnny first came to see me, it was blackmail and a judge."

"I understand if you can't take it any further," Robert's sigh was ambiguously relief and disappointment.

"No. No, I don't mean that."

"So, you can help?"

"Obviously the police won't be investigating anything."

Robert's jaw softened, "Thank you."

"I don't have a lot of time though." Simon reflected. "I've been working with someone, a colleague, a mate... does TV. Can't say exactly, but let's call it racketeering. We're trying to get to the bottom of it... the top really." He paused. "Apart from the odd story to stir things up, yeah, including," he let it fade, "my role's mostly background, whatever I can manage in my own time. I'll get to publish one day. I hope. But for now, my paper and just about everyone else is quite happy to let sleeping dogs lie. And of course, there's the money aspect."

"Always is."

"Well then, first things. We need to find that guy in the back seat. The one you saw."

"I've been thinking about that. Johnny volunteered at a homeless place in Fortitude Valley. They might know something," said Robert.

"And we need all the reports and the officer's statements. That will give us some names. Do you think your policeman might be on our side?"

"Honestly? He came across like he was by the book. I don't know."

"Worth a try." Simon peered at nothing. "Do you think they may have known who Johnny was? From before."

"Deliberately targeting him?" Robert shrugged. "Maybe. I wouldn't put it past them."

They both contemplated this.

"Do you think it would be worth you talking to anyone in politics?" said Robert.

"You joking?" Simon scoffed. "Of course I do. Doubt any of them would talk to me."

Robert explained about his recent henhouse chat, and how his dad had been revisiting the idea of going Independent at the next election. "You'd be getting information from the outer edges, not the inner circle."

"Beggars can't be choosers. But if your dad's willing to spill his guts and get off the Joh Bjelke-Petersen bandwagon, I could probably run some human interest stories to help him climb down, so to speak. See if he's interested. And on that note," Simon extended his hand. "Here's to nailing those bastards."

Robert eased himself back into his chair, searching for a sense of comfort. Simon obviously knew how to keep secrets, and that secrecy was important, but he was on a mission.

Robert looked out of his window. The sunlight was muted. He swallowed a mouthful of cold tea and shivered.

CHAPTER 29

"It's from Judge Matthews," Anna handed him the fax.

"About bloody time."

Anna loitered, "I know about Johnny."

Robert's eyes switched from preoccupied to panicked and the spot midway between his throat and heart spasmed. *Calm the fuck down. She knows he died. That's all.*

"It was on the news." She frowned. "I didn't want to say anything. But on Friday, you said he'd been hurt, and you didn't know where he was."

"The police say it's suicide. But I know it isn't. I'm trying to figure out what happened."

"If you need someone to bounce things off, I'm here."

"Thanks Anna, but didn't you get promoted?"

She didn't smile, "I think I'm more use here at the moment."

"Appreciated but not the point. You're supposed to be doing less, not more."

"All in good time, Mr Carson, and I mean it. You can trust me."

He nodded looking blankly at the document while she closed the door behind her.

There were only two police names on the report. Neither was Nichols or Andrews. He read:

> *Prelim: Officers came in late for shift change. Reported a suspected suicide. Couldn't stop. Had a drunk and disorderly on board. Processed offender. New shift already on a call out, so returned to location of sighting where they found jacket and wallet*

*of John Saunders. Returned to station and logged items.
11.30pm.*

*Body found in mangroves between Kangaroo Point Ferry Shelter
and Jazz Club at low tide around 3pm.*

*Findings: Broken bones consistent with a fall from height. Broken
jaw and laceration to the upper left eye and brow. Possible cause:
debris on entry to the water.*

*Further Notes: Lungs and stomach, minimal ingestion of water.
Possibility that death occurred from injuries sustained from the
fall rather than drowning.*

Estimated time of death: 11pm.

And the coroner's thoughts about depression over the possible outcome
of his pending court appearance.

All nice and neat.

He reached for the phone to call Harry and stopped. He wondered if he
should call Marnie and heard Lauren in his head saying, they're his family
Robert. *You've planted a seed.*

Simon's throwaway, it's worth a try, prodded him and he searched his
wallet for Kowalski's number. He was mentally preparing to leave a
message, when it answered.

"Did you mean it when you said if there's ever something you can do?"
Robert asked.

There was silence and Robert held his curse in check.

"Sorry, I forgot you couldn't see me," said Kowalski. "I was nodding.
But there are conditions."

Robert forced a smile to camouflage the sarcasm, "What kind of
conditions?"

"It can't be illegal."

Of course. "I'd like a copy of the incident report. And if there's a QP9 for
the drunk and disorderly, that too. Anything relating to him and to Mr
Saunders."

Robert interpreted Kowalski's silence as baulking.

"I'm his legal representative. I'm entitled to a copy. Look it up. I'll wait."

There was the hint of hesitation which Robert covered with, "I'll give you a copy of the engagement letter, and if you give me his name, I'll do one for the drunk and disorderly's pro-bono work. I'll bring them in personally."

"His name's Alan John Peters, no fixed address. I don't think there's a court briefing. They arrested him, but they let him go."

"Why doesn't that surprise me."

***

Robert got through most of his clients' requirements with calls instead of rescheduling the cancelled meetings. He was feeling more like Robert the lawyer and less like Robert the liar. Buoyed up, he ignored Lauren, and called Harry and then Marnie and told them emphatically, that the coroner's report was full of vagueness and assumptions and given the time frame, hadn't been done properly, or, it had been deliberately shortened to make the superficial observations match up like facts when they weren't. And there was a big fat why, begging to be answered in either case.

When they agreed he was lifted momentarily, surfing a wave of relief.

By the time Harry called back towards the end of the day to say he'd been able to commission an independent autopsy, and his string-pulling had paid off, the approval for the inquest was being rubber stamped, Robert's euphoria was disappearing.

Determinedly, he reached for a file and started reading. At the end of the page, when nothing had registered, he closed his eyes and was immediately floating in an exhausted half dream. The waves he'd been surfing earlier were definitely no longer curling and friendly. They'd dragged him out and he was struggling in the deep, as the swell of grief and despair rolled over him relentlessly. Floundering and frightened, he looked back towards the land. It seemed to be getting further away. He turned to the horizon, praying for a ship to come and rescue him, and then praying it wouldn't. If it came too close, its wake would knock him off the edge of the flat dismal world. He forced his eyes open.

"Anna, I need a copy of Johnny Saunders' engagement letter, and can you do one for Alan John Peters. And," he glanced at his diary, sitting patiently next to her phone, "see what you can do," he handed her the list he'd been ticking. "It's... I'm feeling sick."

Her eyes clouded.

"I'll be OK tomorrow."

***

An angry horn blast startled him. He yanked himself out of the traffic and the haze he shouldn't be driving in. and into a loading zone to think. The priority was find Alan John Peters. He took the Refidex from the glove-box and opened it at the city maps, searching near Fortitude Valley for the 139 Club. Someone might know something. Someone had to know something.

He looked up at the number, one-three-nine, above the open door and hesitated. Despite its worn but clean appearance, there was something about the place which made his already queasy stomach clench. It was, he realised, the idea of finding himself here as a client because the final threads of frayed dignity had come loose. He thought about Johnny coming here, making friends, joking, laughing, and the guilt-ridden sadness he'd been trying to keep down, rose up.

"You OK? Can I help?"

"I... maybe," Robert looked into pale blue eyes, the wrinkles at the sides, already deep, amplified by thick lenses set in a black plastic frame. Above them a wide expanse of bare forehead and beneath them, a genuine smile.

"My friend volunteered here. He won't be able to come in anymore. I..."

"Thanks for letting us know. People move on. Shame. Anyhoo, life goes on."

He didn't ask what happened or why.

"It's not that," said Robert. "He didn't— he's not coming because he died."

"Your friend? Not young Johnny?"

Robert pressed his lips together.

"Come through. Got something to show you. Fancy a cuppa?"

Behind the apparent choice was a sense of something compelling.

Robert followed him.

Mugs in hand they came to a large airy space. To one side, a dresser, looking regally out of place amongst the plain laminate tabletops and hard plastic chairs. A long cork noticeboard adorned the opposite wall and pinned at the end with brass tacks, was a white poster with a newspaper cutting pasted in the centre, next to a photo. It was surrounded by the names of all Johnny's friends at the Club.

The picture of Johnny and Fuzz was blurry.

Mr Blue-eyes pressed a tissue into Robert's hand.

When he could see again, Robert read:

Nowhere to Go. No Way To Go.

A young man has ended his troubles with the finality of suicide.

A police spokesperson confirmed the body of John Saunders had been found in the Brisbane River. He had been reported missing by his family. The spokesperson commented that this type of copycat suicide was becoming the preferred method for members of the homosexual community to deal with their problems.

Mr Saunders had recently been arrested and was due to face court on criminal charges. The coroner's findings were that Mr Saunders died from injuries sustained after jumping from the Story Bridge. He has, according to the prosecutor, cheated justice by taking his own life.

The civil rights group CAMP (Campaign Against Moral Persecution), are calling for an inquiry into the high number of cases of suicide and self-harm. They claim that the current legislation is discriminatory and leaves them excluded from services, assistance and freedoms that are available to the wider community.

When approached for comment, the Health and Community Services Minister's office issued a statement saying there are available resources in the community for mental health, and that these people have to learn to deal with life's challenges like the rest of us. There are no plans for any inquiry.

Mr Saunders' family declined to comment.

"I hadn't seen that." Robert turned, extending his hand, "Thanks. Robert Car—"

"Ernie," said Ernie. "We don't usually do last names here."

"It wasn't suicide," the words came racing out of Robert to get to Ernie as quickly as they could, in case he tried to stop them. "It might be wishful thinking," he finished, "but I was hoping someone here might know this, Alan. Or where he is."

"Thanks. For telling me. I'll ask around. Usually, I'd say I don't like your chances. But, there was something about your friend." He looked towards Johnny's tribute, "And it wasn't only because they respected him, it was more that he respected them. People can feel that."

Robert tapped his finger against his lips to tamp the looming tears, "I appreciate it. Really. Anything you can do. Would it help to offer some kind of reward?"

Ernie's lips formed a disapproving pout, "There's a kind of code."

Robert nodded.

"Y'know," Ernie mused, "if the police picked him up, it'll probably mean he's had to move on. But, it doesn't mean he did. Have you been back? Checked again?"

Robert looked at him, dismayed.

"Don't beat yourself up."

Robert stood up, "What if his things are still there?"

"I've got a storage area for safekeeping. And I'll put up a notice here. But your Alan, he's more likely to frequent services around The Gabba. Reckon catching ferries over to here might be a bit outside his budget."

Robert missed the cue to smile.

"Anyhoo," Ernie got a notebook and tore off a sheet. He wrote, 'Belongings Are Safe - 139 Club', and put it into a plastic bag with some drawing pins.

Robert frowned.

"Use your shoe." A single soft chuckle from Ernie, "Oh deary me, your face, ahhh, no offence. I take a laugh whenever I get the chance now. I meant like a hammer. Your shoe. Y'know? Put up the sign."

At first the best Robert could do was a halting smile. It surprised him when a huffy laugh spluttered out in three breathy bursts.

"You ever been to a place like this before?"

"No. I feel a bit bad actually. I never even contemplated helping or—"

"Don't," said Ernie. "I mean don't feel bad, not don't come. It's not for everyone. But your Johnny, he was OK. Saw the person not the circumstances. Not everyone does. We'll miss him."

Ernie's head was slowly bobbing yes as they walked towards the door, "That we will," he said. He put his hand on Robert's shoulder, "Normally I'd say check a few other places, but I'll make some calls. Might be easier on you."

CHAPTER 30

Robert headed straight to Kangaroo Point after leaving Ernie at the 139 Club, walking in the shadows of the trees which were well into their afternoon stretch and were busy sucking the hot breath off the city, from across the river.

The ordinariness was out of place.

At the park, he stared at the blank spot where he'd seen the attack. Then faced the swings, empty and motionless. The cars, a muted drumming from the bridge. The cicadas, a chirruping buzz. They became part of the silence. He looked over at the shelter where they would have waited together for the ferry. Waiting to go back to their other lives.

He went and sat, imagining he and Johnny sitting side by side in the shelter. He closed his eyes and it became the Schonell Theatre stage. Another ending. Different.

He'd loved that feeling. The exquisite stillness of the theatre contrasting with the aliveness in him. But it was spoiled. He was so angry. Johnny's big declaration. Completely stuffing up their friendship.

He heard something and peered into the dark crevices of the crimson curtains. Johnny emerged and sat next to him.

He could still feel the tension in his thigh, and how he softened it, so it grazed Johnny's.

"I was waiting for you," Johnny said.

"I was winding down, enjoying the feel of the place. It's like, I don't know. No. I do. It's like here you can play out a different story, anything can happen, and you can be anything."

Neither of them spoke.

"Anyway, it's only been ten minutes."

"Not what I meant," Johnny ran his hand through his hair. "Can I tell you something?"

"If you want."

"I was eleven," Johnny said, "when I came out. Marnie and I, we went together and told Dad. He kind of guessed. Said it wouldn't be easy, and something vague about being true to yourself."

He'd squeezed his eyes closed to shut out the memory of himself at eleven.

He did it now.

And then the past insisted. *Look at this. Don't shut it off.*

He was back there, and Johnny was telling him, "I almost had a cat then too. A stray. It was scrawny, sick. I gave it some milk, and it purred. The next day, I put more milk out and waited, and waited. Dad said to leave it. It might be frightened. So I waited inside, all day, watching until the milk curdled and separated."

Something lapped the edges of Johnny's eyes.

He'd looked away and then the back of Johnny's fingers brushed along his arm.

He didn't move. There was a buzzing inside his inner ear as if he'd just finished a long run. He felt hot, but a shiver starting from the site of Johnny's touch, raced up the back of his neck. It spread across his shoulders tingling behind each ear, and the breath he'd been holding rushed out in an almost silent, "Oh."

The fingers trailed downwards to his hand, and then Johnny's hand closed over it.

They'd sat, silently side by side. Johnny lifted the hand and placed it on his thigh holding it there.

His insides tightened and he listened to Johnny breathing till he couldn't hear it above the blood rushing to his face and between his legs.

"Robert," it was a breathy whisper, "look at me."

He opened his eyes. He hadn't noticed he'd closed them, but stayed looking down.

"Look at me." Johnny said.

Slowly he turned his head and lifted his face.

"I'm going to kiss you." Johnny leaned forward. Their eyes locked and started to close.

At the last moment he'd jerked his head away.

Sensing it, Johnny opened his eyes.

He'd kept his face averted. Then suddenly aware of his hand still on Johnny's leg, he snatched it away.

Johnny lifted himself off the stage and faced him, "You can't be serious."

"Don't."

"Don't what? Why shouldn't I be upset."

"Look, you're my best friend. I love you. OK? But I'm not gay."

Hmmph. There it was. Again.
Keep watching.

"I'm not gay. I don't know how you got that idea. I'm not anti or anything. It's—"

"Marnie said you'd say that."

"What's it got to do with her?" He could taste the spite and paused, softening the next words. "I don't see her like that, in that way. We've been friends since—"

"I know. She told me. You kissed her what, two, three times? Not even a hint of teenage lust. Fuck, Robert. In case nothing else came up and bit you on the arse, didn't that ever make you wonder?"

"What? You discuss the ins and outs of your romantic interests with your sister? Who does that?"

"Don't try and make this about me," Johnny countered. "And that's not what I said."

He clamped his mouth shut and counted in time with his heartbeat. At fifteen he started again.

Johnny held his ground and his silence.

How Johnny? How did you maintain that presence. That dignity? What the hell did you see in me?

On either side of the rows of blank-faced chairs, bands of light from the stair risers waterfalled in a gentle cascade towards them. The Schonell's feature ceiling lights, dimmed now, looked like a night sky twinkling overhead.

He'd looked into it, searching for answers, and fell into the past, into the ceiling mould spore stars in his bedroom. He'd wiped them out of his mind, struggling with a ladder and a bucket, and the bathroom cleaning brush. Bleach running down his arms, and tears running down his face. Scrubbing away the memories that swirled into his mind whenever he forgot not to look. Terry, and the lollies. His birthday treat. Those boys.

He looked down and Johnny's face floated back into view.

"I'm trying to help. You know?"

"Well, thanks all the same," he cringed at his mother's arrogance coming from his mouth. "But you've got it wrong. Or maybe I sent the wrong signals."

"Look," Johnny's hand rested on Robert's shoulder.

Concentrating on its weight and warmth, so different to Lauren's, he thought about how light and normal hers was. It was how his life would be. How he would be. Her face formed in his mind and a raised eyebrow under the silvery-blond fringe questioned him, *What's all this about Robert?* And before he could answer, her face turned into his mother's and the slow creep of self-loathing began its move. He held the shudder in.

"Look," Johnny said again, "I know you're uncomfortable with the idea, but it gets easier."

The hand lifted from his shoulder. He wanted it back. Unanchored, he floundered, "I thought we were friends. Can't you just be my friend?"

Johnny put both hands on the stage and hoisted himself up again.

Their thighs touched again.

He'd felt a wave of anticipation starting with the skin against the floorboards.

154

He felt it now. He clenched and followed the surge of anticipation moving towards his ribcage, as it rippled out across his chest and up the back of his neck. He wallowed in it. Again.

But then Johnny had moved. It was only a hand-width. It felt like more.

Already seesawing, his attention sought the pressing indentation of Johnny's hand gripping the right-angle of the stage floor.

He sucked in a breath. The imprint was still so strong. He could feel it now.

Keep watching.

Thought of anything except feeling its heel wedged into the side of his hip no longer existed. He wondered if Johnny would try to kiss him again and imagined leaning in this time. What would it feel like? His face was getting warm, and his breath was shallowing.

He stared ahead, knowing the truth, but not giving it a voice.

I knew. I knew.

"I can't spend my life waiting for you to be more than my friend Robert. I'm not going to stick around and watch you get married and pretend I'm OK with it. I can't. I just can't."

Silence.

Johnny lifted his chin and staring out over the unresponsive auditorium, "You're going to have to come out one day. Your whole life can't be an act."

He was stone and then the words tumbled, "It's not an act. I'm not gay. I can't be."

Something crept across Johnny's eyes blocking out the light.

"I've been seeing Lauren."

"I know," Johnny's hand raked his hair back behind his ear.

"Anyway, even if I were, it's not just about me. What do you think would happen to my dad? Joh Bjelke-Petersen would bury him. I can see the headlines. There won't be any of Joh's jovial 'never mind, don't you worry about that'. He'd lose his seat. And Mum? It's not that easy."

"I didn't say it was. But it's not that hard either. People deal with it."

"Don't be so naïve Johnny. They don't 'deal with it'. It breaks them. In case you've forgotten, last year. Hah. First ever gay mardi-gras. What a joke. Arrests. Beatings. Even afterwards, in so-called *protective* custody. And that was in Sydney for God's sake, where gay's OK," he scoffed again. "And after? You're a criminal. Forever. Do you get that? It never goes away. How the fuck can I be a lawyer if I'm a criminal, illegal? Huh? Tell me." He'd waited. "See? You can't."

Fear and disappointment, jostled with regret and anger and shame creating a storm in his eyes. "How are you supposed to live, like, a normal life, and be gay?"

Johnny lifted one shoulder, "How are you supposed to live and not be who you are?"

"You still don't get it," the words sharp and jagged, lightning-like.

"I do get it," Johnny's voice was flat in comparison, "*you* don't."

"What? What do you want me to do? Five years. Five years I've spent here, working my arse off to be a lawyer."

"There are other things you can do. We could move interstate. Overseas. You don't have to be a lawyer."

"Are you joking? Honestly?" he snorted. "Sorry Mum, sorry Dad. Changed my mind. I'm going to be a queer instead of a lawyer. You don't mind, do you? The wasted money, the wasted time. I'm moving too. 'Bye."

"But it's all right if you waste your life," Johnny's calm slapped him. "And what about my life? Do you get to waste mine too?"

He was stone again.

Johnny pushed himself off the stage and started walking away.

"I can't."

The anguish twisting his insides was still as raw. Back then, it had transported in his voice. Johnny had heard it. Felt it. It had pummeled his departing back, and the something close to breaking that Johnny had been holding together, fell apart.

Johnny's legs stopped moving. He drew in a long sedate breath and slowly his bunched fists unfurled. It seemed as if their opening held some promise, a change, hovering, hesitant, yet to arrive. And it turned him around and propelled him back, "You can. *We* can. You won't be doing this on your own. It's both of us. We'll find a way."

"There isn't one. Don't you see that? There is, no, way," his mouth set, then quivered. His exhale blew away the remnants of his composure. He looked up and the clouds building behind his eyes broke. He stared ahead seeing nothing till Johnny shimmered, shadowlike through his tears, moving away, and in the blurred dimness, appeared to be floating up the glittering stairs with the muted stars glistening overhead. A silent sob heaved itself from him.

As the door into the foyer opened, the back of Johnny's head, emblazoned with bright light had seared itself.

When the door closed, the stair lights and the soft glistening overhead, again became the only things illuminating the theatre. He rubbed his eyes, sniffed, and forced a breath past the lump in his chest. Gradually his heart remembered its rhythm and as his tears dried, his shoulders retracted, and the mantra from his childhood returned, *Terry will be OK.* He looked up. These stars twinkled, not like the mould ones, "Johnny will be OK. We'll be OK," he didn't realise he'd said it out loud.

He pushed off the edge of the stage the same way Johnny had, and moved forward, his step measured and deliberate. His head nodding with gravitas, as if he'd just agreed to something momentous.

But he'd opened the door and there was no-one there. And he'd abandoned himself and Johnny and become Lauren's husband.

I'm sorry Johnny. I'm sorry. I let you walk away. I didn't know— I didn't want to know what I was missing till it was too late. And now it is. All over again. I'm so glad I told you. I'm so glad you knew that I was coming to you, before this— oh God, I'm so sorry.

I shouldn't have left you by yourself. I'm so so sorry.

He sat in the park shelter. Breathing shallowly and slowly. As if the air was too big to swallow in one whole piece. As if, if he got too much at once, it would burst some small aperture and he'd shrivel up as life drained through the opening, leaving small puddles that evaporated instantly in the heat, or soaked invisibly into the ground. No one would even notice it was happening. He would be a shell. Robert from the outside. Nothing on the inside.

He looked back at the swings and then scanned the park. Through the drying tears he noticed the blue and white police tape winding around the stubby wooden pylons holding the ferry shelter out of the river, and finishing, staked in the grass in front of the mangroves.

Is this where they found you?

His heart had been subdued, weary, but now it started waking up, punching and trying to get out. Standing clear he turned a hundred and eighty degrees, looking up and over towards the underside of the bridge, following it to a place about a third of the way across and down river.

Walking became jogging then a flat-out run.

At Johnny's apartment he went straight to the wardrobe shelf where he'd seen Johnny's camera. *Yes. And a spare film.*

Back at the park, he started clicking. He was microns away from one hundred percent certain they could *show* that Johnny hadn't jumped and maybe... He pushed away the images of that night and was then helpless to stop the dreadful made up ones which might be the truth.

After he'd exhausted the second roll of film, he did what he'd come to do. He put up Ernie's notice and collected Alan John Peters' meagre belongings from the waterside ferry shelter, with a silent prayer that Alan would actually want this stuff, and come to Ernie's to claim it.

Returning the camera to its shelf, Robert pressed his face against the clothes sniffing the fabric for Johnny's presence, then unconsciously he reached up searching. He didn't know what for, until at the back behind folded knitwear he felt a box.

Sitting on the bed, he foraged. When he found a small Monopoly house key-ring, he attached it to Johnny's apartment and garage key, and clipped it onto his own keyring, There were photos at the bottom, he found one of Johnny at about thirteen or fourteen, handsome even at that awkward age, with a wide-smile mouthful of teeth he'd since grown into. And under it, he and Johnny at university.

Robert's mind reeled.

He flicked through and took two more. Johnny on a concrete wall, perched model-like, in a white T-shirt and jeans, and a close up face-view. He'd get copies made.

Then he propped Johnny's close-up against the light on the bedside table and lay on his side so Johnny's face looked at him. After a while he turned onto his back and closed his eyes. His arm ranged over the empty space next to him on the bed, and stilled.

He must have slept, but the sun had barely moved.

Except for his manic run, and his burst of industry at work earlier, everything was lethargic today, as if a day with grief should be weightier and slower. Hard to carry. He turned and looked at Johnny's face and wanted to scream or shout or hit something. But the idea folded in on itself and he put the photos with the film, straightened the bed-cover, and washed the sign of snail trails from his face.

Do something.

He called Anna and apologized, and reaching into his pocket for the cracked face of his watch, took out his wallet instead. The coaster with Pete's number was there.

CHAPTER 31

Robert pushed a beer towards Pete, "This is the one I owe you. Cheers."

The umbrellas over the tables in the beer garden provided protection but not relief from the heat.

"Thanks for the other night," Robert wasn't sure how to progress.

"We're all cut up about this," Pete said, "and I'm not one to pry," he didn't finish.

Robert looked out past Pete's shoulder into a place inside his own head where Johnny was nodding, "Do you remember those guys at the bar? When I first met you?"

Pete's eyes squinted.

"That's who I was running from."

"I figured. That's why Blue took you into the office. We were expecting them. Thought it'd be better if you were somewhere out of sight."

"So why were they coming to the pub. Place was closed," Robert's clarity and training were kicking in automatically.

"If the publican wants to give someone a drink after hours, up to him isn't it?" Pete's eyes narrowed, "Are you a narc or something? A reporter?"

"No. No. Lawyer."

"How about you tell me. What do you know about them?"

"I know they're Special Branch or something. Licensing? I know they're collecting money so the pub can serve, you know…"

"Us."

"Well…"

"The illegal queer folk." Pete added in mock seriousness, "Not you of course."

Robert wasn't sure if he was being laughed at, "And from what I'm guessing and from what I saw that night, they are into a bit of gay bashing and robbery on the side. I think you know that. I think you were warning him off me. Mr Muscles. He disappeared when you and Jimbo came over."

"Fuck," said Pete when Robert finished telling him what had happened. "This isn't fuckin' ancient Rome. We don't kill people for sport, for fun. This is Australia, in the twentieth century. Fa-rk me."

They drank in silence.

Finally Pete spoke, "I know it doesn't help you, but what you just told me, might help me."

Robert's brow creased.

"I can't say anything," Pete's eyes roamed. "You talked to anyone else about this?"

"Tank and Blue. And a reporter."

"You trust him?"

Robert peered into the distance again, he could feel Johnny's approval, "Yeah. Yeah. I do."

Pete swallowed the rest of his beer, his face trying to feign indifference.

Robert wondered if he'd made a mistake, "Tank does too. And Blue."

"So what are you going to do now?"

"Honestly? Don't know. Wait. See what the inquest turns up and hope those bastards get what they deserve."

"Another?" Pete held up his empty glass.

Robert stood, "No. Thanks. Gotta go."

"Stay in touch, eh?"

CHAPTER 32

On the steps of the Government offices in George Street, Robert waited, a little bemused to be hanging around outside dad's work like a teenager.

"Oi," Barry's voice brought him out of his reverie. "Come on. Let's go."

His plan was to chat on the way, and introduce the idea of Simon before introducing him for real, but as ever they were on different wavelengths. He turned his attention back to what his dad was saying. He'd heard it before and cut in.

"What about Mike?" And when his dad turned questioning, "Ahern. I met him at your place."

"In my opinion," Barry puffed up to deliver it, "he's as crooked as a telegraph pole."

"But?" Robert knew there was more.

"But, I reckon Joh still trusts him. Personally, I think Mike knows that to change anything he'll have to be inside the system. It's not the same for me, and I haven't got anything Joh wants. Not any more."

They walked on in silence. Barry interrupted it, looking sideways with a sheepish smile, "Anyway, what did you want to see me for? Is this a special occasion, or are you in some kind of trouble?"

Robert wanted to ask what he meant, but it wasn't the time, and part of him didn't want to know.

"I was thinking about your plan to go independent. Thought perhaps I could help. I've got this friend, sort of friend. He was hoping to hear what your thoughts were about the Nationals, Joh and everyone, and—"

"What? Is he thinking about politics?"

"He's a journalist. Do you remember the betting case? Missing evidence." He waited. "The judge called the police out. The cops weren't too pleased about it. I represented someone in relation to what happened afterwards." Robert stopped talking.

Barry continued walking head down, like he was pacing in his own office, looking up occasionally to check his direction was sound, "Go on."

"It's well, after representing this case, something bad happened. He died. My client. But before that he'd been trying to improve things for some parts of the community… gays," Robert looked straight ahead through the slightest pause, "and he'd been talking about it with my friend, the journalist. So after, when I told the journalist what had happened to my client, and he knew you and I were related, he said he'd like to get some inside perspective, political perspective and…"

Barry maintained his pace and kept listening.

"Well," *Jeeez dial it down, you're babbling,* "I said I'd introduce you. I thought you could help each other, and you'd have an ally in the media. Someone to give you a platform, hopefully a leg up the Independent ladder."

"No wonder you lot get paid by the minute. What's his name?"

"Simon, Draper. Do you know him?"

"Mmmm. Heard of him."

"So you don't mind?"

"Won't know till we talk. You staying?"

"Do you want me to?"

***

Returning to the office, Anna handed him a message, "He didn't leave a name."

Robert read.

"He said you'd know what it meant."

"This just gets better and better," Robert sighed. "Come in."

She walked in ahead of him and waited.

Now that the emotional nerve endings weren't so raw and exposed, Robert could pretend more easily, but he still needed to look away, "It's Johnny Saunders. We'd been friends, a long time."

Anna nodded.

"He didn't kill himself, Anna. Someone did it for him."

"That's how you know he was hurt?"

He nodded, "I'm trying to get information. Anything that can help. And this," Robert waved his hand dramatically, "doesn't help."

"You were supposed to get information from him?"

"Backflipping bastard."

Anna looked confused, "But he didn't say he wasn't going to give it to you. He just said don't come into the station. Assuming it's a police station. He probably doesn't want you there for a reason."

"Bloody hell. You're right. Of course," he smiled. "At least one of us has their head screwed on. You're an angel."

Pleasure and relief sparkled in her eyes.

"His name's Kowalski."

CHAPTER 33

Kowalski stopped pacing when Robert came in.

"Sorry to keep you waiting. Anna can get us some tea," said Robert.

"I won't be long," Kowalski checked the contents in an A4 envelope. "These first. These are from the night before you came in."

Robert started reading.

"I made copies after you left. There's no right way to say this, but it's happened before. Jumping to conclusions and then adjusting the paperwork to match."

"Have you told anyone?"

Kowalski's lip puckered, "No point. My mate, he did. Should have kept his mouth shut. Hounded off the force. And he's not the only one. He reckons bide your time."

"But you're here, so…"

"So, if I *can* do something to help, then I feel like it's my duty."

"Would that duty extend to helping an undercover investigation?"

"Is there one?"

"Not a police one," Robert raised an eyebrow, "I've heard they don't get very far. A friend, journalist. You'd be anonymous."

"I don't know," Kowalski fidgeted, and Robert didn't want to lose sight of what was still in envelopes on his lap.

"Just thought I'd mention it. Maybe when the time's right. When it can actually do some good, eh?" Robert's smile was as reassuring as he could muster given his desperation not to offend. "Like you said, no point now. What else have you got there?"

Kowalski's face flickered from indecision to resignation. Someone not trained to notice would probably have missed the parade. "OK well, here, see the names. Four officers mentioned, plus Alan John Peters, who by rights should've been in the lockup till after 10am, but wasn't."

Robert scanned. Nichols, Andrews and Thompson appeared several times, and the report was signed by Constable Brady, "I can keep these?"

"Do I get those engagement letters?"

"Here you go."

"I've made notes on the backs, to make it easier," said Kowalski. "These are next. They appeared a couple of days later, and those ones," he pointed to Robert's hand, "disappeared."

Nichols and Andrews no longer made an appearance. The charge sheet for Alan John Peters was missing. The incident was marginally different.

They caught eyes.

Kowalski handed over the next envelope, "These are completely different. It's why I said don't come to the station."

Robert read, *'unidentified person running from the scene of an altercation in a known homosexual beat.'*

"I reckon they're gonna pin something on poor old Alan John Peters, if they can find him," Kowalski nodded agreeing with himself. "I bet they're pissed off at whoever let him go."

"Meaning?"

"They have a perfect patsy, but they don't know where he is."

Robert let out a breath.

"I'm no expert," Kowalski handed Robert another envelope, "but, my uncle is. I asked him to look into it. The tides don't support the suicide story. Especially in light of where they found the body." He cringed, "Sorry, I mean Mr Saunders' body. Now there's gonna be a proper inquest, that would've stuck out like a sore thumb. So, their story had to change."

"But Constable Brady, can he do that? Won't he get into trouble?"

"You're kidding me," one side of Kowalski's mouth was imitating a smile, the other side wasn't.

Robert's eyes scanned the document again.

"Look sir, Robert," said Kowalski, "I checked into the whole Judge Matthews thing. The constable that misplaced that evidence, he got promoted." He sighed, "Probably why I'm still plugging away trying to make senior constable."

Robert nodded, "I know, in a roundabout way, what's going on, of course, but it's different when you're hearing it direct and it's people you know. It's sort of frightening isn't it?"

"Yeah. Not easy. I was all inspired after the Lucas Inquiry."

"Heard that before."

"I dunno where this is gonna end up. My uncle, he's told me stories about what it's like behind the Iron Curtain. The SB."

Robert frowned.

"The Polish version of the Stasi and the KGB. He reckons just because it's not snowing in Queensland, doesn't mean it's not a police state. I'm so busy watching my back and trying not to stand on anyone's toes I sometimes wonder if it's worth it. Sometimes I wonder if I'm the only honest bloody cop in Queensland."

"I hope not. You said you have more?" Robert held up the envelope. "Other examples of this sort of thing."

"Yeah, probably never see the light of day. And hey," he pressed his lips together, "apologies. I shouldn't be letting off steam like that. I'll stick with it. And if I hear or see anything else about this, well, you can count on me."

CHAPTER 34

After Kowalski left, Robert sat tapping his index finger on the envelopes. Another head would be useful.

He left a message for Simon. Then he and Anna went over who'd been picking up his slack, and he went to see Duncan.

"Got a minute?" His foot hit the door-frame. "I wanted to apologise. I dropped the ball. Some of my clients are happy to stay with whoever they're with now. I thought I'd see if you needed anything. Gotta earn my keep."

"As it happens, I'd planned some time off. So, yes," Duncan stopped. "What? Don't look at me like that. I'm entitled."

"Yeah. Sorry. You surprised me. Anywhere special?"

"Great Barrier Reef. Cairns."

"I've always wanted to go. What made you decide there?" It was supposed to be a conversational pleasantry, so Robert was surprised by Duncan's slap-down.

"It's a week off. I don't have to justify myself."

"I— of course not. Let me know when it suits for a handover. And thanks."

***

At home after work, he was still unsettled by Kowalski's visit.

"Uni starts soon and if you haven't got someone up to speed," Lauren's brow creased, "you'll start relying on poor Anna to fill the gaps again. Not fair."

"I'm sure she'll have it sorted soon. Did they find a replacement for you yet?"

"Don't know, don't care." Lauren laughed, handing him their empty dinner plates, "Here, make yourself useful."

His mother's words made him wince. He hoped Lauren thought he was joking.

She shook her head in mock exasperation when the phone rang, "Go on, you answer it. I don't know how we'll manage when we're both lawyers."

Robert told Ernie-blue-eyes from the 139 Club, the abbreviated version of his conversation with Kowalski, and asked if he'd seen or heard anything from or about Alan John Peters.

"They're covering their arses," said Robert, "and he won't have a leg to stand on with four police witnesses. I'm worried for him. If they moved him on, they'll know where he is, surely."

"Not necessarily. Might not even be in Brisbane. I'll try further afield."

"Either way, we need to find him before they do. Warn him."

"You're a decent bloke," said Ernie. "I can see why your Johnny kept you around."

"He had a— he was my best friend." *And decent isn't a word I'd use.*

As he started back to help Lauren in the kitchen, the phone rang again. After an overview of the changes in the records and the tide information, Robert told Simon his fears for Mr Peters.

"I'll check the shelter tomorrow. Check the notice is still up. Could you— is there some way of checking, statewide, stories, incidents, through the Paper?"

"Don't you think I'd have thought of that?"

"Yeah. Honestly, I'm second guessing everything at the moment. But what Ko— what I learned today? I'm worried. If they find him first, I honestly doubt he'd make it to an arrest."

"Your source," Simon said, "he doesn't know about you and Johnny?"

Robert looked up.

"They may not be looking for Mr Peters."

"I— You think me?"

"Not you specifically, but someone who was running from the scene."

"Excellent timing," Lauren plonked a saucepan into the drawer. "At least you can pour me a drink."

"Thanks," she said. "I called Marnie today. To see how she was. There's a date for the inquest."

Robert waited.

"In six weeks. So Harry's going ahead with his holiday, trip, whatever. He and Johnny were supposed to go to Cairns. He decided he'd have a complete rest, while he had the chance." Her lip wavered, "I almost said lucky bugger. Oh Robert, this is all too, too sad."

When he hugged her, he noticed his underarms were damp.

CHAPTER 35

"There are a lot more pages in this report," Marnie said when Robert and Harry followed Jack into his study. Her hand trembled as she put the envelope down on the desk, "I couldn't wait."

Jack reached for it.

She looked at him, eyes unfocussed, "It's graphic, Dad. Meticulously graphic. I can feel it."

She absently rubbed her knee. "Remember when I fell off my bike? The pain in my knee. It was like someone stabbing me with a blunt needle, but it wouldn't go all the way in, so they pushed harder. Drove it in."

Jack nodded.

"That was one tiny tiny crack, and it was excruciating." She squeezed her eyes shut. "I can see his face Dad. He must have been in so much pain. He was broken. Everywhere."

Tears plopped onto her cheek. She let them fall.

"Go and make some tea," he said, handing her a glass. "But first have this. Whisky."

He handed one to Harry and Robert.

As Harry read, he kept moving his head from side to side like a captive elephant that believed it was incapable of moving. Stuck in the horror.

It was clear the previously stated injuries consistent with a fall had been naïve at best. The debris causing facial injuries didn't make sense when they were diametrically opposite. There was, as the earlier report said, minimal water in his lungs and stomach. What had been missing was that he had still drowned, in the blood filling his airways. His genitals were a mess of contusions, which in the history of falls had never been documented. His liver had been split in multiple places, more like the result of an explosion

171

than a major fall from height, and the other damaged organs were floating in an internal bloody ocean. It was consistent with multiple blows not one big one. The only injury that *was* consistent with the original report, was a broken collar bone and dislocated shoulder.

Black scuff marks, residue of shoe polish on his jacket, shirt and jeans, was lodged in the fibres of the fabric and visible despite being in the river. Ingrained dirt and traces of grass on the back of his jacket and the inside waistband of his jeans and belt at the back. It was in his hair and the back of his scalp too.

Inside Robert's head was the senseless image of Johnny rolling around on the ground, rubbing his head in the grass and dirt, and polishing his shoes with his clothes before deciding it was time to go jumping off a bridge.

"Good God," Harry interrupted Robert's thoughts. "This can't be whitewashed. Robert, have you got those statements you had from your Candowski? Have they seen them?" he nodded towards Jack and Marnie.

"Not yet. I've got some photos too."

Jack and Marnie leaned in closer.

"I went down to where Johnny was found, and I went back again so I had low and high tide."

Robert handed them the photos. He could feel Johnny watching him from the corner of the room and tried to recall when that had started.

No one said anything as Robert explained the river curving around the Point, and the location of the bridge over it, where Johnny was supposed to have jumped, where his things were found, and where he would have landed; the water's edge, the mud and the roots of the mangroves looking like they were holding the trees up on top of the water, forming a natural fence barrier to anything trying to reach the edges of the riverbank from the flowing waterway. There was the blue and white check tape. There were the patches of bent grass.

Next, he went over Kowalski's information.

In their faces, he recognized the wishful disbelief. He'd felt it in his own face. The layers of information keeping everyone suspended in a net knotted together with grief and anger, sadness and futile longing for a different outcome. He wanted to tell them it was all true. He'd seen it. Some of it. Marnie half knew. He looked at her. She didn't look at him. He looked up at the corner where he felt Johnny watching. The impulse to speak up abated.

"These pictures only show the average difference in the tides. It was super low, the tide the next day, when they found him. I looked it up. Point zero nine of a metre. It doesn't get much lower, ever. I'll get a picture when it's close to that again. The high around nine that night, was two point five. That's a massive difference."

He stood up bending over, "This is the low, and this," he straightened up stretching the other arm above his head towards the ceiling, and their eyes followed, "is the high. If it hadn't been super low the next day, he may not have turned up as quickly. Sorry."

"What?" said Marnie.

"I don't know. I hate talking about Johnny like this."

"But what you're saying," Harry said, "is that whoever killed Johnny, and let's all be clear, he didn't do this to himself, would probably have gotten away with it."

"Because," Jack said, "the water level would have kept him out of sight."

"Not only that," said Robert. "The water was running out towards Moreton Bay, not backwards towards the mangroves. It's in the tide report."

"They may still get away with it," said Marnie, looking at them in turn. "This is the independent autopsy report Harry commissioned. The inquest still has to happen. And from the changes your officer Cam—"

"Kowalski," Robert chimed in.

"Kowalski showed you, then anything could happen," she finished.

"Do you think," Harry said, "he'd make a statement?"

"Do you think it would make a difference? At this point?" Robert asked. "Honestly, I think the less they know about what *we* know, the better. If he speaks up now, he'll likely be sent to the back of beyond. Or worse. We might need him."

"But why would they change their report? There must have been some discrepancy at the start is all," said Jack. "I can understand that they might jump to conclusions at first. But—"

"Dad," Marnie cut him off, "why not just say after further investigations blah blah. Why change the whole report and why did it disappear? The first one."

"We have to trust it will all come out. The coroner, that's his job, and he is, after all, independent," said Jack.

Harry's eyes caught Robert's.

The absence of light in them, the dead dull centre, struck Robert as inordinately sad.

"They've been re-working the story to support the available evidence and vice versa," Harry's elephant nod came to rest. "Even if neither existed five minutes ago."

"What do you mean?" Jack said. "They don't make things up. There are laws, and, this is the police, Australia, not some communist dictatorship."

"This is Queensland Dad. It sort of is."

"Jack," said Harry, "she's right. I'm talking from experience. If they've changed their story, it's because they have a reason. And the only reason they would have, is to save themselves or get someone else into trouble. Or some combination. They're the law, but they're operating completely outside it."

Jack's eyes were a mixture of incredulity and skepticism, till they glazed with panic and then defeat. He'd lost his ideals, as well as his son.

Harry looked away, "What happened to Johnny has, and could, no, to be more precise, will, happen to other people. We should do what Robert said. Keep things to ourselves."

CHAPTER 36

Robert put the folder down open on his desk, pressed his fingertips onto his eyelids and rubbed, then looked out of the window. He could barely see the contours of the office building across the street and got up to leave, catching his reflection. It wasn't just the lighting, the saggy grey half-moons under his eyes were clearly visible. Poking them and watching the skin slowly crawl back into place, he wondered at the promise of Lauren's face cream to soften and smooth. He remembered misreading it as soften and soothe and sighed. He could do with some of that for his soul. At least work was keeping his mind off things.

He jotted down his billing notes on the folder and reigned in his compulsion to call and check with Harry about the inquest. At least this time the coroner had indelible and detailed black and white facts. Once they'd established this was not suicide and caused by, *stop thinking stop thinking*, they'd have to open an investigation. He turned back and looked at the phone. *Leave it. Your job is finding Alan John Peters.*

*

Driving home he kept his mind on kids and stories and hugs and was puzzled at the sallow welcome from the porch light, and that he had to unlock his front door.

The emptiness got louder as he moved from room to room. The oven was slightly warm.

Where was everyone?

He did the rounds again. Looking for a note. The sound of his footsteps bounced off the timber floorboards and soaked into the walls. The pulse in his throat jiggled. People don't write notes if they don't intend to be out long. So where were they? Had there been an accident? Please no. The breath stopped at its usual spot. He forced in more.

He went to Emma and Thomas's bedroom. Their story book was there, but their cuddle toys were missing from their pillows. Toothbrushes. If you're going away, you take your toothbrush, don't you? Unless you're in a hurry. Or you forget. Or you're so upset or angry about something. Or something happened on the way home.

"Oh jeez," he reeled, heading back to the kitchen. What if someone else was hurt? He headed for the phone and then stopped. The door to the dining room was closed.

He opened it, flicking on the light switch. The table was set with the good cutlery. Candles waited on either side to cast their glow on the flowers centred between them. *Idiot. Fucking numbskull.*

He opened the yellow pages. There was a beauty place near Marnie's salon and an upmarket restaurant. He wrote down the details and found an envelope in the bottom drawer. When he propped it against the candlestick, he almost smiled. And with the sharpest corners of his anxiety smoothed he freshened up and dipped his fingers into Lauren's cream, with its promise to do the same for his face.

*

When Lauren came in and stood in the doorway to the kitchen dubiously appraising him, Robert blinked through his own dank grey clouds to hers. They were electric, stormy, and unpredictable.

"Anything I can do?" his voice sounded small.

"Put the oven on. Low, please. I'm having a shower."

He did. And he went to put champagne glasses in the freezer, but she'd already done it, so he took them out.

When she came back her face was softer, or maybe it was because her hair had fuzzed slightly with post shower humidity.

He passed her a glass, and raised his, hopefully, clinking hers.

She sipped, "It was yesterday. Our anniversary. I waited all day to hear from you. Nothing."

He swallowed air with the liquid and it fizzed in his nose as he coughed, "Sorry. I've had a lot on my mind. I thought," his arm swept the room and he avoided looking up, "I thought it was today."

"But not really. You only remembered because of all this." This time *her* arm swept the room. "We need to talk Robert."

He knew a quick make up kiss wouldn't fix this.

"Ice is in the big freezer," she said heading to the dining room with her glass.

"I'll start," her face, momentarily warped as the candle sputtered, "I have only the vaguest idea of what you must be feeling," she said. "I know my mum died, but I was only little. I've never lost a close friend."

He pressed a finger to his lips.

"And I know grief affects people in different ways."

A small nod.

"But you are getting further and further away from us," a pang of wistful making itself known, "and your mind is everywhere, or nowhere. I don't know. Just not where it should be, or needs to be."

She raised her hand when he went to speak, "I think you need help. Maybe *we* need help. I don't want to make this about me, but it is. Anything to do with you affects me too. I'm lonely. You haven't been near me, you know… in months."

Robert's face collapsed into contrition. He lifted it towards her, then put it back down so he wouldn't see her embarrassment, or she wouldn't see his. The speech was rehearsed. But not for polish. It had been waiting for the right time, and in the end, it had to be said regardless. He'd hoped adding student to her to-do list would keep her busy, leaving him free to flounder around trying to figure himself out. Except he hadn't. Floundering yes, figuring no.

"Don't say anything," she said. "Anything you do say may be used," her voice trailed off, the wistful trying to be playful.

When he looked, she was smiling.

"Let's enjoy this," she raised her glass, "and dinner and some alone time. No pressure."

After his inept lovemaking, he pretended not to notice her silent tears, and kissed the back of her head while they spooned, and her breathing stretched out into sleep. He looked out over her into the dark for a while, counting, till at some point it stopped, and he had the best sleep he'd managed in months.

***

"I'll get the kids," said Robert.

They were finishing coffee, sitting on the verandah, the morning sun creeping around the side of the bleached hardwood decking promising a warm day.

She smiled, "Are we OK?"

"We are. I'll try harder."

"That's not the point. I don't want you to have to try."

"It came out the wrong way. I meant I'll try to notice if I'm slipping back."

"Take the kids' swimsuits," said Lauren. "They could have a dip before you come home."

"I assumed they were at Mum and Dad's?"

"That was the plan. But," she put her cup down. "Another?"

"No, I'm going to cut down on caffeine. I slept better last night. But what?"

"Your mum. That's why I was late. I didn't want to bring it up last night. She was drunk. I know," she played with her cup, "that sounds horrible. Barry was AWOL, so I went to Dad's. I thought you should have a word to Barry."

"Do you think she has a problem?"

"Put it this way. I don't think the episode at the barbeque was an isolated event."

***

Jeannie was busy cleaning, "Cuppa?"

He went to take the vacuum cleaner from her, "Shall I—"

"No," she pushed his arm aside, "I don't need any help."

Her breath was stale and sweet.

"Mum?"

"I said I don't need any help."

"My mistake," said Robert. "Come on Mum, let's make that tea. I don't want to upset you."

"Bit late for that."

"I didn't mean—" He stopped and repeated, "Come on. I'll put the kettle on."

"Not in my kitchen. That's my job." Jeannie's face changed to puzzlement, "What do you want?"

"Tea?"

"No, why are you here?"

"We— I was worried about you."

"I'm perfectly fine. As you can see. And I've got work to do."

"Mu-um," Robert hesitated, "it's... last night, the kids were going to stay over, and—"

"Apparently I'm not good enough. Doesn't matter to me. What's that look for? I don't tell you how to live your life. Do I? Do I?" she repeated, her volume rising. "Why shouldn't I have a drink at the end of the day? To relax. I work hard. This place doesn't clean itself. And it's not like your father lifts a finger."

"Mum. Mum. It's OK, no one begrudges you a drink after a hard day. It's, well... sometimes I think the end of the day starts a bit too early. You know?"

"No. As a matter of fact, I don't know." Her eyes were icy. "I think you should go. I've got a lot to do."

"Mum?"

"I said I'm busy."

"Lauren doesn't want the kids coming over. Not when you're— you have a problem, Mum. If anything happened."

"Oh for God's sake, Robert. Nothing happened to you, did it? You survived. There's nothing wrong with me. Go. Go on."

Robert stared. Mute.

"And take that look off your face. Pouting at me like... How dare you?"

Her distress transformed into a sneer, "You think I don't know about you. I do. Pathetic pervert. I should be taking those kids off you. Does she know? Miss Perfect? Hah! Go. Leave me alone."

*

On the drive to Duncan's, Robert kept picturing his mum's eyes fierce with pride at his childhood triumphs, and brimming with compassion because Daddy was too busy to come and watch. He heard her voice soothing, calm, inside the principal's office while he sat outside it, counting to quell the panic every time he heard footsteps in the hall. She'd stroked his hair while he wet her blouse with his sobs. *Had she always hated him?*

He remembered her, proudly saying, "And your dad," she'd sniffed delicately at something in the air that he couldn't smell, "is going to be a Minister."

"God no," she frowned when he asked if that was a sort of priest. "Don't be stupid. Why on earth— It's an important job in the government."

He didn't tell her that Terry had told him about ministers being priests. They'd talked about it after school when he'd told Terry he wasn't invited to the birthday dinner after all, because it was more about his dad's special day because of Joh Bjelke-Peterson being sworn in. They hadn't figured out why people in government had to swear when no-one else was supposed to.

His face softened and he almost smiled as Terry's serious frowning face came to mind.

"I suppose it's OK," Robert said. "Dad and me, we both like roast chook. But jeez… pumpkin cake? I think Mum's competing with pumpkin scones. Dad told her about the Premier's wife. Flo. She makes them."

Terry screwed up his face, "Sort-of glad I wasn't invited."

Robert, standing astride his bike, looked at the clouds.

"It's OK. I've told you before. I know she doesn't like me."

Then Terry laughed, "Hahaha. Flo and Joh." And he'd put on a silly voice, "Want some tea to go with your scone Joh. No Flo. Ya sure Joh. I said No Flo. Haha."

They'd both laughed.

It was good to remember that laugh. He parked outside Duncan's.

And then he remembered struggling home with his and Terry's bikes. He'd put them under the house with all the other stuff that modest Queenslanders hid behind the hedges of mock-orange or lilly-pilly, and gone upstairs to tell his mum what happened.

She was standing next to the hallstand, her back to him. As his voice bridged the gap between them, the cup she was holding banged down onto the saucer, missing the indentation specifically designed to hold it. Everything tipped.

He sat in the car, remembering it now. Seeing it in slow motion.

Amber liquid puddled on the wax-shined wood, shaking, hesitant about what it should do, or where it should go. He held his breath. Without looking at him she jabbed the puddle out of existence with the bottom corner of her apron.

He'd watched her profile. Her upper lip pushed out like she'd bitten a powdery apple and wanted to spit it out. As she faced him, he saw something else he didn't have a name for.

Still didn't. But he'd seen it again today.

"Mu-um," he'd looked at his feet, "I— my— Mum, my friend Terry—"

"I'm on the phone Robert." She waggled the receiver in front of his downturned face, "I've told you before. Don't interrupt me when I'm on the phone."

"But it's import—"

"I won't tell you again. Now go to your room. Get changed for dinner."

He'd sat on his bed, hands pressed between his thighs, and rocked. Tiny movements. He counted in time to them. One, two, three, four...fifteen. Start again.

Saying the numbers in his head, helped stop the feeling that something was trying to burrow into him and out of him at the same time. It stopped him wondering why those boys would do that to him and to Terry, to anyone…

After a while, he'd curled and lowered himself sideways onto the pillow, staring at the far corner of the ceiling. The black and grey dots turned into starbursts, swirling into a white cloud blanket. He let it cover him. But when he blinked, the dots came back. Mould.

He'd read about mould in Mum's *Women's Weekly* and asked Terry if that's how he'd gotten asthma.

"Doofus," Terry had play-punched him on the arm. "Everyone in Queensland would be sick if that was true."

He'd shrugged, squeezing the punch-spot. He wasn't about to argue with his only friend.

Unconsciously, he took one hand off the steering wheel and rubbed the spot again now.

And then after the policeman left the next day, he'd asked if Terry was really dead. She'd nodded and pushed some loose hair back into her bun, and checked her reflection in the hallstand mirror.

"There'll be a funeral or church or something won't there?" he asked the back of her head.

He pressed his eyelids closed so no tears came out, "Can I go?"

"I don't think so. It wouldn't be appropriate," her reflection spoke from the mirror. "Now, make yourself useful. Set the table for dinner."

"OK." Sighing, he brushed his fringe, fine brown and too long like the rest of him, away from his face and looked up at her. "Mu-um," he said with a hint of pleading and defiance in his voice, "what's a poofter?"

She turned around and looked at him, her face like stone, and walked away saying, "For God's sake. I'll do it."

"She has," he said out loud in the empty car. "She has always hated me."

He leaned back against the headrest, eyes closed and heart thudding.

This. This is why you're straight. This is why you don't tell people. Why people can't know.

He thought about Tank, flamboyant and carefree.

Was he? Or was that an act?

He thought about Johnny and Harry separately together. Johnny saying sorry.

Sorry for what? I'm *sorry. I'm sorry I'm not who you thought I was Johnny. I'm not pathetic. I'm not a pervert. I'm daddy. I'm Lauren's husband. I was something you imagined me to be and wanted for a while. But I* can't *be what you want me to be. That's not me. This is me. Is this me?*

He heard tapping on the car window, Duncan saying, "Are you coming in?"

"Hmmph, Yeah. Daydreaming."

"Don't blame you for sitting here in the peace and quiet. Those two are a handful. They're having a sandwich. Fancy one yourself?"

I fancy a drink. A strong one. No you don't. You'll turn into your mother. "Sounds great. Thanks, Duncan."

Playing with the kids coaxed him out of his melancholy. His mum had a problem. He'd talk to his dad. He would lose those words. But he was grateful for them in a way. They'd made him see where he was heading. It wasn't where he wanted to go.

When squeals and laughter turned into teary and tired, Robert started packing up.

"They can have their nap here. Call Lauren to come over. I'm enjoying the company."

"So you weren't serious about peace and quiet then," Robert joked. "You call her. She doesn't say no to you as easily as she does to me."

Duncan was back in moments, "Not happening," he said. "Harry just phoned your place, and Lauren said you'd call in."

"It'll be something about the inquest. He's been attending for Marnie and Jack."

"I know. Go now. I'll take them home. Help Lauren with her homework eh?" Duncan continued chattering.

Robert was only half listening.

183

"Good thing I'm used to talking to myself," said Duncan.

"Sorry. I wonder what he couldn't tell me by phone. Yeah. That would be great Duncan. I'll round up their things."

CHAPTER 37

Harry's face was used to giving nothing away and Robert's gaze shifted to the glass in Harry's hand. A wave of irritation flashed across his own face.

Harry recognized it, "It's not mine," he said, handing the glass to Robert.

"I thought, never mind."

"Come on in. Sit down," Harry sat leaning forward.

After Robert settled uncomfortably into an armchair, Harry continued, "I don't want you to get defensive," he said, "but I know. I've known for a while. I just didn't see the point in bringing it up."

What started as a sip turned into a gulp, and the burn held Robert's attention while it lasted.

"I mean it. I don't want you to feel bad. So you can lose that trapped in headlights look."

Robert lifted the glass again. It didn't burn as much this time.

"I understand you're shocked, but at least as far as I'm concerned, you can be honest. You owe me that. Drink up. I'll get you another one, and," he said getting up, "you can tell me exactly what happened and then I'll fill you in, on where I think this might be heading. What the police are up to. And we'll figure out what to do. You with me?"

Harry's intermittent nodding stopped when Robert's words did, "I can see better now what they're up to. To me, the picture emerging from the inquest has you painted into a corner."

"Me?" Robert frowned. "But..."

"Based on the notion that they didn't really see you, and even if they did they wouldn't know you from Adam. And my guess is, they'd still be pinning it on Mr Peters *if* they hadn't somehow lost him." Harry turned his glass absently, "At the hotel, when you called the ambulance, who knows you were there?"

"It was after closing. There were a couple of people I don't know out on the verandah, finishing their drinks. And Jimbo was outside too. Blue was inside, and so was Pete, Jimbo's other half." Robert told Harry how he'd met them.

"There's been mention of someone called Peter at the inquest. I think it's your Pete," Harry said.

"How do you know?"

"I don't. I'm assuming. The coroner had just finished asking about the pub, and then asked what relationship does this person have with the deceased?' The officer was nervy explaining about new information that had come to light as part of their ongoing enquiries and that Peter, and he stopped and changed it to 'the witness', and said he's not aware of any relationship with the deceased."

"That's it?" said Robert. "I imagine they'd be asking anyone around the area that night if they saw Johnny or—"

"What's worrying me," Harry cut him off, "and should be worrying you more so, is that someone called Pete helps you that night, and before you know it, they're offering information up from Peter somebody. You could bet your bottom dollar it's not something beneficial for you. For a start, you hardly know him."

"I hardly know any of them."

"What about the bar manager? Blue. The bar always knows what's going on."

"He did say once, that Pete had some business or other with Nichols and Andrews. Said he had suspicions. I talked to him. To Pete. I was trying to find out anything I could about Nichols and Andrews. Anyway, I told Pete that I was sure Johnny didn't jump. That I was pretty well certain it was those bastards. He said 'it wouldn't help Johnny, but it might help him'," Robert sighed into his empty glass.

"You're driving."

"Some ginger ale then? Why would he…"

"Alan John Peters is still our priority," Harry handed him the soft refill.

"He's got to be somewhere. Get hold of this Pete and see what he'll tell you. And see if Blue can tell you anything. And," he added, "you've been keeping the gay thing quiet for a long time now. I think you're going to have to keep it that way."

"Honestly Harry, at this point, I hadn't planned to change anything."

"It's not, I don't know," said Harry. "Just keep it all under your hat. I need some time to think it through. And talk to Simon," his lip turned down. "He knows you're gay, so warn him not to say a word. Now who else knows?"

"Marnie, Tank and Blue know for sure. Ernie, from Johnny's 139 shelter, and Pete and Jimbo? I'd say they would have presumed. And," Robert sighed heavily, "Mum, I think."

Harry's eyebrow tried unsuccessfully to stay in place.

Robert repeated the conversation he'd been determined only hours ago to forget, and Harry shook his head in his elephant way, "Big day then?" He didn't wait for an answer, "Go and apologise for upsetting her, and tell her you understand, but don't elaborate. People get defensive. Buy flowers," Harry half-breathed a chuckle and selected an unopened bottle of Scotch from the drinks trolley. "Better still, give her this."

Robert half-smiled back, "How long do you think I've got? Before they come looking for me."

"I'd have thought they'd be wanting you at the inquest. So you could expect that sometime soon. But that's an *if*. It's hard to say with them, the police I mean. They're not exactly interested in justice or truth are they? But the inquest will have to be wrapped up first. Then any investigations will proceed. We've got time up our sleeves. We'll find Mr Peters. Try not to worry."

"I wish," Robert stopped, and all the wishes in his head jostled each other trying to get to the top of the pile. "Johnny's niece," he said eventually, "Nikki. After it happened…"

Harry looked up expectantly.

"She said Johnny had been to visit with Grandma that night. At first, I was over the moon. I remember this surge of relief. Huge. And," Harry's face was blurring, "then Nikki said they were going home together, to her place. To Grandma's. And then I remembered there was no 'her place'. She said," he sniffed, "Nikki said, that he'd watched it happen from the swing. And that he was sorry. I should have told you before. I'm sorry Harry. I'm so so sorry."

Harry's elephant nod was as slow as the trail of silver tear streaks forming lines on his face.

CHAPTER 38

Feeling calm was not what Robert expected. There was a sense of satisfaction arising from applying mental ticks to his must-get-done list, and a sense of something he couldn't point at, but could point towards. And when he looked up into the corner of the room, any room, he felt at peace.

His mum was mollified and if she had doubts, she was keeping them and her whisky under wraps.

By the end of the week, he'd sorted his office, and was heading to see Anna in hers.

"Dropped by to say thank you."

"For?"

"Pretty much that. For not even knowing."

A frown creased Anna's forehead.

"I'll explain. Try to," he smiled to help her relax. "You just, do things, Anna, to help people. Your mum especially, but me too, everyone really. I've used your generosity to cover all sorts of weakness on my part. And you've rearranged, fixed things."

She looked only slightly less uncomfortable.

"I thought I was organising the promotion because I wanted to make things better, but as much as I told myself it was for you, it was because your situation made me feel uncomfortable. Do you see?"

She shook her head.

"It stopped me from looking at my own…" he stopped. "Maybe that's why I do this job… I'm blathering," he half-smiled again. "Stay with me on this."

"No. Stop," she said. "I can see you've been busy. But I've seen some change in you this week. You're calmer. You're not bumping into things."

"Hahaha. I hadn't noticed that bit. But you're right."

"So?"

"So," said Robert, "I have three things to ask you to do. Four. Actually five."

"You sure you don't want to add on a few more?" Anna's sarcasm was delicately applied.

"Maybe. We'll see." Robert turned serious. "Firstly if an Alan John Peters turns up or calls, don't let him out of your sight, chain him to your desk. Whatever it takes."

"The pro-bono?"

"It's pretty important, Anna. I wouldn't trust anyone else. And make sure everyone knows to put him through to you if he phones and asks for me."

She nodded.

"Second. I've put detailed notes on all my files. Clients won't have to repeat themselves. I want them to stay happy with Eldridge's. And could you help Helen find another position? She was a good choice, thank you."

Anna's head tilted under the weight of her questions.

"That's three. Four, Lauren. If anything happens, can you check up on her. Make sure she's OK. I know Duncan will, but someone else she's familiar with and can talk to about me. Stuff she wouldn't maybe ask her father. She'll probably have questions."

"Like I do," Anna said. "What's going on?"

"Well, that brings me to number five. Come and have a drink with me and I'll fill you in. I can only tell you what I know so far. You said 'you can trust me', and I do. As far as anyone else goes, I'm on leave."

CHAPTER 39

Robert looked at the occupied corner of the suitcase. Packing his clothes was easy. Packing for Lauren was a different story. She always took too much, so he was careful to do the same, smiling as he put in an extra pair of capri pants and then smiling even more because he remembered what they were called.

Packing for the kids was even easier.

He looked at the bedside clock and pressed the pocket of his chinos. He didn't have much time.

In the kitchen he put snacks, juice boxes, fruit, staples and treats into a used supermarket shopping bag and made vegemite sandwiches cut into triangles.

He pulled the front door shut as his family pulled into the driveway.

"Come on," he opened the doors to his car, "we'll be late if we don't leave straight away."

He evaded the where are we going questions with, 'it wouldn't be a surprise if I told you,' and 'you'll know when we get there.'

When he looked over at Lauren's face he was pleased to see the skin wasn't tight and resisting, and her forehead was smooth. Looking back at the road ahead of him through the windscreen, he hoped she would remember this feeling.

*

Living an hour from the premier beach-holiday destination in Australia, meant they arrived in time to enjoy some sand and water, before the sun's beach access was blocked by the high-rises lined up along the Gold Coast and their long shadows made the sand cold.

"Lovely surprise," Lauren rubbed sunscreen on the kids. "Totally unexpected."

"That," said Robert, "was the plan."

He turned away, not wanting to encourage the questions he recognised formulating behind her eyes, "Do you mind if I go out a bit further?" he said scanning the ocean in front of them.

She nodded, "Go on. We'll be OK."

He turned periodically, watching the playfight splashes and then Lauren kneeling and Emma and Thomas standing, the three heads disappearing and reappearing, as they ducked under the shore waves.

In the swell beyond the breakers, he faced the horizon while the current carried him sideways and further out. As he bobbed semi-weightless, he thought about letting it take him wherever it wanted, and wondered where he'd end up? He floated looking skywards and closed his eyes. How hard would it be to let go? He remembered Nikki telling him about Johnny watching what happened. Sadness mingled with peace, and water from his eyes merged with its ancient family. And then he was spluttering upright, feet not touching the ocean floor and kicking towards the shore.

*

On the balcony, Robert waited while Lauren put the kids to bed, listening to the consistent swoosh of the waves. Every so often he caught glimpses of their foam edges when the moonlight broke through the clouds.

When she joined him he waited for the questions which didn't come. Perhaps she didn't want this timid happiness to wash away, "How do you like uni?" he said.

"I felt like a fish out of water to start."

"Not possible."

"You'd be surprised," she said. "I think I lost some confidence along the way, being mostly at home in the suburbs. But it's good."

"Why?"

"What do you mean, why?"

"Why is it good?" he said, "Is it the subjects, the people, because it's interesting?"

The wine helped the conversation meander.

"You relax, and finish up," he said and putting down his empty glass, "I'll check on the kids."

He did, but not until after he'd arranged his secretly stowed scented candles.

When he came into the bedroom Lauren was already in bed, "I couldn't find my PJs," she said.

Looking down at her long lean form beneath the sheet, unmediated by a nightie or pyjamas, was strangely erotic. He let the feeling swirl around his abdomen and pulse lightly in his groin.

"I must have accidentally forgotten them," he stayed there standing over the bed. "What a shame."

He peeled back the sheet, slowly dragging it over her skin, watching as her naked body goose-bumped and his eyes moved to the silver threads on her abdomen and a surge of masculinity aroused him further. He sensed her vulnerability competing with her desire, listening while her breath became quicker and shallower. She shifted, tensing, and slightly arching her back, her eyes watching him watching her.

He took off his shirt and sat with his back to her on the edge of the bed, trailing his fingers from inside her knee, up her thigh, and whenever she moaned, he lifted his hand away. He could feel his erection stretching against his underwear. His face was hot. He leaned around so he could kiss her and when she tried to kiss him back, he lifted his face away, bringing it down on her neck, licking under her ear, teasing, then kissing her hard on the mouth.

She moved to roll towards him. He could feel her desperation and arousal. He took her hand tracing one finger exquisitely slowly down her body to the top of her legs and let it slice through the damp. She arched again. He held her hand there and pressed against it with his own, rubbing slightly. As she shivered, he lifted her hand away.

"Slow down," he whispered, and turned her over. "You have plenty of time."

Her bare white skinned bottom and splayed legs made him gasp. He knelt between her legs pressing his fully clothed penis against her. The feel of it straining for release was intoxicating. Finally he let it out, playing, prodding, dipping, before lowering his body onto her back and clenching before turning her over.

After her fingers had scraped him free of his clothes, he thrust, and stopped, his weight pressing down on her, feeling her skin hot and dewy against his. He took her wrists, one in each hand, placing them behind her head, then pushed hard and deep and stopped. He could feel her hips circling. He pushed again and again, until they were both moving together, gasping while the rhythm escalated and released them.

"Shhh," he said when Lauren went to speak. "Shh. Close your eyes."

He pulled the sheet up over her and waited as her breathing lengthened and the dwindling candle-light extinguished itself. Then lay with his hands holding each other on his chest and stared into the dark, feeling the tears edge out of the corners of his eyes. He concentrated on the feel of them trickling towards the pillow and thought about his first time with Johnny. He hoped that's how Lauren felt tonight. His chest tightened.

Easing out of bed, he went to check on the kids. At the door he looked back at Lauren asleep, and then up into the corner of the room. He could feel Johnny smiling. *I miss you.*

***

Emma and Thomas were splashing in the hotel kiddy pool. They'd have to leave soon.

"I don't want to spoil this, but I have to tell you something," said Robert.

Lauren's face turned but her eyes were on the children.

"You know Harry's been going to the inquest."

She nodded.

"He said my name's come up."

"Not surprisingly."

Robert shook his head but she wasn't watching him, "No."

She glanced his way and back at the children, "Sorry, I can't have a serious conversation while I'm watching them."

"It's probably nothing."

She shrugged, "You'll most likely have to make a statement or something. Wouldn't be much to say. You're friends, you're his lawyer, you met up for drinks."

"Just thought I'd mention it. I don't like having secrets." *Fuck. Seriously?* "I don't expect— It's probably nothing," he repeated, adjusting the wince into a smile.

"Is that why you brought us away for the weekend?"

"What? No," he looked down at his hands. "I've been working long hours, I've got tons of leave. I decided to take time off."

She looked at him over her coffee cup.

"Sort of," he admitted. "I felt bad about the other week, and our anniversary and..."

"Consider yourself well and truly forgiven."

PART THREE

1986

CHAPTER 40

Robert's shoulders slumped and his head felt too heavy to hold up. He looked down at his upturned hands, spellbound by the black-grey ink staining his fingertips. Every so often his eyes gravitated to the corner of the holding cell, then back to his hands. *How the fuck did helping with our enquiry turn into this?*

He'd left a message for Duncan with his allotted call. Waiting impatiently, he counted and when he stopped himself, he filled the time with self-torture. The vacuum cleaner screaming. The flash of sunlight hitting metal badges. Emma and Thomas's tear-streaked faces looking at him from either side of a police-woman. A made-up image of Lauren when the police arrived at the lecture hall looking for her at uni. Her face changing from curious to confused to worried to angry. Did she think he'd done something terrible? Maybe. But she knew what they were like.

He consciously willed both the counting and the torture to stop and tried to figure out what was underneath the surface of this so-called line of enquiry. The coroner has no jurisdiction beyond establishing the facts. Cause of death. It can't establish guilt, but it can point to the existence of a possible perpetrator. And that had been his plan.

But geez. Not me.

He tried to imagine the progression, of things being presented. *Harry said I was mentioned so why wasn't I asked to attend? To explain? That should have come first. Shouldn't it?*

The changes in the police records since that night had obviously moved on from what Constable Kowalski had shared. What else had disappeared, or found its way into the mishmash of lies?

He closed his eyes. Johnny's words came. Chess. The changing rules. Then came images, words, faces. A constant flurry, fought for space and dominance in his mind. He resolutely erased them but as fast as he worked more sprang up. He started counting again.

***

"Do you know why I'm in here? Who's said what?" Robert asked as Duncan joined him in the interview room.

Duncan shifted uncomfortably, stretching his neck, his hands bunched tightly until he saw Robert looking at them. "I've talked to Harry," he said, watching Robert's face closely.

Robert was trying to figure out what the tight line of Duncan's mouth meant. "And?"

"And, I'm not going to be able to act for you."

Robert's face drooped, "What exactly do you think you know?"

"No," said Duncan. "You've got me wrong—"

"Look," Robert started out defensively, his voice escalating, "things are a bit… confused. I'm a bit confused. Johnny and I, we were close when we were young. Friends. Good friends. But I married your daughter. I love Lauren. I love my kids. You know that."

Duncan sat still, his hand hovering close to the tabletop, up and down as if it was gently pacifying an infant.

Robert didn't see it. "Haven't you ever done anything stupid or experimental?" He snorted. "Probably not."

Duncan looked past Robert's shoulder and Robert ploughed on.

"If you talked to Harry, you know I could hardly go to the police, could I?" Robert pleaded.

"You're misunderstand—"

"Fuck's sake Duncan? We had a drink and something to eat together. We're friends. It doesn't have to be any more than that. What's on the arrest report? Who's behind it? I have my suspicions, but I have to have an idea of where I stand," Robert was shaking. His eyes met Duncan's, "Don't you care? This is going to hurt Lauren. She doesn't need this."

Duncan's eye squinted.

"I saw what happened. Most of it. Enough. I know who did it. And there's a witness. The police don't know I know that. And I don't want them to. Poor bastard will be the next one to turn up in the river. I'd probably be there too, except for their suicide story. And now that didn't pan out, they need to frame someone. That's what this is. I—"

"Robert," Duncan's hand was doing a traffic stop. "There's a lot at stake here."

"You don't say."

"Harry suggested a course of action. It could work in your favour. And, he thinks it will keep your witness safe until we can locate him."

"We have to find him. He saw it happen. The whole thing. We even have his name and," Robert stopped. "Oh, God, I'm rambling. You know all this. Harry's told you already."

Duncan nodded.

"You don't think *they've* found him, do you?"

"If they have and he's alive, I strongly doubt he's going to be any use to you. Which brings me back to Harry's suggestion."

Elbows heavy on the table, Robert prayered his hands together over his nose with his thumbs tucked under his chin. He closed his eyes.

"You may not like what I'm going to say."

Robert shrugged, rubbed his grey-stained fingertips against his temples, and after a precious moment of no thought, opened his eyes, "Beggars can't be choosers I suppose. What's the plan?"

*

"I can already see holes," Robert's head had been moving in a rhythmic no as Duncan spoke. "If I'm in this frenzied gay panic state because he came on to me, how come we were friends? I *knew* he was gay for fuck's sake," Robert raised a finger with each question. "And why then? And why did I leave him there, at the edge of the water? Why did I take his wallet? And his money? And why on earth, would I leave my jacket on the bridge?"

"We thought about it," Duncan said. "First off, you were panicked. Doesn't matter if you're friends or not. Second. *You* didn't kill him. You fought. He fell. You came to your senses. You checked for a pulse, you checked he was away from the water's edge, and you went for help. Someone else robbed him. His wallet was empty. Maybe they fought too. They hid the body in the mangroves expecting the tide to do its job. They planted the wallet and your jacket on the bridge."

"So I'm a saint? A jury is going to believe that?"

"You were protecting yourself. Saving yourself. That's why it's called Homosexual Advance Defense in the statutes. You're fighting off potential rape. So if someone dies, it's justifiable. Sanctioned even. Look," Duncan's voice lowered into reasonableness, "nothing anyone does is going to bring Johnny back. This isn't hurting anyone."

"Oh?" Robert scoffed. "Johnny's family? Duncan it wasn't a shove, 'get off me'. He was brutalized. I'd have to be some kind of monster. Lauren? My parents. Dad's reputation. Your business. It was me who encouraged Marnie and Harry to pursue this. It doesn't make sense. Oh God. Lauren will hate me. How can someone so violent be around kids?" His words tumbled out.

"I said you weren't going to like it. But it will give you time to find Mr Peters. Do you understand? They're going to blame you anyway. That's why you're here. Gay panic means public sympathy. Some people will think of you as a kind of hero."

"Jeeez! God," he exhaled, pressed his fingertips against his forehead this time. "Let me get this straight." He went over the whole thing again, adding, "The ambulance said there was no-one there? And when I heard it was suicide, what then? Did I just think 'oh dear that's a shame, he probably felt terrible after doing that to me and killed himself. Never mind. What's for lunch?' Honestly Duncan," his eyes begged, "there are too many questions."

"Too many questions is good. It's confusing. It creates doubt. People saw you at the pub, shocked, scuffed, your hand was cut, bruised. But when you heard it was suicide you decided to put the whole thing behind you."

"I feel like shit. Like I really did that to him. I wouldn't. I wouldn't."

"It's a risk," said Duncan. "But…"

Robert put his hands on the table, "If this goes pear-shaped, I could end up in jail. Hah. No. Will. I *will* end up in jail."

Duncan's head was shaking while Robert spoke, "We don't think so. The police who did this want an out. No, they need an out. Your out is their out. I guarantee this will be their offer. They don't want to see some poor straight guy go to jail for killing a," he grimaced, "a poofter. Not when they would rather give you a medal. You even had the decency to go and find help."

The silence between them stretched till Robert found his voice. The words came out flat, "It'd be a lot easier thinking about this, if it was someone else's life."

"We don't see any other way. It can't be them who did it. There were four of them. There's no way that would hold up as gay panic no matter how carefully it was packaged. It wouldn't hold up for *one* of them. This isn't what police officers do."

"And yet this is precisely what they do. And they're getting away with it. Gharrh."

"Another day, another way, Robert. Are you hearing me? Of course, if Harry and I are wrong, and the prosecutor doesn't bring this to you, then you'll have to spell it out for him, for them." Duncan waited for Robert's nod, "Carefully though. Lead them. But for now, don't say anything. Let them come up with it."

"Do I get bail?"

"I'd say for sure, after you make the deal."

Robert shuddered his relief out loud.

"Robert," Duncan's tone changed, "you can't discuss this. No-one knows. You agreed?"

"Lauren?"

"No-one. People can't help themselves. Lip-flapping could de-rail the whole thing." He waited, watching Robert's face. "And of course, you're on leave. Harry's your legal sounding-board."

"What?"

"That's what I was trying to tell you earlier. I can't act for you. No-one can."

Robert's lips turned down and he frowned.

"It's a safeguard. It's *your out*. Trust me. When I leave, I'm telling them you've declined representation."

After Duncan left, Robert sat mute and stunned, until someone escorted him back to his cell.

There, he stared at the walls and bars in turn, clutching onto threadbare strands of reason. He looked up remembering the last time he'd been in a courtroom. What if his judge didn't get the memo, just like Johnny's hadn't. Adrenalin spurted like blood from a cut artery, globs of it splattering the inside of his chest in time with his heartbeat, getting faster and bleeding out into everything. He rocked in time with it, a hand clutching each knee, and tried to breathe past the boulder in his chest. It wasn't working. He sucked harder at the air. *Fuck, fuck, fuck. One, two, three, four... fifteen. One, two, three...*

CHAPTER 41

Robert examined Lauren's eyes. Sleeplessness, hurt, anger and fear were clear. There was something else. Something haughty. He felt her stiffen as his arms went around her, before adjusting her shoulders.

"Can we not talk until we get home?" she said holding up the car keys for him.

He shook his head and got into the passenger side, turning away from the windscreen to the side view. As trees, trucks and tall buildings swished past he counted them into categories.

*

Leaning against the kitchen benchtop, Lauren flicked on the kettle, "Or do you want something stronger?"

"Whatever you want."

"The kids are at your Mum's," she said.

"You OK with that?"

"It's early enough. I didn't have much choice."

"Did she say anything?"

Lauren pursed her lips, "Just that she always knew you weren't 'one of them'. Honestly?"

"So how did she—"

"Know? Well, there's this thing in the living room. A sort of box and when you plug it in and switch it on, people appear, just like they were right there in the room with you."

Robert looked down into his mug, a swirly mix of milky water. He pushed the teabag to the bottom of the cup and watched it try to float back to the surface before pushing it down again.

"It's all over the news, Robert," she put her cup down heavily without lifting it to her lips. "What the hell got into you? I can't believe you'd do something like that. He was your friend."

Holding his tongue still was his only focus. She needed to spew out the questions and comments and judgements and accusations. His job was to hold the bucket.

"Shit. I can barely look at you. Even if you didn't kill him, the fact that you could do what you did. How did you keep quiet about this? No wonder you've been distracted. Hah. Distracted? And all that with Marnie and Jack and Harry. How did you dare? You weaseled yourself into their grief like somehow you belonged in there with them." She visibly shivered, "At least you weren't at the funeral with your fake sad teary face. I feel sick thinking about it. I'm surprised you can look at yourself in the mirror."

She'd been staring at him and turned away.

It gave him time to let the air out.

He thought about how he'd feel if he heard something like this about her. Would he immediately jump to the conclusion that what everyone was saying was true? He liked to think he wouldn't. Maybe he should confide something. Would that help? He unconsciously shook his head, at the same time as she turned back.

"What's that for? Don't you think I've got a right to be angry? I'm furious. This isn't the man I married. This isn't the man I want around my children. Someone who could," she stopped. "Gay panic. Really? That's bullshit. And when I think about how you wormed your way into my—" White hot anger turned to sickening pink shame. "I thought everything was going to be nice. Better. Normal. You knew this was going to happen. Didn't you?"

He looked at her helplessly, Duncan's words repeating themselves, no one can know. No one. "I didn't—"

"Didn't what. Know? Use me?"

"I know it looks bad. But honestly, I wasn't using you."

Her head moved in a slowly repeated no, "Maybe you weren't but I don't know when you're lying any more. Hah! Maybe I never did."

He looked down into the cooling mug of tea and wished it would swallow him.

"I thought about going to Dad's for a while." Her words made him look up. "But then I thought, why should I move out? Disrupt the kids. This is their home. Mine. So, I'm going to get the kids now, and when I get back, I want you gone. I don't want to have to look at you."

Fear and hurt sprang from his eyes. He could feel the damp along with remorse and regret. He lifted his hand to brush them off, but put it back by his side.

"Oh no you don't," she almost shouted, tears springing to her own eyes and her voice catching. "You did this. You! You fix it. This is not on me."

*

After the door slammed behind her, his eyes found their mugs, facing each other, cold and untouched. He poured them into the sink and flushed it clear with tap water, before moving one foot ahead of the other towards the bedroom.

At Emma and Thomas's door he detoured. He picked up sleeping bear and sleeping cow. Touching them made his skin sing for an instant.

He put the toys down on their pillows and turned away.

In his own room his reflection in the mirrored door of the wardrobe confronted him. He flinched recalling Lauren's words and rearranged the sliding doors so he couldn't see himself. His clothes stared back uninterested.

"Shit," he muttered and went back to the hall cupboard for a suitcase.

He started packing things for work and then took them out. He started again, wondering what he needed. *Hah. Besides a new life.*

The suitcase stood next to the front door draped in a suitpack. A plastic shopping bag of shoes propped next to it. He went to the study and took a sheet of paper.

> *Dear Lauren*

He crossed out dear and then crumpled the paper and got a clean sheet.

> *I'll stay at Mum and Dad's. I have something to ask. It's*

extremely (he underlined it) *important for* (he crossed out the trial, and changed it to) *court. If an Alan John Peters calls, please ring me. If you can't reach me. Call Anna. Or Harry. Find out how I can reach him, if you can.*
I don't know what else to say except I'm sorry. I don't know how this is going to turn out, but I never meant to hurt you. I'll update you.
I love you. I love the kids.
R.

He propped the letter against the kettle in the kitchen, trying not to remember the look on Lauren's face.

CHAPTER 42

She'd taken his car. He reversed out of the driveway in hers and pausing for the traffic looked over at the closed front door. An aching cold oozed from the inside of his bones.

Spotting his car still parked in the driveway at his mum and dad's, he u-turned. *Now what?*

He drove unconsciously and found himself in the turning lane for Kangaroo Point and then slowing down at Johnny's apartment. There was a sign outside the building, 'Furnished - To Let', and he pulled over and wrote the number on a scrap of paper he found in the glove box. Then scrunched it into a ball and threw it on the floor. *It would be weird. Wouldn't it? Considering you're supposed to have... stop.* He drove down to the park and turned off the engine. *Anyway, you'll be back at home with Lauren, with the kids, soon. You're disoriented.*

He leaned forward to start the car. An involuntary smile pulling itself into place. *Really? Disoriented? Your whole fucking world's been upended. I feel a bit disoriented.* A soft chuckle bubbled up silently. Then out loud. Quick and jagged, escaping from somewhere around the rock in his chest in rippling bursts. And from nowhere, tears. He sat laughing and crying, hands white-knuckled around the steering wheel.

When the laughter subsided, he let go of the steering wheel, sniffing and looked ahead to the swings. On a whim he got out of the car and went over and sat. Then shuffled back till he was on tiptoe and lifting his legs off the ground, he let the swing carry him forward. With eyes closed, he let it drift back and forth. As it stilled, he stayed there, eyes shut, imagining Johnny sitting there with him on the other swing. Together they were watching what had happened to them both. He felt his bruised heart swell and heard the words, 'Stay here'.

What?

'Stay.'

Here on the swing?

'Fucking dick for brains. No. The apartment. You've still got a key.'

But...

'Talk to Marnie. Go there first.'

Robert got up from the swing still feeling disoriented, but lighter. At the car he turned back. The swings stood side by side. A light breeze breathed across his face. He watched as it moved to the nearby tree. It lifted the leaves. Some of them touched and sighed as they parted.

***

Marnie answered the door, "I wondered when you'd show up?"

Robert blinked, "Really?"

"Nikki said you were coming. Just not when. Beer?"

He looked at his wrist where his watch should be.

"Really?" she said. "Does it matter what time it is?"

Sitting on the verandah watching the sun making its way through the old pines and across the lawn sloping down towards the garden beds around Jack's house, Robert pondered, then, "Did you see the news? Is that why? No. It can't be. If Nikki said... What did she say?"

"When you do things like that you remind me of when we were at school." She looked away from him, back over the lawn, "Do you remember you *not asking* me to the Semi-Formal?"

"I was never really good at that sort of thing."

"I had to drag the invitation out of you. You said, I'm not going. And I said everyone does. You have to. And then you asked me if I was going. If someone had asked me."

"I remember," said Robert. "You said no-one had asked you because they probably thought I had. So I'd better. Because you weren't going by yourself."

"And then I made sure you knew you were taking me to the Formal. Just in case you had any ideas about that."

He sipped his beer and let the bubbles wake up his mouth. It was nice to think about something else.

"Anyway, I'll fill you in," she said, and told him how Nikki kept insisting she call him. "She wouldn't let up. Of course, I couldn't, and I didn't want to say you were in jail. It wasn't till I got cross with her, she told me it wasn't her, it was Johnny."

"You didn't know?"

"I didn't believe her. But I didn't know why she was making things up."

"Except?"

"We were going to box up Johnny's things. We didn't know what to do with them and we didn't want to get rid of…" she looked down. "And Dad thought short-term furnished rental would work, for the apartment, since it's close to the city. Help cover costs. He contacted an agent and they were putting up a sign."

"I just came from there."

"You did?"

"I saw the sign. I even wrote down the number. Then I thought, what did I do that for? I threw it on the floor in the car." He could see her doubt. "Honestly, I can show you."

"You wrote the number down? Why? What's going on?"

"You finish," said Robert. "You haven't told me why you were expecting me."

"OK. Well. Nikki got weepy and more insistent after the sign went up. I did the usual parent stuff, don't be silly, blah blah. But she said we had to wait for you. You were coming over. I said that just wasn't possible, at least any time soon, and she got angry and said you were, and that Johnny said and why wasn't I listening to her."

"So that's when you twigged?"

Marnie nodded frowning, "I had no idea. But after I thought about it, it made sense. She told me about Mum too. Did you know?"

"Mmm yeah, but I didn't know that you didn't know. It's kind of special," he said gently. "Hope she keeps that. Where is she?"

"Sleepover at Grandpa's. They're going to the movies and dinner," she smiled fondly. "And I do too. Hope she keeps it I mean. It's a gift, and it doesn't seem to faze her. She thinks it's normal. So now you. You're here.

Why?"

"Lauren. She can't bear to look at someone capable of…" he looked away.

"She can't think that?" Marnie's voice rose.

"She doesn't know what was happening."

"Even so. She can't think you could turn into a raging violent maniac and attack your friend. That you would even be capable of that. In all the time I've known you I only saw you hit one person."

"Hmmph, I know," said Robert. "Another thing I wasn't good at."

"You were standing up for me," Marnie said.

"But," said Robert, "if I'm honest, it felt rather good. For that first few seconds before he decked me and they all came in and had a go."

They sat, each lost in the past.

Robert remembering trying to dance and noticing Marnie looking at the girl group having fun. He'd insisted she go and join them. She'd said no at first, worried about leaving him alone. And Glen, the big tank from the first fifteen rugby team, chest banging him into the drinks table and *accidentally* spilling Fanta on his shirt, then yanking him with his tie and stabbing at the stain with it. Some of the mums and dads had looked away. Then a mum had tried to rescue him with some paper serviettes.

Glen had grabbed at them saying, 'Thanks. Clumsy.'

He hadn't known who Glen meant, till he'd leaned in saying, 'clean yourself up you dirty queer,' and he'd fumed silently trying not to notice, as people passed laden with drinks and titters.

"You knew it was Glen, didn't you?" he said to Marnie.

"At the formal?" She nodded, "He couldn't keep the gloat off his face. He was a nasty piece of work. I was so glad you were there with me."

"When you said, 'ignore him' and he'd smirked and said, 'do as your little fag-hag says' and done that flick thing where he almost hit your face, I knew ignoring him wasn't going to work. That sort don't let it end there."

"What do you think would have happened if I hadn't gotten that scream out?"

"I was amazed you did. You had three of them holding you," Robert said.

"I had to do something, the other three were laying into you."

"What do you think makes them want to do that?" said Robert. "Why do they want to attack like that? What are they afraid of? That someone gay might fancy them? Or is it just to make themselves feel good. Superior or something."

She didn't say anything for a while, and then, "What upset me just as much, was that dad or whoever, who came out when I screamed for help," she scoffed. "He just looked around and saw you on the ground getting up, and told me off. Missy, he called me. Remember? He said, 'I wouldn't get into the habit of crying wolf, if I were you, missy'. He must've known something was up. He'd just seen half a dozen meaty idiots come outside and then…"

"He didn't want to get involved," said Robert. "He'd have had to confront them, or their parents. Easier to blame the victim. To assume."

"I could talk to her. To Lauren."

Robert's jaw relaxed slightly, "Thanks. No. I don't think now would be a good idea. She's angry. And hurting. And probably worried as hell that I'm going to go to jail. Shit, I am too."

Marnie was quiet.

They sat together that way for a bit longer, then Robert said, "What were your thoughts, when you heard it on the news? Did it cross your mind?"

"That you did it?" She shook her head. "But I've been wondering why you were pushing so hard for an inquest if it was going to be you they'd arrest. Of course *I* know you were pushing, but they don't, the police and whoever. Why didn't you say anything? There's stuff you know, and you've kept it from everyone."

"Yeah, and look where it got me." He faced her. "I was scared. At first it was a mixture of I didn't want anyone to know about me, and if they knew about us, me and Johnny, then… Then Harry. Imagining how he'd… It was bad enough. And the police. They'd deny it. I had no proof. It wasn't going to bring him back. I had to get more information. I had a hundred fucking excuses Marnie. I hoped I could manipulate things behind the scenes and stay hidden. It was all nice and convenient for me. I didn't have to make any choices that would affect my job, or Lauren, Harry, Dad, or anyone. And the longer it went on, the less forgivable it all seemed. I couldn't, I didn't—" he breathed out heavily. "I didn't know how to get myself out. It's like being snagged in a ball of barbed wire in a way. And anyone who comes to help gets ripped to shreds too."

"Look, I get it. The thing with Harry and Johnny. I know about the police. But apart from Lauren, is it just the job?" She took his hand, "You could always retrain. Lots of gay hairdressers, I could put in a good word."

He couldn't help but smile, "Gee, thanks."

"Seriously!"

She went back to subdued, "What were you doing at Johnny's?"

"I planned to stay at Mum and Dad's, but when I got there, Lauren was still there picking up the kids. They were there while she collected me from the lock up. So I drove around and that's where I found myself. Surprisingly. Not."

"You should stay there. It's perfect. It's all set up, and familiar, and you'll need to have some privacy. A phone."

"Hmmph. That's what Johnny said." He said it out loud without meaning to.

"What do you mean?"

"I sat with him in the park, on the swing. He said 'Stay'."

Her head tilted.

"I heard him, Marnie. Clear as a bell. He even called me a dick. Affectionate bastard." And when tears pooled across his eyes he looked towards the clouds, "He said, go and see Marnie."

She reached over for his hand again, lifted it and stroked it. He wasn't expecting to hear an ungracious sounding, "Not fair."

Her eyes were soft, and he knew she wanted to hear Johnny too. He extracted his hand and wrapped her in a hug, "He said he loves you. And thanks."

She sniffed, "Shall I get you the keys?"

He reached into his pocket and pulled out Johnny's Monopoly house key-chain.

She punched him in the arm.

"Marnie?" Robert broke their silence, "I want to apologise."

"What for? There's nothing—"

"No, not for now, except I wonder what would have happened if we'd both been at the ferry stop together. If I hadn't gone back for my watch. That just wrecks me. It was minutes, and…" his voice faltered.

"What actually happened? You never told me. Not exactly."

He told her about the rekindling of their unrequited passion.

How what he'd frozen in time took moments to melt in Duncan's office. How their affair had moved to weekly trysts when Harry re-emerged from hiding. He shared some of the laughs Johnny had at his expense and was able to smile too. He told her how Johnny had declared his life wasn't going to be held to ransom by fear and stupid fucking rules, and a bunch of corrupt cops. He was over it, and looking forward to the future, and that he was actually glad it happened, because it had brought them together. Then he told her about that night, about what he saw at the ferry stop and after. He talked as the sun finished crawling across the lawn and was climbing up the side of Jack's house, and finished with turning up on her doorstep.

They sat together silently.

"I didn't finish," Robert said, "my apology. I'm sorry I wasn't around for you. After Nikki came. It must have been hard, you must've been lonely. And I, Lauren and I, we disappeared. And didn't come back."

"I had Dad. And I had Johnny," she smiled poignant and ironic. And after a pause added, "And you did come back. It's OK. I knew you couldn't be in the same space as him, or me, and keep up the act."

CHAPTER 43

Robert reached towards the lock, then stopped, and stared at the door. This should be like coming home, and he almost conjured the feeling, but part of him felt like he was trespassing. Invading the space of some other Robert, the Robert and Johnny one, which didn't exist without the Johnny part.

Inside, he felt like he was walking through cotton wool.

In the silent heavy haze, he put his suitcase on the bed, and then opened the wardrobe. As he reached to push Johnny's clothes along the rail, his hand paused again. The cotton wool pressed in, whiting out everything. He turned, leaning on the wardrobe door, the heavy weightiness of Johnny's absence pressed down on him. He slid to the floor. The air was too thick. He couldn't breathe it in. And the silence. The silence was unbearable. The damp in his eyes hovered, refusing to fall at first. He rolled to his side, eyes closed, as the tears finally streamed, and he rocked, slow rhythmic and tiny movements. *One, two, three, four... fifteen.* Again. Till the white turned into black-edged red, then dulled to nothing.

When he woke, he called Lauren, gratefully telling the answering machine his number, and that he was in short term accommodation in Kangaroo Point, leaving out that it was Johnny's apartment.

The next call was harder. He interrupted his mum's litany of accusations and complaints, unsurprised that 'putting paid to Dad's chances' came well down the list after 'you're supposed to be coming here, you've ruined my dinner plans', with a firm, "Mum, it's not wasted. Put it in the fridge. I'll pick it up tomorrow. I'm tired, really tired."

He looked at his hands, the ink almost faded. He wondered if she'd even processed his predicament. *Hah. Predicament.* He craved the soothing warmth of a shower, but the thought of Harry or Simon having news about Alan John Peters, sent his hand back for the phone. They had to know how to reach him. The cotton wool was lifting.

*

He quickly unpacked the few grocery items he'd bought with him and took a beer back out of the fridge. The mental list he'd started in the shower needed to be on paper. There wasn't much to write down yet, but the simple fact of holding pen to paper started ideas moving, till they glitched on Duncan's cryptic words about representation. As he flicked the end of the pen, the notion of loophole emerged with 'it's your out'. He put 'talk to Harry' next to it on the list.

Next 'library-research. Gay panic/HAD'. He needed to check everything to do with the preposterous idea that a fuck-off-not-interested wasn't enough; that someone would be tipped into insanity and a blind raging frenzied attack, on the off chance their no-thank-you was ignored. Was it a real thing that people did? How widespread was it? It had never even crossed his mind and now...

'Don't get stuck on this bit. Focus. The list. Come on,' Johnny's words in his ear.

OK.

> *Why me??? fresh leads, new evidence???*
> *Why not AJP? M-I-A!*
> *Why not someone else? Too much work+doctoring more reports?*
> *But... WHY?*
> *Why waste time or effort on a dead poofter?*
> *Seriously— who gives a shit?*
> *The inquest— pointing away from suicide.*
> *People know police were there [AJP arrest]+evidence at inquest*

He got up and poured himself a drink and came back to 'why'.

WHY

He circled it over and over.

> *Why the guilty plea? When they're pushing for not guilty?*

Is this for a precedent?

Have they hurt or killed someone else?

Are they trying to protect someone? Besides themselves?

If this came out, what then?

There'd be a stink? Probably. Maybe not?

His thoughts rolled around on probably. There'd be press coverage. But would the cause become irredeemably visible? There's a chance. If the stink's bad enough who knows, it could lead to… what?

Lines and dots in Robert's brain were joining up.

Case unresolved → another inquest? Trial?

Who? Who would be on trial? Them?!?

He drew a cloud shape around unresolved.

Unresolved=open

They want CLOSED!

Current plan → I plead guilty → not guilty finding

Is this even Possible?

They want: No-one faces any music. They don't. I don't.

Do they really give a shit about me? NO!

They're doing the [looks like] right thing

Evidence:

—multiple police witnesses: me running from scene

—Witness/Pete saying I ran into the pub: banged-up/shit-scared.

BINGO!

—other witnesses? Blue? Drum them up from somewhere!!

Mitigating: for me

—Married/Dad/twins. Creates sympathy

Problem: I'm not at home

Solution: Temporary. Disruptive for wife/children.

—unblemished, likable, suburban professional

—not gay**

—called ambulance/help

→jury busting to let me go

But: guilty plea. No jury!!

Judge only review (any influence? Possibly) → Case closed

"So Johnny," he said to the empty room, "am I up for this? Do we have a choice?"

He lifted the drink to his lips, surprised to find it empty.

In the kitchen he decided that was probably enough alcohol and tipped baked-beans into a saucepan and lowered bread into the toaster, his mind still churning.

The phone ringing surprised him.

As he listened to Harry's voice, his face greyed, "But if Simon's found him, how is that 'doesn't look like good news'?"

"I don't know. He left a message," Harry said. "I wasn't going to call. He said there'd been a rail crossing incident up near Rockhampton. He'd find out more and let us know."

CHAPTER 44

"You holding up?" Simon asked. They were waiting for their coffees at a footpath table outside Tuppy's Takeaway, not far from Johnny's.

Robert felt the sympathy, "Still breathing. I'm not exactly flavour of the month, am I?"

"Not with us liberal minded humanists. The bigots are loving you," Simon's smile faded. "What did your research turn up?"

"Later," Robert waved away the question, "I'd rather hear about yours. Thanks for calling Harry. He rang not long before you did."

"Is he joining us?" Simon adjusted his position on the chair.

"I said I'd fill him in. Are you sure you've found him? Alan?"

Simon nodded, "There were two people in the car when the train hit it. Alan John Peters is dead. The other one is Norman Sparks. Apparently they were friends."

Robert's face tightened, "Fucking great news that is. And someone from the paper called you?"

Simon glared, "No."

"So, if… I'm kind of lost here. Well and truly. How did you find out?"

"By accident. I was doing a follow up story on that rail-crossing incident. The public and the Rockhampton Council are demanding safety barriers. So the Bjelke-Petersen PR team are making it Joh's idea and that he's 'keeping all you Queenslanders safe', when really it's his fault. The state owns the bloody railways for God's sake. Don't get me started. And tragedy sells. I spotted the name."

"I'm gutted. Honestly, I have no idea what the fuck I'm supposed to do now. Do you know anything about this friend? Norm. Can we get hold of him?"

Simon was smiling.

Robert frowned, "You know where he is?"

"He was transported to the PA Hospital. I've just come from there. I thought if I'm going to be there asking questions, I'd throw in a few of my own on your behalf. See if Alan John Peters had told Norm anything. It's the sort of thing people would want to get off their chest."

"And?" Robert leaned forward.

"Well, Norm's been a bit starved for company and loves a yarn," Simon's face became serious. "Sorry, I shouldn't keep you in suspense. I asked him some things about how long they'd known each other. Not long. But they had similar interests. Pubs. And were a similar age. They were heading south to Sarina, to see if there was any work in the sugar mill."

Simon looked at Robert intently, "Then I said did you know if Alan had any family? Where he was from. Did he have any story? He had a story all right, Norm said. I didn't suspect anything at first, but he kept slipping into I, when he should have been saying he. I pretended not to notice."

"Did he say anything about that night?"

"I said loves a yarn, didn't I?" Simon's pause for effect was brief. "He said his mate Alan had been unceremoniously dumped outside a petrol station with none of his possessions by a couple of crooked cops. They gave him fifty bucks from their nightly takings and a warning not to show his face in Brisbane again. Then he went on to tell me about them laying into someone. That he, well, Alan, had seen and heard everything that happened, just acted like he was drunk as a skunk. Apparently it's what you do if you're picked up."

Robert's frown deepened.

"If the cops think you're wasted, they don't lay into you. No fun in it. He said he made them practically carry him into the station, and they had to prop him up for fingerprints. The surprise came afterwards, when they dragged him out of his cell, shoved him in the car, and drove for hours." Simon looked up, "It's called abduction. Anyway, I let him talk on. And then he remembered I'm a reporter, and he'd spilled his guts. I played it down. Said my paper wasn't interested in what happened to Alan, poor bugger. Asked a few more questions about the accident."

"What about Norm's family? Wouldn't they know it wasn't him?"

Robert asked.

Simon shrugged, "Probably. I don't think Mr Peters would have been thinking about that. He must have swapped their driver's licences or taken Norm's, when he had a chance."

"Did you tell him about me? Do you think he'll help us? Me?"

"I wouldn't push him. He's got someone else's ID for a reason," said Simon. "You don't want him to disappear, do you? I'll go and see him again. His leg was pretty bad, obviously, or he wouldn't be here in a Brisbane hospital. He'll be there for a bit longer I'd say."

"But you're going back to see him?"

"That's one of the things I wanted to talk to you about."

Robert looked up as their coffees arrived. They sugared and stirred and Simon continued, "He's going to need somewhere to stay when he gets out."

"Have you got any suggestions?" Robert asked.

"Thought you might look into that. Then I'd have something to talk to him about."

"Not like I've got anything else to do." The joke fell over.

"Speaking of, your research? How'd it go?"

"Yet to find anything where the defendant got off scott-free. That's a worry." Robert rubbed his forehead, "Interesting though, gay panic doesn't hinge on insanity now. Homosexuality was dropped from the DSM-II back in 1973." He answered Simon's look, "Medical classification index. It's not a psychological or psychiatric condition anymore. And on the back of that, you'd expect gay panic to go away. But instead, it morphed."

"Meaning?"

"Meaning, it started as a Freudian thing. Submerged latent homosexual feeling, along comes someone gay, wham, you act out violent self-hatred by attacking the other person."

"And now?"

"Now, it's justifiable homicide on the back of provocation, with an understandable loss of normal self-control." He waited, "Assuming you're a reasonable man, which in legalese is a person of ordinary firmness. Do you think I'd pass for a person of ordinary firmness?"

"Whatever the fuck that means," Simon's head moved from side to side.

"I can't see how the hell they think the plea will lead to an acquittal. A reduced sentence for manslaughter or aggravated assault depending on jeez, any number of things. And still it would be a maybe."

"Tell me," said Simon, "in a similar vein, wouldn't you be perjuring yourself by saying you did it? I know this was sprung on you, but?"

"No. It's a plea. I wasn't under oath for that. It will depend on the questions they ask me in court. It will be perjury if I lie on the stand. But, now I think of it," a look of surprised relief passed over Robert's face. "That's it. Shit. I'm getting it. They'll be steering the questions in the direction they want. Honestly, I should have seen this. My head's constantly being hijacked by my emotions." He twisted his lip in a wry smile, "I'm pretty close to this defendant."

Simon made a face too, "Isn't that why you're supposed to have a lawyer?" He shrugged. "Your choice. But from where I sit, if you do have second thoughts about this plea, you can't let them know."

Robert stirred more sugar into his cappuccino.

"I think you already did that mate," Simon reached over and shifted Robert's cup away. "Sorry, it's annoying. But seriously, they can't find out. Anything supporting you will go up in smoke." He looked at Robert intently, "I can't help feeling that they're just setting you up. Royally."

"I hope to God you're wrong."

CHAPTER 45

Turning away from the microfiche articles, Robert rubbed his eyes, then scanned the rows of books and worn timber banks of catalogue cards in the library, unseeing. His thoughts were full of the idea that people thought he was one of the monsters he'd been reading about. He imagined his face, haggard and startled, flashing across the TV screen, while people balanced dinner plates on their laps, believing they were getting the truth. He wondered what the newsreader thought of it all behind his serious avuncular smile?

As bad as those thoughts were, they had nothing on the shame which surfaced when he remembered the look on Lauren's face, and imagined the same look on the faces of his friends, family, colleagues, Johnny's friends.

He got up wearily. He'd chance it that Harry was home and if not, he'd go and see Ernie. *Hopefully he doesn't hate me yet.*

Robert's mood lifted when he found a parking space near Harry's, and after pushing the button and waiting and repeating, he shrugged. Ernie's it was. He walked, fast. Blood pumping without adrenaline was a welcome change. And once he'd arrived the rich casserole smell and the scent of fresh bread made his stomach gurgle.

He dropped some money into the donation box and headed, tray in hand, towards an unoccupied table, before surprising himself with a change of direction, "Mind if I sit here?"

It was a relief to hear someone else's story. But it was sobering too. The randomness and coincidences, and human frailty, ensnaring people into a life of no fixed abode, no money, no washing machine, shower, toilet, privacy, trying to hold up a diminishing self-esteem.

After listening for a while, Robert ventured, "If I was some rich person, and said here, you can live in this house, no cost, everything in it, would you?"

"Why?" The man turned to face him, and Robert noticed the specks of grey in the pores of his skin. "Why are you asking?"

"I don't know. I suppose I always thought," Robert stopped. "Would you take me up on it?"

"Honestly mate, I don't like to think about it. It would be heaps easier. But wishing for something to be different? Easier to not go there."

"That's kind of defeatist though, isn't it?"

"Wadda you want me to say?" His head followed his eyes around the room. "I'd wanna share it with them. And not all of them are on the straight and narrow. Booze, drugs, things to take away the pain. Stuff in your nice house would go missing, get broken. I'd get thrown out. It's a lot harder to sleep on a bench after you're used to something softer."

Robert looked away.

"But look, thanks for asking. Most people just assume."

"Yeah. We're pretty good at that," said Robert. "Assuming."

"So, what's your story?"

Robert mirrored his table-mate's manner, "You don't wanna know. And looks can be deceptive. You probably think nice clothes, good looking, haha." He was rewarded with an echoing chuckle. "But my whole world just turned inside out, and honestly, I haven't got a clue."

The man nodded getting up, "Oh well, anyway, eat up. Good tucker eh? Barry. My name's Barry."

"Same as my dad."

"Must be a good bloke then."

Robert nodded. He'd never really thought about his dad as a good bloke. He reached over and took Barry's hand, "Robert."

"Well, Robert," Barry said, "you ever need any pointers, you'll find me here, sooner or later. I like the tucker here."

Robert smiled watching Barry turn to shuffle away, and blurted, "Barry, hey. Wait up."

Barry turned back.

"You've been coming here a while haven't you?"

Barry leaned against the chair and nodded.

"You ever come across someone called Alan?"

Barry shrugged, "Should I?"

"He lived over in Kangaroo Point. The ferry shelter. It was only on the off-chance."

"No. I do. I get over to the Gabba sometimes and the pubs around there. Bit cheaper that side of town."

"So you'd know him if you saw him?" Robert kept his voice calm.

"Expect so. Why?"

"It's sort-of got to do with someone. He used to volunteer here."

"The kid with the dog. Yeah. Sad. Some bastard, killing him because he's a woolly." Barry caught Robert's puzzlement. "Woolly. Woolly-woofter, poofter. Ernie told me," Barry scoffed. "They don't hurt no-one."

Robert put his spoon down.

"That boy was a gentleman. Ask anyone here. I'd like to get whoever did it and give them a taste of their own medicine. See how they like it. Only I'd let him live. Bastard," Barry spat the word.

Robert tried not to flinch.

Ernie's appearance broke the chill that had settled on their exchange, "Robert," he said, "what are you doing here?"

Robert started to get up, "I came to, actually, I was just leaving."

"No," said Ernie, giving Robert's shoulder a not so gentle squeeze. "Sit yourself down. You owe me an explanation. Catch you later Barry."

Robert watched Barry go, nervous now, but if there was anyone he could tell the story to, it would be Ernie. He must have heard them all.

CHAPTER 46

Getting everything off his chest into Ernie's open non-judgmental ears was cathartic. but the relief was wearing off. Duncan's words, 'don't tell anyone', thrummed through him with each heavy footfall and by the time he'd walked back to the car parked near Harry's, the guilt and anxiety meter was notching up again. He pushed the call button to Harry's apartment searching for distraction as much as guidance.

Harry listened to all Robert's what-if and could-be scenarios and talked them through in several wine-lubricated exchanges.

"Do you mind me asking a personal question," Robert swirled the glass watching the liquid ride up the sides.

Harry waited, his eyes not specifying yes or no; something he was good at.

"I don't want to pry." Robert hesitated. "But I was wondering, the cancer, are you going to be OK?"

Harry swirled his glass too, "Yes and no. Apparently I'll be around for a bit longer." He took a swallow. "When I first found out, they weren't that hopeful and like I said, I didn't want Johnny nursing me like some old man. Although if you think about it," his eyebrows arched.

Robert shook his head.

"You're a kind person Robert," Harry said. "I was pretty sick. I, well, you know. Anyway, they're giving me three to five years. Maybe more."

"Are you OK with that?" He shook his head again, "Stupid question. I'm thinking more and more about these kinds of things."

"To be expected." Harry's brows knitted, "I know I told you, I didn't mind at all about you and Johnny. The treatment, well you know. Of course, I didn't want it in my face, who would? But as I said, it made me happy knowing he was happy. I'm sorry that it's all turned into this."

"Like it's your fault." Robert looked down then back at Harry, "You know, Johnny didn't even mind about the court thing anymore. Did he tell you? He was happy. He had you. He loved you, you know. I had Lauren. We kind-of had each other. It wasn't about right or wrong with him. It was, I don't know, I miss him Harry, I know it's not really my prerogative, I," Robert looked over at Johnny's partner, lover, friend, benefactor, through a winey haze.

"I do too," Harry pinched his nose. "He was, he taught me to not take myself so seriously. To live a little. I've decided to make the most of things now." He raised his glass, "To—"

As Johnny's name trembled at the edge of Harry's lip, they both turned to the door and without being buzzed up or in, Duncan stepped over the threshold looking like he'd stuck his paw in a trap and couldn't figure out why he wasn't moving.

"Well," Harry sniffed back the emotion, "that was well timed. I was just saying to Robert, that Johnny taught me to lighten up and live a little and in you walk," Harry smiled.

"Are you here for dinner?" Duncan was still recovering, "I have enough."

Robert's bottom lip hung loosely, "I…"

"You might as well stay," Harry said. "Duncan's been trying to reach the very high bar set by Johnny in terms of keeping me fed. Not one of my many talents, but something I hold very dear."

"I never imagined you were into food," Robert was trying to ignore the clamouring questions in his head. In particular, why are you even here?

"I raised a child. I had to cook. Where do you think Lauren got it from?" It could have been a friendly bark.

Duncan headed into the kitchen with his groceries, while Harry watched Robert's face broadcasting the questions playing tag in his mind. Was Johnny's gaydar right? They went to Cairns together. Was that when this started?

Harry chuckled, "I'd love to give you an instant replay of your face."

Robert looked over, stricken with guilt.

226

"Duncan doesn't know about you and Johnny, does he?" Harry asked. Robert shook his head.

"Fair enough. I won't say anything. Unless…"

"I know it's going to come out. We've talked the whole thing through," said Robert. "But it would be a bit awkward. Lauren…"

Harry shrugged, "He can hardly hold the moral high ground."

"So are you two?" Robert let the question ask itself.

"Oh God," Harry chortled softly. "How about I finish a sentence. Are we in a relationship? Yes and no. We might have been, if we'd been able to. But as you know, being a lawyer or a judge in the making, and gay, has some danger attached. He married Lauren's mum and broke my heart. When she died, I'll admit, I held hopes. Now I'm just happy to have a friend and someone I don't have to pretend not to be gay with."

Robert reformatted his face while he thought. His head making the same little forward movements he gave his clients when they had poured their version of the truth into the ocean of doubt that separated them from what was on the other side, and he was reassuring them it was OK to dive in and swim towards it.

"Do you think I should tell Duncan?" Robert asked.

"Put it this way," Harry said, "from what we discussed earlier, he's going to know soon enough. If you come out now, he might be more help to you."

"But what if the gay panic plea works?"

"What if it doesn't?" Harry said.

"Do you think he only suggested I go along with it because he thinks I'm straight?"

"Possibly," Harry frowned. "More like definitely. But it was me who suggested it. You needed time to find Mr Peters."

"I need to tell him, don't I?" It wasn't a question.

"Do you want me to leave you two alone?"

"No," Robert didn't pause to think before it came out. Then, "Maybe. What do you think?"

"Honestly Robert, I think, it's about time we all stopped pretending there was something wrong with us. Gay isn't a disease, it isn't a handicap, and it isn't a choice. It just is."

Robert stood.

"You might even encourage my friend in there to think about it." Harry's chin pointed towards the kitchen.

"Really? He doesn't know?" Robert's brow knitted.

"It's not about do you know. It's about do you want to know. Do you want to be honest about yourself. With yourself. Did you?"

"No," said Robert. "I mean, I think I always knew. I just didn't want to know. I remember when I was eleven, some boys were, were teasing my best friend and me, calling us poofters. My friend was in the water, he had an asthma attack and died. I couldn't," Robert stopped and pressed his thumb and forefinger against the bridge of his nose. "I asked my mother, what a poofter was. The look on her face." He took a long breath, "I'd convinced myself they were wrong until Johnny. That's when I knew. But I still kept it to myself."

They let that sit for a while.

"Did you?" Robert asked.

"Always know?" Harry asked. "It was even harder for my generation, and I liked girls. Their beauty, their gracefulness. I couldn't figure out why I didn't like to be in bed with them. My family pushed me into law. I'd have much preferred architecture or fashion."

"Am I going to spend all night in the kitchen without any libation or company?" Duncan's voice interrupted them.

Harry chuckled, "Coming dearest, friend." He headed kitchen-ward, whispering into Robert's ear as he passed, "I know we said tell no-one, but that was before. We needed time. Do it now."

Robert gulped and followed Harry to the doorway where he didn't pause, "Duncan. There's something you ought to know."

Duncan turned away from Robert, to the cutting board and the colour-categorized mounds of julienned vegetables. He picked up the knife. Robert's eyes found something profoundly interesting on the floor. Duncan put the knife down and turned back to Robert, "Does my daughter have any idea?"

"Lauren," *my wife* Robert corrected silently, "has no idea. At least not from me. I didn't think it would be at all helpful. I thought, why spoil a perfectly good marriage and friendship. I didn't plan any of this Duncan. Hah, that's obvious."

"Understandable," Harry ventured, looking meaningfully at Duncan. "No one deliberately tries to hurt the people they love."

Duncan wasn't accepting anything, "How can you?" He shook his head and turned towards the refrigerator, pulling at the handle. The contents of the door rattled in protest. He thrust a bottle towards Harry saying, "Make yourself useful," and turned back to his vegetables, picked up the knife again and changing his mind again, turned back to Robert, "How *could* you?"

Robert's tone was even and quiet, "Honestly, I thought you'd picked up on it several times, recently. Hand on heart, come on, can you say truthfully that you didn't twig?"

Duncan's shoulders lifted in an uneasy shrug.

"I can totally understand why you wouldn't want to," Robert said.

"What's that supposed to mean?" Duncan came back.

"Nothing," Robert looked at Harry, but he was busy with the corkscrew. "Nothing at all."

In the silence, Duncan turned back to the chopping board.

"I took it to mean that you'd be concerned for Lauren. But," Harry finally chimed back in, brandishing the bottle, now free of its constraints, and pouring, and forcing Duncan to turn back. "What he's really saying my dear, is that sometimes we don't want to know things about ourselves, our faults, hidden desires and agendas, much less share them with other people. And that sometimes," he waited, "the things we don't see in others are the same things we refuse to see in ourselves."

"I'm not gay," Duncan's words reminded Robert of Thomas and Emma at bedtime, 'I'm not tired' while they were sullen, argumentative and slightly hysterical with the effort of keeping their eyes open. He almost smiled, till the memory of teenage Robert surfaced, making the same declaration, to Marnie, and to Johnny.

"Have it your way, my dear," indulgent irony infecting Harry's smile, "but can we eat any time soon?"

"Fifteen minutes, if you help."

Robert watched them from the other side of the island bench, surprised for the second time today to find he was starving. Unnecessarily so. Something had shifted with Harry's words. He thought about Lauren not seeing Duncan's gay and not seeing his gay. *Is that a word? Your gay? Your gayness?* He pictured Tank looking like a blue-sequined princess. *Your highness. Haha.* Perhaps it was the alcohol making it funny. "Hahaha," it was a minor chuckle, signifying amusement not hilarity.

"What's so funny?" Duncan turned away from the stove.

"Maybe Lauren doesn't see gay, because it isn't a thing for her. It's sort of normal. I mean, I'm not *gay*, gay. And they say women go for men like their fathers."

Duncan's face masked in horror, and Harry's mouth turned into a smile, he pointed at Duncan's face and giggled, a happy, carefree, exuberant giggle, "Oh, my dear Duncan," Harry's eyes watered and Duncan could no longer maintain his icy stance, and melted into an amused tolerance. Then a small chuckle bubbled up.

Robert watched them, a bemused smile hovering for a moment longer, before joining them.

CHAPTER 47

On his way to his parents' place, Robert almost turned around twice. Last night hadn't been as hard as he imagined, but fear had been tempered by the consumption of alcohol and the presence of Harry. Did he really need to do this now? Would telling the people closest to him his 'I've been meaning to tell you something' story, ahead of the planned big reveal in court, make any difference to what they thought of him? Did that even matter? Last night's one-hundred-and-eighty degree shift from 'don't tell anyone' had been disorienting, even though it made sense. And after reflecting on it this morning with a coffee or two, it was still making sense.

For him to be able to claim that he was gay and wouldn't have hurt Johnny, those closest to him would have to be able to corroborate his—*what?* He couldn't help smiling. *For corroborating his gayness.* He wondered if there was another word that he didn't know about and then smiled again. *Who gives a fuck?*

Barry's golf clubs were waiting patiently at the bottom of the stairs. Good. Robert turned into the driveway and parked behind his dad's car, perversely imagining at least his dad would have to speak to him, even if it was only to say 'on your way out of my sight, please remove your car, I have to go whack a little white ball around the countryside and pretend it's you.'

"Put the kettle on, Love," his dad ordered, unnecessarily, since Jeannie was already at the sink, kettle in hand. Robert air-kissed her cheek. It wasn't intentional. The cheek was whisked out of reach a split second before his lips were due to land.

"Haven't got long, mate," said Barry.

Robert looked up hiding a cynical half-smile and listened to Johnny, 'Let it go. Be nice. This isn't about you. OK. It is today. But did you ever stop to think he might be so busy with his mates because you make it so bloody hard for him to be nice to you?'

Thank you, Johnny.

"This to do with your court appearance?" Barry tried moving things along, "Bit of a palaver. You all right?"

Jeannie almost patted his shoulder, turning it into a wipe, "Well," she said, "I'm proud of you. What a nasty horrible shock. Groped by that, that... prowling the streets, he could have molested a child if you hadn't come along and stopped it. AIDS too. Can you be sure he didn't infect you? I'd hate—"

"Mum," Robert interrupted her, "Stop. Seriously? You think I could do that? Really?"

"The tea, Love," Barry searched Robert's face as she turned back to the teapot. They held each other's gaze while Jeannie fussed with cups and milk and sugar.

"It does have something to do with the hearing. Sort of. Dad, Mum, there's something I've been meaning to tell you."

After he'd finished speaking, Barry reached for the torn golf glove packet sitting on the table between him and Robert. He picked it up and stepped towards the bin. Jeannie looked at him, wary. Cleaning up was her job.

She opened her mouth, clamped it shut and then it opened, "Leave." It was clear, brittle and bitter.

Father and son both looked at her.

"Didn't you hear me? I said leave. Your sort, you're not welcome here. I don't want you here. I won't have it. No more! If it wasn't for you, your father wouldn't be stuck on the backbench. He'd be somebody. He's been overlooked for years. How could they promote him with you lurking in the shadows? I should never have indulged you."

The two men stared at her.

"I could've been the wife of a Minister, even the Premier. You've spoilt everything."

"I don't think so, Love," Barry said. "Come on. No need for this."

She turned on him, "It's your fault. You never did anything to encourage him. If you'd been a better father. Been there. But no. You were too busy out playing with your mates. You had no time for him. For us."

Robert's eyes found his safe place.

"Come on now, Love. Take it easy," Barry soothed.

"Get out. Get. Out! OUT," she glared at Robert. Her arm stopped poking towards the backstairs kitchen door as she turned for the insides of the house.

Barry took a moment longer then followed her.

Robert picked up their cups, tipped them into the sink, rubbed them with a soapy dishmop and rinsed them with fresh water. After placing them into the draining rack, he stared at the three of them, all matching, perched next to each other, and let himself out.

He was reversing out of the driveway when the tap on the window halted him.

"Got a minute?" said Barry.

"Have you, dad?"

"Don't be like that, son."

Robert's eyes watered. Son.

In his refuge under the house, Barry extracted two beers, taking the tops off with the opener guarding the fridge door from a piece of string.

"Not a word," Barry said. "It's five o'clock somewhere and I want to celebrate. They can play without me today." His spare arm waved at the golf clubs, "Probably be pleased as punch. Might even win for a change." The question mark on Robert's face was answered after a hefty slug, "I'm bloody hopeless at golf." Barry huffed out a half chuckle, "Don't look so surprised."

A beer on top of yesterday's consumption was enough for Robert but Barry, having found his son, wanted a few more. It was only after a promise to at least try golf with another uncoordinated but ever earnest player, that Robert was close to release. That and his confession that Lauren was the only significant other he had yet to tell.

"You can't be serious," Barry's rebuke stung.

"I needed some practice," he said, thinking about the scorn and revulsion he'd last seen on Lauren's face.

"You know," said Barry, "I always sort of suspected. I remember when I came to your room. I didn't know who was more embarrassed. I think it was me. You know. The birds and the bees chat?"

"That never actually happened?" said Robert. "I know," he looked at Barry sheepishly, "I told you we'd learned about 'all that' in biol."

Barry chuckled, "And then I'd made my escape. I said something like 'I'll turn off the light, eh?' I could tell you were going to ask me something." He thought for a moment, "I'm sorry."

Robert waited.

"I didn't want you to change schools. Your mum had you at Grammar after that thing with your friend."

"It wasn't 'that thing' Dad. He died. Terry died."

"She said you couldn't stay there. You had no friends."

"She was right. I didn't."

"I didn't know," said Barry.

"You could have."

"I should have. I know." Barry was silent for a moment, "I insisted you couldn't stay there. An all boys' school. But your mum was insistent too. She went to St Rita's and I went to Villanova. She wanted you to be one better. I was adamant you wouldn't do well there." He took a breath, "That's how you ended up at State High. Courtesy of your brains and your speed and the little bit of clout I had with the Education Minister at the time. But Marnie. When she came along, I thought you two were, you know. Then Lauren. When that happened, I was going whew, at least I didn't put my foot in it."

Robert sat quietly lifting his beer to his mouth. They both did.

"Dad," Robert said, "did you know about Terry?"

Barry put an elbow onto the armrest of the chair and stroked the side of his face, "Not straight away. I dragged it out of your mother when we were arguing about your school situation. She said you'd been bullied. And she said Terry had an asthma attack and died, and you didn't want to go back to that school, you know? Without your friend."

"She didn't know what really happened, because she never asked,"

Robert said. "No-one knows. I never told anyone."

"I'd like to hear," said Barry.

He started then, with Terry and how they'd met, in the boys' toilets when they were only seven. How the boys who'd terrorized him, had terrorized Terry too. How he'd found Terry, pink faced with shame, and crying with his shorts and his hair wet, sitting in the cubicle, his eyelashes tear-glued to his face. How he'd thrown away Terry's torn underpants, and washed his shorts and scrunch dried them in the rolling cloth hand-towel dispenser. And how Terry had said, they called me Ter-ry the Fer-ry and don't tell your dad. If you tell him, it will be worse next time. And then he asked if we were going to be best friends."

Robert took a moment to breathe, "And we were, dad."

"I know," said Barry smiling. "I was surprised when he wasn't home for your birthday tea. Eleven. I was all cheery. It was the day Joh was sworn in and I got a Ministry. Big day. I had no idea he'd died."

"Yeah," said Robert, "neither did I. Not then. That night, you asked where he was. He wasn't invited. Mum didn't say that to you. She said, that boy has a home of his own. And her mouth had smiled. She never liked him. He knew that. I remember asking him if he minded about it. I was looking at the sky not really wanting to hear the answer. He said he didn't care. He was my friend, not hers."

"He had something, that boy," Barry's eyes turned soft. "A special kind of knowing innocence. Maybe I'm romanticizing. I don't know. I liked him."

"He could tell," said Robert, "that you liked him. Anyway, at dinner, Mum started asking about your day, your maiden speech and whether you called the Premier, Joh, or not. I got really angry. I was trying to tell you what happened."

"The potato. I remember," said Barry. "You stabbed a piece of chicken and your fork screeched across the plate. Made a god-awful sound." He shook his head. "The potato skidded onto the tablecloth. You looked at your mother like she was going to send you to the tower."

"Hmph, or my room at least," Robert remembered the strained sound of happy birthday, and blowing out the candles quickly so the melting wax didn't spoil the icing. Terry had said the only good thing about pumpkin cake was the icing. His mum had said she'd pack an extra piece for him for little lunch. For Terry. And he should go to bed. That he looked tired.

As they kissed him goodnight, he felt like a tropical storm had failed to materialize and the air was thick and hot inside him. A cloud needed to crack open. At the door, he turned to try again, but they were on their own island in the sunshine.

"Anyway," said Robert, coming back, "according to mum, it was *your* special day because eleven doesn't count as special, so Terry bought some lollies. We went to the park, to Glindeman Creek to have our own little party after school. We sat on the rocks dangling our feet and ended up in the water, sliding around on the mossy rocks. It was only knee high.

"I got out first," said Robert, "and went to get our shoes and socks, over near our bikes, and saw the boys coming. I didn't know their names, but I knew exactly who they were. Six of them.

"I called out to Terry, to hurry up.

"They dumped their bikes and looked down at Terry's back. He was adjusting his shorts while he turned around.

"I shouted at them to leave us alone.

"The biggest one shouted, 'Gonna make me?' and they all laughed.

"Someone said, 'What's going on here? You two poofs?' I didn't know what it meant. It sounded nasty.

"They snickered. I was willing Terry not to get out. I knew he'd need help and they'd make fun of him. But he tried, and slipped back in. He made a kind of strangled squawking noise.

"The biggest boy leaned forward and said, 'Here. Wanna hand?' and Terry hesitated then took it. He was angled upwards at forty degrees when the boy let go and Terry fell backwards into the creek. His coughing was almost drowned out in their laughter.

"They thought it was hilarious.

"When the laughing died down, Terry's cough seemed louder. And one of them said 'I wanna leak,'. I think it was the big loud one again, and they all lined up on the rocks and pissed on him. On Terry."

"What kind of..." Barry's voice trailed off.

Robert continued, "The ring-leader wiggled his hips, shaking off the drips and said 'This what yous were playing?' and they all started wiggling and laughing.

"I called out 'Stop it. Stop it', and ran towards them.

"The one closest, pushed me over, straddling my chest. I closed my eyes but I could feel something squishing up against my face. I bucked trying to get him off me, but another boy sat on my... On my... groin, and started gyrating. Then I heard this voice in my ear, 'You like that, don't you?' and the other boy shouted, 'Look! He's got a fat. Little poofter.'

"I didn't even know what they were talking about Dad," Robert's voice caught.

Barry's head moved gently up and down, the rest of him still, except the tears invisibly moving up to the surface.

"They jeered. All of them. And the boy stuck his hands into my shorts and started—"

Robert's eyes dampened, he breathed out heavily, "I twisted my head away, so they couldn't see me crying and I saw Terry scrambling out while they were distracted with me. One of them was reaching to help him. I was so... so hopeful, you know?"

Barry continued nodding into the pauses.

"But the big loud boy saw too, 'Whaddo-ya think you're doing?' he said, and the other one, who was trying to help, said, 'I just thought—' but the loud one cut him off with a shove. And then he started on Terry, 'And where do *you* think you're going? You worried you're gonna miss out?' and his chin jutted towards me. And then he was in the water. He stood next to Terry, his hand extended outwards.

"I remember I whispered, 'Thank God.'

"But the hand spread over Terry's face and pushed him under."

Barry sucked in a breath.

"I held my breath," said Robert. "I let it out when Terry's face came up out of the water. And Terry was gasping, trying to get some air in, and then started coughing.

"And the hand pushed him under again."

"Jesus," said Barry.

"I called out, 'Stop. Please. Stop. You're hurting him. Please,' and I started to cry, really sobbing. And the boy shouted at me, 'Shut the fuck up you little cissy.' And then Terry's face came up again wild-eyed. They were all laughing again. But there was this noise. A scraping sound, like someone raking stones. Except it wasn't. It was Terry.

"And they slowly stopped laughing. And the loud boy stepped back. He shoved his old-fellah back in his shorts. They all did. And they rode off, and the big one half-turned back and shouted, 'Nothing happened here. Understand?'"

Robert looked into the distance before continuing.

"And I got back into the water and hauled Terry up against the side of the rock. I scrunched his fingers around a plant and told him to hang on.

"Then I climbed out and pulled him further up, and got his puffer. He'd told me dad, if ever I can't breathe just get some of this into me. I tried to get his lips around it. They were kind of bluey-gray like when you're really cold.

"I squeezed the puffer. My hands were shaking. Maybe I wasn't doing it right, I remember shouting at him to breathe it in, and my eyes were blurring. I blinked, looking down at the water, trying to clear them, and saw the rest of the lollies, bright and colourful, almost cheerful sitting on the mud, and feeling this horrible weight pressing in on me, and all I could think was, Terry will be OK. I kept repeating it in my head, Terry will be OK.

"I told Terry I was going to get help. I'd get his dad. And I ran back to school."

Robert looked at the empty beer in his hand and put it down.

"The principal's secretary tried to stop me, but I burst past her desk, shouting into the open doorway of his office, 'Mr Sullivan. It's Terry.' A chair scraped.

"I remember saying stuff, but it felt like all the words were mushed together. Then I heard, 'Call an ambulance. Where? Where to?' And a hand on my shoulder. Mr Sullivan's. Heavy. Tense, 'Where?'

"When we got to the creek, Mr Sullivan knelt, lifting Terry into a hug, then laying him back down. He breathed his air into Terry. And I breathed in too. Then he pushed on Terry's chest. One, two, three, four, five...

"I counted to fifteen. Then more air. Then pushing one two three... over and over until the ambulance came and put Terry on a stretcher and took them both away.

"After that, I got our bikes and stuff and walked home."

When Robert finished talking, his dad put his face in his hands, and didn't say anything for a moment. Then he blinked, shaking his head, "Oh Robert, I'm sorry. I had no idea. I'm so sorry, Son."

There it was again. Son.

Robert breathed in. A slow breath. And the cords in his neck loosened as his eyes teared up again.

CHAPTER 48

The kids were all over him like a rash, and after the trauma of his revelation to his dad, his heart was flying in what felt for now, like safe air-space. The three of them bounced around on the trampoline, till the syncopated body dumps gradually coalesced into a tumble of arms and legs and joyful contentment.

Lauren came out with Kool-pops, and they sat on the trampoline mat, legs dangling between the springs attaching it to the frame, bobbing softly, and sucking loudly on the frozen cordial. Slowly, Robert's pink faced enthusiasm drained under Lauren's icy stare.

"Hurry up you two, faces clean and nap time."

"Will Daddy be here when we wake up?" said Thomas concentrating on the last of his coloured ice.

Emma looked from one parent to the other.

"We'll see," said Lauren.

"I'll take them in," said Robert.

"Don't be long." It wasn't overly harsh or cold, but definitely not warm.

When he came back, tea was waiting on the verandah at the front of the house, overlooking the street through the leaves of the purple flower tree. Not purple. Mauve. Jacaranda. Between the cork coasters, out of reach of any spills was a yellow Kodak envelope. Robert's heart hammered and he resisted the urge to turn around.

"It was in the box of things Anna brought over from your office. Dad thought it would be better to clear your personal stuff," she said when he sat down. "I thought it was pictures of the kids, or I wouldn't have opened it."

He reached over and picked it up, looking in and then looking at her

240

face. Her eyes weren't angry or sad. They were blank.

"I came over to talk to you about that."

"Did you?" she said. "And, what exactly were you planning to say?"

"Honestly, I—"

"Please Robert. Honestly? That's the word you are using?" she looked out over the front yard.

"Sorry, I," he stopped, put the photos back where she'd originally placed them, looked at the tea, and reached over for it. She turned to face him, and he knocked the cup. They both watched the wave crescendo over the lip and splosh into a pool around the darkened cork.

"Honestly Robert!"

He disappeared into the house and came back with some paper towel.

"What is it?" she said. "Is this whole clumsy uncoordinated incompetence a diversion. Something to hide behind?"

He looked down at the brown-stained soppy coaster.

"You let me think you were some kind of violent depraved," she petered out. "That I'd married someone who could do that to another human being. You never said a word. Was keeping your secret life so important you couldn't—"

"I didn't—"

"Didn't what? Didn't think to tell me? Didn't think I'd notice? I think you need to let me finish. I'll tell you when you can talk."

He stared at the cup on the damp coaster. Lauren picked it up and handed it to him.

"This whole time, you were pretending. Was this, us, the kids, some kind of game?" her retreating anger was regaining traction. "I'm angry, I'm hurt. Humiliated. What did you think? Or didn't you? I thought I married a lovely caring gentle man. Someone kind, like my dad. Now, I don't know who I married. I don't know who you are. Has this been forever? Am I a completely gullible idiot? Am I the only one who doesn't know? Is my whole life a bloody sham?"

The questions came at him like fists.

"When I think about our little holiday. I was so happy. I thought you'd sorted yourself out, you were getting over the grief. I'm... I feel cheap and used and dirty. Like some second rate stand in. How could you do this?

How could you?"

Robert alternated looking up through the leaves and down at his hand clutching the cup, and away from her eyes.

When the silence was long enough, he thought she'd forgotten to say he could speak. He opened his mouth but the apology was mislaid. "I love you," he said. "Always have. I don't know what to say." He paused. "I don't know who I am. What I am. I didn't do that to Johnny. I'm sorry I let you think that. I thought, part of me thought I was protecting you, and the kids. But honest—" he cringed and changed words. "I have to be truthful... I didn't want people knowing who I am. *I* didn't know." His eyes found a gap in the leaves, "I didn't know, because I didn't want to know. And you made it so easy. You were, are, so perfect. When I did finally figure it out, I didn't want to hurt you. And Johnny didn't want to hurt Harry. We thought we'd found a way, to have each other and still have, to still love..."

Lauren looked up into the tree canopy too. Perhaps she was looking for what he could see. She waited.

"None of this was supposed to happen. And when it did, I didn't know what to do. I've been telling myself I was trying to do the right thing, but honest— that's a lie. I was trying to do the best thing for me." He snorted, "Except the joke's on me. All I've done is make things worse. For everyone. Not just me."

She sighed, and her shoulders surrendered their sharp edges, sinking like marshmallows too close to the heat, "Come inside. Help me in the kitchen. I want the whole story. Going right back. Let's start at ten years old. Or five, or earlier. And you stay till we're finished talking.

PART FOUR

1986 - 1987

CHAPTER 49

After finishing his montage, a selective history according to Robert, they ate and he filled in some recent gaps, ending with Johnny turning up in Duncan's office.

Now with the kids tucked into their beds, Lauren turned the lounge into a makeshift one for him, and sat at the end, "But how can you say you didn't know?"

He started to say honestly and stopped himself, "I still don't."

"How can you say that?" Lauren's smooth pale forehead creased with suspicion.

"I don't. Really," said Robert. "How gay is gay? You didn't figure it? Some people don't like me. I'm used to that."

"But Johnny?"

"I know. I know," said Robert. "That's the thing. He's the only one."

She looked down into the diminishing wine glass, and Robert looked to his usual place and said, "I don't know if I'm gay, or it's love. I love you. I love him," he changed direction and looked down at his hands, "I thought I was lucky for a while... I didn't have to make a choice."

And for a while they stayed in the confines of their own thoughts.

"What about this court thing and gay panic. You can't say that."

"Your dad," Robert said, "he, Harry, the prosecutor, I don't know whose idea it was, but I know that's what they want. They've got a reason and I'm pretty sure it's to make sure the scumbags, who did it get off, and I agreed to it. Your dad said not to say anything to anyone. He meant you too. And I'd gotten pretty good at keeping secrets..."

"So you know who did it? Robert," the shock made her voice sharp. "I've got people phoning and knocking on the door asking me how I could live with someone who could— Why haven't you said anything?"

"I can't prove it. Not without the cooperation of people I have no control over." He didn't want to say there was a witness. "It was the police, Lauren."

"But," she stopped herself, "OK. I get it. They know they did it. They aren't going to say so, and you can't do anything about it. They are giving you an out, but if you try to make them own up, which they won't, they can adjust evidence, alter it, lose it, whatever they want. Make it up completely. Like they did for Johnny. You'd be completely screwed."

"That's why I need this up my sleeve. As far as I can see, outing myself could be the only way I can get out of this. It would hardly be gay panic if I'm out as gay. But it has consequences. As well as all the drama that goes with it, I'd be illegal. I'd lose my job. We'd have no income. We'd probably lose the house. I'd find something. I always want to support you and the kids. You know that?"

Her bewilderment softened into confusion. "No," she said. And when she caught sight of his crumpled forehead she added, "I mean, no, I don't know how I feel about us, but also, I mean no, I had no idea this was all going on. My God Robert."

CHAPTER 50

Robert closed the cupboard door on the last dry plate and draped the tea-towel over the sink-edge. In charge of his own kitchen now, he liked the idea of only starting a new mess after the previous one had been completely tidied. With a satisfied out breath he headed for the bedroom, glancing at the clock before reaching into his pocket and rubbing the broken face of his watch.

'Stop it.' Johnny's voice was clear and firm.

Robert placed the watch on the bedside table, his chest deflating.

'In the drawer. Put it in the drawer.'

He pressed the jagged watch-face firmly against his thigh, imprinting the feel of it before placing it in the drawer. He could still feel it in the shower.

The phone was ringing when he got out. He grabbed a towel and fumbling, dropped it with the receiver. He could hear Simon's voice from the floor, "Hello? Robert? Are you there?"

"Yeah. Dropped the phone," said Robert. "Wasn't expecting to hear back, it's Saturday night. Can you hold on a minute? I just got out of the shower. It's a bit breezy."

"Don't need the details mate. What's up?"

"I've got some places that might suit for when Norm's out of hospital, but that's not urgent. What I really wanted was a sounding board. Advice. And, this investigation you're working on, I've got some questions. I thought perhaps this pickle I've found myself in could help you, but I'm not sure how exactly."

Simon laughed, "Pickle, eh? I'd have said you were properly fucked, but that may be misconstrued. How about Monday first up. We can meet at

Tuppy's again. Ten?"

Robert hesitated, "Yeah. Sure. Monday's OK."

He was pulling a clean white T-shirt over his head when the phone rang again.

"It's me again. Tim and I, remember, I told you about Tim, 4 Corners?" Simon didn't wait, for an answer, "We were already supposed to meet. He suggested we both come now. If that's OK with you?"

"Absolutely. Perfect."

"You eaten? We'll bring takeaway."

*

"So," Tim said, "Simon's told me a bit about the story. Johnny. You."

They chatted about Robert's predicament over beers, and Tim began to outline what he was working on.

"I'm calling it The Moonlight State," he said. "You can't breathe a word."

Robert raised his eyebrows.

"Yeah sorry. Habit," said Tim. "It's slowly coming together. People were a bit shy about fessing anything at first. But there's been a bit of a shift recently."

"How come?" said Robert.

"It's getting to be too much," Simon jumped in. "But every time we get anything into the paper, all that happens is 'We'll be investigating further' and then someone resigns, gets promoted or disappears. And the further investigating fizzles."

"Or the PR team from the Premier's office, discovers some proposed protest which might end up as a street march and endanger all our lives, and any heat is doused in iced water. But, where it was cold feet before, I think people are genuinely getting scared now. Worried. Like where is it all going to end? Is it ever going to end?"

Simon weighed in, "Not just them. Some of the politicians too. I've been talking to Robert's dad. He said the mood is subtly shifting. No-one would spot it. And no-one's saying anything, but..."

Tim dropped a piece of black-bean chicken back into the opaque plastic

246

container, "Can I raid your kitchen for a proper fork, this plastic stuff is shit."

"I'll get it," said Robert. "More beers?"

The conversation was still on politics when he came back. He passed the beers across and resumed listening to the ins and outs of the Premier's mysterious trips to Charleville to see a disgraced Terry Lewis, who instead of being chucked out of the Police Force altogether, on the back of his role in some scandal, was suddenly brought back to Brisbane and elevated to Assistant Commissioner.

"And no-one knows who owed who, or who's paying the rent," said Simon. "All we know is that Whitrod resigns straight after that appointment, and we've conveniently got a new Commissioner."

"Nobody ever thought for a moment that Whitrod was part of anything shady," said Tim. "My guess? He was getting too close, but couldn't do anything. I mean even if you're head honcho, you still can't do anything if everyone under you and around you aren't playing by the same rules."

"Johnny said something similar when we were stymied at his hearing. You told him about that didn't you?" Robert looked at Simon, but the nod didn't come. "Johnny said it all still looks like a chess game, the pieces look the same, so everyone thinks it's chess, but it isn't. The rules are made up on the go, and no-one, none of us mere mortals anyway, knows who's making them."

"We kind of know," said Tim. "Proving it? That's another kettle of fish."

"And getting them to stop," one side of Simon's lip curled.

After the subdued pause, Robert asked, "So, how close are you to getting your story out there?"

"Close," said Tim. "But that's where I was going before I got sidetracked. I think your stuff is too big to lump in with what I've got. It's an hour time slot."

The spark in Robert's eyes faded, but his face kept its composure.

"It's not that I don't want to, mate. It won't all fit. It needs its own headline. And it needs an investigation. I'm sort of up to my armpits."

"What if I help get it all for you. Work on it, with Simon," Robert looked hopefully at Simon. "Some of the people Johnny knew. They know things."

Simon looked down for a moment and nodded, "Could you do some on-camera interviews?"

"I don't see why not," said Tim. "And I'll run it by the boss. Maybe we can make it a follow up."

Robert considered for a moment and said, "I know it doesn't completely tie in with your main storyline, but there are links. I'd need to delve a bit deeper, but... I think Kowal— my policeman would step up if he thinks it will go somewhere at last. And there's a possible, no, almost certain link on the narcotics front. Abduction, Mr Peters," he looked at Simon, "murder, Johnny; Harry, evidence tampering. It ties in. The homophobic strand is an element, granted, but... Am I clutching at straws here?" he said.

Tim pressed his lips together, his head nodding slightly, "Let's work on it. We'll do the interviews. We can pixelate the faces and do voice distortion."

"But," Simon frowned, "without something big happening as a result, everyone'll be in the shit. Big time. The cops will know who they are. Pixelated faces or not."

"What about the Feds?" Robert sounded hopeful.

"Lost cause," said Simon. "The Joh and Terry show have been out-maneuvering them forever. It's jurisdictional. Federal involvement has to go past the Police Commissioner first, and our mate Terry Lewis, he's the one who doesn't want them involved."

"Maybes aside," Simon said, "we're living in a fascist nightmare, and because it smiles at us in our sleep, we wake up every day thinking it's a democracy. We have to do something don't we?"

"Here's to wiping the smile off their faces," Tim raised his glass. "Let's hope we all get out of this in one piece."

Three beers were lifted in agreement and emitted a pleasant to the ear ting-t-ting as they clinked together.

"Bring on the revolution," Robert laughed.

"Don't laugh," Tim said. "It is one. Or the start of one. Hopefully."

"Well," said Robert, "since we're talking about big changes, and I never thought I'd say it, but hand me the flag, I'm stepping out."

"Are you?" Simon's eyebrows emphasized the question.

Robert started naming the list of people who now knew his secret.

"Yeah, mate, well done," said Simon. "But a rabid throng of homo-hating, bible-bashing, card-carrying National supporters ready to tear you to pieces. Are you ready for that?"

"When you put it like that," Robert's face dropped. When he lifted it, he was smiling, "Why not? Maybe I should shimmy up Queen Street in a tiara and tights, hand in hand with Harry and Tank. We could have our own mini Mardi-Gras on the way to the Courthouse."

"Or maybe it's the beer talking," said Tim, waving his empty in the air and going to the fridge. "May I? You don't strike me as the sequins and sparkle type. But you're right. You need to be visible. You need to stand up. But I think a straight looking gay man with all the credentials of mainstream social values is going to be a more powerful image. They won't be able to hold you up to ridicule."

"Are you really coming out?" Simon asked.

Robert grinned. It was lopsided, "I'm going to have to. I sort of hinted before, but I'm planning to spring it on them in court. A why would I go all gay panicked if I'm gay? Why would I kill Johnny? We were, well— I kept it quiet because of Harry, and he knows. So…"

They tink-t-tinked again and drank.

CHAPTER 51

Beer-induced bravado had turned into doubt and anxiety in next morning's sunshine.

Robert opened the kitchen window, flicked on the kettle, slathered butter and smeared Vegemite on his toast, and started to feel better.

He put down a half-eaten piece and reached across for the message pad near the phone, putting a line down the middle and a plus and minus sign at the top of his columns.

He started with Kowalski. Everyone had a separate page and a list of reasons to support him or not. It was different with the coppers. His anger and revulsion sprouted. *Can I do this?* As the question arrived so did an image of Johnny, wandering through a garden, dabbing weeds with a poison wand. Robert watched the weeds shrivel, and the seeds they'd been choking pushed through the soil, fresh and green.

The gardening image was totally unexpected.

He frowned, wondering where it came from. Suddenly he could smell fresh cut grass, and his mind sourced a lawn mower and wheelbarrow and from somewhere the garden shed from his childhood backyard appeared. It was hardly a shed. A rickety line-up of timbers with a roof and a door that would bang in the wind if you forgot to push the bolt across.

He let go of the image and wrote his own name at the top of the next blank page and before he had time to formulate any words, the door on the derelict garden shed was swinging open and he peeped inside it.

With his eyes closed, he could see himself as a child, a little Robert in there alone, huddled under a grubby blanket, clutching it fiercely around him, his eyes squinting as the sun pushed its way through the holes in the corrugated iron roof.

An overwhelming softness swelled in Robert's heart and he saw himself go into the shed and sit next to the child. He pulled him close and held him, rocking him gently. He realised they were both sobbing.

When they stopped, he held little Robert's hand and then Johnny was there on the other side and took little Robert's other hand. They sat together. He could feel little Robert's fears slowly evaporating as the last tears dried on their cheeks.

Robert's real tears found a path through his morning stubble, and fell onto his t-shirt. He didn't want to brush them aside. Finally he opened his eyes and looked at the clock on the stove. Time to get to work… back to work.

***

"You know," Kowalski's voice was loud in his ear, "the hardest part of my job has been playing dumb enough that everyone thinks I'm some stupid Kraut. And you don't have to explain. I knew it wasn't you. Call it intuition if you want."

"Remember," said Robert, "I asked you whether you'd talk to a kind-of friend of mine, a journalist?" Robert held his breath in the silence.

"I didn't mean to leave you hanging," said Kowalski. "I was nodding. It's a bit of a habit. Maybe it's time I met him. Where are you? I'll come to you."

He called Simon and left a message. *Robert. Meeting police contact, 2pm at mine.*

*

His next call was his dad.

"How's Mum?"

"You didn't ring to talk about Mum, did you?"

"No. Is she OK though?"

"She will be," Barry said. "What's up?"

251

"I met Mike Ahern at your place a while ago. We had an interesting chat about hen houses and foxes and, it's a bit cryptic but he said there wasn't much hope that things would improve, till we found a vegetarian fox."

"And?"

"I think I have one," said Robert. "Almost certainly. And Simon, remember—"

"I haven't succumbed to dementia yet. Go on."

"He's working on something. Did he tell you about that, after I left?" Robert stopped. "Doesn't matter, he is. And he's going to need some help. Information. Not necessarily anything that would cause you or Mike any problems, but... Do you think he'd be open to a call, from me? Mike? I don't want to scare him off."

"Why don't I talk to him first. I'll say I'd been talking to you about the poultry thing. See what his reaction is."

*

After calling Tank and arranging to meet somewhere besides the pub, so they wouldn't inadvertently run into any collections, Robert grabbed his wallet and headed towards Tuppy's.

He bought some custard and jam-filled donuts, and got home in time to boil a kettle and display his thoughtfulness on a plain white dinner plate.

"Pretend paczki," Kowalski smiled when he saw them. "The Polish favourite. Is this how you intend to bribe me?"

Robert held his smile.

"It's not possible. It's been tried. It's how I got moved out of Licensing and sent on my downward career trajectory."

"I read about them," Robert pointed towards the paczki with his head. "These ones have either custard or jam inside. I wanted to get on your good side, or at least impress you. Coffee?"

"Thanks. Black."

"Sit down," Robert headed into the kitchen. "So, how is it you have all this information? Is it from then? When you were in Licensing. I didn't know."

"How would you?" Kowalski countered, and as Robert's head appeared in the doorway, "What's happening? Really. I mean, the journalist."

"You're not the only one who wants to change the world my friend. Hang on. I'll be back in a minute."

"My uncle has a solution for that," said Kowalski when the coffee sloshed over the sides of the cups in Robert's hands. And without waiting for a what, "Don't fill the cups up so much."

Robert laughed with him.

When he'd finished outlining of what Simon and Tim were working on, and that they were keen to get an insider viewpoint and hopefully something solid to back it up with, and it could all be done anonymously, Kowalski had finished one donut and was trying to distance himself from another.

Robert pushed the plate towards him, "Don't hold back."

Kowalski sighed and reached over, "All this bribery and corruption eh? Little did they know they could have had me with something soft, sugarcoated and stuffed with custard. Go on. I can tell there's more."

Robert went on to explain his own dilemma, followed by the pros and cons he'd considered from Kowalski's position, "What do you think?"

"I've been thinking," Kowalski rubbed the excess sugar off his fingers, it fell in miniscule white flakes onto the empty plate, his candid blue eyes on Robert, "about what's going to happen, if I don't, if *we* don't do anything?"

"So you'll do an anonymous interview? Fantastic."

"No—"

"But I thought—"

"You have to let a man finish his sentence. I meant no, I don't want it to be anonymous. The stuff I've got. I've been sitting on it. And I've got a few friends who've been feeding it to me. Special Branch too. If I don't reveal who I am, I might as well disappear myself now. They'll know who it is, and they'll want to shut me up. Being highly public and highly visible is probably the only way I'll keep myself alive."

"I hadn't thought of that."

"You don't know the half of it, but I'm sure your Simon and Tim are getting a good idea. I knew it would go nowhere until the right people came along. How's this going to work?"

"I told Simon I was meeting you at two so you could make your getaway if you weren't interested in talking to him. I expect he'll be buzzing to get in soon." Robert's shoulders relaxed, "I know this is weird, and a bit late to ask, but, I don't even know your name."

"Walter. Wally," said Kowalski. "Wolly Kah-wolly-skey. I had a great time at school. My uncle used to say not to take it personally," he faded off into his own thoughts.

"You talk about your uncle a lot. I remember at the station."

"I've got two. We're a pretty close family, stick together. The migrant experience," Kowalski smiled. He turned his head at the sound of the buzzer, "That'll be him. Pity there's no paczki left."

"You're not smiling," Robert said when Simon arrived.

"Yeah, well, there's a reason for that. And I didn't want to tell you on the phone. I'm not gonna beat around the bush. Norm discharged himself. I went to Gillies House, where you'd set up a place for him, but he never showed. If you ask me, he's not likely to."

***

Tank and Blue exchanged looks throughout Robert's list reveal.

"It's all so intense," Tank fretted.

"Not really," said Blue. "But I think your policeman's right. The more visible we all are the better. At the right time though."

"So Lovey," said Tank, "how are you feeling? This whole thing. It's pretty fucked up."

"One of the hardest parts was my wife. For a while she really thought it possible."

"Is she OK with it now?" Tank asked.

"Sort of. Not really."

Blue was shaking his head, "You're gonna have to wear it a bit longer."

"It's OK," said Robert. "I feel better knowing we're going to have a go. But they're deadset arseholes and they make my skin crawl," he shivered. "Especially Nichols."

"I'd like to, I dunno," Tank's lip curled. "He'd have been the kid who tortured baby kittens for fun. Now he's moved up. Now it's people. What do you do with that? Cunt."

"What's the go with interviews and stuff?" Blue steered them back.

"I'll give Simon your number and he'll sort things with you. But if you want to know anything in the meantime. Give me a call. Here," he passed them his card with his work number crossed out on the front and handwritten on the back.

"Go on, you've got things to do, Lovey." Tank leaned forward and gave him a hug. "It'll get easier," his voice soft. "Let's do this for Johnny. He deserved better. We all do."

Freed from Tank's slender embrace, Robert stood and rubbed his eyes.

Blue stood too, "Come here."

Being held was comforting. He felt supported, in something strong he could trust. And the swift unexpected release of emotion calmed him for the second time today. He wasn't in this alone. Johnny had friends. He had friends. He sniffed. And smiled.

***

Robert waited at one of Tuppy's outside tables staring intermittently at the dried lacework milk bubbles and powdered chocolate, congealing on the sides of the used coffee cups.

"Thanks for meeting me," he said when Mike arrived.

The waiter sailed past.

"Oi," Mike called and the waiter turned, struggling with a tray full of used crockery. "Cappuccino?" Mike looked at Robert, and turned back to the waiter, "Two thanks."

Robert sent a silent apology to the waiter, and Mike shifted the dirty cups on their table further to the side, shaking his head, "Your dad coming?"

"No. I thought if you wanted to up and leave no-one would have to know you'd seen me. But to be clear, I'm here on behalf of friends, reporters. They thought it would be better to start with, if you weren't associated in any traceable way. And I'm happy to help them. I'm not working at the moment, so I've got plenty of time."

"Nasty business you've gotten yourself into."

Robert raised an eyebrow.

Over coffee he told Mike that all they really wanted was an impression of the support Joh had, or didn't have, inside the party room, and who might call for, or back, an inquiry, "A proper one," said Robert. "Not one whose teeth had been extracted before they could bite."

Mike stared at his imaginary horizon then turned back, "Names or just numbers? And what about the Opposition?"

"No-one has to own up unless they want to. My dad of course. He hinted there might be others. But it's also about the timing. They, my friends, want to know when to air the dirty linen. When Joh's likely to be out of town. Way out of town."

"So he can't shut it down, or play around with the terms of reference," the corners of Mike's mouth had finally lifted. "He's riding pretty high right now, reckons he'll be the next Prime Minister of Australia. Arrogant bastard."

"Seriously? He's going to give up running Queensland and take over the country? Is this common knowledge?"

Mike grinned, "Not yet. Bush telegraph. His rich developer mates have been filling his head with crap."

"But could it happen?"

Mike's smile was one sided, "The rest of the country aren't idiots."

"And Queenslanders are?"

"Don't get me wrong," Mike said. "He's a master manipulator. Been wheeling and dealing and wheedling and twisting things for nearly twenty years. He might call his press conferences feeding the chooks, but he's been feeding us all bullshit and convinced us it's delicious. That we love it."

"True," said Robert waiting.

"So I'll be seeing who's in cahoots and who's just pretending to be?"

"Subtlety *and* insider knowledge. It'll be important," said Robert. "Although Dad's not so subtly pushing an agenda for some other friends of mine."

"Civil liberties," Mike's head tilted. "Yes I know. Brave. I'll be in touch."

Robert extracted a card from his wallet and said, "My number's on the back."

Mike looked at it frowning, "Oh. Right. Yeah. How about I get these then?"

Robert put an overly generous tip on the table before leaving. It was reactionary. The 'my treat' ending had left Robert shrinking instead of expanding. And despite the feel good of playing investigative journalist and detective, his thoughts turned to his promise to look after Lauren and the kids.

Guiltily he decided he'd have to be more frugal and to walk into the Gabba and visit the Commonwealth Employment Service. Surely there was something he could do. After that he'd bite another bullet and call Pete too.

CHAPTER 52

The two people ahead of him in the CES queue were quickly shepherded into waiting cubicles. Feeling completely out of his comfort zone, he contemplated what he should tell the consultant about his state of affairs. Did you have to say you'd been arrested, or your employment might be cut short when you went to jail or got your old job back.

Do what you tell clients. Answer the questions. No extraneous information.

"So, you studied law?"

"Yes. Yes."

She jotted a note and ticked a box, "And your last job?"

"I was working in a law office, but they let me go."

"Interests?"

"Commercial and financial, mainly. Corporate. A little bit of family law. Not much criminal. But I'm interested in social and environmental issues."

"I meant types of jobs," the eyebrows twitched. "At the least, transformable hobbies."

"Oh." *What happened to your plan, idiot.*

"Done any bar work?"

He looked blank, "Like?"

"Pubs, or restaurants, waiting tables?"

"Oh, of course." He touched his forehead, and looked down at his damp fingertips, "Honestly? I'm a bit clumsy."

"Do you have your own transport?"

"I do. Can I ask you a question?" He waited for confirmation. "Is it possible to get something close by. I live in Kangaroo Point. I might have to sell the car if, um, if I don't get work pretty quickly."

As he answered the questions and there were no more frowns and eyebrow wiggling, Robert decided it was kind of nice to have someone sorting his life out for him, even if it was only on the surface.

"There's not a lot happening, but here," she handed him a card with her name on it, and his client ID number. "Keep this. If I'm not here someone else can look up my notes. And," she handed him some forms, "fill these in and bring them back tomorrow afternoon. If we haven't got anything for you, at least you'll be in the system for unemployment benefits."

"Shouldn't I do them now?"

"If you'd come in earlier," she smiled. "But I don't get paid as much as a lawyer, so I don't do unpaid overtime."

"Thanks. Thanks a lot." Robert's outstretched arm nudged the pencil holder.

They both watched it wobble, before righting itself.

"I'll see you tomorrow?" He smiled apologetically.

Her words followed him out, "Try not to worry, we'll sort something."

On the walk home he looked up to a sky which felt like a different coloured blue and blinked away what he told himself was exhaust dust. He'd call Lauren too, he decided, and tell her he was looking for a job.

***

His momentum was frustrated by a lack of response from both Pete and Lauren, but looking out over the river, watching its progress to Moreton Bay he had a sense of moving somewhere too.

Coming back to the kitchen after showering, he noticed the red flashing message light.

Pete. He pushed replay twice, 'Hi mate. Tonight would be OK. Maybe. Not the pub. Thanks for calling.'

Robert wondered why Pete didn't simply say where and when? He sounded nervous, but that was understandable. He must know I'd figure out who got me arrested. It could also be that he didn't want to say anything on the phone. That someone was listening in. So, was he saying tonight? Regardless, he was saying yes.

He mulled over his reply. If Pete was worried about someone listening in, then he should be too, "Hi mate. Yeah, great. I was thinking of trying that new place in Chinatown for a feed soon, but it might be a bit upmarket. Anyway, let me know. Soon though. See ya." Hopefully Pete would decode the message and if not, at least he'd have a cheap meal.

*

Robert's tension turned down marginally when Pete and Jimbo peered into the shabby cramped restaurant. He'd been getting looks from the owner stationed at the cash register near the door. It wasn't the type of place you took a leisurely meal. Two recent neighbours had already come and gone and the beer he'd been nursing was warm and stale. He wasn't game to ask for a water.

"Bit bloody cloak and dagger eh?" Pete's face was drawn, he looked at Robert in the eye and then turned aside.

Robert followed Jimbo's eyes to the doorway checking, and said, "Come on, let's order. I've been getting looks."

As soon as they picked up the menus, the owner's son appeared and wrote down the English numbers in Chinese characters and disappeared.

"I have to ask," Pete's gaze wavered. "That night, what happened to Johnny, it isn't what they say, is it?"

Robert's face soured, "Are you for real?"

"Sorry," Pete's eyes drooped. Tired and trapped.

Jimbo was looking past Robert's shoulder at a faded framed print.

"I'm going to get straight to the point," Robert said. "Blue told me Nichols and Andrews make regularly scheduled visits to see you. That you've got some kind of arrangement with them. And, the only other people who knew I was there that night, were Tank and Blue and they didn't say anything. I even told you Pete, what happened, what I saw. Are you two narcs or snitches or something?"

They both looked at him and said nothing, so he continued, "The name Peter accidentally slipped out at the inquest. Any ideas?"

Pete's eyes stayed on the red plastic tablecloth nailed into the sides of the table.

"This whole thing with Nichols is a shit-fight," said Jimbo. "Well and truly."

"Why don't you tell me about it."

"It was a plant," Jimbo said, not waiting for Pete. "That's how it started. Pete never even touched weed, let alone anything else. Neither of us did. He was at a march. Got wacked around the head with a baton and thrown into the back of a paddy-wagon. And surprise, surprise, when he's being processed, you know, 'empty your pockets, sir', there's a big fat joint. Like, really? Who'd be so stupid? So of course, next thing there's a search warrant and under the mattress they find a plastic bag of white stuff. Could've been baby powder, you know, talc, for all we knew."

"Why you then?" Robert said, "Just curious."

"Buggered if I know," Pete said. "Dumb luck? Most likely it's because when you're gay you can't make waves."

"Turns out the police have special powers and it can all disappear," Jimbo did a magician's wave of the hand with his chopsticks. "Including the original arrest for the heinous crime of walking down the street with a sign saying 'make me legal'. But not yet. There's conditions. You gotta do something for me. We'll give you the product. You sell it. If you don't, you'll go to jail."

"They don't exactly give you time to think it through," said Pete. "I said yes. Sorriest day of my life."

"Bastards," Jimbo's lip curled.

Their food arriving gave everyone a pause.

"Can you bring another round of beers?" Jimbo smiled at the waiter.

"So," said Robert, "they supply you with drugs they've taken off other people and you have to sell them."

They nodded, "We get a cut. A small one," said Pete.

"That's what you thought I was at the pub for," said Robert. "When we first met. You thought I was a new customer, looking for you."

They both nodded.

"And when you said you thought you had an out, when we talked about Johnny, that's what you meant. You thought if you told them you knew it was them, they'd simply let you go. Let you out of the arrangement?"

"Fucking second sorriest day of my life," Pete said.

When the beers arrived, Pete told Robert that he'd organised a meeting with Nichols, and after having his arm almost twisted off his body, and several whacks into his mid-section, they'd demanded a name. "I didn't tell them," Pete shook his head. "And then he started with this idea that it was me who'd been running away. That they'd all seen me. They'd been watching me because they knew I was selling drugs, and that I'd gone to get the money Johnny owed me. He hadn't paid up since his rich sugar daddy disappeared. And when he didn't come good, I beat the crap out of him. And then when he didn't get up, I threw him in the river. They said they'd followed me and watched me when I planted his wallet and jacket on the bridge."

"They were going to pin it on Pete," Jimbo said.

"We pretty much knew all this gay panic thing wasn't true," said Pete.

Robert had been shaking his head while Pete told the story, "Nothing surprises me about them any more. But, I might have a way of getting you out of it. All of it," he said. "But this next step is all in. From right now. I'll go for a bathroom break. You think about it," he pushed his chair back. "You can give me your answer when I get back. Then I'll explain."

"We're in," they unisoned, before Robert had finished standing.

CHAPTER 53

The morning light was soft on this side of the building and Robert ignored his headache and overly full bladder, and pretended he could stay like this all day. He tensed his neck and shoulders and deliberately left them to soften of their own accord, into the pillow and mattress. Once relaxed, his mind wandered back onto the bridge and his walk home.

He'd stopped at the spot where Johnny was supposed to have jumped. An icy panic gripped him, even though it wasn't true. It wasn't just the shocking nature of the act, it was that those sick bastards could do this. Consign the families of the people they'd hurt or killed to the horror of forever being guilty of not seeing the signs, of not having reached out, of not having done anything to help. The callous disregard. No, the disdain.

He rolled over in bed, physically turning away from the thoughts. Anyway, there was no point to understanding them or why they did it. He didn't want to know.

'Yes, you do,' Johnny urged him, 'Come on. Pretend. Be the prosecutor.'

And he was there, seeing it like he was on a stage, playing his role in their drama before drifting back into a deep doze that started lifting as he became aware the light had moved. With it came the dawning realisation that his headache was MSG, not too much beer after all. He smiled. He was almost sure Dad used that excuse. And thoughts of Dad wound around strands of semiconscious thought.

He recalled their latest conversation when his dad told him the recollections of Joh he'd been sharing with Simon. How Terry Lewis had been the bagman for *his* boss, Commissioner Bischof, collecting bribes and protection money. At least till Bischof was dismissed and Lewis was banished to Charleville. Maybe being shipped off to the back of beyond wasn't a punishment after all.

"I reckon," his dad said, "it was to protect him. Out of sight out of mind. And then Joh, with his hypnotic balm of 'don't you worry about that', deflecting questions about why he, the Premier, was dashing off to Charleville. Lewis knew the ins and outs of the whole corrupt operation, so don't tell me he isn't up to the same caper now." His dad's eyes had gone stony, "And Joh, with his pompous smirk, and 'next question'. He knows all right. That's why he put Lewis in charge. That's why Terry Lewis *is* the Police Commissioner."

Clever. Machiavellian even. But what, Robert mused, was the story behind it? It couldn't be a simple blackmail. There had to be something equally and mutually threatening about disclosure. Not only did they, do they, keep quiet, they support each other. If it was one sided, or even lopsided, it would never have gotten this far. But what?

One thing was certain. There was no way Lewis wasn't involved in this. What wasn't clear was how much he knew about Johnny and what was happening before. And after. Robert shook his head. He knew the endless circle started with these questions, and got out of bed because regardless of whether it was beer or MSG produced didn't matter. His headache wanted paracetamol.

*

Bored with waiting and bored with the housework he was doing while he was waiting, Robert walked to the employment office. Did arriving early count as keen?

At the head of the queue, he took the card from the pocket of his jacket and glanced at the name, Gemma Thomas. The similarity hit him with the reminder that Lauren hadn't called back yet. Or if she had, she hadn't left a message. He shifted his focus to the kids.

"You seem happier today?"

Why would she say that? "I was thinking about my kids, Emma and Thomas."

She pointed at the chair.

Something wasn't quite right, despite the sun in her greeting.

"You may not have told me everything yesterday," she said.

Robert's hand came up and confirmed the furrow in his brow. The other hand was tightly bunched out of sight, by his thigh. He loosened it, stopped rubbing his forehead, and took the filled-in paperwork for unemployment benefits from his pocket. *There's always the car.*

"Don't," Gemma started, and changed track, "It's not the end of the world."

He hazarded a look.

"I thought I'd heard your name before, that's all," she said. "And… it's not that easy, when you have a reputation like yours."

"Here," he handed her the completed forms. "I won't keep you."

"No, please," she sighed, taking them. "I looked into a couple of things. There's a cleaning job at QIT."

"What?"

"The Queensland Institute of Technology? Maybe you've heard of it," her smile was a friendly condescending. "It's not exactly world shatteringly interesting but it's—"

"I meant," Robert interrupted. "Doesn't matter."

"It's walking distance, if you get the ferry across. But," she brightened, "I have a sort-of olive branch, if you're interested. Only, it's unpaid."

"Volunteer work?" he hoped he didn't sound too disappointed.

"You never know where it could lead though."

He held his shrug in check, "Go on."

"Callum O'Connor, at QCCL," she paused to check he was with her.

"Queensland Council for Civil Liberties?"

She nodded, "He wants someone with legal experience to work on gay rights issues, a kind of liaison person with CAMP."

"And why me?"

"Do you want me to spell it out?"

This time he didn't stop the shrug.

"Look if you're not interested."

"I am. But you know who I am. So why? Some kind of poetic justice? A joke? Send the gay panic killer to work on gay rights?"

"I don't think you get it," Gemma's face was serious and something else.

"Get what?"

"I don't buy it."

"Buy what?" he leaned forward.

She sighed, "Gay people sort of know other gay people."

He frowned, "So you're…"

Her eyebrows rose. "And you know, most of the people I know, don't believe you did it. And now I've met you, I'd guarantee it. You're just not the sort."

"And that would be?"

"Thug," she shrugged now. "Violent, macho, punch now, ask questions later. Why did you say you did it?"

"No choice. It's a long story. Anyway, that's the deal I've got, and if I'm not believable as straight, I'll end up in jail."

"Or not?"

"I'm working on it," his eyebrows pulled tighter together. "Is it that obvious?"

"That you're gay?" she shook her head. "But did you ever wonder why people pushed you away, growing up? Put it this way, when did you realise?"

"Should we even be having this conversation?"

"Suit yourself."

He looked around at the line of people growing behind him, "I don't want to take up all your time."

"Classic," she said. And when he frowned, "Avoidance. Would it be life threatening to actually come out?"

Her face was open concern, nothing more. It was encouraging, "Right now?" he said. "It just may be. I told you. I have to be convincingly straight. They have to believe it."

Her eyebrows did a quick well-then lift. She placed his form into a folder with a number black-inked onto a tab alongside his name and put it on her pile. Then held out her other hand, "Here. Do you want these or not?"

He reached over and took the paper slips with the position details.

"Let me know," she said. "I need the work stuff of course. But I mean let me know what happens. If you need help or, I don't know. Let me know. OK?"

"I will. Thank you, Gemma Thomas," his eyes softened. "I won't forget that name."

He caught her words as he was walking away, "Bet they're cute kids."

They are.

***

At home he put the two job cards on the coffee table and stared at his future. So what do you want to be when you grow up? Fireman, astronaut, doctor, international sports star, part time cleaner at the Queensland Institute of Technology.

The wry attempt at humour fell over. He saw himself in primary school, hands bunched at his sides, as usual, while everyone else was excitedly stabbing the air with theirs. While he'd listened to them, all he could think was 'normal'. A boy who's good at being like other boys. Who the other boys don't pick on. In his mind he moved from the classroom to home and then to the backyard and the garden shed. What was it about the garden shed? He had no idea. He looked up. The pinpricks of light merged suddenly and fiercely bright, and he opened his eyes. The breeze lifting the living room curtain had let in the afternoon sun.

He got up and dialed the QIT Maintenance Department.

No, he didn't have commercial experience. *Not that sort.* But he knew what a mop and broom were, and had used them. And he could follow instructions. And he could do the paperwork and orientation today at 4.30. Yes pm. And he could start tomorrow morning, 4.30 till 9.30. *So much for public transport.* On the bright side as interviews went, he'd passed with flying colours, and without even having to make an appearance.

He looked at the number on the next card. *Do I really want to do this?*

'C'mon. Get on with it,' Johnny insisted.

He dialed.

Yes, he could come in this afternoon and meet Mr O'Connor.

A lot less questions. Great. Not. He needed something to settle his nerves. Tea. The mum version. He laughed out loud and put on the kettle. He would have tea and talk to Lauren.

He left her another message and took the tea to the bathroom, sipped and examined his face with his hand, avoiding the mirror but catching sight of his face anyway. He ran a tidying-up razor over it, dry. At least his shirt was wrinkle free. He pressed cold water onto his face and then sat on the bed ruminating about the civil liberties job, before leaving for the ferry.

It might all amount to nothing. But there's every chance no-one else will even want it. It's unpaid. What if they haven't heard about me, and then find out? Would it be a public hanging, or will I just slink off quietly back into the mud?

'Stop it.' Johnny's voice. 'Think. What do you know about civil liberties and gay rights?'

Only what you said while I half listened. Too busy watching your hair fall over your eye. And your mouth moving. And thinking about other things.

It wasn't clear if his groan was desolation or desire.

He imagined Callum O'Connor's face when it dawned on him who was sitting there, pretending to be a serious candidate. He'd be angry about one thing at least; his wasted time.

He considered phoning up to cancel when the rebuke in his head came in Johnny's voice again, 'Or you could stop thinking about yourself. Tell them who you are and ask what you could do to help them.'

He reached for the extension and called the house. *How many times now?* Still no answer. He left another message and looking for a diversion, he called Marnie.

She hadn't heard anything from Lauren. Yes they can meet up tomorrow and talk about the flat. Yes, Nikki's good. He put the receiver back. Maybe Nikki would be home and he could ask her what Johnny meant.

'You know what I fucking mean,' Johnny's voice in his head was loud and clear. 'It's time to stand up, not just pretend to. Come on. You can do this. You have to do this. You can't wimp out on me. No isn't an option.'

He stood up, and felt his shoulders adjust. He wasn't alone. A sense of settled and quiet determination cloaked him in calm.

'Time to go.'

He glanced briefly towards the wardrobe. *And time to be real.* He'd tell Mr O'Connor a tie wasn't needed at his paying job.

***

The fact there were two people waiting in the meeting room didn't disturb Robert's calm. A tinge of elation wafted around the edges of it. He felt gracious, as if he was making Callum feel comfortable and he smiled extending his hand, then presenting it to Callum's guest.

"Alex Maddison, from CAMP," said Alex.

"Alex arrived and I didn't have time to call you back," Callum apologized.

"Well, that's good," Robert said. "I understand we'd be liaising. But before I get ahead of myself, there's something you should know."

He told them the bones of his story, and that he wouldn't have come at all, if he didn't think it, or he, would be useful.

Callum and Alex exchanged looks.

"For a start, there's the media interest," said Robert. "I'm led to believe gay panic and my story is already causing a ruckus. I must admit I've been avoiding it till now. If nothing else, it's polarizing, and that makes press. Plus, even though I can't practice, doesn't mean I don't know the law. And I'll have ample time. My paid job, I'm on my way to confirm it after I leave here, is part time and finishes around ten, and is only a short walk away from here."

"Oh?" Alex's head tilted.

"I'll be gracing the halls of QIT with a broom and mop, as long as they're happy with me," his smile fresh and disingenuous.

Callum's eyes narrowed.

Alex looked slightly confused, "You know I knew Johnny, don't you? He'd been coming in, doing whatever," he waited for Robert's confirmation. "So the panic thing? That's what they want you to say?"

Robert nodded.

"But why? Why don't you just say you're gay."

Callum looked like he was going to say something, and Robert deferred, "Because, with no witness to the contrary, all they have to do is point a finger. The presumption of innocence isn't all it's cracked up to be in situations like this. Besides that, evidence isn't exactly reliable these days. By pleading guilty to gay panic, you've got more of a chance. And for that you'd have to definitely not be gay."

"I know you're trying to be helpful, but at this point there's not much anyone can do, and," said Robert, "since I'm my own client, I really shouldn't be discussing his case."

"Of course. Of course," Callum repeated. "Alex, what do you think?"

"Mind boggling," Alex dropped the pretense of being a corporate style interviewer.

Callum's mouth curled at the edges, "I meant about our new liaison officer?"

"Oh. He'll be great. For as long as we have him. But," Alex's eyes were troubled, "given the circumstances..."

"How about you leave us to it?" Callum looked at Alex pointedly, and then the door.

When he'd gone, Callum spoke, "Were you serious? You're representing yourself?"

Robert nodded.

"I can help. We could sit down now and have a proper lawyer client meeting."

"I was told I shouldn't have a lawyer," Robert's frown apologized. "It's not that I wouldn't want you to."

"Who advised you?" Callum could see Robert's hesitation.

"It's not exactly that he said I shouldn't have a lawyer," Robert was looking back on his conversation with Duncan at remand. "He said, I was choosing to be unrepresented. He stressed it. Said it was my loophole. It took me a while, figuring it out. I believe his intention was that if I had a lawyer, to represent me, I couldn't change my plea."

Callum scribbled on a blank sheet of paper, before passing it to Robert.

Robert read, "For the purpose of this and subsequent meetings, I Robert Carson, do not appoint Callum O'Connor as my legal representative. However, all the confidentiality provisions of the lawyer client relationship apply."

"Haha, OK then. You've got me," Robert signed. "Thanks."

They talked, with Callum taking notes until Robert looked at the clock on the wall of the small conference room and said, "Hey Mr O'Connor, I have to go. I don't want to be late."

"Callum," he said. "I've got enough for now, see you tomorrow."

*

On the walk over to QIT, Robert wondered about Gemma Thomas, whether she'd had any inkling that working for Callum O'Connor for free, might have turned out this way. He decided it didn't matter whether she did or not, and that sparkling and flowers might be a nice thank you. Lauren liked bubbly. And with that thought his mood flatlined.

***

Next morning after his QIT job, Robert bought the daily paper on the way to QCCL. It seemed like it might be a good time, and the fact that his story was old, and his photo was probably mopping up fish and chip oil while he mopped up floors, appealed to his tentatively re-emerging sense of humour. Not that it had ever been particularly raucous. He tucked the paper into his briefcase with his cleaning clothes, and swapped hands, deciding he needed a backpack and hoping Lauren would answer his call and let him take one from the cupboard at home, when he visited.

When he arrived a petite brown-eyed, brown-haired teenager was watching someone in a suit precede Callum into his office. She turned to Robert, "I'm Rose, I wasn't here when you came yesterday. But we spoke on the phone."

She had a way of making a statement into a question.

"I remember."

"I'll show you around." Again the question.

It didn't take long, and they stood in the tea-room nook waiting for Rose to think of what to do next. "Do you want to put anything in the fridge?"

"No. Thanks."

"What about a tea or coffee?" she asked.

"Tea sounds good."

"OK then," she started back towards the reception area. "Milk's in the fridge. Yell if you need anything."

271

He collected himself, "Do you want one?"

Her bottom lip pushed forward, reminding him of his kids, "Nup. Thanks. When you're ready, you can watch over my shoulder for a while."

To one side and under the desktop of the reception area, was a cabinet like a library catalogue. A drawer was open, and Rose was typing the contents of one of the cards in it, into a form on the computer screen.

"You can use a computer. Wow," he said.

"Once you know the ins and outs it's simple. Like typing," she said. "Wanna try?"

*

Callum peered at them over the counter-top after seeing his appointment out, "Ah, upskilling. Good idea, Rose. You've got some catching up to do Robert, I'm her star pupil. We'll all have to know how these things work soon." He turned towards Robert, "Got a minute?"

Robert thanked Rose.

"Really," said Callum, "take the opportunity. She's here Monday, Wednesday, and Friday. How was the new job?"

Robert looked surprised to be asked, "I'll probably be aching this time tomorrow. I didn't realise how physical it would be."

"First things," Callum pushed a folder towards him. "Have you ever done a submission before?"

Robert shook his head.

"Thought not. Read through this. It's one we did recently. It'll give you an idea of how we put them together."

Robert started to reach for it, but there was also an expanding file in front of him, so he waited.

"And this, is a bunch of notes, affidavits, declarations, reports, articles, you name it," he smiled. "You'll also need to access Hansard. No need to go right back to the beginning. Alex has a summary in here of the early years. But the recent stuff needs to be logged and summarized. And there's rather a lot of it."

"We're working on?"

"Legalising my gay brothers and sisters. Go through all this first. You'll probably locate the parliamentary debates in Hansard more easily using the news cuttings for indicative dates." He pointed his head towards the expander file, "Not so much guff to get through."

Robert nodded.

"I want you to note who's saying what in the debates. For and against obviously, but it's the fencers… we want to know who they are too. And from both sides."

"I'll go see my dad. He'll—"

"Of course, yes, Carson. Barry Carson. Taking it he's on our side?"

Robert nodded again, "If you'd asked me not so long ago, I might have had a different answer. But what's even better is, he's a fixture. He knows what's in people's heads, not just what comes out of their mouths."

"I knew you'd come in handy," Callum joked. "Now, for you. I have an idea."

CHAPTER 54

"Want a drink?" Marnie offered as he started sitting down. There was an open bottle of wine on the coffee table and a spare glass.

He wanted to say yes, but he had to get up early. Way early. "Better not. I'm driving."

She poured anyway, "In case you change your mind."

"What's going on?"

She picked up the glass and handed it to him, "It's only one, and I've got something to tell you. Two things actually. But one you're not going to like."

He sniffed the contents, "OK?"

"I spoke to Lauren today. There's a reason she hasn't been answering your calls. She isn't there."

He put the glass down. It hit the table with a thick clunk.

"Sorry. I didn't know how to break it to you, so I blurted," Marnie watched his confusion. "She moved into her dad's. Packed everything up. Put it into storage. Except it seems, the phone."

"But she never said anything, I don't understand."

"She said you'd have tried to talk her out of it."

"But," Robert repeated, and ran out of words.

"Yeah. But. I know," Marnie's lips pressed together. "She said she was going to call you after things had calmed down a bit. It's all a bit confusing for the kids. They need to be settled. People are moving into your place."

"I should go and see her."

"Don't. Not now. She'll know I told you."

"And?"

"And I wasn't supposed to. No-one else knows. Except Duncan. And she is always going to come before you." She handed him back his glass, "And as much as I don't want to be in the middle, I kind of have been from the start, so don't go racing over there. Call Duncan tomorrow and tell him you're worried. He'll tell you then, and I'll be in the clear."

The glass wavered on its way to his mouth.

"This way she'll still talk to me. It might be useful to have me as a go between."

He put the glass down gently this time, "Who does that? Who takes your children, packs up your life, and doesn't tell you? Not even a message."

"There's something else," her shoulders caved forward watching his pain. "It's not bad this time. It's the apartment. Technically it's mine. Johnny left everything to me," she leaned forward and took his hand. She gave it tiny strokes, trying to wipe off some of the hurt, "It's actually a little bit good."

He felt his nose prickle, and he could see the teary sheen in her eyes, because none of this was good.

"Johnny had insurance. He took it out because of the mortgage. Anyway, when the *new* coroner's report was tabled, the insurance company had to turn around and pay after all."

"Because it wasn't suicide." The comment had as much life to it as a pool of tar. He picked up his wine and drank the rest. She reached for the bottle, and he shook his head, "No. Thanks though."

Ignoring him again, she poured a tiny amount into the empty glass. "I know you don't want to celebrate. Neither do I, but," she clinked his glass, "to Johnny, and his foresight."

"You know," he said, "if those bastards had gotten away with faking suicide, that money wouldn't be there. Harry and I even talked about it. The trauma is bad enough. The guilt, the blame, the grief. The loss. They've literally taken someone you love. The emotional cost. But they steal your money too. Imagine if there were kids as well. How dare they Marnie? How dare they? They have to be stopped. This has all got to be stopped."

They were both silent.

Then Marnie said softly, "There was just a little bit more. Since I don't have to try to find the money to pay for the mortgage..." her voice faded away.

He looked at her, his eyes swimming with sadness against a tide of anger.

"You don't have to pay me any rent. If you can cover the rates and things. At least until you're on your feet."

She shuffled over on the couch and wrapped her arms around him. He lifted his around her, and buried his face against her shoulder, and she buried hers against his.

A few droplets of sad and grateful were spilled.

CHAPTER 55

Arriving home with a packet of spaghetti, a container of frozen Bolognese sauce, and no inclination to talk to anyone, Robert didn't even look at the answering machine.

He put water in a pot to boil, and the container of sauce into the microwave. He heard Marnie in his head saying, 'it has to breathe'. *Don't we all?* The newspaper went onto the coffee table in front of the TV. Now that he wasn't going to be confronted with his own face and circumstances, and given his current roles, he wanted to know what was going on. His QIT-MD for maintenance department shirt went into the washing machine.

The spaghetti water was still dithering, so he showered. The microwave beeped as he was drying off. He started wrapping himself in a towel and stopped, letting it fall to the floor where he stomped on it. He could go to the kitchen naked if he wanted to.

'Well, well, well. Look at you,' he heard Johnny.

The bravado reduced to a confident nonchalance he hadn't felt in a while. *Or ever?* He decided not to think about that, but slightly too late. The feeling moved down to nonchalance without the confident bit. He still felt good as he spurted wine from the box, into an oversized glass and surveyed the fridge interior. It looked lonely in there. Butter, vegemite, milk and bread, a dehydrating carrot and yellowing broccoli reminding him to eat more vegetables. And an unopened packet of cheese. He found a grater.

Tomorrow he'd take some money from his and Lauren's joint account and buy more groceries. He wanted a fuller fridge. Lauren wouldn't mind. *Would she? No. But. No.*

He hacked open the pasta packet, with a not very sharp knife and felt a tinge of naked vulnerability. He doused the feeling with a slosh of wine and went back to the packet. *How much? Half?* It splayed outwards from the centre of the saucepan. He'd watched Lauren do that. *Salt.* He prodded the resistant strands pushing them under. The thought arrived from somewhere, that he might even need his own bank account, and he told himself to do that tomorrow before going to the office. And call Duncan. Then he wondered if it would be OK to use the phone at the office? Did Anna use the office phone? What would he have said if she asked? He saw Callum's face instead saying are you kidding me? OK. OK. Sorry. Slink off.

The glass was empty.

The pasta bubbled in white water. He opened the microwave. The sauce was a frozen floating island. His skin goose-bumped. He put the sauce in the fridge and tipped off the pasta water. Spaghetti escaped into the sink. His fingertips recoiled when he tried to pick it up. He ran them under the cold tap, chilling the pasta underneath. He lifted some into a bowl with tongs and doused it with salt and pepper and a mini mountain of cheese, and shivered.

In the bedroom he got a pair of boxers and a t-shirt and stared at the damp towel for several seconds before hanging it up.

Feeling heavier but more comfortable, he sat and scanned headlines, but he'd never been a fan of overcooked cool spaghetti and half-melted cheese, and half-eaten, it joined the other lonely fridge dwellers while he went to bed. And slept.

***

The light from the answering machine was throbbing like a slow pulse as he walked towards it.

Jeez. Who was he going to call back at four in the morning?

Outside the front door, he stopped. *What if— the kids? Fuck's sake, stop it. Duncan, Harry, Marnie? No they'd have called back. Probably just Lauren with her moving out moving on message.* He closed his eyes to shut off the noise inside his head, and felt a weirdly one-directional swaying pulling him towards the phone. *No.* You can't be late on day two. You need an income. *Still?* He shook his head. *Knowing right this minute won't make any difference.*

*

The flashing red light of the answering machine seemed to appear against the grey lino flooring as the mop changed direction.

He ignored the urge to go home between jobs, but sitting at the conference table reading, he noticed he'd been drawing a series of circles alongside the notes he'd been taking.

When Callum came in, he asked if he could work from home sometimes. When he had personal calls to make.

"You can make calls from here you know," he registered Robert's relief. "But yeah, it's OK, as long as someone's here. And?"

"And?"

"And, what else?" said Callum.

"I have to go to the bank."

"Go. I'm here," Callum's hand flicked towards the door. "Don't be all day. Not sure if I'll be able to figure out how to use the phone on my own."

Robert's mind went to Anna again. *Shit.* He hadn't even called to see how she was going, "Sorry," he said to Callum. "I won't be long."

*

The first bank teller looked him up and down, sneered, and walked away. The next one was gushy.

Robert wanted to stand on a chair and shout 'I didn't do it'. Instead, he looked down a lot and tried not to catch anyone else's eyes, before leaving in a hurry and forgetting to get any money out.

Shit. Shit. Shit. At least the spaghetti sauce will be defrosted.

*

Back at his QCCL office his mood drizzled further. Anna wasn't at work. And 'No, Mr Eldridge is with a client.'

He pushed the phone away. And pulled the notebook and expanda-file towards him. *Come on. Concentrate.*

And he did. There was so much. The history. The lives. The lies.

*

"Nice to see your dedication," Callum was leaning on the doorframe of his office. "But there's no-one here to impress except me. Shouldn't you be going home?"

Robert smiled.

"Rose is in tomorrow. Why don't you work from home? In fact, why don't you not. You have to follow up on your Alan-Norm."

"You sure?"

"Look," Callum came over and stood in front of him, "I can feel your anxiety."

Robert winced.

"Even if you don't want my advice, I'm going to give it to you," said Callum, "This tippy toe-ing around. It doesn't make you invisible. It makes you stand out. For the wrong reasons. It makes you look guilty," Callum's lips pressed together while he considered continuing. "Stand up." He stopped and waited. "Come on, I mean now, let's do this. Look straight ahead." He planted himself in front of Robert. "If someone looks at you, don't turn away or look down. Hold their gaze. When they lower their eyes, walk on. You don't have to say anything."

Robert stood and resisted the powerful compulsion to look away or lower his head. Callum's eyes were steadfast and glistening with conviction.

"You don't see Terry Lewis or Joh Bjelke-Petersen, looking down. The only time they look away is to say 'next question'...*after* they've dismissed you. They ooze honest and trustworthy. You ask anyone in the street," Callum's fist bounced on the tabletop. "Practice it in the mirror, and while you're at it, start telling yourself, I didn't do anything wrong. They did."

"But, if—"

"The only thing you did was stay hidden. I don't blame you. You had a lot to lose. Not least your own life. And you got that second inquest."

"Yeah. That worked out for me."

"What do you think we're doing here Robert? Your average Queenslander is terrified of people like you. They think their children will be molested. And what about all those poor babies who are going to die from AIDS simply because there's such a thing as gays. People believe that shit. How do you fight that?"

"Keep making submissions?"

"It's going to take more than that. I know some politicians have half a heart, just not the ones who have a voice."

"It's more than that," said Robert. "From the political standpoint, Joh controls things. If anyone looks sideways at anything he doesn't support, they're history. His news machine's talking up your replacement. Local papers are full of stories about all the fuckups you've made. They don't dare."

"We've got work to do then."

*

At home, a finger wobbly with lack of food and an overload of adrenalin pressed play. Lauren's recorded voice saying hello and that she couldn't put up with the nasty letters, threats, and a constant stream of door-knocking intruders that simply hadn't stopped. Robert's shoulders sank back into place.

He called Duncan's home number.

"I'm really sorry. I had no idea. Why didn't you say anything. I—"

"Oh come on Robert," she interrupted. "What? What would you have done?"

"Well…"

"Exactly. Well, nothing." It didn't sound like Lauren. The voice drooped like it was bored.

"Are you OK there? Has anyone been around bothering you?"

"No. No. I feel safe enough here."

He waited for her to say something about renting out the house. "I thought we should catch up, make some plans." He paused. "I've got a job. It's only part-time. I can come over, see you, the kids."

"I don't think that's such a good idea."

"But—"

"Look," she interrupted again, "I've got something to tell you."

His heart tripped before falling flat.

*

After staring at the wall for an indeterminate period of time, he stopped counting, and walked into the kitchen and stood outside the fridge. The thought of Marnie's spicy rich red sauce waking up in the microwave made him feel sick.

He went back to the answering machine and his finger hovered over the delete button. He didn't fancy listening to more of Lauren's bored condescension, but at the last moment, his finger veered over and hit play, expecting more of 'for God's sake Robert, answer the phone,' but heard Anna's voice. Three, four, five times. Finally, 'I'm not at work today, call me at home, here's the number. It's urgent.' He grappled with the drawer for a pen, and missed the number, 'Here it is again.' *Thank you, Anna.*

A man answered the phone.

Robert wondered if he'd got the number wrong and checked, and the man said, he couldn't say for sure but then he asked, "Are you Robert?"

Robert stared blankly at the wall again. There was no Mr Anna. A cousin? An uncle? Did that mean something happened to her mum? She'd said urgent and rung a gazillion times, "Yes. I'm Robert."

"Good. Finally. She said if the phone rings answer it. It would probably be Robert, and to tell you to come over ASAP. I'll give you the address. Hang on."

CHAPTER 56

Next to a plate of cheese, olives and crackers, was a bottle, dribbling condensation onto the fabric napkin under it. Four champagne flutes stood to the side. Robert frowned.

Anna led him by the elbow to meet her mum. The hand with its delicate fingers danced rhythmically back and forward as she extended it towards him. He wondered if he'd confused MS and Parkinson's but decided they were as bad as each other. He grasped her hand gently and felt its resisting tremor and winced. She had Anna's smile and eyes, or rather, Anna had hers.

"So now he's here," she said, eyeing the bubbly.

"Hold your horses, Mum."

The nerve on Robert's right eye fluttered. He didn't know if it was impatience or confusion or fatigue.

"OK," said Anna, "you can come out now."

Someone was limping towards him.

"Robert," said Anna, "I'd like you to meet Alan. Norm. This is Robert."

"Oh my God," he said. "You found him."

"To be truthful, he found me," said Anna.

Robert's eyes brimmed with gratitude. After several eye stretching blinks he said, "I don't believe it. Do I call you Alan or Norm?"

"Suit yourself," said Alan. Then added, "Probably better you call me Norm."

The cork popped and Robert's questions started, "Where have you been? Why didn't you go to the hostel, to Gillies?"

Alan's face tensed, "Let's just say they'd have been trying to sort me out with the dole and things, which might not have quite matched up with my new name."

"It doesn't matter now. But I am curious how you found Anna."

"I ended up at Club 139 for a feed, and hopefully the directions to a bed, and was checking the noticeboard, and the guy there, blue-eyes, glasses, he started talking to me."

"Ernie. And?" Robert encouraged him.

Alan downed the rest of the glass and glanced hopefully towards the bottle.

Anna pretended to ignore the look, "Go on."

"So, he told me the story. I didn't say anything, but I reckon he twigged. Said there was a similar notice in the ferry shelter at Holman Street, and the fellah who'd put it there had brought Alan's things in. That they were in the back and did I want them now or after I had something to eat.

"I asked him how he knew it was me, and he said no-one had spent more than a passing moment looking at the notice since it had been there." Alan nodded, as if he was hearing it all again. "Anyway, so then I told him *my* story, and he brought out my stuff, and I started going through it. Except it was a bunch of new stuff. New pillow, plastic tarp sheet, sleeping bag. Even socks still in their packets. Stuff you'd put in there for me."

Robert twirled the stem of the champagne glass.

"Then Ernie told me what happened to you. Those," he looked over at Anna's mum then back to Robert, and mouthed 'fucking' "bastards." He scowled, "I saw what happened. I saw the whole thing. I couldn't," he broke off, and swallowed. "I couldn't do anything. I was locked in the car with the window half open. Handcuffed. But I had a clear view of everything with the shelter light, and I listened. I knew something was up because, well— It was weird. Normally they would have just had a go, you know, laid into me or taken me in and charged me, but they were backwards and forwards to the park and spaced out in the shadows and…

As Robert listened to Alan the images came alive with the horrible reality which he half knew and didn't want to see.

*

Johnny watched the dark swallow Robert. The wind was stronger now, and the fig's tendrils clutched the air with long witchy fingers. He shivered muttering, "Should've gone back with you, relaxed with a glass of wine. Then got a cab."

"Fuck it," he looked back again, along MacDonald Street and then half turned towards the alternate route, where Holman Street joined Main Street with its superior lighting.

"Which way would you come? My luck we'd miss each other." He listened in the quiet, to the river edge sloshing against the mangrove's feet, noticing a couple of cars at the Jazz Club as he passed. They were parked in the drive about halfway down towards the building, which was close to the ferry's landing pontoon. He peered towards them. The light was on in one. Someone was in it. He wondered why anyone was there on a Thursday night. Band practice? Maybe a meeting? At least there'd be someone else around. It made him feel slightly more comfortable. And then anxiety swooped in again. He didn't know which shelter to wait at. Park or waterside? They hadn't said.

He headed over to the waterside one to see if he could spot the ferry from the pontoon. If it was close enough, he'd stay and ask the driver to wait. If not, he'd come back to the park-side one where it was easier to spot Robert. From there he'd still hear the ferry approaching.

The smell of urine was strong at the entrance and he held his breath till he'd passed. The light inside had died. The outside one illuminating the pontoon and walkway, was trying to make up for it. The moon wasn't much help, lolling behind the clouds.

At the safety barrier Johnny peered over the side. The water could be any depth. You wouldn't know. The filmy black sheen, broken by sudden flashes as the surface of the water changed shape in the tide or the wind, gave away no hints.

As the prickle of a shiver climbed up his back, he spotted the ferry on the other side of the river. It was swinging around. The port light was visible, but Robert should have plenty of time.

Turning back through the shed he noticed a blanket spread over something under the bench-seat. He reached out and lifted the end. The punching inside his chest eased at the sight of a striped plastic zip bag, an ancient pillow, mismatched socks and a brown paper bag from which the neck of a bottle poked its empty head. 'Pity', he thought, 'a lookout would have come in handy.'

Back at the park-side shelter he sat, re-folded Robert's jacket onto his lap, and waited.

A car door closed. He ran his hand through his hair. "Get a grip," he muttered, realising it was probably the musos loading their gear.

Then a shuddering waterside. He stood up. The reverse thrust of the ferry engine, slowing it down for the deckhand to jump off, tie up, and lower the passenger ramp. But it couldn't be. He'd just seen it on the other side of the river. He looked around. Two men were standing close to the big tree near the driveway to the Club. 'Odd place to wait for the ferry.' One of them had something tucked under his arm. The flickering of the ferry light caught the edge of his vision. "Shit. Shit. Stupid. You were watching the wrong ferry." *He shook his head remembering that on the turning or strong outgoing tide, the ferries motored further up-river for their approach to the pontoon. He'd been watching the one getting ready to head home to Bulimba, as they changed to an hourly service.* "Fuck. Come on Robert."

He sat down.

Another door closed.

He looked around reflexively stroking his hair. The two under the tree, were making their way over towards him. He breathed easier thinking that they'd seen him and noticed the ferry leaving. They were checking he was OK.

"Hey," one of them called, putting on the hat he'd had tucked under his arm. *"You waiting for the ferry?"*

They weren't musicians after all. Well one of them wasn't. Had something happened at the Club? A break-in. His breath came out in a short rush, "Yeah. Officer. Sir."

They were getting closer. Not smiling. Concerned.

He stood up.

The sound of a car engine starting up. Johnny's head turned towards it and the headlights. They lit up the area enough to see through the bushes. The engine stopped. The lights stayed on. He could see two men leaning back on the car. Something stirred in his mind.

"Well," the man bulked full of muscle standing with the police officer sneered, *"why didn't you get on it?"*

This wasn't what Johnny expected to hear. He brought his attention back from the car and the two figures.

"I said," louder now, the lip twisting further, *"why didn't you get on it?"*

Johnny's hand started its move towards his hair and stopped, "I was waiting—"

"You went down to the pontoon. Why didn't you get on the fucking boat?"

Johnny's eyes flicked back to the car. He contemplated running. Now there was only one figure leaning on the car. He didn't dare look around for the other. A match torched the end of a cigarette and lit the face. He took in the shape and heard the tsunami of adrenaline roar in his ears. Nichols? What did he want? Why was he here? He thought about Robert's encounter. Had he gotten in the way of something?

"Hey. Are you looking for someone?" It sounded slightly nervous trying to be aggressive.

Johnny shook his head, looking at his interrogator, "No. Sir."

"You haven't answered the question," the non-uniformed one sounded too soft and soothing for such a muscled physique. "Why didn't you get on the ferry?"

"Look," Johnny forced himself to sound normal, compliant. They were trying to put the wind up him. He'd ignore that. Play it like they were trying to help. "I— I was meant to, I went to check where it was. It's just that I'm waiting for someone. A friend."

"Well, it wouldn't be a girl would it?" This from behind him. Familiar.

Breathy snickering from the other two.

And then with leisurely drags on his cigarette, Nichols approached.

"You're not a filthy poofter are you?" again from behind. And a laugh, "I think you ar-are."

Andrews? The way the voice sing-songed. It had to be him.

"Not who we were expecting, but we've got a live one." It was the muscle guy.

The air thickened in Johnny's chest, turning solid.

"The homeless man. I saw his stuff," Johnny found his voice, but it came out in ragged spurts. "He must be around here, somewhere." They wouldn't try anything. Not if there was a chance someone would see them. Would they?

"He's not going to be much use to you. Drunk as a skunk. Anyway, wouldn't have thought he was your type. Haha."

Then from Andrews, behind him, "You wanna join him? Hey? You could be cell-mates tonight. Would you like that? You slimy poofter."

A muscled non-uniformed arm pushed his shoulder. He stumbled, dropping Robert's jacket.

"Oh, what a shame, it'll be all dirty now." Fat grey snowflakes fell onto the jacket. The cigarette followed, and a black steel-capped shoe butted it out.

"How about you introduce yourself prop-er-ly," from behind. Definitely Andrews.

"Where's your ID?" from the uniform. Then a hesitant, "F-fag."

Johnny's hand obeyed, moving to the pocket of his jeans, but he stopped it. "I really should be asking for yours. Shouldn't I?" It surprised him to have said it. Robert couldn't be too far away. He had to keep them talking, slow things down. If he was carted off, Robert wouldn't know where he was. "I'm minding my own business, waiting for the next ferry, I'm not doing anything wrong."

"Did everyone hear me ask for ID?" the uniformed officer didn't wait for an answer. "And-um, did, did anyone see him give it to me?"

"A police officer asked for your ID fag," scorn iced the words.

As Johnny resigned and reached, the muscled arm poked, "Hands where I can see them."

'Don't defend. Stay calm,' he told himself, and tried again.

Another shove.

'Don't say anything. Pray,' Johnny glanced towards the car. 'No... run.'

He started towards the road, then twisted away, mindful there could be more of them at the cars. The river, over by the playground, seemed like the better option.

But Andrews and Nichols had relocated, taking up field positions like some bizarre cricket game.

Johnny had barely moved when he was grabbed in a chokehold, catching the nauseating whiff of nicotined fingers. He struggled, gasping for air and freedom.

The blow to his solar plexus came without warning, and the choke released as he fell forward with an air sucking grunt. Half-kneeling, half-crouching, he saw a black lace-up boot coming towards his jaw. He turned away. It caught his eye. The pain was momentarily masked by the shock of blood spurting from the gash. He couldn't see the warm drops splodge rhythmically onto the back of his hand.

Blindly, he moved the hand tentatively upwards to explore his face, while he coaxed air past the other point of impact. A foot crashed against his raised arm, then a knee with the full force of a body behind it, pinned his arm and shoulder to the ground. Someone else's foot kicked his other shoulder, tipping him completely back before planting itself on him, so he lay spreadeagled, face up, one leg straight and one knee half bent under him. A steel capped boot exploded into his groin and behind his bloodied unseeing eyes, a flash of searing white arced and lit the blackness. Every nerve in his body spasmed, and what breath he had restored, expelled itself in silence.

"Let's see who we've got here."

Johnny couldn't see through the slick bloodied curtain of eyelashes, but somehow through the pain-haze, he felt a hand reach into his jeans pocket and take his wallet.

"That wasn't so hard, was it?" Nichols' matter-of-fact voice paused, then chuckled. "Well, whaddo-ya know. Thought I recognised you. Not following a police order is a crime, isn't it John Saunders?"

Johnny couldn't move or speak.

The voice turned cold and sinister, "And so is being a mangy filthy fag, isn't it? You fuckin' animal."

Silence.

Then another voice, sing-song, "And what do we do with these animals, boys?"

There was a titter, nervously eager.

He continued, answering his own question, "We have a re-sponsa-bil-ity. We gotta teach them to behave like normal people, don't we?"

Johnny could hear muscle man's sick smile.

"And how do we do that s-sir?" The uniform.

Sinister and matter-of-fact, Nichols voice, "Aversion therapy."

A chorus of harsh laughter preceded the next kicks. Johnny flinched. His arms still pinned. At first the assault came from one direction. Over and over in the soft tissue of his side between his ribs and his hip. Then when he couldn't bear it, a stomp on his chest. He heard a cheer over the sound of the crack. Then stomping on his shoulder and pinned arm, so even when it stopped, he couldn't move his arm.

Pain was searing and sudden and unpredictable and exhausting and everywhere.

He heard them grunting with effort. A savage kick to his jaw took the pain from the other side of his face, and he tasted blood. Another smashed his cheek above it. An invading viscous drizzle clogged his airways. He coughed, and gagging coughed again. Blood splurted out of his nose and mouth.

"Look what he's done to my shirt. Where's your fuck-ing manners. How am I supposed to clean that off. Fuckin poofter."

The tirade finished. The blows didn't.

He couldn't breathe. He couldn't feel. He coughed again.

Another blow to the side of his head and a roar inside it.

From somewhere else, he watched as the boots connected with his body.

It continued to jerk limply, unresisting with each kick.

Nothing hurt anymore.

*

…"And then I saw you. Remember?" Alan looked at Robert. "We caught each other's eyes, but I had to look back. And I heard you yell at them, and I thought holy shit, this isn't gonna end well, and two of them started to come at you and you took off like the clappers. When I turned back I saw the other two half carrying and half dragging Johnny towards the river. I lost sight of them at the shelter. I figured they be back soon enough, so I lay back over on the seat like they'd left me. I knew what happened. Their shoes were muddy, and the bottom of their trousers was wet."

Robert's face had grayed, his half full glass of bubbles was hot and flat, his words were small and soft, "I'm sorry Anna, I can't finish this." He put the glass down. He wondered if he'd ever be able to drink champagne again.

Anna didn't say anything. No-one did.

Robert forced thought back into his blanked mind. *This has to end, Johnny.*

The colour started to come back into his face, and he turned to Alan, "How did you find Anna?"

"Your business card. Ernie had it."

"And luckily," added Anna, "I happened to be passing the reception desk, and heard your name."

"I'd been coming in every day. Asking for you. Dumb girl at—"

"He kept getting told you didn't work here and would he like to make an appointment with someone else," Anna interrupted again, "even though I'd given instructions."

"So Anna comes over all polite," said Alan, "and says 'Come with me,' and we went to the conference room and she made me a cuppa, and rang you."

"And rang you, and rang you, and rang you," said Anna, "But there was no answer. I couldn't figure out why you weren't returning my calls. I was starting to worry."

"You were ringing home. Lauren had gone to Duncan's and... but I rang. I left my number for you. The new one."

Anna raised her eyebrows, "Yes, well. Eventually I asked Mr Eldridge. And then I rang and rang and rang that one."

"And you've been staying here?" Robert looked at Alan then Anna.

"She insisted," Alan nodded towards Anna. "Said she'd been given strict instructions not to let me out of her sight. It was a godsend."

"Not just for you," Anna's mum piped up from across the room.

"I've been helping out a bit is all." Alan's jaw jutted upwards, "I'm no bludger. Gonna get some cards made up and sort some tools. Won't be long and I'll be paying my way."

"You're staying?" Robert looked from Alan to Anna, "Here?"

"For as long as I'm welcome," said Alan.

"He's hardly stopped," Anna's face was soft. "Seems he was a bit handy with a hammer in a previous life."

"Cabinet maker. I was a subcontractor. Got shafted though. Head contractor went under and couldn't pay me. Couldn't pay anyone. But miraculously finishes the job with a new business name. Big government job. Ask me why I don't trust politicians. Anyway," he looked over at Anna's mum, "what is it we say?"

"Onwards and sideways," her smile was sad.

CHAPTER 57

"Seriously had my doubts," Callum's head made a slow no.

Robert's grin almost split his face before contracting again.

"And he'll testify?" said Callum.

"It's tricky, since he's supposed to be dead."

"Have you told anyone else? Simon Draper?"

Robert shook his head, "Haven't seen him. He's been busy. I... it's confidential."

"I am your not-lawyer," Callum's eyebrow lifted. He opened the Sunday Mail, pointing, "Anything to do with this?"

Robert skimmed the piece.

"A few stories like this have been popping up," said Callum. "Hopefully people will start asking questions. Or more questions."

"I'll call him," said Robert. "Actually, you two should talk. And I should touch base with some other people too. See what they know about all this."

"Your mates from the pub?"

Robert nodded.

"Do you think that's wise?"

Robert shrugged, "Probably not."

"I know it's frustrating."

"Understatement." Robert looked at his wrist where his watch should be, "I should get to work. I'm supposed to be meeting Alex at CAMP shortly. Weren't you scheduled for that?"

"No. Do you know who's going to be there?"

Robert shook his head, "Committee Progress Meeting. My first one."

"Do you think they'd mind if I turned up?"

"I'll call."

"I'll do it. You get going. I'll be fifteen minutes or so behind you."

*

"Oh my God," Robert grinned, when he walked through CAMP's door, thinking this is becoming a habit. A nice one.

Tank had lunged, wrapping him up, and only let go when Blue nudged him aside. Simon avoided the hug, and gripped his hand.

Alex smiled, "Good to see we all know each other. And Callum's on his way. I'm sure you'll find something to talk about while we wait. There's tea and coffee in the meeting room."

*

"Should I take the notes?" Robert looked up from the previous minutes, as they finally got down to business.

"This latest legislation affecting pubs," Alex started. "Any progress?"

"Progress?" Blue's top lip puckered, "We got a notification from the Hotel Association. The law is official now. Assuming they mean gays when they're talking about perverts and deviants, and along with child molesters and drug users, it's illegal to serve them."

"But how do they police it? How can you tell who's a child molester?" Robert asked.

"Can't," said Blue.

"Of course, we sometimes know who the gays are," Tank turned his head to one side and arched his eyebrow. "I know. Missing the point."

"Which is?" Callum asked.

"More opportunities to collect money. They're getting greedy. Greedier. You want to stay open? Pay up." Blue shook his head, "It's worse than ever."

"Did you hear anything from your dad on this?" Callum's eyes were on Robert and the question hovered over the despondent silence.

Simon put his hand up, "If I may? We spoke over the weekend. Cabinet was unanimous as you'd expect, they just do everything Joh wants. The opposition had a word or two to say against it, at least they try to be a voice for reason. The rest of Joh's lot didn't even whimper. I don't know why they bother turning up."

"What happens now, besides it costing publicans more money to keep the cops off their backs?" Callum again.

"The QHA, the Association, are going to issue a press release," Blue said, "saying the legislation is untenable. That even if we ask patrons to verify they aren't any of the excluded categories, we have no idea if they're telling the truth, and that staff and owners, can't be held responsible. They'd be open to fines and prosecution. And of course, there'd be the cost of 'we'll keep it between ourselves, nudge-nudge', and the accompanying cash donation."

Callum's eyes narrowed, "How did the Commissioner even think this would work?"

"Don't you worry about that," Simon impersonated the Premier and laughter temporarily lifted their spirits. "I asked your dad if he could shed any light on the origins of this unholy Joh and Terry alliance. I mean really? Politics and policing this close together in any other language would be a dictatorship."

Robert stopped writing, "I've asked him that too. All he says is, the old bastard has a lot of secrets. Did he tell you that Joh never signed up to the superannuation scheme. If he leaves the job, he won't have his salary or a pension."

"Which explains this, I suppose." Simon nodded towards the paper, "And how the likes of Iwasaki and other shady developments get approved, despite planning permissions being denied at the regional level where they actually should be. Smells a bit like Joh's retirement plan to me."

"Speculation," said Robert. "Makes sense, but still speculation. We need proof."

"Working on it," said Simon.

"Well get a move on," said Alex. "And while you're at it, a bit more action on our behalf would be good. I'd like to be alive when I'm legal."

"You could move interstate," Tank offered.

"That's why CAMP's here. Why I'm here. We shouldn't," Alex stopped when he recognized Tank's sarcasm, "Oh."

"Simon," said Robert, "next point we were hoping you'd be able to do something with in the paper. AIDS. This business of outlawing condom vending machines. It's tantamount to lining people up and shooting them if you ask me. And fobbing off research funding requests. Can you do anything?"

"According to my editor, people aren't interested in quote, civil liberties shit."

"What are they interested in then?" Callum snorted.

"Whatever he decides. And that of course, depends on who's paying for advertising. In this case Joh and his buddies. The Nationals."

"It's an uphill battle," Callum scoffed.

"But we have to keep trying," said Alex. "It's people's lives."

"Yeah. People's lives," Robert's eyes clouded, and his face had a sheen over its pallor.

"You don't look crash hot," Simon frowned.

"I'm OK," Robert looked up and felt a hot flash before an icy damp formed on his forehead. "No, actually, I'm not. Here," he passed the minutes to Alex and rushed to the bathroom.

After heaving up the brown slime of regurgitated coffee and nothing else, Robert looked into the mirror. *Are you a grown man? Are you capable of feeding yourself? Then why the fuck aren't you doing it?* He took some plain biscuits from the jar in the kitchen and headed back to the meeting, catching the tail end of what they'd been discussing in his absence. Him.

"…janitor," said Callum and Robert's face scrunched, "and working with me on this. So keeping busy. And bail conditions. It's not a walk in the park is it?"

"And I suppose the less people he sees, the less he hears what they're saying about him," said Tank.

"Exactly," said Simon. "It's not pretty. The letters to the editor are still coming in. Some of them want to give him a medal, but, there's a lot of people who don't. They don't get much space. But I wouldn't want him to come face to face with any of them."

"I don't know which is worse," Tank's voice sank. "Being the poster boy for poofter-bashing bigots, especially, well, Johnny. Or being vilified by your own kind. Being blamed for killing him."

"They don't know," Robert's voice came from the open doorway.

"I'm sorry Lovey," Tank's remorse was stark. "We weren't—"

"It's OK," said Robert. "Honestly. At least with all of you I feel safe. But it's sort-of lonely, and, demoralizing. Thinking about them getting away with what they did to Johnny."

"And to you," Tank's tone had shifted. "They did this to you. You've got no Johnny, no kids, no wife, no career."

"I appreciate your support, Tank," Robert said. "And it's a bit of a list..."

"But?"

"But I did this. If I hadn't ventured out with Johnny, none of this would've happened."

Blue's head was shaking, "No mate. You've got that all wrong. If it wasn't you and Johnny, it would have been someone else. And, if it happens to one of us, it happens to all of us. That's the way it is. Understand?"

Alex patted Robert's vacant chair, "Come on."

"We'll get there," said Callum.

And Simon added, "They're not going to get away with bloody murder forever."

"I certainly hope not," said Robert. "Not if I can help it." He looked over to Callum, "But right now, I need to go home, I'm definitely under the weather."

"We'll take you," Tank offered.

"My car's at QIT," Robert said. "I'll need it to get to work in the morning."

"No, honestly," Robert insisted when they stopped near the parking area at QIT and offered to swap around and drive his car home for him. "But thanks. I do feel a lot better."

Tank checked Robert's temperature with the back of his hand, "OK then."

Savouring the cool air coming off the river through the trees and drying his perspiration, Robert watched them go.

He had almost made it to the car park when he heard the voice, angry and accusing, "Hey you!"

He instantly forgot Callum's advice.

Someone pushed his shoulder. Someone else stepped in front of him. He saw a pair of faded brown leather shoes, and a pair of grubby trainers.

"It is him," another voice. Excited. "Hey, it's him. It's the gay panic killer."

Tucking his briefcase under his arm, he pushed trying to get past.

A blow to his middle stole his breath. He bent over trying to find it, and someone pushed him to the ground. A foot connected with his ribcage and he grunted.

He heard, "Over here. Quick," and "Bastard," and rolled away from the next kick, getting up on one knee and then making a break for it.

"Come on," a voice.

And another, "Don't let him get away."

More shouting. He changed direction, away from the carpark, heading for the Botanic Gardens. It was big enough to get lost in. He hoped.

Almost on the other side of the Gardens, he veered towards the city to Johnny's old workplace, The Park Royal, and stopped running. *Be normal.*

Inside the building he locked himself in a cubicle in the men's toilets sitting hunched over on the lid, while the memory of Terry interrupted the hammering in his ears.

He'd get the car later, he decided, when it had all died down.

***

At home he swallowed a glass of water then lay on the bed and drifted into a black heavy and welcome sleep. Until suddenly he heard shouting. He jerked to avoid the shoulder push he thought was coming, but for some reason it didn't. Then he saw the boots and coiled into a giant foetus as they swung towards him. He braced against the anticipated blows, turning sharply. And woke up.

The sun was still hanging over the city. Just. He pulled the gray uniform shirt from his case and smelled the underarms. *Oh well.* He pulled it on over his office shirt and went back to get the car. Cleaners were invisible. And when people did see them, if they didn't look away, they looked beyond them. Even so, he'd have to be more alert. Perhaps he could get a haircut,

297

or a cap. *Or another fucking life.*

He forgot to check the answering machine.

CHAPTER 58

Safely out of the carpark with his car, still didn't feel safe. Robert drove distractedly trying to lose sight of the dream he'd had, and not wanting to return for a repeat. On autopilot the idea of an in-person thank-you to Ernie and the prospect of a 139 Club meal appeared, and then he was driving past Harry's and a parking space beckoned. A scotch and dry without the scotch might help settle his stomach.

After the buzz wasn't answered, Robert stepped back and waited for someone else to have a turn, and then someone else, and buzzed again.

"Harry. It's Robert. Want some company?"

The hesitation was almost imperceptible.

"It's OK, if you'd rather give it a miss. It was just a whim. I'm not exactly—"

No. No," Harry interrupted him. "Give me a minute Buzz me back in a minute."

He turned away from the panel and waited.

The door opened, and Duncan came out. Robert couldn't help but smile realizing just how invisible cleaners were as Duncan sailed past him, and this time when he buzzed, the door opened for him. His smile faded in the elevator. Did Harry not want company because Duncan was there? Is that why Duncan left? By the time he'd reached Harry's foyer, he'd decided that if Harry and Duncan wanted him to know there was a Harry and Duncan, Duncan would not have left.

To confound his theory, Harry's first words were, "Duncan left two minutes ago."

"Oh," said Robert, "that's a shame. Honestly though, I'm not so sure he would want to see me."

"Why not?" Harry said motioning Robert to come in.

"Family solidarity. Lauren. She doesn't want to talk to me, and I can't see the kids. It will *unsettle* them."

"You can't be serious? Would it help if I said something? Scotch?"

Robert shrugged, "I don't think so. Saying something I mean. Make mine plain ginger ale. Harry, are you and— Forget it. None of my business."

Harry handed him the drink, "It's OK," he said. "You know it's no secret I'd like to say yes."

"He spends a lot of time here now. Duncan."

"He loves your kids Robert, but I think full time is a bit much for him. He's quote, giving Lauren some space. But she had some special presentation she wanted to be at for uni. She wanted a babysitter."

"I saw him leave. I thought it was because of me?"

Harry looked at him sideways, "It isn't all about you."

Robert started to lower his eyes and stopped, "I probably deserved that. How are you?"

"Better for having been asked," said Harry. "Duncan prefers not to talk about it."

Harry looked at his scotch, "I've been thinking about a lot of things lately. Having a deadline does that."

"Shit. Seriously? I'm sorry."

"No. I didn't mean it like that. Not at all. Nothing's changed on that front. But I was so easily threatened. I could have— should have told those, I don't like to swear... pricks, to fuck the hell off. None of this would have happened." He paused, "I've been feeling a bit down. I wasn't really looking forward to company."

"I've had a bit of a day myself. I'll go hey?"

"It's all so futile. Depressing," Harry ignored the offer. "You have to hide away. Pretend, for your whole life, that you aren't you. You're not entitled to have what everyone else takes for granted."

Robert waited for Harry to find what else was picking at the sore on his soul.

"It wasn't my first choice, I told you, but when I started in law, I was inspired by this ideal of justice that's ethical and compassionate. But law isn't that. I kept wanting it to be. It's a bully. As robust and overbearing as it is fragile."

He reached over for his glass, pulling it soundlessly on its green felt-based coaster. Inside the glass, the liquid thrashed against the sides.

"Maybe it was me that wanted justice. Here I was, part of it, upholding it, and always outside it. I had this power. Hah. Thought I did. It was all an illusion. A lie." He looked as if he'd pulled back the curtain and seen the fetid mess it had been hiding. And without the thick pleats holding it in, the smell had hit him smack in the face. "I gave him up for that. No. Pushed him aside. For that despicable… that appalling lie."

Robert held tightly to his glass.

"My whole life," Harry's voice turned wondrous, "a lie. Yours too. And Duncan's. So many lies. So much lost happiness. No, not lost. You can't lose what you haven't got… Forsaken… We can't keep paying for who we are, like it's some kind of reparation. Like we've caused some," Harry searched, "some irreparable and monstrous damage to the world."

The stench of Harry's words was overpowering.

Robert's face drooped, "We will Harry. I don't know how, but we will." As he finished, he had a sense of Johnny saying 'thank you, for trying.'

"I should go," Robert swallowed the last of his ginger ale.

Harry sighed, "Not much company."

"Not your job," Robert's face softened. He held Harry's eyes, "Harry, if there's anything you need, want to talk about, I'm here. I don't mean to fade into the background. But honestly, I haven't been on top of the world lately either. Don't hesitate. OK? I feel like I should've, I feel bad. If—"

"If. If, if, if. No more. No more. We didn't do anything wrong. They did."

It was the second time Robert had heard the same words.

Something lifted in Harry and his face set, "You need to call me as a witness."

"You sure?"

"I'd be under oath."

"Do you think that matters to them?"

"It matters to me. The truth," Harry peered at something only he could see. Then reset his eyes, "The truth will out, as they say. Eventually. This way, it might be sooner rather than later."

PART FIVE

1987

CHAPTER 59

Robert's mind was drifting dangerously on the drive home from Harry's. He slammed on the brakes, when he noticed the traffic light he was about to pass was red. With his forehead resting against the steering wheel, he let out an audible sigh, grateful no-one was behind him, or in front. When he recovered his composure, he counted, refusing to think about anything until he got home.

Once there though, thoughts crashed around him again as he autopiloted. Dousing his grey overshirts with washing powder; and dousing vegetables with oil and putting them in the oven. His mind kept flicking back to Harry and Duncan. If Harry was feeling so down about Johnny and what happened, what was the thing with Duncan? *None of your business is what.*

He ate in front of the TV and fell asleep.

Music from the television woke him. Turning to switch off the living room light to go to bed, he saw the answering machine flashing red, and groaned.

Are you going to have to stick a fucking note on the fridge door?

He pushed play. Lauren asking him to stay with the kids. She needed to go somewhere.

"Fuck. Fuck." *That was your pass back in, and you missed it. You idiot.*

*

At work the next day, he called. After the third call he left a message. He was beginning to feel that normal, his new normal, was wobbling precariously on a crescent-shaped slackwire. He couldn't get to the little platform on either side. It was exhausting, and frustrating, and there was nothing to hold on to. And the only thing he wanted to hold on to right now were his kids. He called back.

"Forget it," he told the machine. "Don't call back. I'm coming over after work."

He left not long after Rose arrived back from lunch, telling her he'd work from home. He was vaguely aware that the threat of a 'no you're not', hadn't set his adrenaline spurting as he raised his hand in good-bye.

At home, he dumped his briefcase on the coffee table, checked the answering machine with a satisfied smile, and checked the clock. They wouldn't be home from Crèche yet. An hour or so of sleep would be welcome, but sleep wasn't cooperating. Instead, he took out a cleaning cloth and spray bottle. He thought about his mum and squeezed the trigger, spraying and wiping surfaces as he went room to room.

When he got to the bathroom mirror, he remembered Callum's words and looked himself in the eye and sprayed, watching the lavender-scented chemical bubbles blot out his image. They sagged, but still clung on. He swiped them and they smeared.

While he rubbed at the smear, he thought of his dad standing up for himself as an Independent and for gays; of Tank and Blue and brown paper bags and CAMP; of Jimbo and Pete, two birds breaking out of their cage, determined to fly despite their clipped wings. He saw Terry, and a line of bullies and felt his spare hand gripping the cold edge of the sink. And then he thought of Simon, and Tim, Kowalski, and Ernie and Alan, Anna and

Callum, Harry and Duncan. Marnie and Jack. And little Robert. And Johnny.

Johnny. Tears welled unspent and his nose prickled. He kept wiping, staring ahead.

As the smears cleared completely, he stared at the face looking back at him and thought about his mum again, lost in her haze of misplaced disappointment. *It's not your fault. She used you. She hid behind you.*

And Lauren. What the hell?

The cloth was balled up in his fist. He looked at it, then back to his face in the mirror. His eyes were different. The syrupy wallow in them had solidified.

'We weren't doing anything wrong,' said Johnny. 'Being who you are isn't wrong. We weren't hurting anybody,'

Robert stared a moment longer. He felt different. A wave swept over him. It was powerful, but it didn't knock him down. It came again, lifting him with it.

***

His car was in the driveway of Duncan's house. Robert parked behind it in Lauren's. *Fuck it. It's not like you need a fancy car.*

Lauren held the door frame, "I don't think this is such a good—"

"Idea? Time? What?"

She went to answer.

"It was rhetorical, Lauren," he said. "There's never a good time and it's never a good idea. We just have to do it anyway."

Her eyes clouded, "Are you coming in?"

"Are you inviting me in?"

After the squeals died down and he'd spent the first half hour of the visit with Emma and Thomas, he told them it was Mummy's turn. He promised them a bedtime story even if it wasn't bedtime.

"Are you really, really promising?" said Thomas.

"What if Mummy says no?" Emma had spotted Lauren in the doorway.

"Well, sometimes," Robert said pretending he hadn't seen her, "daddies get to say yes even when mummies say no. It depends on what's in the best interests of the child."

"But there's two childs," Thomas's bottom lip stuck out.

"You, little champion," Robert mussed his hair, "are not going to miss out," and poking Emma softly in the ticklish spot of her ribs, "or you. Is that clear?"

She giggled, and they both nodded.

"The kids seem settled," Robert held Lauren's eyes. "That's good. But I'm sure they'd enjoy some of my company from time to time."

"I don't know—"

"Know if that's such a good idea," Robert finished for her. "And why is that? You were happy enough to ask me to be with them last night."

She looked down, marshalling her words into their practiced order, "It's not that you haven't been a good father, but all this... You'd be sending them the wrong message."

He didn't interrupt.

"What happened to Johnny was demented. People believe you did that."

He stayed silent, balancing on the controlled wave he'd moved to from the slackwire. His heart beating steadily.

"We need to distance ourselves. From you. Think about Emma and Thomas. Kids at school will tease them, bully them. And the police, even if they've made a mistake, people will still say where there's smoke there's fire." Her voice was prancing into its high-horse mode, "I don't want the kids growing up knowing the kind of person who's been accused— could have done something like that, let alone be around them all the time. Or whatever time he thought he should have. Why did you have to say you did it?"

"Have you ever said you did something, and you didn't?"

"This is different. This isn't 'I ate the last piece of cake' for God's sake."

"I said it because there was no choice," Robert said. "And we have no idea how this is going to come out in the wash. Clean I hope."

There was silence.

"My take on all this," he said, "is that you're angry with me for being gay, and for telling you. Not that I blame you."

"No. Absolutely no way. I was in a street march supporting gays. I was locked up. How is that anti-gay?"

"I didn't say you were anti-gay," Robert's tone was even. "I said I think you are anti *me* being gay. And this is your way of punishing me."

"You never seemed gay," she looked down. "Not to me."

"Did you ever think you might not be able to tell if someone is gay or not?"

"Of course I would. Johnny is— was, most definitely gay," it came out with a swagger.

Robert shrugged.

"You can't be gay." Her voice escalated, "You're not. Not really."

"How do you know?"

Lauren turned and ran water over her cup in the sink.

Robert talked to her back, "Do you ever feel cheated Lauren? For not having a mum."

Her fingers clamped over the sink edge.

"Why do you think your dad never re-married?"

She released her grip and turned around.

"Why do you think he never even dated after your mum died?"

"How dare you?"

"I'm only asking you a question."

She stared.

"I'm serious."

She tried to take his cup.

"No, I mean it," he said. "Look at me. Why do you think you picked me to marry? You were the most stunning girl at uni. Men were falling over themselves, and each other. You could've had your pick."

She frowned.

"You picked me. The gawky uncoordinated totally-not-jock who liked everything they didn't. Someone like your dad."

"What are you saying?"

He rinsed his own cup, wiped his hands and took hers, "If I'd had more of a clue back then, I wouldn't have brought you down this path with me. Freud has this theory, that we choose a mate resembling our opposite sex parent. Particularly when we idolize them."

There was a hint of something in her eyes, and he kept going, "I wasn't even looking, Lauren. I was confused. You adopted me. When you picked me, I thought maybe I was OK. That I'd gotten it all wrong. That the kids at school who'd teased me and bullied me had gotten it all wrong." He squeezed her hands, "It was no great burden to fall in love with you, believe me. I thought I'd hit the jackpot. For once in my life, I was what everyone envied instead of what they kicked into the corner." He could see her tears pooling, "You gave me confidence. I tried. I became a younger version of your dad. But you know, don't you?"

She wrenched her hands free and hit him in the shoulder, and then bathed the spot with her tears.

"I didn't want this to happen, Robert. I don't deserve this. I didn't do anything wrong."

He held her. He could feel the hurt trying to push its way up.

"Why couldn't you just leave things as they were. I liked my life. We had a good marriage. I was going to work with you and with Dad. You've taken the lovely future I imagined and destroyed it. Completely wrecked it. It's gone."

He waited.

"I love you, Robert. It's not fair. It's not fair." The tears ran freely and she punched his shoulder again before burying her face back on the spot.

After a while she lifted her head, and stepped away, "I don't want to share my husband, Robert. I don't want our— my children sharing their dad. I loved Johnny. But I don't want him or anyone else in my marriage."

Robert stood still arms by his side.

"And," she continued, "I don't think you can keep trying to be what you aren't."

"So?"

"I think we should get a divorce."

He nodded, "I thought you'd say that."

"And given the circumstances, and the fact that you aren't exactly legal and would be deemed unfit by any court, I want custody," her eyes were brittle.

He shook his head, "I'm not a violent man. I only ever punched one person in my life, and I only hurt his pride. And all of this will disappear. Soon I hope. And," his eyes set, "if it's the fact that I'm gay? Then I'm not prepared to let Duncan have my kids, when for all intents and purposes, he's as unfit as me."

"That's not fair," she said.

"None of this is fair," he said. "You just said so. None of it. It's not your fault. And it's not theirs. And there's this thing… a term bandied about in the family court… in the best interest of the child. I think we should be going down that road, don't you?"

Her head had been moving slowly side to side, and stilled.

"Hopefully," he said, "by the time they've grown up, there won't even be a conversation like this. I'll do the paperwork and drop it off. Someone in the office can file it on our behalf. And now, I've got a story to read."

"I made casserole for dinner. I'll put some in a container. You can take it home with you."

He smiled, "That'd be nice. Thanks."

***

The kids had skewered him with their pointy questions at first, but over the next few months, they'd adapted and settled into a pattern for visits. They loved the bunk beds he'd bought and took turns in the top one, and for the most part Robert had adapted to aloneness without feeling lonely. His paying job was a long meditation, and the slow progress of anything to do with his real-but-not-paid job, meant that any small win was inordinately satisfying. Lauren had seemed more contented. She was doing well with uni. Maybe it was a confidence thing with her too.

These thoughts driving home from the last drop off at Duncan's, felt comforting and comfortable. He looked at the Tupperware container on the passenger seat and allowed himself to feel happy. And he didn't have to cook tonight, thank-you Lauren. His skill in the kitchen was improving, but he was grateful for his uninformed palate and simple tastes. Have to be OK with simple on my pay. He laughed to himself, locking the garage door. And thinking of money, he detoured to the letterbox. It was electricity bill time.

Inside the apartment, he glanced at the answering machine, then flicked through the junk-mail and found the electricity bill. Vindicated. The smile slid from his face when the next envelope appeared. His breath caught. Yellow. No stamp. Government logo.

He breathed again and tapped it against the hand holding the rest of the mail. *It's hardly unexpected. Come on. They had to set a date some time.*

In the kitchen, he set it down, threw away the junk-mail, poured a large glass of wine, drank some, put the glass down, flicked open the seal, and found the date.

After putting it aside, he was mildly surprised that his heart was beating faster anticipating the numbers on the electricity bill.

CHAPTER 60

"Got caught up," Simon said, arriving at CAMP.

Robert liked the way Simon never offered reasons.

"Go through to the meeting room, I'll get us a coffee."

Back with a half-full mug in each hand, Robert nudged the door open with his foot. He smiled, realising he hadn't done his habitual kick and cringe in ages. He'd latched onto the idea from Lauren, that it was an acquired affectation, something stopping him from appearing to be gay by appearing to be clumsy. But was it? What was it?

His eyes unconsciously headed up, looking for an answer.

Holy shit.

His mum screeching, 'Get them off. Get them off. What do you think you're doing? You'll ruin them. You ruin everything.'

He'd been prancing around the living room. One of her scarves draped around his neck, her glam Jackie O sunglasses sliding off his face, and wearing a pair of shiny high heels. She'd lunged. He'd stubbed the delicate point of her shoe on the doorframe scraping a chunk of shine off. 'Get out. Get out of my sight.'

He'd kicked off the shoes, running out of the house. Ripping off the sunglasses and scarf, dropping them on the back stairs on the way to his cubby. The dilapidated shed at the end of the garden. The smell of cut grass was overwhelming.

"You OK?" Simon asked.

Robert closed his mouth, "Yeah. Yeah. Thanks. Here," he put the mugs down, and showed Simon the official notification of the court appearance.

"Beginning of May. This works in well," Simon said, "Joh's going to be away around that time, a little jaunt to the USA which the trade minister isn't to be trusted with. Tim can go to air with no bluster and redirect."

"Gotta hand it to Joh. He does that well."

"Years of practice and a reptilian mind," Simon shook his head. "Doesn't seem to matter what we've put out there to date, nothing sticks."

Robert started naming a list of the Premier's crimes, "If I take off my shoes we could include more. The Daintree got to me. No-one would even have known if Joh hadn't wanted footage so he could brag about it." Robert's eyes narrowed. "If the government in Victoria did that to a community on the Murray, there'd be hell to pay. But Joh cooks up a story about these people are up to no good, with not an ounce of proof, and everyone's applauding him for a job well done. He burnt down people's homes, destroyed their lives. For nothing. A diversion. A stunt. I should stop there. And I shouldn't let it get to me."

"Welcome to my world," Simon shrugged. "You're pretty passionate, you could do worse than pursuing stuff like this if you've got the stomach for it."

"Enough on my plate," said Robert, "for now anyway. What about Pete and Jimbo's story? Did you get any further with that?"

"Tim's been working on it."

Robert's nod slowed, "This'll sound weird, but do you think Joh is actually human?"

"What?"

"That lizard-like skin of his. Nothing sticks. Do you think he was born with a Teflon coat?"

Simon laughed, "It's gotta be wearing thin though, eh?"

"Jeez, I hope so."

"Don't we all? I tell you," said Simon, "if the shit doesn't hit the fan after everyone's seen *The Moonlight State*, I give up."

"You can't," Robert said. "Every story, every single one, has an impact. Even if people are totally anti, some part seeps in. Pour water on a rock and it runs off but leaves a damp stain. Keep pouring and," he stopped. "Shit, listen to me, telling you your job."

Simon laughed again, "That's the idea. Anyway, you're up next, ready or not."

Robert shrugged, "Are you going to run another lead-in on gay panic?"

"What do you think?"

"As much as I hate to be standing in that particular spotlight," said Robert, "I can't help thinking it would be a good idea."

"You're right. It really can't hurt you, can it?"

"I don't care. No. I do. But if we don't get people talking. Just the ordinary everyday usually don't-give-a-rat's-arse people, then what's the fucking point?"

"Is there anything I can do?" Simon asked.

"Just be there. I've got a general plan. Some of it isn't even clear, but without anyone reporting it…"

"Are you still planning on a big reveal, to catch them out?"

"Yeah. Why?"

"You might be cutting your own throat."

Robert frowned.

"When you told us, that night with Tim, I thought, good idea. But recently? I don't know. My take, is that if you say I didn't do it because, guess what, I'm gay, we were having an affair. They've got you with motive. You were viciously silencing him. They'll well and truly stitch you up."

CHAPTER 61

Robert stopped looking around the slowly filling courtroom, and stared ahead wondering whether forgoing a jury trial with a guilty plea, had been the right choice. Then he reminded himself, there'd been no choice. At least with a judge-only trial, there'd be no jury to fact check and convince, just one man presiding over the admissibility of the evidence, and concluding that evidence was insufficient for a conviction.

He reminded his shoulders to lower. The case was cut and dried. No surprises. Except the ones he wanted. And at least with Simon's warning he wouldn't fall into their trap. No. There had to be no suspicion that he wasn't out of his depth, and simply and seriously confirming the facts according to the police reports. *Facts. Hah. Call them points.* Through closed eyelids he searched for Johnny. It wasn't working. His eyes flew open.

'Close your eyes. I'm right here.'

For what seemed like no particular reason, Robert placed both hands at the spot above the stone in his chest. He could feel the thud, thud, thud becoming quieter, more centered. His pulse slowed. He waited for the calm blanket to descend around him, but this time he felt it arise from within. Wavelike. Lifting him. And he remembered he'd felt it before.

'You've got this,' said Johnny.

No. We've got this. The guilty plea is good. I'm compliant. Not wasting the Court's time or resources. But…

'Stop there,' said Johnny's voice, 'You can always appeal.'

Not with new evidence.

'Why the fuck not?'

Because that's the rule.

'Fuck the rules. No-one else is playing by the fucking rules,' Johnny's

314

words clear. 'Fucking chess. If you can't change the rules, just stop playing their game. Better still, make up your own fucking game.'

Johnny, I hear you. But I need you calm. I need to be calm. We've got this. We have.

The judge entered. As everyone bowed, Robert glanced sideways at the prosecution and noticed their eyebrows drawing together. Whispering followed.

"Gentlemen of the prosecution, if I may have your attention," the judge waited while they un-huddled. "Is something disturbing you?"

"Your Honour. We were expecting—"

"Quite. Yes. My colleague is indisposed."

"May I request an adjournment until—"

"For what purpose?" The judge waited for two whole breaths before turning to Robert. "Now, Mr Carson. I see you are not represented. Is this going to cause the Court any problem?"

"I don't believe so, your Honour."

"Your occupation?"

"Um-now... cleaner, your Honour," Robert tried to keep his eyes looking straight at the judge's, and faltered.

"Hmm. Nothing to be ashamed of. My concern is your capacity to understand the processes. I don't want to have to act as interpreter, but if anything is unclear on a point of law, you should ask." He turned away from Robert to the prosecution, "And I caution the prosecution to maintain the role of providing a fair presentation of facts for the jury."

"I'm sorry, your Honour," the prosecutor stood, "this is a no-jury trial. There was a submission. The defense agreed."

The judge flicked through the papers in a timbered tray and extracted it, "Quite. However, under these circumstances, and with an unrepresented defense, a Jury of peers is my preference."

The prosecutor's legal counsel stood too, "With all due respect your Honour, the defense has pleaded guilty. It isn't required."

"Your respect is noted." The judge's eyebrow relaxed its arch. "However, it is my prerogative, and we have people outside waiting to be impaneled. Bailiff, would you bring them in."

The Bailiff stood.

"But, your Honour, the police checks? We haven't vetted these jurors for this case."

The judge frowned, "I'm not sure what you mean. Let me assure you, *you* might not have vetted them, but the mandatory name, age, and absence of unresolved criminal matter checks have been done."

"Yes, your Honour. But, our checks, we have to exclude anyone who doesn't meet our criteria from the possible selection," the solicitor's cheek colour was progressively brightening.

"Whatever procedure you've been following with regard to assessing juror suitability, I can assure you, again, the legally *allowed* assessments have been made. Am I clear?" He waited and as the solicitor sat, "Hmm. Quite."

The judge turned to Robert, "Does the defense have any objection?"

"No, your Honour." *Maybe. I don't know.*

"Go ahead Bailiff."

Robert's mind was rummaging for meaning. The prosecution was clearly unsettled too.

'New game. Way to go,' Johnny sounded almost happy.

Robert was still rummaging. He couldn't help thinking that if the stitching holding the seams of the prosecutor's story came loose, they could all be left exposed. Their plan, at least in his mind, was to lead the judge to the conclusion that justifiable self-defense had an unfortunate and unintended consequence, and that there was no substantiated proof to implicate the defendant. Him. His plan was to wait till that was assured, and then spring some serious questions on them. Get some kind of justice. Maybe. Hopefully.

That might have had a chance of working, as long as he went along with them to the point of deviation. If he did that now though, with twelve people to convince instead of one? How the hell was he going to do that? They didn't even have to tweak their story, which they could. All they had to do was tweak their questions, and he'd be totally fucked.

'That was always the case,' said Johnny's voice. 'And don't start getting ahead of yourself.'

Robert nodded, calmer.

'And remember, the police don't give a shit about you. This game is about them, getting themselves off the hook. Get inside their heads. You've gotta look like you're playing along.'

Robert let the jury selection from the assembled candidates go unchallenged. They were picking likely support for a poor accosted straight guy. *Well good on them. Keeping up their end of their own self-serving bargain.*

*

The air was still. The smell of warm dust and warm bodies mingled and hung in the air till the judge cut through it, calling the Court to order. There was a sharpness now, as he read in Robert's direction, "You are charged under the Criminal Code 1899, section three-zero-three with Manslaughter. How do you plead?"

"Guilt—"

"Your Honour," the prosecution solicitor stood, "in all fairness, there are mitigating circumstances."

"Approach the Bench."

"So is this a hearing or a trial?" the judge's face was uncompromising.

"We weren't expecting a jury, your Honour."

"A fact I am already aware of."

"The defendant agreed to a plea of guilty with diminished responsibility. Namely HAD."

The judge continued, his face neutral, "Homosexual Advance Defense, yes, I've been briefed."

"And also referred to as Gay Panic. And you said we should be fair to the defendant given that he is unrepresented. So, if I may?"

The judge nodded.

"There was no intentionality. And coming back into his right mind, he went to summon help. An ambulance. And the victim was discovered in the river. Not where the accused had left him. So there is a possibility some other party was involved."

"And yet you have charged this man."

"Your Honour, we had planned to explain all this to you."

"But now you have to explain it all to them," the judge nodded towards the jury. "Is there really a case here?"

"It was sent up," said the prosecution solicitor.

"That wasn't my question," said the judge.

"The accused has made a plea of gay panic. But we're expecting the jury will find for him."

"You mean not guilty?"

The prosecutor nodded and it echoed down the line, "It will become clear."

"And you are OK with this?" the judge's eyes bored into Robert.

Of course not, I'm not an idiot. But I don't want them to get away with murder. Arseholes. Robert's head moved once to the side, seemingly saying no of its own accord. He stilled it, "Yes, your Honour."

"You don't want to change your plea?"

"Your Honour, honestly, I believe this is the best way." This time he held the judge's eyes.

CHAPTER 62

Robert listened as Constable Brady gave a verbatim version of his report. He had a chiseled face and physique. His arm and chest muscles were visible beneath the fabric of his shirt when he moved his arm for the oath. No wonder they used him as the bait in their gay-bashing racket.

When asked if he wanted to cross examine, Robert hesitated as if he was going to decline and changed his mind.

"Constable Brady, would you mind confirming for me that it was only yourself and one other officer on duty with you, a Constable Thompson?"

"Correct."

"And you are both uniform officers."

"Yes."

"Were you wearing your uniform that night?"

"No. I wasn't."

"Is that usual? Can you tell us why?"

"I was doing a special surveillance type of job," Brady's chest inflated and pressed harder against the fabric.

"So only you, not Constable Thompson."

"Correct."

"Would you tell me about this special surveillance job?"

Brady's eyes flickered to the prosecution, "I'm not at liberty to say."

"That's OK," Robert pre-empted the objection, "So, is it usual? I'm confused. You're both on special surveillance but Constable Thompson was wearing his standard normal uniform. Do you know why?"

"No," said Brady, "I just do what I'm told. I didn't tell him what to wear or anything."

"I understand. Just taking orders. And-um, you'd done this job before.

Is that why you were there. You had specific experience of this, surveillance?" Robert eased over the word.

"Yes."

"But you hadn't worked with Constable Thompson before?" Robert sounded like he had no compelling reason to ask.

"No."

"So was this like a training session or something?"

"I don't know."

"OK," said Robert, "But this was his first time doing this particular surveillance."

"Yes," Brady sounded relieved.

"Sorry," Robert fussed with some papers on the desk, as if he couldn't find something. "Tell me, do you still do this special work?"

"No," Brady shrank back into his clothes.

"Oh?" Robert's forehead wrinkled and he repeated, "Oh, so, what work do you do now?" He looked at his paperwork, "Yes, here it is. You were promoted straight after that job."

The chair scraped, and the prosecution lawyer stood, "Objection, relevance your Honour."

"Mr Carson," the judge cautioned.

Robert's head bowed deferring to the judge, "Can you please describe for me what you were wearing."

"Dark pants, casual, and a white sleeveless t-shirt."

Robert looked down at his own shoes and Brady added, "Oh, black lace up shoes, same as for work, I mean in uniform."

"No further questions, at this time," Robert finished.

Constable Thompson's testimony was similar. An almost word for word of the QP9. When it was his turn to question Robert asked, "Would you could confirm for me, and the jury, that there were only the two of you, Constable Brady and you Constable Thompson who were there when you say you saw me attack Mr Saunders in the park."

His eyes darted to the prosecution desk, "C-correct. As I recall."

"And what were you wearing?"

"What was I wearing? My uniform."

"Can you describe it?"

"What?" Constable Thompson frowned and looked over at the prosecution. Eventually he looked back at Robert, "My standard issue uniform. Light blue short-sleeve shirt, dark blue pants, black lace-up boots, and my hat."

"It was late. Ten-ish? Why were you wearing your hat?" Robert kept his voice even.

"I'd come from an earlier shift, I-I didn't go home—"

"Objection. Relevance your Honour," the Prosecution interrupted.

"Mr Carson?" the judge queried.

"I'm hoping to show relevance your Honour." Robert sounded contrite and waited for the judge's nod. "So you unexpectedly came straight from a full shift and it was unusual for you. Can you tell me how it came about and what your extra shift entailed?"

Thompson fidgeted, and again looked at the prosecution desk.

When the judge prompted him to answer the question, he said "I don't recall exactly."

"Had you ever been requested to do this, Constable Brady called it special surveillance work before?"

"No."

"OK, so, you were new, and you didn't know what to wear?"

"Yes, correct," Thompson seemed soothed.

"And you weren't forewarned or told what your surveillance job entailed?"

"I don't recall."

Robert sighed, moved some papers, and looked up, "Can you recall what I was wearing?"

Thompson looked away and back, "Light chinos and a light polo shirt. White."

"Shoes?" Robert queried.

"Deck shoes. Light. Like natural," Thompson was getting short tempered.

"I won't be much longer," Robert held up a pair of deck shoes, "Like these?"

Thompson nodded, adding, "Yes."

Robert nodded to the Bailiff, then continued, "And where are you stationed now?"

"What?"

"I want you to tell me, after your introduction to special surveillance, what you are doing now."

"Your Honour," the prosecution counsel bleated.

"I'll allow it. Mr Carson try to stick to the relevant line though."

"I was promoted. Second in command in Edmonton now. North Queensland."

"So you're *Senior* Constable Thompson. Congratulations," Robert smiled. "How long have you been in the Police Force?"

"Six months."

"Wow. That's quick. Double congratulations," Robert's smile broadened momentarily. "And was it cold that night?" he said, reverting to serious, "I remember I took my jacket off. And you said I wasn't wearing a jacket, and I can't seem to find it anywhere. I thought, I was hoping you might have seen it."

"No. Not that I recall."

"Oh? Never mind. But you said you saw me attacking Mr Saunders. I might have put it down or dropped it. Are you sure you didn't find it? Later or something?"

Constable Thompson scanned the room looking away from Robert and not answering, and Robert removed his frown and said, "Just to be clear Constable Thompson, there was no-one else in the area at all, and you know this because you were there in that area on special surveillance."

"Correct."

"Are you sure? Except the person you saw attacking Mr Saunders, who you allege was me."

"Yes."

"And that person was in a blind panic."

"Yes."

"Can you describe what I was doing in that panic state?"

"You-you were fighting off your assailant. Punching and kicking him."

"Oh? Both? I wonder how would I do that," Robert moved his foot, then bent, leaning towards the ground. He shook his head, "Never mind.

And did Mr Saunders defend himself?"

"What? I, I don't recall."

"But you recall running after me? Both you and Constable Brady."

"Yes," his shoulders loosened.

"And Mr Saunders, you left him there. Was he lying down? Standing up?"

"I," Constable Thompson scratched his ear, "I don't recall."

CHAPTER 63

Blue was the next prosecution witness called.

He testified that Robert had come into the Story Bridge Hotel not long after closing, upset and wanting to call an ambulance. Someone was hurt. And yes, Robert had injuries to his hand. He was put into a cab home, moments before the ambulance went the other way towards the park.

Robert questioned him briefly, "And would you tell the Court, why did you call a cab and send me home."

"Strictly speaking I didn't call it. Someone else did. I didn't think it was safe for you."

"Where were you then? Why did someone else make the call? Oh, don't worry. That's not important is it?"

"I suppose not," Blue shrugged.

"What did you mean though, it wasn't safe for me? Why would you think that?"

"You were running from something or someone. You'd called an ambulance. I figured you were running from someone in the park."

"But what if I had hurt someone? I don't understand. Why didn't someone call the police?" Robert only paused a moment, "Had this happened before? Someone running into the pub for help, like I did?" Robert looked like he was just beginning to see a connection, he hoped the jury had too.

Blue opened his mouth to speak, and then it came, "Objection."

It was Pete's turn next. Yes, he'd seen Robert at the pub. Yes, after it closed. Yes, he had an injured hand. Yes, he looked panicked. Yes, he'd called an ambulance.

"And it was you who called the taxi?" It was Robert's turn.

Pete nodded, "Yes."

"And it was after the pub had closed?"

"Um-yes."

"So. Do you work there?"

"No."

"But you were inside. They were closed. Why would you be inside?" Robert shook his head like he was trying to connect something and not getting the pieces to fit, "I'm not... had we ever met before that night?" Robert asked him.

"Yes."

"Can you tell the Court when we first met."

Pete smiled, "It was some time before. You'd come into the pub. I don't think you knew it was a gay bar."

A chair scraped at the prosecution desk.

"Sorry," Robert circumvented the objection. "How long did I stay?"

"You finished your drink and left. You were in a bit of a hurry to leave."

"So you'd say I was uncomfortable there?"

"Speculation."

"I withdraw the question. No further questions," Robert finished.

*

Robert could smell the metallic aftermath of adrenaline every time he shifted his arm too far away from his body. He tucked his elbows close while the prosecution rested and the judge addressed him.

"Mr Carson, the prosecution, having closed its case against you, I must ask you if you intend to adduce evidence in your defense. This means," he shifted his gaze to the prosecution as their muted mumbling escalated, "this means you may give evidence yourself, call a witness or witnesses, or produce evidence. You may do all or any of those things, or none of them."

The hissing whispers from the prosecution became louder and the jury was looking from them to the judge.

Robert ignored what was happening and started to speak.

"Gentlemen," the judge interrupted him. His eyes wearily on the prosecution, "You obviously have something to discuss. We will adjourn for a recess," he looked up at the clock. There was no second hand. The minute hand jolted silently onto the eight, "And reconvene in one hour twenty minutes. Bailiff, two pm."

The prosecution still huddled, watched as Robert swept his papers together with one hand, grabbed his briefcase with the other, and zig-zagged around the departing jurors.

No-one noticed Simon sitting off in the corner, still making notes.

CHAPTER 64

Outside, Robert made his way around the edge of the courts building, and then down a narrow one way street towards the main city grid and the anonymity of a lunchtime city crowd. Crouching down between a delivery van and an industrial bin, he pushed the papers he'd been holding into his bag, and walked more slowly, untangling the various strands of his tangled strategy.

A few more runs on the board were definitely needed. All he'd done so far was set himself up as agreeing with them, in a rather confused way. But the threat of estoppel he'd been caught up in, wasn't really applicable. So what if he broke their so-called contract. So what if it caused them some detriment. This wasn't commercial litigation. This was a criminal case. Estoppal didn't apply. His chest expanded.

Then it contracted.

They could still close down the case. He'd felt them wanting to. Just waiting for the right moment. Would the judge allow it? And where would that leave him? It would leave them in the clear. His lips pressed together. *That can't happen.*

He wondered how much the prosecution team actually knew. The bare minimum, he suspected. But you wouldn't know. And he wondered who they'd taken instruction from. Nichols? Or someone higher. Would the Commissioner be involved? He imagined Terry Lewis with his condescending smirk, the eyes, beady, almost leering, and the words, hard and even saying, make this go away.

Now he was clearer, he realised the prosecution team may have no idea what sort of miscarriage of justice was on the table. But that wouldn't help him, would it? And he'd need the judge on side.

Deep in thought he almost passed the mini-mart.

Now with some deodorant in his suit pocket, he headed towards his old office, wishing he still had access to the bathroom, and going into Lennon's Hotel next door instead. He rinsed off the underarm portion of his shirt and his body, smiling grimly. Wouldn't be the first time he'd washed off clothing in the toilets. *This is for you too, Terry.*

'Don't count chickens,' Johnny warned. 'Wouldn't be the first time something out of the blue turned up in a courtroom.'

***

As expected, the prosecution weren't sending out sunbeams of goodwill when Robert formally claimed his right to bring forward witnesses. He placated them with the argument that he needed to strengthen his mitigating circumstances to show that despite his plea, he wasn't actually responsible for Johnny's death. They had no choice. This was supposedly their intention anyway.

He called Norman Sparks.

His questions were benignly supportive of the story so far, and assiduously avoided anything which might lead Alan to perjure himself.

Were you at the park the night of—? Did you see Mr Saunders being attacked? Did you see me? Did you see the men in these photographs? Yes, yes, yes and yes. Everyone in the jury got their turn to look. "The witness has confirmed he recognizes Constable Brady and Constable Thompson."

"By the way," Robert interrupted himself, "did you see my jacket?"

Doubt or confusion passed over Norm-Alan's face.

"You might not have known it was mine," said Robert. "If you saw one, would you describe it for the Court."

"Mr Saunders had one on his lap," Alan shrugged, "I could see it quite clearly in the shelter light, it was light-coloured, maybe beige? It stuck in my mind because Mr Saunders was wearing one already, except it was navy I think, or black. I remember thinking that's gonna stain, when he dropped it, and when the—"

"Thank you, Mr Sparks," Robert cut him off and moved quickly on to did you see me running away, then was there anyone else there in the park that night?

"Yes," said Alan.

"There was? But," Robert paused, "Oh, well perhaps Constable Brady and Constable Thompson just didn't remember. I... never mind. I'd like to be able to recall the witness later, your Honour."

The prosecution huddle broke, reserving the right to question the witness later too. And Robert wondered why they didn't cross-examine Norm now about his location during the attack. But then, he could see how not questioning him kept the status quo.

Robert called Harry.

"Mr Matthews, would you mind telling the Court your occupation."

"I'm a judge, retired."

"In what capacity did you first know me?"

"Relevance," the prosecution objected.

"My point, your Honour, is to show it wasn't me who killed Mr Saunders," Robert allowed exasperation to drip slowly into everyone's consciousness.

The judge waived down the objection.

"The firm you worked for was representing my boyfriend, Mr Saunders."

The jury shifted in their seats making a point of not looking at each other.

Ignoring the fact that he was supposedly a cleaner and hoping no-one else had noticed, Robert continued quickly, "When you were first informed that Mr Saunders was deceased, what were you told."

"Nothing. I'm not considered immediate family. They shared the coroner's findings with me, that Johnny's wallet, emptied of cash, and his jacket had been found on the Story Bridge. That his body had been found in the river with injuries consistent with a fall from that height. The coroner concluded it was suicide, given the state of his mind, leading up to his trial on charges of homosexual soliciting," Harry paused for effect, "of me, his boyfriend, lover. We lived together. We were out having a drink together."

When the murmuring quieted, Robert continued, "You said that Mr Saunders was committed to stand trial on charges of soliciting. But it is clear that he wasn't, so why and how did this happen?"

The prosecution solicitor stood, and the judge waved him down.

Harry almost smiled and unfolded his story with a captivating melodic rhythm, while Robert scanned the jury. They had reached a stage beyond embarrassed wariness and shock, and looked curious.

"My one regret was caving to the pressure, to conceal I'm gay," Harry's eyes held each of the jury members in turn. "I'd been doing it for so long. This whole nightmare has made me re-evaluate. We shouldn't be frightened of being who we are. Our lives and livelihoods, our relationships, we shouldn't have to sacrifice them to outdated and ill-informed sensibilities and rules. I'm not going quietly. Not now."

When he spoke, Robert said nothing about Harry's story, "Judge Matthews, would you tell us who the arresting officers were that night?"

The prosecutor called, "Immaterial, your Honour."

"Mr Carson," said the judge glancing at his watch, "is this leading anywhere?"

"Sorry your Honour," said Robert, "I didn't think it would be polite to interrupt Judge Matthews. And yes, it is going somewhere. I hope."

Harry didn't give the judge much time, jumping straight in with, "Detective Senior Sergeant Nichols and Detective Senior Constable Andrews of Licencing Branch."

"Is this them?" Robert handed the Bailiff photos of Nichols and Andrews, keeping an eye on the prosecution. Harry confirmed them, and the pictures went over for the jury to view.

"You said earlier," Robert waited for Harry's attention, "that I knew the deceased, Mr Saunders, Johnny," Robert looked down and pinched the bridge of his nose. When he'd recomposed his face to neutral, he turned back to Harry, "The Johnny Saunders who I'm supposed to have viciously attacked."

"Correct."

"So, I knew Mr Saunders, and would you say I had any reason to attack him in the manner of which I have been accused?"

"Calls for speculation," the prosecutor said.

"I'll rephrase that," said Robert. "To your knowledge was there any reason for me to attack Mr Saunders."

"No."

"Would you tell the Court why."

"Because the two of you were in love."

The whispering hubbub escalated to murmurs to babbling. Robert half turned towards the public seating so he could see Simon, whose thumb appeared, bouncing with excitement next to the notebook he'd been writing in.

The judge banged his gavel while the Bailiff called for order.

Some of the jury fidgeted.

"That will be all, thank you." Robert waited without breathing for the axe to fall.

It didn't.

The prosecution reserved their right to question the witness later.

Calm returned.

Robert's parade of witnesses progressed.

Pete, Jimbo, Blue and Tank all confirmed they knew of and could identify Nichols, Andrews and Brady. Incrementally, snippets of Johnny's story, his personality, his commitment to gay rights, his passion for helping people, his kindness and his joy emerged. Now the jury knew about a person named Johnny in place of 'the deceased'. Also emerging was the whiff of corruption. Some of the jurors had stopped swiveling their heads to see if anyone else was smelling it.

Robert's fingers pressed the pocket where his broken watch would have been, and looked up at the wall clock. He'd let people talk and it was getting late. His nerves were stalking. He wasn't sure how long he could maintain the slow information drip before the prosecution took more than offense. He could feel their tension. It felt more like they were holding back waiting for the right moment, not that they weren't going to pounce at all, and most of this testimony, pretty much all of it, had absolutely nothing to do with the case at all. He saw the judge following his eyes to the clock.

Should he approach the bench with his change of plea now?

If he did, the judge would call it a day so he could review the documentation. And that could be it. The prosecution strategy was looking less feasible, but with Harry's testimony, so was his. But that could be good. Give them a sense of we've got this if he goes too far. But if they abandoned the case now, they'd never face a court themselves.

'Now,' Johnny's voice was resolute. 'Call him now.'
"I'd like to call Alan John Peters."

CHAPTER 65

There was audible consternation when Norm followed the bailiff into the courtroom and swore to tell the truth.

This time Robert started with, "Would you please state your name."

"Alan John—" he was cut off by the chair scraping the floor underneath the prosecution lawyer.

"Your Honour, this must be a mistake. This is Norman Sparks. We've only just heard testimony from him."

"Bailiff," the judge's arm waved at Alan, "would you please escort Mr Sparks from the stand and call the witness."

As the bailiff started towards him, Alan raised his hand, "Excuse me sir, your Honour, I *am* Alan John Peters. I've been pretend— I've been temporarily known by a different name because—"

"Objection, your Honour."

"Indeed," said the judge, "Mr Carson, would you please approach the bench."

Robert felt his chest moving again as he did.

The judge leaned forward so their whispered conversation didn't reach the jury's ears. Robert apologized and confirmed the subterfuge and that Norm, Alan, would justify it during his testimony.

"It is highly unusual," the judge commented, "but I'm inclined to allow it. The entire case has been highly unusual. I suspect there's an outcome you are trying to steer us towards, and it would make it easier if you simply changed your plea. Had you considered that?"

Robert's nod was slight, in contrast to the enthusiastic bouncing of his heart, "I have your Honour. I have the submission in my briefcase."

"Is there a reason you haven't approached me before this?"

"Yes, your Honour."

"Would you kindly share it."

"Your Honour, I don't want to risk the prosecution shutting down the case, on the grounds I reneged on the plea deal. There is a lot at stake..."

'Miscarriage of justice. Say it.' Johnny prompted.

"Not just for me and not just for Mr Saunders." Robert looked up, "And if it doesn't come to light here in your courtroom, it will be buried forever. There would be a," he paused while he omitted 'whopping', "miscarriage of justice. Can I ask you something?"

"No, you can't," he said, "unless it's on a point of law. I suggest you get that submission now, so I can announce it."

Robert took deliberately unhurried steps back to the defense table, took the paperwork from his briefcase, and back, handing it to the assistant.

"Members of the jury," said the judge, taking the papers from the assistant, "the accused has entered a petition to change his plea to not guilty. In light of—"

The screech of chair legs moving too fast cut him off, "Your Honour, we have a plea. He can't—"

The judge raised his hand, this time cutting the prosecution off, "He can, and he has. It is up to me to allow or disallow it. You may be seated."

The prosecution lawyer started to sit, then unfurled, "Your Honour, we request the motion to change be denied. Mr Carson can't change his plea if he's had legal advice. He's a lawyer. Wouldn't that constitute legal advice?"

"I thought you were a cleaner, Mr Carson," the judge's head angled towards Robert, but he kept one eye on the prosecution.

"I am, your Honour. But I was a lawyer, as Judge Matthews has already stated."

Satisfaction and relief began flexing and stretching across the prosecution desk.

"But you are a cleaner now?"

"Yes, your Honour."

"Your previous occupation is immaterial, and you are unrepresented. Did you take— ahem, excuse me, did you engage counsel with regard to your plea or your defense?"

"No, your Honour," Robert could feel the damp hidden by his suit-jacket.

"Quite," the judge turned back to the prosecution. "Your motion to overturn the change of plea is denied. An unrepresented defendant has the right to change their plea."

Still standing, the prosecution lawyer moved his arm to include the presence of his colleagues, "Your Honour, we request a *nolle prosequi.*"

Robert stopped breathing and clenched his fist by his side, keeping his face expressionless.

The judge looked from the prosecution to the clock and then over to the jury, "The prosecution has asked that the case be dismissed, unless or until they bring further evidence," and turning back to the prosecution, "your request will be considered."

"But your Honour," the lawyer continued, "we don't want to continue to prosecute the case at this time."

Robert watched on as if from a platform in the distance.

The judge tilted his head gecko-like. One eyelid partially lowered, the other eye flicked at the bailiff and a miniscule chin drop nod. The entire process was barely discernable.

"Mr Sparks, Mr Peters, you may step down for now. This court is adjourned until ten am tomorrow."

The gavel echo bounced off the woodblock.

CHAPTER 66

Nerves didn't affect Robert's sleep as much as he thought they would. He felt like somehow navigating between the waves and the unpredictable currents of yesterday, he'd discovered a bay, put out the anchor and at least while it held, he could look out from the deck. He could still sink of course, but at least the view was nicer here.

*

Next morning when he was asked to meet the judge in camera, he wasn't surprised. Having to explain his position made perfect sense.

"You've a compelling case for your plea change. To deny it would indeed cause a miscarriage of justice."

Robert could feel the 'but' on the horizon.

"But I want to hear your reasons I should deny the nolle prosequi. Especially since that's the subject of my next appointment with the prosecution."

"It's complicated, your Honour, but I'll try to be brief and to the point."

The judge's hands opened in a be-my-guest gesture, "Proceed."

"First," said Robert, "as you know, with a nolle pros the case isn't closed. It just looks like it. Evidence, new witnesses, could magically appear from anywhere," he checked to see if the judge understood the hidden meaning. He was non-committal. Robert proceeded anyway. "Every knock on the door could be a 'you're under arrest'. And honest—" he saw Lauren's eyebrows arching, "and given my current situation, and how it came about, that knock will be a when, not an if."

The judge's head moved slightly.

"Second, the record would always show my criminal status. I couldn't do a lot of things. That's not how I want to live."

"There's a few needs and wants of your own in that argument."

Robert looked down feeling like he was going to be given three Hail Marys as penance.

'Come on,' said Johnny. 'Don't give up.'

"It's, well, from a purely legal perspective, a nolle pros means there simply isn't enough evidence *yet* to prove I'm guilty, and the only way around that is to prove my innocence. Definitively. And to do that, I have to show the Court who *is* guilty. And I know they aren't on trial so," Robert raised his hands in a what-can-I-do, "but then it will be up to the police or someone, to act."

Robert looked ahead, searching for any additional words which might be usefully employed out in the space between them.

The judge found them, "And the Court will have the evidence and sworn testimony of the witnesses, once and for all."

"Irrefutably," Robert's enthusiasm unleashed itself. "And there'd be public pressure brought to bear if they do try to refute it." Then he subdued the zeal with a shrug, "I don't know. All I do know—"

The judge interrupted him, "And did you have this in mind all along?"

"Sort of," Robert wondered how far his honesty could go. "Given the choice I wouldn't have. But, you know how things work."

"Tell me."

"If I hadn't pleaded guilty, I'd certainly have been *found* guilty. It was contrived this way to protect those who did kill Mr Saunders. I don't know how much you know, but this is tip of the iceberg stuff and... well, there's a lot more to come out. Anyway, going back to your question. As it turned out, being forced to plead guilty, made the whole thing manageable in a convoluted way. If things aren't expected, they can't be pre-empted."

"Thank you for your brevity, Mr Carson," the judge pushed his seat back, and as Robert stood, he added, "and your candour."

The prosecution team were seated outside the chambers awaiting their turn. As Robert passed them, he mustered the courtesy of a nod. It was hard to think they might have no idea what they were doing.

CHAPTER 67

It was a late start, but eventually the jury was called in and the judge gave them direction.

He selected his words and delivered them with measured seriousness, starting with reminding them about the presumption of innocence and reasonable doubt and continued with, "In this case, the defendant has requested to change his plea from guilty to not guilty, which in the circumstances and in accordance with the law, he is perfectly within his rights to do. And you," he scanned their faces, "are still charged with determining a verdict: guilty or not guilty."

They sat, a collective sponge.

"However," he made a tent with his fingers, "the prosecution requested they be released from prosecuting the case. They can do this if they know the burden of proof will not succeed at this time. They are then free to find more facts and re-start the proceedings. It also means, that Mr Carson isn't a free man, just that he is free for now, if you will."

They watched him, waiting for the next instalment.

"Stay with me for this," he said. "Mr Carson must, at this time, present evidence and testimony showing you if or where there is some, or any, doubt about his guilt. Now, and this is the important bit for us, if this is what is missing from the prosecution's fact gathering, and he has it, then it is not merely about the desirability of establishing this, but it is imperative, in the interests of justice, of obtaining the fullest possible access to all the facts relevant to the case, and presenting them to you, so that you can make your determination. Now, if everyone is clear," he turned to Robert and the prosecution, "we will proceed."

Robert's dinner companion from Club 139, Barry, identified Alan John Peters. Then Robert presented the Court with officially confirmed proof that the fingerprints on record for Alan John Peters matched the ones that had been done on Norm, before everyone knew he was really Alan. So when Alan John Peters reappeared, and told his story of what happened that night and subsequently, up to the reclamation of his name, the seeds of doubt which Robert had planted before this appearance, sprouted. But it wasn't a triumphant spring.

Alan finished with the dismal, "It will stay with me forever. After the first bit where they held him, and took turns, it got worse. The only thing I could do was bear witness. I didn't look away. Except when I saw you," his chin pointed at Robert, "I mean, the accused, and you called out and they all stopped kicking, and those two," he pointed at the pictures of Brady and Thompson and the Bailiff showed the jury, "took off after you."

"Then these two," Alan said, pointing at the photos of Nichols and Andrews, "when I turned back, I watched them prodding the body, Johnny, with their boots." He waited while the jury looked at the photos, then continued, "They didn't even bother to check his pulse. He could have been alive. And they dragged him, half carried him, to the river. I lost sight of them at the ferry shelter where my things were. I lay down on the seat of the police car and went back to pretending I was almost out-cold drunk. I didn't want to end up in the river with him. But when they came back to the car, I saw their shoes were muddy, and wet. So were their pants, up past the ankles, mid-calf. Andrews, the tall one, put his jumper on. He had Johnny's blood on his shirt."

"Just to be sure," Robert said, "Is this the person you saw being beaten?"

As Johnny's photo was passed around, Robert's fist bunched by his thigh and with the other hand, he pressed a finger to his lips. He found the ceiling and his composure, then reminded Alan about seeing the jacket, and that he'd been going to say something else, "Yes, the stain, I was worried, but then I knew it would be ruined anyway, when this man," he pointed at Nichols' photo, "stubbed out his cigarette on it."

Robert bent down and took a plastic bag from the seat next to him, pulled out an item of clothing and raised his arm, "Is this the jacket?"

Robert asked, turning to the jury, and for what appeared to be no significant reason said, "Johnny was a size medium. I'm a large."

After checking the burn, Robert put it on, "Would you look at this," he started taking things from the pockets. "Phone messages for Mr Carson, and presumably my missing after-hours entry swipe-card for the office, which can be confirmed, and the power bill with my name on it. I wondered where that had gotten to." He put everything back into the pockets.

The Court was presented with the original coroner's report and the revised and detailed one, and thanks to Officer Kowalski and his testimony, the changing charge sheets, records, statements and logs. Kowalski also confirmed the jacket had originally been logged as part of the framework supporting the abandoned suicide story.

"Would you tell us where my jacket was subsequently found, Constable Kowalski?"

"Lost property at Licensing."

"And what do you think it was doing there?"

"Objection. Speculation." It sounded tired.

"What made you look there?" said Robert.

"A hunch," said Kowalski. "I knew Detectives Nichols and Andrews. And their names were on the original paperwork that disappeared when Mr Peters did. I'm just going to spell it out. Johnny was holding a jacket, yours. He was alone. Either they didn't give much thought to the fact that Johnny was already wearing one, or they thought it was his, and it was going somewhere with him. I suspect they didn't even check the pockets before planting it on the bridge. Then it disappeared when the suicide story looked like it would fall over. Maybe they lost it or maybe they realized and thought they'd be able to use it against you. Who knows where it might have ended up if I hadn't gone looking for it. But it's sloppy. Honestly, there were four of them. Anyone with half a brain—"

"Speculation, your Honour."

Robert knew it was coming.

"The jury will disregard the last statement." The judge sighed and spoke to the court stenographer, "From I suspect they didn't even check."

Robert placed the jacket back into the original evidence bag, and passed it to the bailiff and proceeded. He knew the jury would have been thinking exactly what Kowalski had been thinking.

His orderly presentation had been layering and cementing into something hard and solid. Objections were few and cross examination perfunctory. And because they had no choice, the judge having taken that away, to Robert it felt like the mood had shifted in the prosecution camp. These were the missing facts that they didn't previously have access to, and weren't aware of. They had to allow them, and they seemed as blamelessly interested as everyone else in the unfolding story.

As Robert's re-call of witnesses progressed, Simon scrawled busily into his notebook.

Pete, then Jimbo, were close-to-tears-relieved and didn't know how high up all this went, but wanted to see an end to it, especially their forced coercion into drug trading.

"Immaterial," the prosecution tried.

But not really, Robert argued, since it formed part of the framing of an innocent man. *And was now on the record.* He was feeling more confident as the mostly irrelevant to this case but nonetheless captivating details of protection payments and illicit substances, and Nichols and Andrews involvement in it all, was being recorded officially by the Court's stenographer.

Blue corroborated the involvement of Nichols and Andrews in the collection of protection money for running a gay bar, and what he'd seen of Pete's police-sponsored confiscated drug reselling enterprise. He then confirmed Brady was involved in the baiting operation targeting gays.

"Yes," Blue said. "It was a regular occurrence, especially for a new patron to be bashed and robbed, and probably blackmailed." He looked up waiting for an objection which didn't arrive. "More recently the regulars knew what was going on and avoided Brady, we nicknamed him Muscles. Early on people reported it to the police. But instead of getting help, they mostly got beaten up again at the station. Sometimes they were thrown in jail and charged too. I started warning people, you know, new customers at the pub, if I saw them being approached by Brady. There wasn't anything else I could do."

Robert felt a chill run from the side of his jaw and down his back. He shivered, "Did you warn anyone that night?"

"Yeah, I did. I asked him if he was meeting Muscles, down at the beat. He was a bit, mind your own business, y'know?" said Blue. "But then I told him what they were up to and not to go. There would have been an ambush waiting for him after the last ferry."

Robert's shoulders sagged, draped in the burden of remembering exactly who ended up ambushed.

"Objection," it came after the sound of the chair scraping, and gave Robert a few extra moments to collect himself.

The prosecution's objection was valid, the police weren't on trial here, but Robert pointed out that as he was, and that if it was others who attacked John Saunders, it was relevant.

"Overruled." The judge nodded at Blue, "Proceed."

'Yes, keep going,' Johnny's energy reverberated.

Robert was sure now that Thompson was being trained as the new bait, given everyone knew the old one. Blue was a star of forthright brilliance. But it was a hollow light in Robert's eyes.

"The prosecution had previously asked you whether I had been injured," Robert waited.

"Yes. Your hand," said Blue.

"Like I'd been fighting?" Robert asked, watching the prosecution eyebrows.

"It was your palm," said Blue. "I've seen a few fights in my days. It's usually swollen and split knuckles, not gravel cuts on the palm."

He asked why the police thought it might be an idea to claim a gay man had killed his gay lover and then claimed he'd lashed out in gay panic.

"Calls for speculation."

"Was I panicked, when you saw me that night after closing."

"You'd just seen Johnny Saunders killed mate—"

"Objection."

Everyone waited for the judge, "Overruled."

Blue continued, "And they were coming after you. I would've been panicked."

"Is that why a taxi was called to send me home?" said Robert.

"Bloody oath. Sorry. Yes. Nichols and Andrews were in the pub. They were picking up Pete's takings for the night. And ours. You weren't safe. Probably still aren't, if you ask me."

"Objection."

CHAPTER 68

It wasn't a long recess in which to plan his next moves. Robert walked, briefcase in one hand, and sandwich and soft-drink in a plastic bag in the other. A half-smile emerged at the thought of being a high flying lawyer on his lunch break, and he headed towards the river and Coronation Drive. There were benches. He could sit and think.

He debated calling Nichols and Andrews to the stand. They wouldn't hesitate to lie. How many of their false facts would hold? To him, it was more than clear that he wasn't guilty, but would the one lone Kowalski, a few gays and a drunk, be enough to get a result for him from the jury? They hadn't been picked for their support of gay anything. And Kowalski had been made to sound like a loser grinding a blunt axe. He'd need something else. An admission.

He shook his head. *Not bloody likely.*

They were bullies. Was there something about the type which made them want to be police? He thought of Kowalski again. They're not all bad eggs. He watched the river and tried not to think. In the absence of thought, Terry's face appeared. So did the line of bullies with their pants down and their bare arses facing Robert.

As he walked back into the Courtroom the image of Terry and the boys, wouldn't disappear.

What is it? Come on.

He looked around, at the jury, at the judge.

Come on. Think.

'Change your focus,' he heard Johnny.

He closed his eyes and the images changed from Terry and the lineup of

344

boys, to later, to the one boy, the boy bending forward and stretching out an arm, before being pushed aside.

"I'd like to recall Constable Thompson."

*

"Constable Thompson, remembering you are under oath, I want to ask some further questions."

Robert started with benign and disarming confirmations, interspersed with teasing out of the lesser lies with questions using referencing statements.

"In your earlier testimony you said..."

"You didn't recall, but now you've had some time to think, can you tell the Court..."

"If I was wearing light coloured deck shoes, how do you suppose black shoe polish was found on Mr Saunders' clothing?"

"Objection. Calls for speculation."

Robert turned the question into an inescapable maze of what colour shoes was I wearing? What colour shoes were you wearing? What colour shoes was Constable Brady wearing? DS Nichols was there too? Was DS Nichols wearing black shoes? And DS Andrews, what colour were his shoes? What colour were the shoe polish marks on Mr Saunders' clothing? Was there any other colour polish on Mr Saunders' clothing?

Good. Much more precise. He glanced at the prosecution. *Thank you.*

Then he started mixing the questions up.

They stopped following any particular sequence.

"Who briefed you on your role in this operation?"

"Isn't it standard procedure for..."

"How did you first hear about this surveillance work?"

"When Constable Brady said..."

"What did you mean when you said..."

"Can you tell me why DS Sergeant Nichols' name was on this report dated..."

"Can you tell me why DS Sergeant Nichols' name was not on this report dated..."

"Where was DS Andrews when…"

"Whose idea was it to say that Mr Saunders had jumped off the bridge?"

"Who was responsible for removing Mr Peter's arrest from the record?"

"Why wasn't an ambulance called for Mr Saunders from the police radio?"

"What were your concerns when…"

"Can you tell us how…"

"Who was…"

"How did…"

"Would you please tell us in your own words…"

He chased and prodded and confounded and doubled back and then he said, "Why did you become a police officer, Constable Thompson?"

"I— I'd always wanted to be one. I remember the police coming to school when I was a kid. They helped people. Made it safe. They uphold the law. And to me it seemed kind of…" he searched for the word, an embarrassed pink suffusing his neck, "important and… and noble. I wanted to do that."

"Do you know that perjury is an offence punishable by time in prison?"

Constable Thompson's flustered pink deepened, "Yes."

"Is there anything you have now remembered which previously you couldn't recollect?"

"Yes."

"Let's start with this then. Was Mr Saunders alone in the park before you arrived, on the night he disappeared?"

"Were you alone?"

"Who was with you?"

"Why were you there?"

Constable Thompson started to talk.

After telling the Court about getting Mr Peters out of the way, the history of the assaults of the gay men came out. He hadn't wanted to, he explained. It wasn't what he'd signed up for, but he wanted to get ahead. And they, homosexuals, were illegal and the things they were doing were illegal. It was only roughing them up, a bit of fun, he'd been told. He knew he shouldn't, but if you didn't go along with it your career was over. They're my superior officers. I had to. I'd be kicked off the force. That's what happens if you cause any trouble for them.

"Who's them?" said Robert.

"I— I don't know. I honestly don't know. I mean DS Sergeant Nichols, he must have orders from someone above him. It's like… you do as you're told. If you don't, you're in trouble. But if you do, then you're in trouble too. Except there's no one to tell. And then it's more. It gets deeper. There's no out. And if you leave. Who's gonna listen to you. And if someone does listen, they soon stop, when things start happening to them."

"What do you think is going to happen to you now?"

"I don't know. I don't care. No. I do. And this," pride and guilt, the anguished confusion, were visible to everyone, "this shouldn't have happened. You know?"

"Why don't you tell us what shouldn't have happened," Robert said softly.

And then the brutality was laid before the Court, in Constable Thompson's own words.

They came like a light mist, and turned into a shower and then a torrent.

When they stopped falling over the Court in their hurry to escape from where he'd been holding them in, hiding them from the world, his eyes were still looking out, unseeing, over everyone's spellbound heads.

It was difficult to breathe.

The air was thick with them.

He lowered his eyes and stared at his hands, white against the deep brown and highly polished timber, and then he looked up again, straight ahead as if there was no-one in the room, and he was talking to himself.

"That poor man. Johnny. He wasn't doing anything. Nothing wrong."

His lips sank against each other, and his cheeks sagged. He was still, and then his head rolled softly from side to side, a look of tortured incredulity stark on his face. He opened his mouth and sucked in a breath. It got stuck on the way, and his chest shook. His shoulders jerked forward involuntarily. Just the once.

He didn't notice his tears, "We kicked that poor man to death."

And, as if he couldn't quite believe it, "And then we threw him into the river."

No one moved.

Robert swallowed, and looked up into the corner of the Courtroom. On Johnny's face, a wistful smile.

Robert's fist unclenched, and he released the words, "The defense rests, your Honour."

The End

NOTE FOR READER

Although this story and its characters are fictional, my research includes reference to the very real efforts of some brave and visionary and steadfast people who worked to bring about much needed change.

Phil Dickie, a *Courier Mail* (Queensland) investigative journalist and Chris Masters, an investigative reporter for ABC's (Australia) *4Corners* make their appearance in *The Outing*, as Simon and Tim. Their reporting, particularly the programme *The Moonlight State* [https://www.abc.net.au/4corners/the-moonlight-state---1987/2832198] which aired on May 11, 1987, sparked the Fitzgerald Inquiry which brought down the Premier of Queensland, Sir Joh Bjelke-Petersen and the Police Commissioner, Sir Terry Lewis and ended an era of audacious corruption.

Nigel Powell was a former UK policeman in Queensland, who inspired the fictional Constable Kowalski.

The story is based on real life tragedies, in particular the apparent suicide of Scott Johnson, a PhD student in Sydney, which over thirty years later (in 2020), was re-classified as a hate-crime murder; and the death of Adelaide university professor, Dr George Duncan, who was thrown into the Torrens River by the police because he was gay. He drowned. No-one was ever charged. Scott and George of course, were not, are not, the only casualties.

An early inquiry into police corruption, The Lucas Inquiry, is mentioned. It was prompted by the Queensland Council for Civil Liberties (QCCL), which is also featured in the novel with the fictitious Callum O'Connor in place of Terry O'Gorman. It was a case of the police being in charge of investigating the police, so when it failed, it added a heightened sense of invulnerability and arrogance to the people involved, and escalated the corruption.

Being gay in Queensland, (Australia) was a crime until 1991 and it wasn't until 2017 that gay panic was removed from the Statutes in Queensland, where the novel is set.

Although Equal Opportunity legislation exists in many places, the reality falls short. A gay nurse in Spain was beaten to death at a Pride Rally, horrific hate-crimes have occurred in Ireland, and police subcultures of discrimination and bigotry have all surfaced while this book was being written.

What is clear, is that legislating the prohibition of discrimination, doesn't make it go away. It tends to go underground, where it can become insidious and micro and unprovable and still impacts the lives of so many gay people. So, while some of us are celebrating gay rights, the fact that there are any at all, that they have to be given a name at all, is a reflection on the need for them in the first place.

When I read about Scott Johnson and George Duncan, I was moved to tears. It brought up all the fears I'd had for my own son. I wrote this especially for him, but it was written because we can't forget that today's freedoms are necessarily tied to the struggles to attain them.

***

Thank You

Thank you for reading my book. If you enjoyed it, please take a moment to leave me a review at your favourite retailer.

ACKNOWLEDGMENTS

Sharing your words with people for the first time is both harrowing and exciting and it's hard to know the difference. So a big thank you to my early readers. Your feedback on both my writing and the story's merit gave me the confidence to continue.

To all my CBC writing buddies, it is a joy to share your thoughts, your progress, your tribulations and your achievements and to hear your suggestions and ideas. Richard Carden, Ellie Salked and Kate Bentley who've been on this painstaking path since our early courses together... I'm overwhelmed by your generosity. Likewise, Ally Zetterberg, Abi Bruce, Emily Howes, Aoi Matsushima, and Melissa Eschalier, who've also given the manuscript the benefit of their perspective, experience and expertise. You've all made me a much better writer than the one you met in the beginning, and even though The Outing may still have been finished and published, it certainly would be without the finesse that your critical eyes, and wise words helped steer me towards. Thanks also to Charlotte Mendelsohn and Zanni Louise who encouraged me to be a brutal editor and to go the extra distance.

Madelaine Baddiley, Tom Jones, and Paul Foley, my family, thank you for your multiple reads; your tireless and what must have seemed like endless support; for your very trustworthy gut feelings; for packaging your critique so carefully; for your steadfast belief, and for sharing your delight with the finished novel. Admiration to Paul, who has added marketing and publishing to his CV on my behalf.

My heart goes out to Scott Johnson and George Duncan, and to everyone else who didn't make it, were damaged in the process, or stood up, so that the changes and freedoms and inclusiveness that we are becoming accustomed to are there in the first place, to be maintained and improved on, and most of all cherished.

Tommy, I wish you could have read this too.

ABOUT THE AUTHOR

Fabian is Australian, and loves to travel. She's been meandering in Europe for the last few years in a caravan, with occasional stints house and pet sitting, which she and her husband Paul blog about on
http://www.anotherdaymeandering.com
Besides traveling and writing, she loves reading, eating (especially authentic pizza and anything with parmesan and truffle) and dabbles in cooking. Read more about her and find out what she's working on next, at
http://fabianfoley.com

Made in the USA
Middletown, DE
27 June 2023

33790916R10215